HER
DEADLY
TOUCH

BOOKS BY LISA REGAN

HER DEADLY TOUCH

LISA REGAN

bookouture

Published by Bookouture in 2021

An imprint of Storyfire Ltd.
Carmelite House
50 Victoria Embankment
London EC4Y 0DZ

www.bookouture.com

ISBN: 978-1-80019-633-9
eBook ISBN: 978-1-80019-632-2

In loving memory of the most extraordinary human I've ever known, my dad, Billy Regan. I let them tell me no, Dad, and they didn't.

CHAPTER ONE

The bus was full but Wallace and his little sister, Frankie, and super annoying Bianca from his class were still sitting along the wall outside school. The bus kept belching out fumes, making Wallace's stomach feel queasy. Frankie tugged at his wrist. "Wallace, come on! We have to get on the bus or we're going to get stuck at school. I don't want to get stuck at school. It's like, my worst nightmare."

Bianca laughed. "We wouldn't be stuck here. Eventually someone would come find us and take us home."

"Like your mom?" Wallace said. "She works so many hours she can't even take you to your own appointments."

Bianca reached across Frankie and punched his arm. It hurt a little, but he didn't show it. "Don't talk about my mom."

"Why not?" Wallace sneered. "What're you going to do?"

Frankie jumped up, her brown ponytail bouncing. She shifted the straps of her hot pink backpack. "Come on, you guys. Don't fight."

"I don't take orders from fifth graders," he told her.

A stern female voice from behind them said, "But you will take orders from me, young man."

The principal. Cringing, Wallace turned and pasted a smile on his face, wondering how much she had heard. But she didn't reprimand him. Instead, she made a shooing motion with her hands. "Go on, then. The three of you. Onto the bus."

Bianca stood up. "But today we were supposed to—"

The principal didn't let her finish. "You're supposed to be on the bus. That's what I was told. Now get going, and no fighting."

CHAPTER TWO

Dr. Paige Rosetti's office was designed to soothe. The walls were cream-colored. The couch and chairs were soft and gray. Wall art showed paintings of faraway places that looked too beautiful to be real. Josie counted at least fourteen potted plants even though the large bay window to the left of her seat looked out onto a well-tended garden. It was August and the lush colors of the various flowers were difficult to tear her eyes from, even as she squirmed beneath Paige Rosetti's patient stare. She couldn't quite get comfortable. She'd never felt at ease in therapy although she'd only been coming for two months.

"Josie," Paige said softly.

Josie's heel tapped out a muted beat on the carpet making her knee bob up and down frenetically.

"Josie," Paige said again.

Slowly, Josie met Paige's gaze. Crow's feet gathered in the corners of her brown eyes. She was old enough to be Josie's mother. In fact, Josie had gone to high school with her daughter. Her long, wavy blonde hair and open manner made her seem more youthful than her age.

Paige smiled. "This only works if you talk to me."

She said that every session.

Paige added, "You are paying for my time. I'd like for you to get as much from it as possible."

She also said that at every session.

"Sorry," Josie said. She leaned forward, resting her elbows on the tops of her thighs, trying to still her jumpy leg. "What—what were we talking about?"

Paige smiled again but this time, Josie could see a tightness at the corners of her lips. She was getting impatient. "I was asking you how you felt about going back to work tomorrow. You've been on suspension for almost four months."

"Right," said Josie.

Josie was a detective for the Denton, Pennsylvania, police department. Denton was a small but bustling city in Central Pennsylvania nestled among several mountains, resting on the banks of the Susquehanna River. The population, which swelled when Denton University was in session, was large enough to keep the police department consistently busy. Her last case had been a double homicide that happened on her wedding day at her wedding venue. She and her husband, Noah Fraley, who worked as a lieutenant for Denton PD, had been thrust into the case when they realized that Josie knew the murder victims. During the course of the investigation, Josie's grandmother, Lisette Matson, had been murdered. Afterward, when she was supposed to be grieving at home, Josie had left her gun and badge and gone looking for a missing person associated with the case. She hadn't told anyone on the force, not even Noah, where she was going or that she had figured out the location of the person.

"Josie?" Paige prompted.

The next day, their Chief of Police had suspended her for not looping in the team on her activities. The official report had said she was insubordinate. He'd kept her out far longer than anyone expected. Josie suspected it was because he wanted to give her extra time to grieve her loss.

"I'm not worried about it," Josie murmured, looking out at the garden again. A brightly colored cardinal flitted through some low-hanging tree branches at the outer edge of the yard.

"You're not worried about returning to work after being out for four months?" Paige echoed. "Isn't that the longest you've ever been out?"

"Sure," said Josie.

The truth was that she hadn't minded the four months off. For the first time in her life, she didn't care about work. She didn't care about anything, really, besides her husband and their dog, Trout. The world without Lisette—who had basically raised her—was hollow and colorless. Joyless. Josie felt muted inside and out, like she was trapped beneath a mile of sludge and too exhausted to fight her way up and out of it.

From her peripheral vision, Josie saw Paige check her watch. She gave her credit for not letting out a lengthy sigh. Paige changed topics. "How are you sleeping?"

"The same," Josie said.

"So you're not, then?"

She shrugged. "I keep having the nightmare," she offered.

"The one where your grandmother gets shot?"

Josie looked at her. "Yeah. I mean I guess it's a memory, not a nightmare. Only this time, I know what's coming. I try to throw myself in front of her, to take the bullet myself, but my feet are stuck to the ground. I can't move at all. Then the shots come, and I…"

She trailed off. *I wake up screaming*, she continued silently. *Crying, soaked in a cold sweat.* Then Noah would hold her while their sweet Boston Terrier whined and tried to lick her face. "She shouldn't have been out there," Josie would cry again and again while Noah rocked her like a small child. It was the only time she allowed herself to cry and that was mostly because she woke up already in tears. Unfortunately, she couldn't control her dreams or her body's response to them.

Paige said, "Josie, eventually we are going to need to really talk about this. We need to go deeper. This is a safe space for you. You can cry and scream and rage and freak out here with me and I won't judge you. I won't be scared. I won't be upset. My feelings won't be hurt, and I'll never tell another soul."

Avoiding Paige's eyes again, Josie returned her gaze to the window. The cardinal was gone. Her eyes traced the flowers, some of their petals limp in the searing August heat. "I know," she said.

Paige's chair creaked. Josie turned her head in time to see her stand up and walk over to her desk, where she placed her notepad. Not for the first time, it was blank. "I think that's all the time we have for today, Josie."

Josie stood up. "Same time next week?"

Paige's chin dipped toward her chest. Finally, she let out the sigh that Josie knew she'd been holding in the entire forty-five minutes Josie had been there. "Josie, I'm glad you're here. I really am, and I want to help you. I think you could benefit from therapy a lot. I'm happy to continue seeing you, but again, I'm not sure that you're getting anything out of this."

"Dr. Rosetti," Josie said, smiling for the first time that morning. "Are you dumping me?"

Paige looked at her and laughed. "No, not at all. I'm just—" she broke off, wearing that tense smile that Josie seemed to provoke with every session. After a few awkward seconds, she said, "How about this? In the next week, I want you to make a list for me."

"What kind of a list?"

"A list of things that make you feel…"

"Sad?"

"Out of control."

Josie felt a small flutter of discomfort in her chest. "Out of control?"

"Yes," said Paige. "Three things. At least. When you come back, we'll discuss them."

Josie swallowed, throat dry. "Sure," she said.

She left without thanking the doctor. So far, she'd managed to avoid doing what Dr. Rosetti kept telling her was the "heavy lifting" in therapy. She knew that the doctor wanted to ask her why she kept coming if she wasn't going to fully engage in the sessions. The truth was that Josie wasn't going for herself. She was going because of a little girl she'd helped during her last case. That little girl had lost just as much, if not more, than Josie on that case and yet, she'd faced up to the trauma with grit and steely determination. She always, as she had described it to Josie, "felt all the feelings until they were gone." She had even done it toward the end of the investigation when Josie had asked her to recall some particularly traumatic moments. The girl had since moved away with relatives, but Josie felt like a fraud having asked that courageous little girl to face her demons so that Josie could solve a case when she could not even bring herself to go to therapy to try to resolve a lifetime of trauma and then, most recently, Lisette's murder.

So Josie had gone to the sessions with Paige so she could live with herself. *I'm trying*, she kept telling herself. If she talked with the girl, which she did about once a week via Zoom, she could tell her that yes, she was still in therapy. Still trying to work up the nerve to feel all her feelings even though after two months of therapy, she hadn't shed a tear in Paige Rosetti's soothing office.

"Next week," she muttered to herself as she got into her car and fired up the engine.

She put the AC on full blast and then turned up the radio as loud as it would go, hoping for some music to drown out her thoughts, but instead the host of one of their local FM stations was giving their hourly news report. "Denton police are still searching for Krystal Duncan, a thirty-two-year-old legal secretary who went missing three days ago. Duncan was reported missing by her boss when she failed to show up for work last week and didn't answer any calls. Authorities are asking anyone with information to contact Denton police. You can find a photograph of Krystal Duncan on our website."

Josie punched at the buttons on the console until she found a station playing eighties music. Noah had mentioned the Krystal

Duncan case at home, but Josie hadn't asked any questions. Together they'd watched local news coverage of Krystal's disappearance. Josie had studied the photo of the woman as it flashed across the screen. It had been taken from the website for the law firm where Krystal worked. In it, she was dressed in a casual skirt suit. She was posed artificially beside a large mahogany desk, her long brown hair cascading over her shoulders. Close-set brown eyes peered over her nose, which had a small bump on it, as though it had been broken once but not properly fixed. Her smile was thin and forced. The woman's face stayed in Josie's mind for three days and still, she asked Noah no questions. It was that strange, muted feeling again that she'd had since Lisette's murder. She knew she should be interested in the disappearance of a local woman. Before Lisette's murder, Josie would have been obsessing over it—even if that meant, because of her suspension, she had to comb the internet for news coverage from home while her colleagues solved the case.

But now she pushed thoughts of Krystal Duncan out of her head. Josie knew the investigative team at Denton PD were already working Krystal's case and they were the best. If Josie ever went missing, she'd want them looking for her. She knew she'd be elbow-deep in all the details tomorrow when she returned to work. For now, she didn't want to think at all. She wanted to be swallowed deeper into the mental and emotional sludge that kept her from the empty ache of real life.

A bead of sweat ran down Josie's spine. Her fingers toggled the AC dial again but there was no more cold air to be had. With a sigh, she pulled away from Dr. Paige Rosetti's house, which doubled as her office, and weaved through the streets of Denton. Noah was at work and although Josie knew their Boston Terrier, Trout, would be ecstatic to see her, she didn't feel like going home just yet. Instead, she drove to the cemetery where she'd buried her first husband, Ray. Josie's grandmother, Lisette, had requested to be cremated and her remains now sat in a shiny urn on a shelf in Josie and Noah's living room. But Josie had come to see Ray as she often did when she felt like life was spiraling away from her.

"I guess I should put this on my list," she muttered to herself as she parked the car near Ray's headstone and got out. Why was she feeling out of control now, she wondered. She didn't want to examine it. What she wanted was a searing shot of Wild Turkey. But she'd given up drinking long ago because she made poor choices when she drank and while alcohol dulled her emotional pain temporarily, it never made it go away.

The sun beat down on her as she weaved her way through the headstones to Ray's grave. A light breeze drifted past, but it gave little relief from the oppressive heat and humidity. By the time she stood before Ray's stone, her shirt was damp beneath the collar. It had been six years since Ray's murder, and things between them hadn't ended well, even before his death, but Josie had known Ray since she was a child. They were high school sweethearts. For most of her life he'd been her anchor, her North Star, much the way Lisette had been. Josie usually felt a sense of peace when she visited this place. Closing her eyes, she let her body sway slightly in the breeze. Around her birds chirped and the only other noise that could be heard was the faint sound of cars whirring past on the road that led to the cemetery.

Until the screaming started.

CHAPTER THREE

Before Josie's brain had a chance to catch up with her body, her feet were propelling her forward, deeper into the cemetery toward the sound of a woman shrieking. As she dodged through headstones and up to the crest of a hill, the cries became louder. They weren't the keening wails of grief, Josie realized, but the sharp, serrated screeches of shock and horror. Scrambling down the other side of the hill, Josie's sneakered feet slid along the soft, overturned ground where someone had recently been buried. She fell backward, arms flailing, but caught herself on a nearby stone. Righting her body, she saw the source of the commotion: a woman in khaki shorts and a purple T-shirt standing among the gravestones. Her hands clutched at the dark hair on either side of her head. Her body curled in on itself even as she stood, as if protecting herself from some sort of attack. A bouquet of colorful flowers lay discarded on the ground at her feet.

Josie ran ahead. Sweat poured from her brow. The woman turned as Josie reached her. "Help!" she hollered. "There's something wrong with her! She needs help!"

Josie looked beyond her to where a second woman sat beside a headstone. Her legs were folded beneath her, and her arms wrapped loosely around her waist. At first, Josie didn't understand what had alarmed the first woman so much. A step closer brought the kneeling woman's face into focus. Her head was canted to the right. Some of her long brown hair was matted to her left cheek. The rest of it hung limply over her shoulders, mussed in some places and knotted in others. Although her skin was pink and vibrant, her eyes were fixed and lifeless, staring straight ahead. A breath shuddered through Josie's body as she tried to process the tableau before her. The woman looked alive, almost normal—except for her eyes—as though she'd dozed off in a seated position and her head had lolled, or as though she were meditating. Except that she was dressed in business attire. A silky, short-sleeved cream-colored blouse, light gray skirt, torn nylons, black flats. That telltale bump on her nose was barely noticeable, except that Josie had been looking at this face on the news for the past three days.

Krystal Duncan.

Here she was, dressed as though she'd come from work. But Josie knew she'd been missing for three days. If there was any doubt in Josie's mind, a quick glance at the headstone beside her squashed it. *Bianca Duncan*, it read, *Beloved Daughter*.

Hands pushed at Josie's shoulders, urging her forward. "Help her!" the living woman screamed. "Something's wrong with her! Can't you see?"

Josie stumbled closer, already knowing that there was no help she could offer the woman kneeling before them. She had seen enough dead bodies in her time as a police officer to know that it was too late. Still, to pacify the hysterical woman behind her, Josie leaned over and pressed two fingers into the dead woman's throat. As she suspected, no pulse. Gently, Josie nudged one of her arms. It didn't budge. She was in full rigor, which meant she'd been dead at least two hours, maybe more. There was also something on her lips. Froth? Josie wondered. She leaned in to get a better look. Not froth. Something else.

Josie's heartbeat skidded to a halt and then kicked back into overdrive.

"She's dead, isn't she?" came a voice from behind Josie. "Why does she look like… like that?"

Josie stood and herded the woman away from the body. She pulled her phone from the pocket of her shorts. Her fingers dialed a 9, then a 1, and froze. If she called 911 or even dispatch, the call would go out over the police scanner, which the local press routinely monitored. Krystal Duncan's disappearance had garnered a great deal of press coverage. Not only because of Denton's sordid history with missing women but also because she was the mother of a girl who had been killed in a tragic school bus accident two years ago, and the trial of the bus driver was only weeks away. Josie cleared the numbers and instead, called Noah directly. "I need units," she said when he answered. "At Vincent Williams cemetery. I've got a body. I'm pretty sure it's Krystal Duncan. Female, mid-thirties. Suspicious circumstances." She looked around them and tried to fix their location so she could tell Noah where to find them. Once she gave a general description, she said, "We need the Evidence Response Team, an ambulance for transport, and Dr. Feist."

Dr. Anya Feist was the county medical examiner. Noah said, "We'll be there in ten."

"Keep it off the radio," Josie instructed. "Unless you want the press crawling all over this place."

"You got it."

Josie pocketed her phone after hanging up. "Miss," Josie said to the other woman. "We need to get away from here."

She pointed to the body. "What's wrong with her? Why is she just sitting like that? How is she—how can she be dead? What happened to her? What's that… what's on her mouth?"

"What's your name?" Josie asked instead of answering her questions.

For a second, the woman looked dazed. She blinked twice and focused her gaze on Josie. "Dee," she said. "Dee Tenney."

Josie took hold of one of Dee's elbows and walked her several feet from the body, turning her away from the spectacle. Beads of sweat dotted Dee's upper lip. Her skin took on a slightly green hue. Josie wished she had some water with her, but she didn't. The best she could do was get Dee into the shade beneath a large oak tree nearby. "Dee, let's wait here for my colleagues."

Dee rested her back against the tree trunk and used a forearm to swipe away the sweat on her face. She looked Josie up and down. "Colleagues?" Her eyes narrowed. "You're that detective, aren't you?"

In the small city of Denton, Josie had gained some fame and notoriety for having been instrumental in solving several cases so scandalous that they had made national news. Between that and her own shocking family history, which had been featured on *Dateline*, she was often recognized by strangers.

Josie opened her mouth to speak but Dee continued, "No, wait, you're the reporter. You have to be the reporter. Why else would you be here?"

Josie held up a hand. "You were right the first time. I'm a detective with Denton PD. My twin sister, Trinity Payne, is a journalist. She lives and works in New York City. Dee, my team will be here in a few minutes. Why don't you tell me what happened?"

Dee looked over Josie's shoulder, out at the cemetery, but then she quickly squeezed her eyes shut. Her words came out high-pitched and fast, spilling out into the space between them. "Nothing happened. I was here. I saw her. I thought she was just sitting at the grave, you know? Except something wasn't right. She wasn't facing the headstone. I called out to her and got no response. I walked over to touch her shoulder but then I saw her face. She looked alive but dead. I don't know how to explain it."

"You don't have to," Josie said.

Dee kept her eyes tightly closed but shook her head hard. "It was her color. She looks alive," Dee went on. "But she can't be. She's not, right? You felt for a pulse. She's really dead, isn't she?"

"Yes," Josie said. She reached out and gently touched Dee's forearm. "Dee? Can you open your eyes for me?"

Dee took in a deep breath and on the exhale, opened her eyes again.

Josie pointed to her own face. "Right here, Dee. Stay focused on me, okay? You're doing great."

A tremble started in Dee's arms and quickly encompassed her torso. She hugged herself but maintained eye contact with Josie.

"Good," Josie told her. "That's very good." Josie took exaggerated, slow breaths in through her nose and out through her mouth, her chest rising up and down in an even rhythm. After a few seconds, Dee began to mirror her. When Josie felt Dee had regained some of her composure, she asked, "You were here visiting a loved one's grave?"

Dee nodded. "I was on my way to my daughter's grave. I had brought flowers. I got a lot of yellow dahlias this time. She loved those. Anyway, that was when I saw Krystal. It was so odd. I knew everyone was looking for her. I felt this rush of relief, you know? I had found her. Until I got close… Jesus."

Tears streamed down Dee's cheeks, but she kept her gaze locked on Josie's face.

Josie quickly panned their surroundings and noticed a gray Honda Civic parked on the shoulder of the nearby cemetery road. "Is that your car?"

Dee nodded. "I know there's a parking lot at the entrance to this place but it's too damn hot to walk all the way out here from there. I figured it wouldn't matter if I just pulled over. I was only going to be here for a few minutes. I didn't expect to see anyone really. Certainly not Krystal."

"Do you know her?" Josie asked. "Or did you recognize her from the news?"

"I know her. I knew her. My God. She lives down the street from me. Our kids… oh my God."

Finally, Dee broke eye contact, looking down at her feet. Slowly, she slumped until she was sitting at the base of the tree. Josie watched as sobs shook her body. Searching her shorts pockets, Josie came up with a folded tissue and handed it to Dee. She didn't press her any further. There would be plenty of time for questions later, after the team arrived and began a formal investigation. Josie wasn't even due back to work until tomorrow.

As she waited for them to arrive, she turned back toward Krystal Duncan, her stomach twisting as her mind labored to process the scene once more—the unnerving dissonance between Krystal sitting upright, her skin a healthy shade and those dead eyes, that substance clinging to her lips, hardened drops of it stuck to her chin. Turning back toward Dee, Josie tugged at the collar of her shirt. Every square inch of the fabric slicked to her body with sweat. Even in the shade, the heat was oppressive. Josie moved her body so that she stood directly in Dee's line of sight. What would cause a person's skin to look so healthy after death? Josie searched her mind for some explanations from cases she'd worked in the past, but it was a struggle to focus. In this heat, decomposition would be accelerated. Yet, Krystal looked as though she had simply folded her legs beneath her and sat on the ground, which meant that she had not been dead for very long. Yet, she'd been missing for three days. Where had she been during that time?

The sounds of tires over asphalt reached Josie's ears just before police vehicles crested the hill on the nearby road that looped through the cemetery. Josie looked down at Dee, who now held her head in her hands. "Dee? Can you stay here for a few minutes?"

A muffled "yes" came from behind Dee's palms.

"I'll be right back," Josie told her.

She threaded her way through the graves to the road and waved for them to stop. A patrol vehicle and ambulance rolled up first, their lights off. Then came Noah driving his vehicle with their colleague, Detective Gretchen Palmer, in the passenger's seat. Behind them was the marked Denton police SUV used by the Evidence Response Team. Josie saw the head of their ERT, Officer Hummel, and his colleague Officer Chan in the front. Bringing up the rear of the caravan was an old white beat-up pickup truck that Josie recognized as belonging to the ME, Dr. Anya Feist. They all came to a stop in line behind Dee Tenney's car. As they disembarked, they gathered in a loose circle in the middle of the road. Josie brought them up to speed and then Gretchen took over, giving instructions for the uniformed officers to set up a perimeter and to stand sentry outside the crime scene to ensure no mourners who might show up would come close. She instructed Hummel and Chan to get to work processing the scene.

As Hummel and Chan dragged equipment from the back of the SUV, Dr. Feist said, "I'll go with them." She smiled grimly at Hummel. "And don't worry, I'll stay out of your way until you're ready for me."

Josie watched them walk off, each of them pulling a suitcase marked "Property of Denton's ERT" behind them. She was keenly aware of Noah's gaze on her. "Visiting Ray?" he said.

Josie nodded, feeling awkward telling her new husband that she'd been here visiting her old husband the day before she was due back at work. A day they both knew was a big deal for her. Then again, before they had even started dating, Noah had been the only person who knew about her visits to Ray's grave. She didn't tell people because she didn't think they'd understand. Ray had died a disgrace—corrupt, dishonest, and cowardly—but he had died trying to save her from someone even worse, and Josie had never been able to stop grieving the man he was when they got married, or the boy he had been during their childhood. Once, he had been good. Until he wasn't.

Noah smiled, hazel eyes twinkling, and reached over to smooth a lock of hair out of her face. His touch was so soothing that she felt like melting into the asphalt.

Gretchen looked in the direction from which they had come. "I had a uniformed unit drive up to the caretaker's office to let them know what's going on and find out if anyone saw or heard anything, or if there are cameras anywhere on the premises." She took out her notebook and pen. "You sure it's Krystal Duncan?"

"As sure as I can be," Josie told her.

Gretchen used the top of her pen to scratch her chin. She sighed. "Shit. All right, then. Let's get started."

CHAPTER FOUR

Gretchen spoke with Dee Tenney for several minutes before sending her to the police station with Noah to give a formal statement. Processing of the crime scene would take several hours, and Josie knew Gretchen wanted to get Dee out of the heat as soon as possible. They watched as Dee handed Noah the keys to her Civic, and he drove away with her in the passenger seat.

Josie said, "I think she might be going into shock."

Gretchen began walking toward the edge of the crime scene tape. "Noah will keep an eye on her. Get her comfortable, get her into the AC, make sure she's okay before she leaves the station. You want to stick around or go home?"

Josie kept pace with Gretchen. "I don't know," she said honestly.

Gretchen stopped walking and shielded her eyes with her notepad. "You serious?"

A bead of sweat slid down the side of Josie's face, along the thin scar that ran from her ear to the center of her chin. She rubbed it away. "Yeah."

A few seconds ticked by. Gretchen said, "You still going to therapy?"

"Yeah."

Now that they were out from under the shade of the tree, the heat felt more stifling. Josie's black hair was wet and stuck to the back of her neck. She was acutely aware of the sweat staining the underarms of her shirt. Again, she tugged the fabric away from her torso as Gretchen continued to stare. Gretchen was dressed in jeans and a Denton PD polo shirt and aside from a light sheen of sweat along her hairline, she appeared unbothered by the temperature.

"What?" said Josie finally, unable to bear another moment of Gretchen's scrutiny.

"Tomorrow morning you'll report to the station, and I'll have to bring you up to speed on everything we've learned here today. Save me some time, would you? Stick around. You are a witness, after all."

With that, Gretchen turned away and trudged toward where one of the patrol officers stood sentry at a strip of crime scene tape, a clipboard in hand. Beside him, Dr. Feist waited to be admitted. In her arms were a Tyvek suit and booties. She'd already fitted the skullcap over her silver-blonde hair. She nodded at Gretchen and Josie. The officer lifted his pen to sign Gretchen in but she held up a hand. "Not yet," she told him. "Wait till the ERT says it's okay."

Josie followed her as she circled the perimeter, trying to get a better look at Krystal Duncan's body. From where they stood, Josie could see strands of Krystal's brown hair blowing in the breeze. Again, the sight of the mother kneeling at her daughter's grave—looking alive but most definitely not—sent a ripple of discomfort through Josie's heat-addled body. Within the crime scene tape, Hummel and Chan took sketches and photographs and laid evidence markers. A flash of brilliant color caught Josie's eye. The flowers that Dee Tenney had dropped, now wilting in the heat. She'd been bringing them to her daughter's grave, she had said. But Dee was so young. She couldn't be older than Josie—mid-thirties. How old had her daughter been when she died?

Josie said, "Dee knew Krystal. She said that Krystal lived down the street. Their kids—"

Gretchen stopped walking, pocketed her notepad and pen, and pressed her middle against the crime scene tape, straining to get a good view of Krystal Duncan's body. "Their kids were both killed in the West Denton bus crash two years ago."

Just like everyone else on the Denton PD, Josie was aware of the bus accident. Five middle-school children had been killed in West Denton on their way home from school. Their Chief of Police had sent Gretchen to the scene to take point on the case. In her late forties, Gretchen was older than her colleagues, but more importantly, she'd had fifteen years of experience working for the Philadelphia police department's homicide unit before coming to Denton. She had seen more grisly death cases than the entire Denton police department combined. Child deaths were the most difficult cases in their line of work. The emotional toll could be catastrophic but Gretchen, with her signature stoicism, had handled the bus crash with grace and forbearance.

Josie said, "The odds of Dee being here to find Krystal's body are—"

"Pretty good," Gretchen filled in. "All the kids are buried here. But I'll check out Dee's alibi for this morning and the last couple of days nevertheless."

Josie nodded. "Who was the last person to see Krystal Duncan alive?"

Gretchen kept staring across the cemetery. "Her boss. She stayed late to finish up some pleadings on one of their cases on Thursday afternoon. He locked up after she left. She was due in the next morning and didn't show. Him and one of her coworkers called her several times on Friday but got no answer. The boss called dispatch and asked for a welfare check."

"After less than twenty-four hours?" Josie asked.

Gretchen nodded. "Krystal lived alone. She was a single mother. Never married. No boyfriends. She's got no close family. Never knew her dad. Mom lives several hours away. No siblings. According to coworkers, her friendships fell away one by one after her daughter died. Evidently, she met regularly with a support group for the parents of children killed in the crash. I called several of them over the weekend to find out when they had last seen her. All the other parents said the same thing: they saw her at their last meeting, which was the Monday before she went missing. They said she was upset but then again, they all were with the bus driver going on trial soon. Krystal's coworkers said she'd been become very emotional the last couple of months. Volatile. Weepy. When she didn't show up on Friday, they thought maybe she'd harmed herself."

"Dispatch did send someone out for the welfare check, then," Josie said.

"Yep. Her front door was unlocked. Car in the garage. Purse, cell phone, and house keys on the coffee table inside. Nothing disturbed. It was like she just walked out the door and didn't come back."

But no one went anywhere without their cell phone anymore.

"Neighbors see anything?" Josie asked.

Gretchen shook her head. "A couple of them reported seeing her come home on Thursday evening—pulling into her garage, getting the mail from her mailbox, but that was it. A few of them had home security cameras but no one picked up anything. None of the cameras are positioned within view of the front of her house anyway."

"You get anything from her phone?"

"Nope. Nothing unusual. Calls to and from work, to and from coworkers. A couple of calls to and from the district attorney's office. I spoke with their office. She was preparing to testify at trial so they'd been in touch with her to make sure she would be ready. Other than that, all we could find were appointments with doctors, that sort of thing. No red flags. The only thing that was unusual was that her boss said she logged into their firm's database on Saturday night."

"Meaning she was at the office?"

"No. She did it remotely, they said. They don't know why or what she was doing on it. They have a remote feature so that employees can work from home when necessary. They can login and access all the firm files, download or upload work, that sort of thing. The system shows who logs in and out and if they make any changes to a file, it will record that."

"But Krystal didn't make any changes to any files," Josie guessed.

"Right. She logged in at 9:08 p.m. and logged out at 11:14 p.m. We have no idea what she looked at or why she was in there."

"Can you tell where she logged in from?"

"We've got a subpoena out to the company who handles the firm server to see if that's information they're able to provide. If we can get an IP address, we can probably pinpoint where she was within a reasonable degree of certainty when she accessed the database. Other than that, there have been no leads in her disappearance, and you know how hard we've been hitting this in the press."

"Yeah," said Josie. "You can't turn on the TV or the radio without hearing about her. You get any leads from the coverage?"

"Nothing solid. A few people thought they saw her on Friday, but all the sightings turned out to be other women with long brown hair and an average build."

Josie sighed. "She hasn't been seen by anyone since Thursday night, but she was obviously alive until a few hours ago."

Gretchen said, "Now that she's been found dead, I'll have another conversation with her boss about which cases she was working on."

They turned toward the road at the sound of tires over asphalt. Another patrol unit pulled up and parked behind Dr. Feist's truck. A young officer got out and jogged over. Josie recognized him before she was able to see the name on his uniform. Brennan. "Detective Palmer," he said as he reached them. "Detective Quinn."

"You talk to the caretaker?" Gretchen asked.

He nodded. He took off his hat, used a sleeve to wipe his brow, and put it back on. "He said to take as much time as we need. He was here at six a.m. when he opened the front gate—that's what time it's opened every day for mourners. It's closed at ten p.m. Four employees showed up at six thirty and he put them to work getting a burial site ready, but they were on the opposite side of the cemetery and didn't see anything unusual. Anything at all, actually. Not even any vehicles. Also, there are no cameras on the premises."

"Not even at the entrance?" Gretchen asked.

He shook his head.

Josie said, "They've never had problems here. Not even with vandals. That's why we chose this place for Ray. This part of West Denton is the safest part of the city. They wouldn't need cameras here."

With a sigh, Gretchen looked back over her shoulder where the ERT continued to work. "All right," she said. "Brennan, drive us over to the caretaker's office, would you? We'll need formal statements from him and from the employees about when they arrived, when they left, and that they didn't see anything of note."

Josie was grateful to get into the air-conditioned car for the ten-minute ride to the office. The Vincent Williams cemetery was the largest in Denton. As she watched the rolling hills dotted with gravestones flash past, she realized it was entirely possible that the crew working on the other side of the premises really hadn't seen anything. The location of Krystal's body was closer to the main entrance. It would have been relatively easy to slip in, leave her at her daughter's grave, and slip out unnoticed, particularly if it was done early in the morning before any mourners arrived. At the caretaker's office, which was a sprawling, single-story, stone building, four men waited inside the lobby.

Again, Josie was grateful for the air conditioning as she and Gretchen met with each worker and the caretaker to get formal statements. Josie knew that as soon as they returned to the stationhouse, Gretchen would run each one of their names and other personal information through various databases to see if there were any red flags in their histories or connections to Krystal Duncan.

Gretchen was finishing up with the caretaker when Josie felt her phone vibrate in her pocket. She took it out to see Dr. Feist was calling and swiped answer.

Dr. Feist said, "I've been trying to get Gretchen but she's not answering her phone."

"She's been taking statements," Josie said. "What's going on?"

"We're ready to move the body back to the morgue, but you two are going to want to see this before we do."

CHAPTER FIVE

Dr. Feist waited beneath the tree that Josie had led Dee Tenney to after she discovered Krystal Duncan's body. Crime scene tape still cordoned off the area and the patrol officers remained in place, guarding the scene. In the road, Hummel and Chan packed up their equipment as well as several bags of evidence. Dr. Feist held a skullcap, which she waved back and forth in front of her face, trying to move some of the hot air. When Josie and Gretchen reached her, she started walking toward the body. They trailed behind her. The officer with the clipboard wrote their names down and lifted the crime scene tape so they could duck under it.

Two EMT workers stood behind Krystal's kneeling form, a gurney between them, waiting to take the body away. Josie was relieved to see that neither one of them was Sawyer Hayes. Sawyer worked for the city's Emergency Services department as a paramedic. He had been Lisette's grandson, although he and Josie were not blood related. The night that Lisette was shot and during her last days in the hospital he had been angry with Josie, all but blaming her for Lisette's death. Josie hadn't seen him since the funeral although she had called him several times to check on him. He never returned her calls. A swell of relief rose in her chest that she wouldn't have to confront him now in a cemetery hotter than hell next to a kneeling dead woman.

As they drew up in front of Krystal Duncan, Dr. Feist said, "Chan thinks the substance on her lips is wax. She scraped some to have it analyzed, and I'll save the rest when I do the autopsy and enter it into evidence."

Gretchen said, "Someone poured melted wax into her mouth?"

"I don't know," Dr. Feist said. "I have to get her on the table, but it sure looks like it."

"Why does her color look so good?" Josie asked. "She's been out here for hours since we found her and probably a few hours before that."

Dr. Feist frowned. "This kind of color in a body—the bright-pink appearance of the skin—in the absence of prolonged exposure to a cold environment, suggests death by carbon monoxide poisoning or cyanide poisoning."

Gretchen raised a brow. "Twenty years on the job, don't think I've ever seen a death by cyanide poisoning. With carbon monoxide poisoning, it's usually accidental or suicide."

"This is not a suicide," Josie put in. "There's no way this woman poured hot wax down her throat and staged herself kneeling by her daughter's grave."

Dr. Feist said, "Indeed. She went into rigor while she was in this position."

Josie said, "You're saying this is how she died? Kneeling like this?"

"Obviously, I can't say that for certain, and I do need to perform my autopsy to give you any official findings, but it seems most likely. Even if someone had propped her up like this before she went into rigor mortis, it's unlikely that her body would have stayed upright. But if she had died like this and then gone into rigor without being moved, it would account for the positioning."

Gretchen said, "Will you be able to tell on autopsy if this was carbon monoxide poisoning?"

Dr. Feist nodded. "I believe so. If she died from carbon monoxide poisoning then her internal musculature, tissue, and blood will all have a cherry-red appearance, which is typically found with carbon monoxide deaths. Even the removal and embalming of the tissue doesn't get rid of that color. There will also likely be lesions in certain specific areas of the brain that are characteristic of that cause of death."

Josie tried to wrap her mind around this potential news. Krystal Duncan had been home on Thursday evening. Then she wasn't home. No one saw her leave. No one saw someone abduct her. All her personal items were left behind. Yet, she was still alive on Saturday night and probably into Monday morning, just hours before Dee Tenney stumbled upon her. That meant she had been held somewhere. Had someone intentionally killed her using carbon monoxide or had it been accidental?

Another glance at Krystal's sealed lips told Josie that nothing about Krystal's demise was an accident.

Dr. Feist said, "I'll have a better idea of her time of death after I've taken her internal temperature and done some calculations based on the temperature out here today, but I can tell you that in this heat I would have expected to see a greater rate of decomp by now or even by the time she was discovered."

Gretchen said, "You think she was kept somewhere cool before she was moved here."

"That would be my guess, yes."

Gretchen scribbled notes on her pad while Dr. Feist kneeled beside Krystal. From the pocket of her Tyvek suit, she pulled a pair of latex gloves and snapped them on. "I could have waited until after the autopsy to let you know about this, but I thought you'd want to see it now."

Josie watched as she gingerly pulled Krystal's right arm away from her waist. The rigor mortis made it difficult, but Dr. Feist held the forearm away just far enough and for just long enough that Josie and Gretchen could both see why she had called them over.

The inside of Krystal's forearm was stark white compared to the pink of the rest of her skin. As if reading Josie's mind, Dr. Feist said, "It's called contact blanching. Basically, with the onset of livor mortis, a person's blood settles into the lowest parts of their body—dependent on their position. That's usually when you see the deep purple color in a person's skin once livor mortis sets in. If they're found on their back, it will usually all be along their back and legs. If they're found on their stomach, then you'll expect to see the blood settle in the front of their body. You can see where livor has set in here on Krystal but, because I suspect this is carbon monoxide poisoning, the color is a cherry red rather than a purple. Anyway, contact blanching is when certain areas of the body are compressed so that the blood doesn't settle there. That's why it looks white."

But the white area of skin on the inside of Krystal's forearm was not the reason that Dr. Feist had called them back to the body. Across the pale expanse of Krystal's arm someone had used what looked like black magic marker to write something.

"Is that a name?" Gretchen asked, dropping her notepad and pen so she could snap some photos with her phone.

"I don't know," said Dr. Feist, letting the arm snap back to its original position. "My job is to tell you as much as I possibly can about how this woman died. This is a mystery for your team."

Josie studied the letters, again trying to decipher something that seemed to make no sense at all. Capital letters spelled out: *PRITCH.*

CHAPTER SIX

Josie and Gretchen stood near Bianca Duncan's gravesite, watching as the EMT workers struggled to get Krystal Duncan's stiff, kneeling body into the back of the ambulance. Rigor mortis could be broken by flexing the joints but that was something that Dr. Feist would handle prior to performing the autopsy. For now, the EMTs would have to transport Krystal's corpse in its current position. Once they were gone, Josie turned to Gretchen. "Does that mean anything to you? 'Pritch'?"

Gretchen flipped through several pages in her notebook. "No. I've got nothing. I'll have to go back through the missing persons file but I don't remember any person, place, or thing called Pritch."

"What about someone called Pritchard?" Josie wondered. "Maybe Pritch is short for that? Or whoever wrote it didn't finish? Or maybe Krystal wrote it, and she was trying to tell us something about who did this to her but didn't get a chance? If she was in rigor when the killer moved her with her arms wrapped around her waist like that, there's a chance that the killer never saw it."

Gretchen nodded and began walking toward the road. "That's a possibility although it would be pretty sloppy on the killer's part. It could also be that the killer tried to write it after she went into rigor but couldn't finish the word because it was too much of a struggle to pull her arm away from her body."

"You're right," said Josie.

Gretchen said, "I'll talk to her boss and coworkers again. Maybe try to get access to her work files to see if there's anything about 'Pritch' there. I can also try to get some handwriting samples from

Krystal's boss and see if they match up or not. This detail is not being released to the press, though."

Josie followed behind her, wrinkling her nose as she smelled her own body odor after nearly an entire day out in the heat of the cemetery. "Good call."

Over her shoulder, Gretchen said, "You coming back to the station?"

Josie paused at the road, looking back and forth between the vehicle Gretchen had arrived in and her own. "If it's all the same to you, I'd like to go home and shower."

Gretchen stood next to Noah's car, which he had left there for her. She fanned herself with the notebook. "Want to come in after? Write up your report?"

"No, I..." Josie trailed off. What was it? Any other time in her life she would have done anything and everything to be back at work. Normally, it would have been a dream come true to get to come back a day early. What was wrong with her?

From Gretchen's puzzled expression, it seemed she was wondering the same thing. She didn't press Josie. Instead, she said, "First thing tomorrow, then. If the Chief gives the okay, you can work with me on this. I'm sure Dr. Feist will have autopsy results by tomorrow. I'll see what I can come up with in terms of this 'Pritch' business."

Josie gave her a weak smile as she retreated to her car. "Thanks. I'll see you then."

She got in and drove away before Gretchen could change her mind and try to coax Josie into the station that evening. She meant to go home but instead found herself outside the liquor store ten minutes later, staring at its glass storefront. The air conditioning vent blasted her face with cold air. Now that the sweat had dried on her body, goosebumps rose along her flesh. A memory of Wild Turkey burning its way down her throat and into her stomach, warming her, settling her muddied thoughts, called to her. A siren song. She hadn't felt this kind of thirst in years. *Just one shot*, said a voice in the back of her head, *two at the most*. They made small bottles now. She could buy them, drink them, toss them in the trash can right here in the strip mall and go home. Noah was still at work—Gretchen had his car. No one would know. She could shower and brush her teeth long before he got home.

Josie groaned. In the weeks she had been attending her therapy sessions, Dr. Rosetti had probably talked more than she had. Josie had given her the no-frills, emotionless version of her horrific childhood. Even after Paige probed with her several variations of the question "How did that make you feel?", Josie refused to attach her emotions to the events she recounted. Still, they had come up whenever she discussed Lisette's murder, no matter how hard she tried to compartmentalize her grief and trauma. The thing Paige liked to say over and over again was, "Just sit with it. Sit with the feeling. Let it pass through you."

Downing two shots of Wild Turkey was most certainly not an effort to sit with any of her feelings. What she wanted was to erase them, obliterate them, push them to the far ends of her consciousness. White-knuckling her steering wheel, Josie let the feelings swirling inside seep out from the place in her mind she dared never go. The discomfort became physical. A weight pressing on her chest. A pounding in her temples. A thickness in her throat. Was there a way to stop it, she wondered. Once she unleashed the feelings, could she stuff them back in? Or would she need Wild Turkey to do that? Dr. Rosetti always said they were just feelings, and they would pass, but the tightness in her chest and the tingling in her fingers told another story.

The images that unfolded in her nightmares were real to her now in the daylight, crowding her vision. Her grandmother's body jerking as the first round of buckshot hit her. Lisette falling and rising up again, taking the second spray of buckshot, putting herself in front of Josie with the kind of superhuman strength born of a mother's love.

A mother's love.

In all of Josie's childhood only Lisette had loved her with such ferocity. Now she was gone. Josie felt the chasm yawn open inside her, and it was dark and bottomless. She didn't believe Paige Rosetti when she said that the feelings were only feelings and could not harm her. The demons rising from the cleft in her soul would consume her. Hands shaking, she turned the car off and opened her door. What was a few shots of Wild Turkey to this pain?

Her sneakered feet touched the ground of the parking lot. Shaky legs straightened, bringing her to her full height. Then she heard a noise. A small clink but so unfamiliar that it registered immediately, even through the panic building inside her. Panning the ground, she saw the small, beaded rosary bracelet that her Chief had given her when Lisette lay dying in the hospital. She bent to pick it up, closing her palm around it. The beads were dark green and polished— lovely, really—with a medal that showed a woman in flowing robes. Around her head were the words: *Our Lady Untier of Knots.*

Josie wasn't Catholic. She wasn't even particularly religious. Between her childhood and the atrocities she saw in her job, it was difficult to believe in anything besides the depravity of human beings. Her Chief wasn't Catholic either. He wasn't even nice. Bob Chitwood had been hired by the Mayor four years ago. He was abrasive and quick to anger, and in the years he had been with them, he hadn't seemed to warm up to anyone at all. But in his way, with this bracelet, he had tried to either help or comfort Josie. She wasn't sure which. She recalled the conversation they'd had outside of the hospital as her grandmother was inside, fighting for her life.

"I don't understand, sir."

He reached forward and curled her fingers over the bracelet. "Someday, I'll tell you the story of how I got that thing. All you need to know right now is that even if you never prayed a day in your life, when someone you love is dying, you learn to pray pretty damn fast.

Someone who believed very deeply in the power of prayer gave that to me, and at the time, it was a great comfort. Maybe it won't mean shit to you. I don't know. Regardless, if this is Lisette's time, nothing's gonna keep her here, but you? You're gonna need all the help you can get. You hang onto that until you're ready to give it back to me, and Quinn, I do want that back."

"How will I know when I'm ready to give it back?" Josie asked.

Chitwood started walking away. Over his shoulder, he said, "Oh, you'll know."

Josie still had no idea what he'd been trying to accomplish or how she would know when to give it back. It felt like some kind of test, and as she frequently feared when it came to Chief Chitwood, she was afraid she'd fail.

What she did know was that it wasn't time to give the bracelet back now. Not yet.

"I'm not ready," she muttered, squeezing the warm beads in her hand.

"Miss? You okay?" said a man walking past. He stopped a few feet away from her.

Josie looked around, her reverie broken. Her car door hung open and she stood beside it, clothes rumpled and now stiff with dried sweat, fisting a rosary bracelet. She forced a smile for the stranger.

"Yeah," she said. "Thanks. I'm fine. I—I need to go home."

She got back into her car and tucked the bracelet into her pocket again. At home, she let Trout, their Boston Terrier, cover her face with kisses. She petted him and gave him all the requisite attention. Then she showered and ordered a pizza. By the time she was settled at the kitchen table googling Krystal Duncan, Noah came home. He greeted Trout and walked into the kitchen, planting a kiss on Josie's head before snatching up a slice of pizza.

"You had an interesting day," he said.

"I did," said Josie. "Any news on the Krystal Duncan case?"

"Nope," Noah said. "Gretchen's trying to figure out what 'Pritch' means. She's meeting Dr. Feist at ten tomorrow morning to go over the autopsy findings."

"I'll be there," said Josie.

CHAPTER SEVEN

The city morgue was located in the basement of Denton Memorial Hospital. The hospital itself sat high on a hill overlooking the city. All the other floors provided beautiful views of the small metropolis of Denton and its surrounding mountains, but the basement was windowless and looked like something out of a horror movie with its grimy yellowed floor tiles and drab, white-tiled walls, now gray with age and dirt. It was by far the quietest place in the building. Josie's and Gretchen's footsteps echoed in the long hall as they made their way to the morgue, which consisted of one very large exam room, a walk-in freezer area for holding bodies, and Dr. Feist's office.

They found Dr. Feist in the exam room, leaning over a laptop on one of the stainless-steel countertops that lined the back wall. She wore her usual dark blue scrubs. Her silver-blonde hair was tied back in a ponytail. "Detectives," she greeted them with a smile. "Come in."

The smell of the room, even absent any dead bodies, always curdled any food or drink in Josie's stomach. Even the chemicals that Dr. Feist and her assistant used to routinely disinfect the place could not cover the ever-present stench of putrefaction. Still, Josie managed a smile for the doctor. "It's good to see you back, Josie," Dr. Feist said.

Josie nodded. Her gaze wandered to the examination tables. One was empty but the other held a body lying flat, a sheet covering it.

"That's her," Dr. Feist said. "I was able to break the rigor mortis. I was also able to positively identify her with ID provided by your department, which I understand was found in her home."

"Yes," said Gretchen.

"Cause of death is as I predicted: carbon monoxide poisoning. The findings are pretty characteristic. Her organs, musculature, and viscera had the cherry-red coloring typically seen in those kinds of deaths. She also had characteristic pulmonary edema and organ congestion. A measurement of her level of carboxyhemoglobin will tell us how much carbon monoxide she had in her blood, but I don't have the equipment to do those tests here, so I've sent some blood samples off to the police lab, but the results may take some time. My report won't be finalized until I've got those and the other standard toxicology results back, but I can tell you with certainty that this woman died from carbon monoxide poisoning. The manner of death is homicide. Officer Chan was correct, the substance on her mouth was wax. As I told you yesterday, your team sent some off for analysis, but it looks as though it was candle wax. Whoever did this to her poured it into her mouth."

Josie winced. "Were you able to determine whether or not they did that while she was alive?"

Dr. Feist shook her head. "It's very difficult to determine. There are some burns deeper in her throat. It took me a long time to dig the wax out, and I wasn't able to get all of it. There's damage to her uvula, epiglottis, and pharynx—all the structures toward the back of her mouth— but not so much her gums or inside of her cheeks, or even her lips."

Gretchen's notebook was out, and she scribbled as Dr. Feist spoke but now she paused, pen in the air, and said, "How is that possible? Wouldn't she be struggling? Thrashing? There's no way I would let someone pour hot wax down my throat without a fight."

"Unless someone was holding your head while someone else poured," Josie suggested.

Dr. Feist nodded. "Yes, that could be, but given the partial burning, it's more likely that the wax was used as she expired."

"You mean in the moment of her death," Gretchen said.

"Yes. You must remember she would have been extremely disoriented. Carbon monoxide poisoning causes headaches, nausea, dizziness, weakness, fatigue. If the wax was poured into her throat as she was dying, it's likely she didn't even know what was happening at that point. That would account for how carefully it was poured, so as to injure the structures deeper in her throat and mouth but not so much inside her cheeks or her lips."

Josie asked, "Is there any way to know how long she was exposed to carbon monoxide?"

Dr. Feist shook her head. "It depends on the size of the structure the person is in when they're exposed and the concentration of carbon monoxide. It could take less than an hour or it could take several hours. There's really no way to know for certain. In all of the cases I've seen in my career, they've either been suicide or accidental and the person was found where the poisoning and death occurred. With Krystal Duncan, I have no idea."

Gretchen sighed. "What about time of death?"

Dr. Feist frowned. "That's a little tricky. I can't narrow it down as much as I'd like but I can tell you this: when she was found, she was in full rigor, which usually appears between one and six hours after death."

"That's a huge window," Josie said.

Dr. Feist held up a hand. "But the average is two to four hours. Livor mortis and rigor mortis are usually seen together. As you know, livor mortis is when the blood settles into the lowest parts of the body and causes the discoloration. This occurs within thirty minutes to four hours after death and becomes fixed between eight and twelve hours. When livor mortis becomes fixed, moving the body will not change the area of discoloration."

Gretchen said, "But before it's fixed, if you move the body, the area of discoloration will change."

"Right," said Dr. Feist.

Josie said, "What happened when Krystal Duncan's body was moved from the cemetery to the morgue?"

"The blood settled elsewhere," Dr. Feist said. "Here." She folded back the right side of the sheet to expose Krystal's arm, which now lay at her side, palm down. Dr. Feist lifted the arm so that they could see the word "Pritch" written on the inner forearm. Where the skin had been pale at the cemetery, it was now a bright red. "Livor was not fixed when Josie found her yesterday morning. She was, however, in rigor. She would have had to have died and been left posed for some time in order to go into rigor while in this position. It's likely that whoever brought her to the cemetery probably had the same trouble that the EMTs had with her yesterday."

Josie said, "You mean she was in the kneeling position when the killer moved her."

"I believe so," said Dr. Feist. "The way that you found her in the cemetery is the way she was positioned when she died. The killer poured wax down her throat as she was dying, then left her like that for somewhere between one and four hours, at which point she went into rigor and then she was moved."

"So the killer exposed her to enough carbon monoxide for long enough to kill her, sealed her airway and her lips with wax as she was kneeling, and then left her like that for hours."

"Yes," said Dr. Feist. "That's my assumption."

"She was moved after rigor set in but before livor was fixed. That means when the boss found her in the cemetery yesterday morning at ten, she'd been dead less than eight hours," said Gretchen. "That's not a very narrow window, doc."

"I'm afraid that I can't narrow it much more than that. Even her body temperature doesn't tell me enough for me to give you a more specific time frame. Typically, the body temperature falls about 1.5 degrees Fahrenheit per hour after death, but it will fall faster if the body is left in a cool area. Assuming she was moved from a cool area to the cemetery, the temperature would have begun to rise again the longer she was out in the heat. It's simply not a reliable factor in determining the precise time of death in this case."

Josie said, "Any sign of sexual assault?"

"No, none."

"Was there anything else? Skin under her nails? Anything?"

"I'm afraid not," Dr. Feist said. "Nothing that would help you identify the killer. But there is one more thing of note." She reached for Krystal's hand, separating her middle finger from the others and holding it so they could see the side of the first knuckle. "I think that Krystal was right-handed. You can see a callous here, which is exactly where a pen or pencil would rest when she was writing."

Gretchen said, "I write with my right hand. I don't have a callous."

"Not everyone does. It's possible she just held her pens too tightly and developed one, or did a lot of note-taking at her job. She also has a scar on her palm from what I believe is a carpal tunnel release surgery." Dr. Feist gently turned Krystal's hand up so they could see her palm. It was cherry red from having lain palm-down in the morgue until livor became fixed, but Josie could see the thin silver scar in the center of her palm where it met the wrist. "Carpal tunnel syndrome is most likely to develop in the writing hand."

Josie said, "If she was right-handed then she most likely did not write on her own arm."

"Precisely," said Dr. Feist. Her hand lingered over Krystal's body. Her head gave a small shake. "Sad," she muttered, almost as if to herself. Then she forced a smile and turned to them. "I'm afraid that's all I can give you, detectives."

"We'll work with it," Gretchen promised her.

CHAPTER EIGHT

In the parking lot, they sat in Gretchen's car with the air conditioning blasting while Gretchen took a few more notes. It was going to be another scorcher; the heat and humidity were already nearly unbearable and it wasn't even noon.

Josie said, "This killer is trying to send some kind of message."

"I agree," said Gretchen without looking up from her notes. "The wax seals her lips. You don't pour wax down someone's throat when they're already taking their last breaths for nothing."

"The carbon monoxide poisoning is strange, don't you think?" Josie asked. "I've never seen this—not a murder. Like you said, it's always accidental or suicide. Whoever did this would need an enclosed area that they could fill with carbon monoxide."

"Right. The easiest setup would be a garage, I'd think. Pull a car right in and leave it running," Gretchen replied. She looked up from her notes, tapping her pen against the pad. "What are we looking at here, psychologically? Did he use carbon monoxide because it was less violent and messy than a shooting or stabbing?"

"Less intimate than strangling or smothering," Josie added. "Or did he use it because he wanted to watch her suffer and decline slowly?"

"Good point. Given the wax and the message on her arm, leaving her at her own daughter's graveside, I'm not sure this killer is turned off by overt violence."

"We're back to the message he's trying to send, then," said Josie. "Was he trying to shut her up with the wax?"

Gretchen set her notepad and pen on the console and put the car in drive, slowly pulling out of their parking space. "That would make sense but then why leave a message on her arm? Why leave her in a public place like that?"

"Because the killer wants us to know whatever Krystal knew," Josie said. "Maybe it's not that he was trying to shut her up but that he wanted us to know that she was hiding something? Her lips were sealed because she was keeping a secret?"

Gretchen drove down the long road that led from the hospital back into town. "Then why leave such an obscure clue? Pritch. What does it even mean? Is it a name? A place? Some kind of inside thing?"

Josie said, "Did you talk to her coworkers again last night?"

"I talked to her boss," said Gretchen. "Everyone else was gone for the day. He didn't know the significance of 'Pritch,' but he said he would have someone on the staff make copies of all the files Krystal was working on when she disappeared." She glanced at the clock on her dashboard. "Actually, we could probably swing by there now and talk to a few more people, get those files."

"When Krystal went missing, you went through the usual questions with the rest of the staff, right?" Josie asked.

"Yeah," answered Gretchen. "I went through those questions with every person who knew her: coworkers, neighbors, the parents in her support group. Was she prone to disappearing for long periods of time? No. Did they know of anyone who might have been giving her trouble? No. Had she been feuding with anyone or had bad blood with someone? Friends, ex-boyfriends, neighbors, clients, anyone? No. Had she expressed any concerns about being followed or stalked recently? No. Could they think of anyone who might have wanted to hurt her? No. We were looking at all dead ends before Dee Tenney stumbled on her in the cemetery."

"I know you said she was a single mother, but did she have any kind of contact with Bianca's dad? Child support? Anything? What about boyfriends or ex-boyfriends who were giving her trouble?"

"Nothing," said Gretchen. "One of her coworkers—a woman named Carly who was evidently closest to Krystal—told us that Bianca was the result of a one-night stand while on vacation in Florida. Krystal never even got in touch with him to tell him about the pregnancy, so that was a complete dead end. That same coworker told us she had had a couple of boyfriends when Bianca was a toddler but stopped dating once Bianca was school-aged. Not enough time or patience. Her focus was on her daughter. The only thing Carly said was that Krystal was not the same since Bianca's death and that all of them worried about her possibly trying to kill herself. We were able to get into her work and personal email as well as her social media accounts, but we didn't find anything useful. You can look at her Facebook page. We got full access to her account but there wasn't much more than what she made public."

Josie took out her phone and pulled up Facebook to search for Krystal Duncan. Her profile picture was of her and a young girl Josie assumed was Bianca Duncan. The girl had looked like a near carbon copy of her mother save for her nose, which was wider and flatter. In the photo, Bianca was dressed in a pair of jeans and a black T-shirt with the word "*Love*" emblazoned in gold across it. One hand rested on her narrow hip. On her other side, Krystal, wearing khaki capris and a pink open-shouldered blouse, leaned in so that the two were cheek to cheek. Both smiled brightly. Josie felt a suffocating sadness. She had lost a lot of people in her life, and although she had never had children of her own, she couldn't imagine anything worse than losing a child. Now both daughter and mother were gone.

Why?

Josie scrolled through Krystal's page, but her privacy settings were strict, and all Josie could glean from it were a few more photos of Krystal and Bianca. "These are all old posts," Josie said. "All focused on Bianca."

"Exactly," said Gretchen. "Bianca was her life and once she died, it was like time stopped for Krystal. Here we are."

Josie pocketed her phone and looked up. The law firm that Krystal Duncan had worked for was housed in a four-story, gray brick building in an area filled with office buildings where West Denton bled into South Denton. Josie followed Gretchen inside. They took the elevator to the third floor and found the suite housing the law offices of Abt and Defeo. Just inside was a swanky guest area with long, shiny leather couches surrounding a teak coffee table. Along one wall sat a small coffee bar with stacks of clean mugs that had the firm's name emblazoned on them as well as various options for coffee and tea. A glass partition separated the guest area from the rest of the suite. A young woman with short blonde hair sat on the other side. As they approached, she slid the window open. Her smile faltered as Gretchen gave her a wave.

"You're here about Krystal again, aren't you?"

"I'm afraid so," Gretchen said.

Josie offered the woman her credentials as well. She took a cursory look and handed them back. To Josie, she said, "I'm Carly Howe. We had a staff meeting this morning about Krystal. Mr. Defeo wanted us to know before the press found out."

"I'm glad that he told you," Gretchen said. "The press got wind of it this morning. They've been calling our press liaison since six a.m. It will probably be on WYEP's noon newscast."

Carly shook her head slowly. "It's just awful. I just can't imagine… Mr. Defeo said you suspect foul play. I don't understand who would want to hurt Krystal. She'd already been through so much."

Josie said, "That's what we'd like to figure out. Can you tell us if everyone who worked with Krystal is here today?"

Carly nodded. "Yes, everyone's here today. Mr. Defeo said you'd be coming by for some files and that you might want to talk with us. Why don't you come on back?"

She leaned to the right and then they heard a buzz and the sound of a lock disengaging. Gretchen reached for the handle of the door beside the window and opened it. Inside, Carly's desk was stacked high with letter boxes. She walked around the desk and pointed to them. "These are the files. I can help you carry them out to your car when you're ready to leave."

"That would be great," Gretchen said.

Josie pointed to the door they'd just walked through. "That's a lot of security for a personal injury firm. Have you had problems?"

Carly laughed. "Nothing serious. We just have a lot of clients who love to show up without an appointment and want to stay and chat for hours. It's easier to tell them the attorneys aren't here when they can't get past the front lobby."

Josie looked beyond her where several desks were arranged in an open area. Only two were occupied—one by a woman in her sixties and another by a woman in her forties, from what Josie could tell. Both spoke on their phones although they shot furtive glances over at Josie and Gretchen. Beyond the desks were several rooms, each labeled with the names of the firm's partners, Gil Defeo and Richard Abt, as well as their function: a conference room, a file room, and a break room.

"I'm sure we can set you up in the conference room if you'd like," said Carly.

"Yes," Gretchen said. "That would work."

Josie said, "Detective Palmer here tells me you were closest to Krystal."

For the first time, Josie saw a crack in Carly's sunny receptionist façade. Her brown eyes glimmered with tears. "Yes. I'm the one who told Gil he should talk with the police when Krystal didn't come to work. It just wasn't normal for her to not answer any calls. I mean, work was all she had left after Bianca passed. I never thought that someone would hurt her though. I mean I thought maybe she did something to herself, but never… I don't know who would do such a thing."

Josie said, "Your boss told Detective Palmer that her friendships deteriorated after the bus crash."

Carly nodded and leaned back against a stack of boxes. "It's terrible, really, but I think people didn't know what to say to her. Like, how to talk to her. It's really hard. What do you say to someone who loses a child?"

"What did *you* say?" Gretchen asked.

Carly blinked slowly, as if surprised by the question. "I didn't say anything. I listened."

Josie said, "She was lucky to have a friend like you."

Carly threw her arms in the air and let them fall back to her sides. "Fat lot of good it did. I wasn't there for her when she needed me most."

"What happened to Krystal is not your fault," Gretchen assured her.

Carly chewed on the nail of one of her index fingers. "I guess."

Josie said, "If Krystal had met someone new or had been having trouble with anyone in her life, do you think she would have told you?"

"If you asked me last week, I would have said yes, but now? I'm not so sure," Carly confessed. "I mean, I thought she told me everything. It seemed to help her when she talked with me. Krystal was really high-strung, you know? Even before Bianca passed away, she was always anxious. Wound real tight. Stressed about everything. I thought we were really close, but who knows? She had other friendships—before Bianca died—but they were mostly superficial. That's why she smo—"

Carly broke off. A hand flew to her mouth.

Josie said, "It's okay, Carly."

She removed her hand from her face and shook her head. "I'm so sorry. That was private. I shouldn't—Krystal wouldn't want me to say anything."

Gretchen's expression was grave. "Carly, Krystal is no longer with us and someone very bad killed her. At this point, we don't know what's going to be important to finding her killer so we need to know everything, even the private stuff. I promise you, you're not doing anything wrong by telling us."

Carly looked over at her coworkers, but they were still speaking on their phones. Her shoulders slumped. She hugged herself. Lowering her voice, she said, "It's just that they're still going to talk about her in the press, you know? Between the trial for the bus driver and now her murder—this is media gold. I don't want her reputation ruined. I know that sounds stupid, but she was my friend."

Josie said, "We'll do everything we can to keep anything you tell us out of the press."

"They'll make it seem like she was a bad mother, and she was not. Not at all. That bus crash was no one's fault but the driver's. He was drunk. But that won't matter to the press. They'll make it out like it was Krystal's fault that Bianca died or that she was on the bus just because—look, it's not a crime to let your kid ride the school bus, no matter what you do in your private time."

"Carly," Gretchen said. "We'll do everything we can to protect Krystal's reputation. I promise you that."

Carly sighed, took a beat, and then said, "She smoked pot, okay? Like, a lot. Every day. But never when she had to be at work or care for Bianca. It was at night, once she and Bianca were in for the day. She said it was the only thing that helped her."

"Medical marijuana?" Josie asked. "Prescribed by a doctor?"

"No," she said quietly.

Josie glanced at Gretchen, who gave her a curt shake of her head. It was their work shorthand. Silent communication. Josie was asking if they'd found any marijuana at Krystal's house, and Gretchen was answering that they had not. To Carly, Josie said, "Did she take anything else?"

"No, never. She drank wine sometimes but that was it. But the press won't see it that way. If they find out she was a pothead, they'll blow it way out of proportion and the story won't be about those kids dying or Krystal being murdered, it will be about Krystal being some kind of drug addict and terrible mother, which she was not."

Gretchen asked, "Do you have any idea where she got her supply?"

Carly hugged herself tighter. "I don't know. Some guy under the East Bridge. That's all she told me."

"Thank you, Carly," Josie said. "That is helpful."

Carly didn't look convinced. After a second, her eyes widened. "Do you think it was her dealer who did this to her?"

Gretchen said, "We really can't say at this point, but we'll look into the person who was providing her with marijuana and go from there."

Josie asked, "Is there anyone else she talks to? Anyone else she might confide in?"

"Not that I can think of. I mean, other than that support group she's in—the one for the parents of the kids who were killed in the crash with Bianca."

Gretchen said, "You mentioned that the last time we spoke. I did talk with the other parents, but no one had seen her since their last meeting, and no one had any ideas where she could have been. It might be worth talking to the person who runs the group to see if they've got any information. By any chance, do you know who that is? Or where the group meets?"

"No, I'm sorry. But I'm sure if you ask one of the other parents, you could find out."

"Thank you," said Josie. "One last thing before we talk to your colleagues. Does the word 'Pritch' mean anything to you?"

Carly's brow furrowed. "Pritch?" she said. "What is that? Like, a name?"

"We don't know," Josie said. "We were just wondering if it meant anything to you? If you'd ever heard Krystal talk about a person or place called 'Pritch' or maybe something close to it."

"No, I'm sorry," Carly said. "Where'd you get that from, anyway?"

"We're not at liberty to say," Gretchen told her.

CHAPTER NINE

They spent over two hours at Abt and Defeo interviewing the rest of the staff as well as the two attorneys. No one had anything to add to what Carly had told them and none of them recognized the word "Pritch"—as a name or a place or even the partial name of a person or place. Josie and Gretchen loaded almost a dozen boxes into the back of Gretchen's car and headed for lunch.

"First day back," Gretchen said as she pulled up in front of Josie's favorite restaurant. "I'm buying."

Josie gave her a smile as they walked in and found a table in a back corner of the place where they could discuss the details of a murder case without being disturbed or alarming anyone.

"Have you seen the Chief yet?" Gretchen asked Josie after the waitress took their order.

"No. I was in early this morning, but he didn't come out of his office."

"He's still pissed," Gretchen told her.

Josie reached into her pocket and felt the rosary beads, warm against her fingertips. "As opposed to what?"

Gretchen snorted. "Good point." She put her notebook onto the table but didn't open it. Instead, her gaze bore into Josie. "You okay?"

Josie shrugged, feeling the saliva in her mouth dry up. She thought about yesterday's near-miss in the liquor store parking lot. *But I didn't go in*, she reminded herself.

"Josie," said Gretchen, and Josie knew Gretchen was serious because she almost never called her by her first name. It was always "boss." Josie had been the interim Chief of Police before Chitwood was hired and everyone in the department had called her "boss." She was the one who had hired Gretchen. Even after Chitwood came on as Chief, the staff still called her "boss."

Josie swallowed, willing her voice not to crack when she spoke. "I'm—I'm—"

"Don't say fine. That's not an acceptable answer."

"Why does everyone want to talk about stuff all the time?" Josie asked irritably, the words pushing out before she could moderate her tone.

Gretchen laughed, a good old-fashioned belly laugh.

"I'm being serious," Josie said when Gretchen didn't stop.

"I know," Gretchen said finally, settling down with a sigh. "I know you're serious. The easy answer to your question is that we're worried about you. The reason I asked is because I think that when we are dealing with stuff—big stuff, hard stuff—we don't even know what we're feeling until we try to say it out loud. I mean, sometimes. To be fair, asking you if you're okay after you lost Lisette is a pretty stupid question. So let me rephrase: what's your level of not being okay right now?"

This time Josie laughed. In the four months since Lisette's murder, this was the best question anyone had asked her. "On a scale of one to ten? Ten being I can't even function and I want to die? One being a mild feeling of discomfort? A six. Although it seems to change each hour."

They fell silent as the waitress brought their drinks. Once she left, Gretchen said, "That sounds about right. You ever get to an eight or nine and you call me, you got that? I know you've got Noah, but I'm here, too."

"What do I say?" Josie asked, only half joking, because she wasn't good at dealing with her own emotions. "'Hey Gretchen, I'm at an eight?' Or do I need a secret word or something?"

The waitress came back and set their entrees in front of them. Again, Gretchen waited until she was gone to speak. "Sure, why not?" Looking at her plate, she said, "You get to an eight and all you have to say is 'ravioli' and whatever we're doing, wherever we are, I'll get you the hell out of there. Or come get you. Whatever the case may be."

"Ravioli," Josie said, unable to suppress her smile.

"You got it," Gretchen said, digging into her plate of pasta.

Josie watched her eat for a few seconds. Then she took a bite of her burger and turned her thoughts back to the case. "The support group that Carly talked about for the parents of the kids killed in the bus crash—how long had Krystal been going to that?"

Gretchen dabbed her chin with a napkin. "About eighteen months. Maybe a little longer. The crash was over two years ago. I'm thinking that if she met with these people every week for nearly two years, at least one or two of them might know more about her personal life than they initially let on. Now that we've got a murder on our hands, I'd like to talk to them again—this time in person."

"We can start with Dee Tenney," Josie said. "When Noah took her back to the station yesterday to get her statement, he didn't know about the 'Pritch' thing yet so he didn't have a chance to ask her."

"We'll go after lunch. But first I want to get over to the East Bridge and show Krystal's picture around, see if anyone will admit to selling her drugs or at least to seeing her down there."

Denton had two bridges that spanned a branch of the Susquehanna River. One was located in South Denton. It was small and saw little traffic. The other was the East Bridge, which was much larger and well-used by motorists. Due to its more central location, the area underneath it was home to a good deal of the city's homeless population as well as its drug users and dealers. No matter how much time and resources Denton PD spent trying to eradicate the drug activity from beneath the East Bridge, it never quite went away. The sun was high in the sky as they parked near the bridge and picked their way down the incline to the bank of the river, dodging rocks, weeds, discarded food wrappers, and empty beer bottles. Josie spied some used needles and tiny plastic bags used to hold a number of different drugs.

On the bank of the river, the air was cooler, for which Josie was grateful. A light breeze lifted the hair from the back of her neck. A few people stood near the water. When they noticed Josie and Gretchen, they started walking briskly under the bridge where a cluster of tents and lean-tos made from cardboard boxes and blankets sat like crooked decaying teeth in the maw of the hollow beneath the bridge. As the people they'd seen on the bank disappeared among the shelters, Josie saw some blankets and other types of coverings ripple as the occupants peeked out to see the new arrivals. Beyond the tent homes, a group of people scattered, running up the hill and away from the bridge. It was typical of any time the police visited the area.

They spent an hour flashing Krystal's photo around to the reluctant occupants beneath the bridge. No one under the East Bridge ever wanted to speak with police, but over the years and the course of various cases, a handful of people had come to some sort of grudging trust in Josie. One of those people was a woman who informed Josie that she had seen Krystal there about once a week for several years and that she always talked to a man named Skinny D. Josie texted Noah and asked him to check their database for anyone by that nickname who had been questioned, detained, or arrested in Denton in the past several years. If he'd been selling drugs under the East Bridge for any length of time, chances were good that he'd had contact with their department at some point or another.

After getting a description from her and searching around a little more, they found Skinny D along the top of the bridge. He'd been with the group who had fled when Josie and Gretchen first showed up. As Josie's informant had told them, he wasn't skinny at all. She put him at about five foot eight and three hundred pounds. A white tank top hugged his thick frame. His khaki shorts were wrinkled and bore a myriad of old stains. Greasy black hair had been pulled behind his head in a messy man-bun. Thick glasses with black frames sat on his narrow nose. Josie couldn't decide if he was in his mid-twenties or his mid-forties. It was hard to tell. His face was unlined and yet, he had the look of someone who had seen a lot in life. His bridge enterprise was probably his full-time job. He leaned against one of the concrete barriers that separated the start of the bridge from the shoulder of the road. A cigarette dangled from his thin lips. Dark beady eyes tracked their approach.

"You Skinny D?" Gretchen asked as they drew up a few feet from him.

"Depends," he replied.

"What's your name?" Josie asked.

His gaze lingered on her for a beat too long. "You're that cop, aren't you? The one who's always on TV?"

Josie showed him her credentials. "We're not here to jam you up if that's what you're worried about, Skinny D."

He laughed, his voice a rasp. "Don't sound too good coming out of a cop's mouth."

"Then tell me your real name," Josie said. "I'll find out eventually anyway."

"You here to arrest me for something?"

"We're here about Krystal Duncan," Gretchen said.

His eyes narrowed. "Who?"

Josie took out her phone and pulled up the photo of Krystal that had been used in the press since her disappearance. She held it out for him. Leaning in toward the screen, he cupped his hands over his eyes to shade the sun. "Oh shit," he said. "Lady K."

Josie heard her phone chirp with a text message and took it back. She swiped to see that it was from Noah. A booking photo for one Dorian Kuntz from three years earlier. In it, Skinny D was considerably thinner. He'd been arrested for possession with intent to distribute schedule-two narcotics. Scrolling down, Josie saw that the charges had been dismissed. He was thirty-eight years old, and he'd been arrested almost two dozen times on drug charges. Only twice had he been prosecuted, taking a plea deal both times and receiving nothing more than probation.

"That's what you called her?" Gretchen said.

"Yeah, she was a reg—I saw her here a lot."

Josie pocketed her phone and sighed. The sun beat against them out here in the open. Sweat gathered on her forehead and along her neckline. "We already know she bought pot from you, Dorian."

His eyes widened at her use of his formal name. "Hey, not so loud, okay?" His eyes darted around them but up on the road, they were alone.

Josie glanced at Gretchen whose mouth twitched. Dorian noticed as well. "It's not funny," he said.

Gretchen flattened her lips into a straight line. She wasn't sweating at all. Josie said, "No one said it was, but you're right, Skinny D is probably a better street name than Dorian."

He rolled his eyes and flicked his cigarette onto the ground. "What do you bitches want?"

Gretchen said, "When is the last time you saw Krystal Duncan?"

He folded his arms over his protruding stomach. Josie could see sweat stains in the places his shirt had creased into his skin folds. "Last week."

"What day?" Josie asked.

"Tuesday. She always came on—I always saw her around on Tuesdays. Wait. Well, last week she was here Tuesday and Wednesday."

Gretchen asked, "How long had she been coming here on Tuesdays?"

He shrugged. "Like, a long time. Years."

"More than five?" Josie asked, wiping the sweat from her brow with the back of her forearm.

"I guess."

"You said last week she was also here on Wednesday. Did you talk to her?"

Dorian said nothing.

Gretchen said, "Listen, Skinny D. Krystal? She disappeared from her house last Thursday and then yesterday she turned up murdered. We're trying to figure out who killed her."

His eyes widened. "Lady K is dead?"

"You don't watch the news?" Josie said pointedly. "Or go on social media? Her face has been everywhere for four days."

He motioned toward the underside of the bridge. "Does it look like we get TV down here? Are you telling me she's really dead? Like someone offed her?"

"Yes," said Gretchen. "That's what we're telling you. I'm not interested in arresting you because you sold a dead woman some weed. I need to know what you know about Krystal. I need to know where you've been since Thursday night, and then I need to talk to anyone who can corroborate that."

He reached up and rubbed his chin. "This is bad," he muttered, almost to himself. "But look, I didn't have nothing to do with anything that happened to Lady K. I been here all weekend just like I am all the time. A buncha people down there can tell you that."

Josie said, "Great. We'll get some statements after we talk with you. What can you tell us about Krystal?"

His head hung. He seemed genuinely saddened by the news of Krystal's death, but Josie couldn't tell if it was because he had had some affection for her or if it was because he was losing a regular client. "She was a good person, that's what I know. She treated me like… like a human being, you know? Not like some guy she met up with here but was too good to actually talk to."

Josie noted his vague wording—he still wasn't willing to admit to a couple of detectives that he had been selling Krystal drugs. But she wasn't sure that made him a murderer. While he might have been able to hold her somewhere under the bridge for a few days with no one being any wiser, there was no place nearby he would have been able to poison her with carbon monoxide.

"You have a car?" Josie asked him, changing the subject quickly, wanting to keep him off guard. A fat drop of sweat slid from the back of her neck down her spine. She resisted the urge to pull her polo shirt away from her body.

"Nah. If I need a ride somewhere, I ask someone. There's a guy from one of the local churches who comes out here all the time. Brings us food, takes us to doctor's appointments and shit like that."

Gretchen said, "You said that Krystal came on Tuesdays but last week she was here on Wednesday as well. Why was that? Did she talk with you about anything? Anything at all?"

He shrugged again. "Lady K always wanted weed, okay?"

Still, he put the responsibility on Krystal. She had wanted weed. He hadn't sold it to her.

"Fine," Josie said. "She came here on Tuesdays looking for pot. Was there ever anyone with her?"

"Nah, she rolled solo. Always."

Josie asked, "What did she want on Wednesday?"

"Something more potent, she said."

"Like what?" asked Gretchen.

"Like painkillers or something. Like oxy or ketamine."

"Did she get it?" Josie asked.

"Nah. There wasn't any."

What he really meant, Josie thought, was that he hadn't had any to sell her and he didn't want to send her to another dealer and risk losing her as a client.

"Besides," he added. "I didn't want her getting into all that. I told her that. She was a nice lady. Had a good job. A good life.

Weed is one thing but once you start taking oxy or ketamine on the regular, it's not good, you know?"

Painting himself as the hero, Josie thought. Yet he clearly didn't know Krystal that well if he described her as having a good life. Losing her daughter had shattered her life, so much so that her coworkers worried she might harm herself.

"Sure," Josie said without sincerity. "Had she ever asked about painkillers before that?"

"No," said Dorian.

Gretchen said, "Did she say why she suddenly wanted painkillers?"

He pulled a crushed pack of cigarettes out of his back pocket and fished one out, putting it between his lips. As his hands searched his front pockets for a lighter, he said, "Don't really remember. I mean she said a lot of shit that night."

"Was she upset?" Josie asked. "Or did she always talk a lot when she came here?"

A lighter appeared in his hand. He lit his cigarette and took a long pull. On an exhale of smoke, he said, "She was upset that night. That's why she wan—that's why she asked about painkillers. I told her, 'nah, you don't want to get into those,' and she said, like, she was upset and needed more than just weed or she was gonna lose it or some shit like that."

Gretchen said, "Did she say anything at all about why she was upset?"

Dorian pinched the cigarette between his thumb and index finger and held it away from his mouth. Smoke blew back at him and he blinked several times. "I don't know. She said she found something out or something like that."

"Found what out?" Josie asked.

He took another drag of his cigarette, held in the smoke for a second, and exhaled. The heat from the smoke made Josie feel like she was in an oven inside of another oven. She waved the smoke from her face. Dorian said, "I don't know. She didn't say. I didn't ask. She just said she found something out, and she couldn't deal with it. Said she needed something to forget everything even if it was just for a few hours. I just told her she couldn't get painkillers down here. That was it."

Gretchen and Josie exchanged a look, and Josie knew they were thinking the same thing: Dorian Kuntz didn't look good for Krystal Duncan's murder. Still, they had to do their due diligence.

"Dorian," Gretchen said. "Does the word 'Pritch' mean anything to you?"

He tossed the butt of his cigarette onto the ground, close to the first one. His lips puckered momentarily. A crease appeared between his eyebrows. "What?"

"Pritch," Gretchen repeated. "That mean anything to you? Sound like someone you know? Someone around here?"

"Never heard of it."

CHAPTER TEN

Skinny D found three people under the bridge willing to corroborate his alibi. While Gretchen took down their personal information, Josie spoke with Noah on the phone to get as much information about Dorian Kuntz as possible. As it turned out, he was homeless, which made it even more unlikely that he could have abducted and held Krystal Duncan from Thursday evening through Monday morning. He had also told the truth about not owning a vehicle. As they got back into the car and pulled away, Josie said, "I don't think he's involved."

Gretchen rolled down the windows and blasted the AC. Hot air rushed from its vents as the air conditioning system lumbered to life. "Me neither. I think the question at this point is, what did she find out that sent her to the bottom of the East Bridge looking for something that would get her obliterated?"

"According to Carly, without Bianca, she only had three things in her life: work, weed, and that support group."

"Which is why we're going to go talk to Dee Tenney right now," Gretchen said. "I texted Mettner and had him message me her address."

The drive to West Denton took longer than expected due to traffic. It was nearly dinner time and motorists all over the city were headed home at the same time. What should have been a fifteen-minute drive took nearly forty-five minutes. Josie tried to keep her mind on the case, but it kept wandering to Lisette and the night she'd been murdered. Trying to push those images out of her brain, she forced herself to find a memory of Lisette as she had been in life. Vivacious, grinning, a mischievous gleam in her eyes. Gray curls bouncing at her shoulders as she threatened to mow over anyone in her path with her walker. Without her realizing it, Josie's hand had found its way inside her pocket and clasped the rosary bracelet. The medal dug into the flesh of her palm as they pulled up to a large, two-story, tan stucco home with a two-car garage and basketball net in the driveway.

This part of West Denton was the quietest and safest part of the city. In all the years that Josie had been on the force, she'd only been called out there twice—once for a car accident and once for a stolen bicycle. On the street where Dee Tenney lived, the houses were quaint and well kept, like something out of a magazine. The families that lived here were somewhere north of middle-class but south of affluent.

Josie followed Gretchen up the front walk and let her ring the doorbell. A moment later, Dee Tenney opened the door, her tight smile failing once she realized she was staring at two police detectives.

"Can I help you?" she asked.

Gretchen said, "Mrs. Tenney, we need to speak with you about Krystal Duncan."

Dee looked behind her momentarily before turning back toward them. The skin around her eyes tightened. "I have someone here," she said. "But I guess, well, just come in."

They followed her through a dimly lit foyer into a large, open kitchen with shiny hardwood floors and granite countertops. There was an island in the center of the room on which Dee had obviously been making a salad, given the large bowl of lettuce and around it, other vegetables in various stages of being cut up. To the right was a large wooden table with four chairs around it. A teenage girl sat in front of a laptop, earbuds plugging her ears. Her long blonde hair was pulled into a ponytail. She looked at them as they walked in, blue eyes wide and curious.

Dee stood awkwardly between the table and the island counter-top, hands clasped at her waist. "Well, I…" she began. She gestured to the counter. "I was making dinner."

"We won't be long," Josie promised.

Dee motioned toward the girl at the table. "This is Heidi. She's… Well, I'm just looking after her for Corey. That's my neighbor. He's a single dad. Long work hours and all that. She's a junior counselor at a summer camp, and she comes here after for dinner."

Heidi took out her earbuds and said hello.

"It's good to see you, Heidi," said Gretchen.

Josie took a moment to search her brain for how they might know one another, but Dee filled in the blanks. "Heidi is the sole survivor of the bus crash," she told Josie.

As if she didn't want any more of the narrative to be constructed without her input, Heidi said, "My dad is single, always has been, and I get shuffled around to the neighbors. Well, not anymore, not since the accident. Only Mrs. Tenney wants to see me."

Dee looked over at Heidi, stricken. "Oh, Heidi, that's not true."

Heidi laughed. "Yes, it is, Mrs. Tenney. It's fine. I get it."

Dee didn't look mollified. She kept staring at Heidi with a mixture of horror and sadness on her face. Shaking her head, Heidi popped the earbuds back into her ears and resumed typing away on her laptop. Dee focused her attention on Josie and Gretchen but didn't ask them to sit or offer them anything. It didn't matter. The air conditioning alone felt heavenly. Josie plunged ahead. "We're here to ask you about the support group that you and Krystal belonged to. I know you spoke to my colleague here over the weekend, but I was hoping you could tell me about it."

"Oh," Dee said, her posture loosening a bit. She walked over to the island countertop and began dicing tomatoes. "It's just a few of us. Not everyone goes to it. We've been meeting once a week, sometimes more, since after the funerals. Honestly, I'm not sure if it hurts or it helps but this…" She waved the knife in the air. Josie saw tears gather in her eyes. "This experience—losing a child—it's not something people understand or even know how to respond to. It's a very lonely place to be, in the aftermath of something like this, and so we found that we could only talk with one another. Faye Palazzo, one of the other mothers, she had been seeing a psychologist and she set it up with that doctor."

"Who is the doctor?" Josie asked.

"Paige Rosetti."

Josie felt a jolt. She'd been going to Paige's house for therapy for a couple of months now and had never seen any of the bus crash parents nor had Paige said anything. Then again, Paige wouldn't say anything. Privacy was paramount in her work. Plus, Josie was only there once a week for forty-five minutes. She only ever ran into the patient who left before her. "Do you meet at her office?" Josie asked.

"Yes," Dee answered.

Gretchen had her notebook out. "Tell me again who attends these meetings? You said not everyone goes."

Dee went back to work on her tomatoes, her eyes downcast. "Well, obviously, Corey doesn't go."

Corey hadn't lost a child, Josie thought, looking over at Heidi. He was the lucky one.

"Then there's Nathan and Gloria Cammack. They're divorced now. Gloria came at first but then once they broke up, she stopped coming. Sebastian and Faye Palazzo, and Krystal."

"What about your husband?" Gretchen asked.

"Miles rarely comes to meetings." She dumped the sliced tomatoes into the large bowl and rinsed the cutting board in the sink. "We're separated," she added over her shoulder.

Josie knew that many marriages didn't survive the loss of a child so this came as no surprise. "When do you meet?" she asked.

Dee brought the cutting board back to the counter and started slicing cucumbers. "Monday evenings. Always Monday evenings."

"Did you meet last night?" Gretchen asked.

Dee froze then gave a stiff nod.

Josie said, "It's okay, Mrs. Tenney, if you told the group what happened."

She looked up at Josie, tears now streaming freely down her face. "I'm sorry. That other officer, the good-looking one who took me back to the station, he said not to talk to the press. He didn't say I couldn't tell friends or family. You have to understand what a shock it was to find Krystal like that. We've all been through so much. It's so hard. Every day is a struggle." She used the back of her free hand to wipe the tears from her cheeks. With a sniffle, she lowered her voice to a whisper, probably so Heidi wouldn't hear her, and added, "It's excruciating."

Again, Josie found the rosary beads in her pocket. "I understand," she told Dee. Of course, she could never understand. While she'd lost many people in her life, none had been her child. She did, however, understand the ways in which grief could paralyze and cripple you, make you do things you normally wouldn't, the way it sometimes physically attacked you so that you could barely breathe.

Dee swallowed, straightened her spine, and kept slicing cucumbers. "I had to tell them. I couldn't possibly pretend I didn't know. Especially after the way things ended at our last meeting."

Gretchen said, "How did things end at your last meeting? I spoke with Faye Palazzo over the weekend, and she said that Krystal had been upset but that you all were."

Dee swiped a pile of sliced cucumbers into the large bowl and rinsed off the cutting board once more. As she dried it with a dishtowel, she said, "She's right. Krystal was upset." She gave a dry laugh. "That sounds so stupid. We're all upset, all the time, and group is where we come to be most upset with one another."

Josie said, "But Krystal was more upset than usual? Is that what you're saying?"

Dee nodded. She placed the cutting board back onto the counter but made no move to continue her work. "I don't want to say too much about the group. It's private. I'm not sure the other members would be okay with me telling you things that we talk about."

"Understandable," Gretchen agreed. "But Krystal's been murdered, and we need to find the person who did this to her. Anything you can tell us about what she said would be extremely helpful."

Dee took in a shuddering sigh and braced her hands against the countertop. "In broad strokes, I can tell you that we were talking about the fact that the district attorney had asked each of us to be prepared to testify at the trial of Virgil—the bus driver. That's coming up in a few weeks. Did you know that?"

Gretchen grimaced. "Hard not to know about it—it's been all over the news. Also, I was the lead on that case so I'll have to testify as to the contents of my reports."

"Right. Of course. Well, testifying at the trial was the main topic of discussion that night. As long as we've waited for Virgil to be punished, it still means reliving that day again. It's hard, you know?"

Josie and Gretchen nodded in unison.

Dee continued, "Everyone was just talking about how they felt, like we always do, but Krystal was silent. That was unusual. She's a little high-strung. When she gets really anxious, she tends to talk more, not less. Then again, the meeting before that one, it had come out that she had met with Virgil in jail. That would have been a little over two weeks before she went missing. Everyone was very upset with her. We all came down pretty hard on her initially."

Josie said, "I'm surprised she was allowed to meet with him."

Dee shrugged. "Apparently his attorney allowed it. They taped the meeting so there would be no question as to what was said. I think Virgil's attorney was hoping she'd offer some kind of forgiveness, something that he could use at trial to Virgil's benefit."

Gretchen asked, "How did it come up that she had visited him in the first place?"

"She told us," Dee explained. "She was afraid we'd find out some other way, and she wanted us to hear it from her. I mean, in a way it wasn't a surprise. Before the crash, Virgil was a good friend and neighbor to all of us. That's why it was so hard when we found out what he'd done. But anyway, Krystal said it was a mistake, and that she didn't get what she went there for so we should just forget it."

"What had she gone there for?" Josie said.

"I don't know," Dee said. "She never told us. Never had a chance. Everyone was so angry with her that the whole meeting was spent berating her until she left early. Then she came back the next week, her final meeting, and like I said, she was completely silent. Then about halfway through the meeting, she stood up and started screaming. Just screaming at all of us."

"What did she say?" Josie asked.

Dee's knuckles were white against the countertop. "She said, oh my, excuse my language, but basically, 'Screw you. Screw all of you. Bianca wasn't even supposed to be there that day. She wasn't even supposed to be on the bus.' Things like that. Dr. Rosetti tried to calm her down, but she was completely out of control. I never saw her like that before. She told us we could all, you know, screw ourselves, although that's not the word she used. Then she stormed out and we didn't hear from her again. The next thing we knew, her face was on the news and she had gone missing. I'm sorry I didn't volunteer this when you called me over the weekend, but like I said, the things we talk about in group therapy are very private. I probably shouldn't even be telling you now except that Krystal's been murdered, and I . . ."

Gretchen scribbled in her notebook. "You're doing the right thing," she assured Dee.

Josie said, "Besides Krystal, which support group members were there that night, Mrs. Tenney? Specifically."

"Me, Faye, Sebastian, Nathan, and actually Miles was there, too. He likes to avoid me, but I know the upcoming trial is bothering him a lot."

"Do you have any idea what was behind Krystal's outburst?" Gretchen asked.

Dee shook her head. "Not at all. I wish I did. I wish I had. I should have gone after her, tried to talk to her. But all of us are bowing beneath the awful weight of this thing. It's hard to be there for one another when each one of us is…." Again, she glanced at Heidi. She whispered her next words: "barely hanging on."

Josie asked, "Do you have any idea why Krystal would say that Bianca shouldn't have been on the bus that day?"

"No. Bianca rode the bus every day. Krystal's work schedule would allow her to get home at the same time as the bus dropped the kids off around the corner, but she could never get out early enough to pick Bianca up from school. That day was no different than any other day."

"Was there someone in the support group that Krystal was closer with than everyone else?" Gretchen asked.

"No, not that I am aware of. She was always working so much, she rarely had time to socialize even before the accident. Afterward, she withdrew even more. I was glad she joined the group. I thought it was good for her to have some human interaction besides work." She shook her head, and said, almost as if to herself, "Who knows if it's any help? We just keep going. What else are we supposed to do?"

Although her voice was low, Josie noted from her periphery that Heidi was no longer focused on her laptop but on Dee. Was there even anything coming through her earbuds? Had she been listening to them the entire time?

Gretchen said, "One last thing, Mrs. Tenney, and then we'll leave you for the day. Does the word 'Pritch' mean anything to you?"

"Pritch?" Dee asked, a puzzled look on her face.

"Yes," Josie said, spelling it out.

"No, I don't know what it means. I've never heard it before," said Dee.

From the table came Heidi's voice. She said, "I know what it means."

CHAPTER ELEVEN

They all turned toward Heidi. She closed her laptop and took out her earbuds, setting them onto the table. Dee walked over and stood across from her. "Heidi? What are you talking about?"

Heidi looked past Dee, toward Josie and Gretchen. "Pritch was a nickname we had for Wallace Cammack."

Quietly, for Josie's benefit, Gretchen said, "He was one of the kids who died in the bus accident."

"Gail never told me that," Dee said, her voice tremulous.

Heidi gave her a pained smile. "I'm sorry, Mrs. Tenney. It wasn't one of those things that we talked to our parents about. Plus, it was a combination of two words you probably wouldn't approve of."

"Like what?" asked Gretchen.

A slight flush spread across Heidi's cheeks. "Prick and bitch."

Dee's hand flew to her mouth. "Oh," she said.

Josie walked over to the table and looked at Dee. She touched the back of one of the chairs. "Do you mind if we sit, Mrs. Tenney?"

Dee pulled out the chair closest to her, not taking her eyes off Heidi. Taking that as a yes, Josie and Gretchen sat down. Gretchen said, "Heidi, how old are you now?"

"I'm fourteen. You want my dad's permission to talk to me, right?"

Josie said, "Since we're not questioning you as either a suspect or witness to a crime, we don't technically need his permission, but we do always prefer that parents are aware that we're speaking with their children."

"I don't have a mom," Heidi said bluntly. "So you have to get permission from my dad."

"That's fine," said Gretchen.

"Heidi," Dee admonished.

Heidi rolled her eyes. "What? It's true. I don't have a mom." She looked earnestly at Josie and Gretchen. "Adults like to say—" Here she lowered her voice in a tone of mock seriousness. "'Heidi's mom is *not in the picture*,' but what really happened is she was a one-night stand, and she'd just turned nineteen when she had me so she decided that the whole baby thing wasn't for her, and she left me with my dad. I don't even know if she's still alive or not. So, yeah, it's just me and my dad."

Dee pressed a palm to her forehead and closed her eyes briefly. When she opened them, a strained smile spread across her face. "Heidi, I don't think this is the time to get into that. How about if we just ask your dad for permission for these detectives to talk to you?"

"Fine," said Heidi. "I'll text him."

From a backpack beside her chair, she produced a cell phone. Her fingers flew across its screen. They heard a series of beeps and then Heidi slid the phone over to Josie so she could read the text exchange.

Dad, the police are at Mrs. T's to talk about Krystal. Okay if I talk to them about kids I knew at school?

The response was a single letter: *K*.

Gretchen leaned in and took down the number Heidi had texted. Josie knew she'd double check to make sure it belonged to Heidi's father later.

"Okay?" Heidi asked.

Gretchen said, "Tell us about Wallace Cammack."

"He went to my school. He was in my grade."

"You rode the bus with him every day," Gretchen prompted.

"Yeah," said Heidi. "There were six of us that got dropped off last. Me, Gail—that's Mrs. Tenney's daughter—Wallace and his little sister Frankie, Bianca, and Nevin. When the accident happened, Gail and Nevin were in the sixth grade, Frankie was in fifth, and me, Wallace, and Bianca were in seventh grade. But like I said, we were all on the bus together every day. Anyway, Wallace was a bully, and we got tired of it and some of us came up with that nickname for him."

"Pritch," said Josie.

"Yeah. Because he was mean as a prick—" She broke off and looked at Dee, but Dee seemed to have disconnected, her eyes suddenly vacant, her body still. Heidi continued, "But when any of us stood up to him, he would whine like a bitch. He was a pritch."

"You said he was a bully," Gretchen said. "What kinds of things did he do?"

Heidi gave a half shrug. "I don't know. The stuff all bullies do. Call us names, say mean things to us, knock stuff out of our hands. Once, when we had a substitute teacher, he wrote his name in for Student of the Month, which was a joke because he was always in trouble. But the regular teacher never did anything about it. Sometimes he'd pull girls' hair."

Dee blinked and cleared her throat. "He pulled Gail's hair once—really hard. Actually, they got into an altercation. It was right before the accident. Apparently, he pulled her hair in the hall at school. It wasn't the first time. My husband had told her not to take any crap from Wallace Cammack so she hit him. Not hard, just a slap, but he became very angry and pushed her pretty hard into a water fountain. She fell and hit her head. I had to take her to the emergency room. She had quite a lump. Everything was fine but before we had a chance to properly deal with it, the accident happened, and, well…"

She drifted off, eyes going glassy and blank again.

Heidi said, "I know he's dead, but he was a jerk. I mean, I'm sorry he's dead. He was a bully sometimes, but he didn't deserve what happened in the accident. No one did. Still, he caused a lot of trouble for a lot of kids before the crash. A bunch of kids started calling him Pritch. He hated it so much."

Gretchen said, "Did any adults know about his nickname?"

"I have no idea," said Heidi.

Josie asked, "How many kids knew? How many called him Pritch?"

Heidi said, "Well, the kids on the bus. Probably everyone in my grade."

"Who came up with it?" Josie asked.

"I don't know exactly. I mean, it just kind of happened. A few boys in our grade started calling him a prick 'cause he was always messing with everyone. Then one day, on the bus, he kept kicking the back of Nevin's seat—Nevin Palazzo—and Nevin got really mad and stood up and yelled, 'You're such a prick!' Nevin was small and always so quiet and it was kind of funny to see him that mad, you know? Anyway, everyone on the bus started laughing—not at Nevin, at Wallace. They were like, 'Damn, little Nevin's gonna kick your ass' and Wallace got upset and said he wasn't. Then a few of the other boys started chanting 'prick,' and Wallace looked like he was about to cry. That's when Gail said, 'Look at him, he's just a little bitch' and someone in the back of the bus—I don't know who—yelled, 'He's a pritch!' Then everyone on the bus cracked up and Wallace never bothered Nevin again. But the nickname stuck."

"What was the bus driver doing while all this was going on?" Josie asked.

Heidi shrugged. "He was driving. Mr. Lesko didn't pay much attention to what was going on as long as we all stayed seated."

Gretchen said, "Were there a lot of problems on the bus?"

"No, not really. I mean it wasn't like an everyday thing that people were getting bullied on the bus. Maybe at school, but the bus wasn't so bad."

"How long before the crash did Wallace get the nickname Pritch?" Josie asked.

"I'm not sure. A couple of months, maybe?"

Gretchen continued to scribble in her notebook. Josie slid a business card across the table to Heidi. "My cell phone is on there," she said. "If you need anything or if you think of anything else having to do with Wallace and his nickname, you'll let me know, okay?"

Heidi picked up the card and stared at it. "Sure," she said. "Hey, how did you know about that in the first place?"

For the first time in a few minutes, Dee's eyes seemed to take on some life. Her head swiveled in Josie and Gretchen's direction, awaiting their answer.

Gretchen said, "We're not at liberty to say."

CHAPTER TWELVE

Denton's police headquarters was housed in a large, three-story, gray stone building. It was on the historic register and had been converted from the town hall to the police station over sixty-five years ago. It was both beautiful and imposing with its ornate double-casement arched windows and bell tower in one corner. Gretchen circled the building and parked in the municipal lot out back. Normally, the sight of it brought Josie comfort. It was her second home. It was the one place where things always made sense. Here, she was guided by protocol and purpose. Here, she was kept busy with cases to solve—puzzles that kept her mind fully engaged so that it had no chance to dwell on the demons of her past.

Now, she felt a small bud of anxiety bloom inside her as she got out of Gretchen's vehicle and walked toward the entrance. Gretchen was ahead of her, almost to the door, when Josie stopped. The sun had fallen closer to the horizon now that it was after dinnertime. The heat was less oppressive and at this hour, the parking lot was mostly shaded. Still, Josie felt a sheen of sweat envelop her body. She didn't want to go in. But why? She'd been there this morning. She'd been fine.

Gretchen turned back toward her. "Boss?"

Josie swallowed. She willed her feet to move but they wouldn't. It was as if the soles of her shoes had melted into the hot asphalt. She thought about what Dee Tenney had told them about the last support group meeting, how Krystal had come unglued. *Bianca wasn't even supposed to be there that day.* Josie closed her eyes as a wave of feeling washed over her, so strong that her knees trembled. It was the same mantra that had played on a loop in her mind for months. Since the night Lisette died. *She wasn't supposed to be out there.* Josie said those words to Noah almost every night when she woke from her nightmares. If Lisette hadn't been out near the woods, she'd still be alive, and Josie wouldn't have to go back to work and carry on with life as if it was perfectly normal when it wasn't at all.

"Josie," Gretchen said, closer now.

Josie opened her eyes and looked at her friend. Her skin felt hot all over and yet, her limbs started to shiver. "I'm not ready," she whispered to Gretchen.

Gretchen nodded and moved beside Josie, putting a hand under her elbow. Josie didn't need to explain. Gretchen understood. Josie wasn't ready to keep working, to return fully to life as she knew it without Lisette, even though she had no choice. Throwing herself into the Duncan case, returning to work with her whole heart in it, getting back to normalcy, felt like she was accepting Lisette's murder. But she would never accept it.

In her ear, Gretchen said, "This isn't an either-or situation, Josie. You're still here. You have to move forward. It doesn't mean anything except that you're still alive. Lisette lost both her children, and she kept doing all the things that living people do."

Josie nodded. She closed her eyes and took several deep breaths. Dr. Rosetti had made her do a deep-breathing exercise every time she went to therapy. Josie had always thought it was bullshit, but now it seemed to help. A sweet sense of relief filled her as the tidal wave of feelings swept through her consciousness and numbness replaced them again. The sludge. She knew Gretchen was right. Josie had lost her first husband to violence. Even though they were separated at the time, his death had still devastated her. She'd carried on. Why did this feel so different?

Gretchen gave her arm a squeeze. "Besides, we're here to help the dead. Krystal Duncan's killer needs catching. Are you with me?"

Inside her shoes, Josie wiggled her toes, feeling her legs once more. She took in several more deep breaths, shoring herself up.

She reached into her pocket and fingered the rosary beads again. "I'm with you," she said.

Gretchen let go of her arm and stepped toward the door again. "Good. Now let's go see if we can get a few bodies to help carry in all these boxes from Krystal's law firm."

A half hour later, the boxes had all been moved up to the second-floor great room—a large, open area filled with desks where detectives and other officers could make phone calls and complete paperwork. Josie, Gretchen, Noah, and Detective Finn Mettner had permanent desks. They'd been pushed together in the center of the room. Off to the side was the only other permanent desk, which belonged to their press liaison, Amber Watts. Only three uniformed officers remained after helping Josie and Gretchen carry in all the boxes. Noah had gone home for the day and Mettner had the day off. Watts had likely left for the day as well. Josie looked to the Chief's office door, but it remained closed.

Gretchen put one box on Josie's desk and another on her own. Together, they began to sort through the documents that Krystal's boss had given them.

Josie said, "These are all cases she was working on recently?"

"Yeah. I'm not sure what we're looking for exactly though."

"Yeah," said Josie. "I figured this was an I'll-know-it-when-I-see-it situation."

Gretchen laughed. It took them an hour to take an initial pass through all the documents. Neither of them found anything that seemed unusual or that might have upset Krystal Duncan enough to send her down to the East Bridge to get something more potent than pot. They were personal injury cases: car accidents, slip and falls, medical malpractice and product liability cases. Neither Josie nor Gretchen recognized the names of any clients or witnesses. Nothing stood out.

"Maybe this thing that she found out had nothing to do with work after all," Josie said.

"But then why log in to her work database on Saturday? What was she looking for?" Gretchen said.

"Maybe she wasn't looking for anything? Maybe she was trying to signal to someone that she was alive."

"Then why wouldn't she leave a message of some sort? Her boss said no files were even opened. If she wanted to leave a message, she could have opened a file, typed something in, and saved it."

"She was just looking, then. Could the files be viewed without opening them, though? Sort of like a document-preview type of thing?"

Gretchen said, "Yes, Carly showed me how to preview the documents without opening them. It's very possible that Krystal looked around in the files and found whatever she was looking for without opening anything. But this stuff is… not exactly scintillating. Guy breaks his wrist falling in the supermarket. A lady gets rear-ended by a guy driving while texting. What could she possibly have been looking for?"

Josie said, "Maybe she wasn't looking for anything at all. Maybe the killer had her looking for something."

"If that was the case, I'd be more inclined to look at the law firm as the source of whatever trouble that Krystal stumbled onto, but why would the killer write the nickname of Gloria and Nathan Cammack's son on her arm?"

Josie said, "True. We should ask Carly to do a search of all their clients and witnesses to see if the Cammacks' names come up."

Gretchen scribbled on her notebook. "First thing tomorrow, I'll call over there. Then I'm going to talk with Wallace Cammack's parents. In the meantime, I'm going to take another look at these files to see if there's anything we missed."

"You think it's significant that she met with the bus driver just over two weeks before she went missing?" Josie asked.

"I would not have except that the killer left her at her daughter's grave, and now we've got the connection to the Cammacks, whose children were also killed in the accident. I'll leave a message for Virgil Lesko's attorney and see if he'll agree to either let us talk to him or see the video of the meeting with Krystal."

Josie's stomach growled loudly. She smiled sheepishly. "Want to order takeout?"

Gretchen peered at her for a long moment. Then she said, "Why don't you call it a day? I can go over the files myself. I'm sure Noah and Trout would like to see you at the end of your first day back."

"I'm fine," Josie protested, but it sounded weak even to her own ears. After a few awkward moments, she gathered her phone and keys and went home.

Trout greeted her at the door, his bottom wiggling. He let out a series of howls and moans as she knelt to give him attention. He jumped on her again and again, his body a blur of black-and-white fur, frenetically trying to lick her face as he cried out. Noah appeared in the kitchen doorway. "Hey," he said over the din. "Sorry about him. I think he had a hard day."

Josie stood up and Trout jumped again, putting his two front legs on her thigh and kneading with his paws. Noah walked toward her, pointing to his left. Josie looked toward their living room and saw destruction. During the four months she had been off, she'd tried a number of things to keep busy: crocheting, jigsaw puzzles, painting, candle-making, and indoor gardening. Now the remnants of all those hobbies lay demolished and littered across the living room floor.

Noah said, "I'll clean it up, I promise. I just wanted you to see it."

Josie looked down at Trout. As if sensing the shift in her mood, he sat and flattened his ears against his skull, doing his best baby-seal impression. His bulging eyes looked sorrowful and pleading.

"You were home with him for four months," Noah added. "Then today we were both gone all day. He has to get used to the old work schedule again. He's just acting out. At least he didn't destroy the furniture. We might have to start putting him back in his crate though when we leave the house, at least temporarily."

Josie looked down into Trout's mournful brown eyes and felt a relief so palpable that it literally felt like a weight being lifted from her shoulders. This little soul got her. He often seemed to mirror her feelings, and today was no different. She dropped to the floor and crossed her legs, letting Trout climb onto her lap. She leaned in and wrapped her arms around his warm little body. "You had a bad day, too, buddy?" she whispered. "It's okay. It will be okay."

Noah sat down across from her, cross-legged as well. "You had a bad first day back?" he asked.

Josie stroked Trout's back and looked up at her husband. "No. I mean, I don't know. It was… tough." She didn't want to talk but then again, she never wanted to talk. That's what had landed her in therapy. She forced the words out anyway. "I miss her, Noah. I miss her so much, and I feel—" Her throat felt clogged, but she kept going. "I feel so damn guilty, still. Why should I get to just go back to my regular life as if everything is fine when she's dead? Because of me, she's dead."

In her lap, Trout whined. Josie felt his warm tongue on her forearm.

She waited for Noah to say all the things she knew he was supposed to say—the things he had said to her in those first weeks at home when she was rudderless and barely functioning. The things Gretchen, her sister, her brother, her biological parents, and Dr. Rosetti had all said to her in the last four months:

"It wasn't your fault."

"You didn't do anything wrong."

"You have nothing to feel guilty about."

"The killer bears all the responsibility."

But he didn't say any of those things. Instead, he touched her cheek. His hazel eyes were somber and pensive. "I know," he said.

In that moment, Josie believed him. She knew that he was just as familiar with this unique sort of pain and guilt—losing a loved one to violence—as she. His mother had been murdered, and Josie knew that even years later, Noah still asked himself whether she would still be alive if only he had arrived at her house ten minutes earlier. If only Josie had told Lisette to go back to the hotel instead of letting her walk toward the woods, she would still be alive as well.

As if reading her mind, Noah said, "It's a wound, Josie. It doesn't heal. It just scabs over from time to time. But I promise that you will get used to it."

"I don't want this awful feeling to be normal," she choked out.

Again, Trout whined. She scratched between his ears.

"I know," said Noah.

He leaned in and they touched foreheads, making a steeple with their bodies over Trout. They sat like that, breathing into one another until Josie couldn't feel her legs anymore. She wondered if this was what Dr. Rosetti meant when she said to sit with her feelings. Except that this wasn't the crush of horrifying emotion that was so overwhelming that Josie felt it might physically destroy her. This was just the ache and the sadness. This was missing Lisette. This was the knowledge that every day ahead of Josie for the rest of her life now yawned open before her, empty, without her grandmother. This was the hollow feeling that came with unfathomable loss. It was a slow agony, a torturous drip, drip, drip of the new reality. This was the amount of feeling she could handle mostly because Noah didn't try to make any of it go away. He didn't try to gloss over her pain or displace it or distract her from it. He knew none of those things worked. But sitting here with her, with these feelings; this he could do.

He stretched his neck and adjusted his head so he could kiss her lips. "You want dinner?"

"Sure," Josie said. "But first I want to go upstairs."

CHAPTER THIRTEEN

The next morning, Josie met Gretchen in the municipal lot behind the police station and Gretchen drove them back to West Denton. She took a slightly different route since the Cammacks' house was a block over from Dee Tenney's house. As they turned onto the road that ran perpendicular to both the Cammack and Tenney houses, Josie noticed a memorial that had been set up for the five children who had perished in the West Denton bus crash.

"That's the bus stop," Gretchen said. "Before the crash it was just a corner with a big sycamore tree in that front yard right there."

Josie looked at the house that sat on the corner, a split-level brick rancher set back about forty feet from the pavement. There was no sycamore tree now. Instead, paving stones had been laid into the grass, forming a circular patio and around the edges of the patio were five seats, sculpted in bronze. They looked almost like stools twisting up and out of the paving stones. There was room to sit on each one and rather than backs, each stool was fitted with a bronze vase. The children's names had been carved into the vases. Gretchen lingered at the stop sign on the corner and Josie read the names: Bianca, Gail, Wallace, Frankie, Nevin. All the vases were filled with flowers. Bianca's stool also held a teddy bear.

Gretchen said, "The neighbor felt so awful that it happened in his front yard, that he had what was left of the tree removed and donated that space for the memorial. The community raised money for it and a local artist got together with a landscaping company and built it."

"It's beautiful," Josie murmured. But she wondered if it made it easier or harder for the parents to drive past it every single day, probably multiple times a day. Grief was different for everyone, and it changed over time. The memorial, while well-meant and quite lovely, could serve as either a happy reminder that the memories of the children were being honored and kept alive or it could serve as a horrific reminder of all that had been lost. Josie couldn't help but wonder whether all the parents had been consulted. Had they discussed it in their support group?

Gretchen pulled away and two blocks later, turned right onto the Cammacks' street. It was similar to the houses on Dee Tenney's street, which was a block over, filled with mid- to large-sized two-story homes with two and three car garages and large front yards. All the properties were well tended. The Cammack house had cheery cream-colored siding and white shutters. Calla lilies of various colors lined the front walk. Two large stone planters bracketed the front door but both were empty. Josie rang the doorbell, and they waited.

"I thought Dee Tenney said Gloria and Nathan Cammack were divorced."

Gretchen fished her credentials from her pocket. "They are. Gloria got the house. Nathan lives in an apartment downtown. We'll talk to him later today."

"Does she know we're coming?" Josie asked, pressing the bell again.

"I spoke with her this morning," Gretchen responded.

A few minutes passed and Josie was about to ring the bell once more when the door swung open. Gloria Cammack stood before them in a sharp black pantsuit with a pink camisole beneath her jacket. Her shiny black heels were at least six inches. Her blonde hair was slicked back away from her face. In her ear was a Bluetooth. One hand held her cell phone while the other waved them in. She talked rapidly, her tone strident. The effect was disconcerting at first until Josie realized she was talking to someone via the Bluetooth and not them.

"And get those orders out today. I'm not kidding. I don't want to lose this client. They're huge. You hear me? Huge. I know you can do it, okay? You just need to take a minute, center yourself, and refocus. Remember, we don't limit ourselves. We push forward and through. Got it? Okay, yeah. No, I can't. I've got a meeting here at home. I'll be there in an hour."

They followed Gloria deeper into the house. On the walls that led from the foyer to what looked like the kitchen were dozens of framed photographs. Josie slowed to study a few of them. All of them were of Gloria and Nathan's children. Wallace resembled his mother, tall and blond with blue eyes. His hair was shaved short in the back with a sheaf of blond locks nearly covering his eyes. A quick scan of the photos revealed that sometime between toddlerhood and adolescence he had stopped smiling—at least for photos. In what must have been the most recent pictures, where he looked oldest, his face seemed to hold a challenge, as if he were daring someone to mess with him. Was this a typical male, preteen attitude or something more, Josie wondered?

His sister seemed the complete opposite. With brown hair and a wide, infectious smile, Frankie Cammack shone from every photo she appeared in. For every picture that her brother brooded in, Frankie grinned. In some, she stuck out her tongue or struck a sassy pose. There was one photo taken in front of the house where Frankie was doing a handstand and Wallace holding onto her legs. Frankie's face was bright and smiling. Wallace looked to be in the middle of an eye-roll. Each photo she passed made Josie's heart ache even more.

Gloria Cammack's kitchen was surprisingly homey with honey oak cabinets and blue gingham hand towels that matched the curtain over the kitchen sink. Gloria yanked the Bluetooth out of her ear and tossed it onto the kitchen table together with her phone, letting out something between a groan and a small howl of frustration. Turning her back on them, she went to the countertop and poured herself a cup of coffee. "These people come to you with these resumes that make it seem like you're underpaying them. Then they get into the position, and you have to hold their hand with every little thing."

She slammed the coffee pot back into its place with such force, Josie was surprised that the glass didn't shatter. She watched as Gloria took in a breath, staring straight ahead at the cabinet in front of her as if they weren't even in the room. It was almost like she was looking into a mirror. Josie saw her struggling to force a smile onto her face before turning back to them.

"Detective Palmer," she said to Gretchen. "I wish I could say it was nice to see you again, but I'm sure you realize that it's not. No offense."

She took a sip of her coffee, black.

Gretchen smiled. "None taken. Mrs. Cammack, this is my colleague, Detective Josie Quinn."

She took a few steps toward them and extended a hand to Josie. "Gloria Cammack," she announced. "I'm the owner and CEO of All Natural Family and Child."

After they shook hands, Gloria reached up to smooth her hair back although not a single strand had fallen out of place. "I'm so sorry. My manners. Would you like some coffee?"

They declined and Gloria motioned for them to sit at the table. She remained standing, leaning against the countertop, her coffee mug in hand. "This is about Krystal, I'm guessing. I don't know why else you would be here unless you came to tell me that Virgil Lesko was killed in jail while he was awaiting trial."

Gretchen said, "We're here about Krystal."

Gloria tipped her head back and gave a mirthless laugh. "We wouldn't get that lucky, would we? For that bastard to die in jail and spare us all this circus of a trial. Now, with Krystal's murder…" She returned her gaze to them. "I already know she was murdered.

Dee told the group, and Nathan called me afterward because he thought I'd want to know. I don't go to the group. I went once and didn't find it helpful. I'm not sure how I can help, though. Or are you here because Dee told you there was bad blood between Krystal and me."

Gretchen and Josie exchanged a furtive look. This was new information. Josie said, "Why would Dee think that?"

Gloria rolled her eyes. "Oh, come on."

When neither Josie nor Gretchen spoke, a spark of rage flashed in Gloria's blue eyes. She slammed her coffee mug onto the counter and the liquid sloshed over. A few drops got onto her wrist, but she didn't seem to notice. "Really?" she said. "I know that Dee was the one who found Krystal's body. Nathan told me. Which means you talked to Dee. You have to talk to the person who calls in the body, right?"

"Yes," said Gretchen. "We talked with Dee."

"You expect me to believe she didn't tell you? She and Krystal were practically BFFs, at least after the kids—" She broke off and turned her head to the side. Again, she seemed to be going through some private ritual to compose herself. When she spoke again, her voice was calmer. "After the kids died."

Josie said, "Dee Tenney didn't characterize their relationship that way."

Gloria waved a dismissive hand. "Whatever." She stalked over to the fridge and opened the door, stared for a moment, and closed it. Returning to her coffee mug, she took a sip and then said, "Maybe Dee didn't tell anyone. She was never a gossip. Or maybe Krystal didn't tell her. If I'd done something like that, I wouldn't be bragging about it."

Josie said, "Something like what, Mrs. Cammack?"

"Krystal had an affair with my husband."

Gretchen took out her notebook and flipped to a fresh page. "How do you know that?"

"Because she told me."

"When was this?"

"I don't know. A few weeks ago. Or maybe a few months ago. All the days blur together now." She pointed to a corkboard affixed to the side of the fridge where a calendar hung. Josie saw it was still set to May from two years earlier. The month her children had died. Almost every box was filled with what Josie assumed was Gloria's handwriting, graceful and loping. Soccer, birthday parties, drum lessons, softball, dental appointments, art classes. Gloria continued, "My days used to revolve around them and their schedules. Now, there's just… work." She said the word "work" as if it were a prison sentence. Then again, life without your child was a prison sentence, Josie imagined.

Gretchen asked, "How did the conversation with Krystal regarding the affair come about?"

Gloria walked over to the back door. Its windows were covered by blinds, so she threw it open. Josie and Gretchen stood and walked over. Just outside was a wooden deck with wrought-iron patio furniture and more empty stone planters. Beyond that was a fairly large rectangle of grass hemmed in with chain-link fence.

Gloria said, "I had the swing set taken down and removed. I couldn't look at it anymore. I donated the soccer net we used to have back here for Wallace to practice. I just couldn't—" She broke off.

Josie looked over to see her eyes clamped shut, her lips pursed, and her chest heaving. Fists clenched at her sides. For a moment, it seemed like she might break down completely, but she pulled herself together and opened her eyes again although her hands remained balled up. With her chin, she motioned toward the backyard that was directly behind hers, on the other side of the chain-link fence. It was nearly identical to her backyard, just a postage stamp of grass except for a large wooden play structure. On one side it had a slanted climbing wall with bright yellow grips for hands and feet that led to a small deck. There was a slide and a tiny area that was shaped like a house. Access to the faux treehouse could also be gained via a rope ladder. Thick beams extended from the deck and out over the open yard. Two swings hung from them. Immediately, Josie thought of her friend's son, Harris. He was almost five years old. He would love something like this.

Gloria said, "That's Krystal's yard."

Josie raised a brow.

"That's right. Our yards touch. The unlucky five, right? The five children of the famed West Denton crash. Four families in total, since I lost both of my children." Her voice dripped with bitterness. "We all live pretty close to one another. On that street, about seven or eight houses down, is the Tenneys' place. Another block over are the Palazzos. Guess what? That son of a bitch Virgil Lesko's house is only four more blocks in that direction. It was never sold. Did you know that? His son lives there. His son! I mean he's a grown man, but still. Can you imagine staying in the same neighborhood after your father killed five children?"

Trying to get Gloria back on track, Josie said, "Did you speak with Krystal often, since your yards connect?"

Gloria met Josie's eyes for a moment before turning back to the playset. "No. I don't talk with her. We weren't close when the kids were alive, and we weren't after. But I wanted to be able to come out to my yard and sit on my deck and not think about what a shitshow my life has become for five goddamn minutes once a day or even once a week and that fucking playset is there. I didn't say anything at first. For almost two years, I didn't say anything. But then I couldn't look at it any longer. Why would she keep it?"

Gretchen said, "Did you ask her?"

"I couldn't take it anymore, so yes, I asked her. A few months ago. I asked her to have it removed. I even offered to cover the cost. I know she's not as financially comfortable as some of the other families who live here."

Josie said, "But she didn't have it removed."

Gloria shook her head. A flush crept from her throat into her cheeks. "No. She said Bianca loved that thing. I said Bianca was almost thirteen goddamn years old. She hadn't touched it in years. I told her. I said, 'Krystal, we're both going through the same thing, and if something over here that you had to stare at every day bothered you that much, I would get rid of it in a heartbeat if that meant easing some of your pain.' Do you know what she said to me?"

No answer seemed necessary. Gloria was on a roll, as if she'd been aching to tell someone about the situation. She went on, "She told me to go fuck myself. That's when she told me. She said for years she had to stare at something that bothered her, which was my husband playing house with me and our kids while he was having an affair with her. Every night, she said, he climbed over the fence to be with her."

"Were you aware of the affair?" Josie asked.

Gloria's rage dissipated slightly, the tension in her body loosening. Her fists uncurled. "No," she admitted in a tone of resignation. "Of course not. I wouldn't have tolerated that. But I was so busy with my company and the kids." She turned her body to face them. "But look, the affair didn't even bother me that much."

Gretchen said, "Really?"

"If I had known about it at the time, well, yeah, I would have gone scorched earth on both of them. I would have been devastated. But by the time Krystal told me, Nate and I had already been divorced for a year. What bothered me was that it seemed like she only told me to be cruel. I mean, my marriage is over. It's been over for a long time now. Why even bother telling me now? Unless she was mad that once it ended, Nate didn't end up with her. I don't know. You have to ask him." She threw her hands in the air and shooed them back to the kitchen table. After closing and locking the door, she turned back to them and let out a heavy sigh. "I'm sorry. I haven't even let you talk, have I? Is this what you came here for? To hear about how my marriage was a sham, and I didn't even know it?" A laugh escaped her lips.

Josie said, "Mrs. Cammack, please sit down."

Gloria didn't protest. Instead, she took a seat across from the two of them. Again, she reached up to smooth her hair although it still looked perfect. "You think I'm crazy, right? I know I'm all over the place, but I'm trying to keep my company going and this trial is coming up, and believe it or not, Krystal's murder is upsetting to me. No, I didn't like her and I'm not happy that she and Nate were... you know, but I lost both of my kids. I'm tired of death. So tired of it."

With that, she slumped in her seat.

Gretchen said, "You're not crazy. No one thinks you're crazy, Mrs. Cammack. We understand that you're still grieving. Believe me, we're sorry that we even have to be here. But we do need to ask you some questions."

"About what, then?" said Gloria.

Josie said, "About your son."

CHAPTER FOURTEEN

The corner of Gloria's mouth quirked upward. She looked from Josie to Gretchen and back. "This is a joke, right? I'm supposed to laugh?"

Gretchen said, "I'm afraid not, Mrs. Cammack."

Gloria straightened her posture and leaned her elbows on the table. "You remember that my son is dead, right? You said earlier you were here about Krystal's murder. What does my son have to do with her murder?"

Josie said, "Does the word 'Pritch' mean anything to you?"

Confusion passed over Gloria's face. "What? What is that?"

Josie spelled it for her. "Evidently, it was a nickname given to your son by the other children at his school. Did you know about it?"

A line creased Gloria's forehead. "You're talking to me about a mean nickname that children gave to my dead son? Are you serious right now?"

Gretchen held up a palm. "Please, Mrs. Cammack, I know this is upsetting. We don't want to be here any more than you want us to be here. The word 'Pritch' was found at the scene where Krystal Duncan's body was located. We've been over Ms. Duncan's home, family, and work life extensively and can find no connection between her and the word 'Pritch' other than your son. Do you have any idea why your son's nickname would be associated with Krystal Duncan?"

Gloria stared at them, as if she were waiting for some kind of punchline. When it didn't come, she laughed. "You're kidding me, right? I mean, you're actually kidding me. What was it? Like, stapled to her forehead or something? Was it spelled out in her blood or something? I think Dee would have mentioned something like that to the group. What do you mean it was 'associated' with her? What does that even mean? I don't know what you expect me to say to this."

Josie said, "We don't typically release all the details of a crime scene to the public. Dee was not aware of the presence of the word because it was in a location that she could not see. But I can assure you that it was found, and it was prominent. It was meant to be found."

"Found? What does that mean? Found? Did someone write it? Was it part of a note? Maybe Krystal wrote a note. Are you sure she was even murdered? Because every single one of us has thought about killing ourselves since the accident—numerous times—and Krystal? Well, she was more alone than any of us."

Gretchen maintained her stoic expression. "We know she was murdered, Mrs. Cammack. We're trying to figure out who did it and why. Can you think of any reason why someone would want to draw attention to your son with her murder?"

Gloria shook her head slowly, eyes wide with shock. "I honestly have no idea. Maybe someone is trying to hurt me? Torture me? Maybe hurt Nathan? Have you talked with him yet?"

"No," said Josie.

Gretchen added, "We're meeting with him later today."

"There are a lot of crazies out there," Gloria said. "Do you know that we actually got hate mail after our children died? Hate mail. Can you imagine that? It was from the press coverage, I'm sure. There were people who thought we should burn in hell for wanting charges pressed against Virgil Lesko. As if he shouldn't be held accountable for drinking and then driving a bus full of kids around. Then there were people who wrote letters—people who didn't even know us—saying that maybe if I hadn't been so focused on my company, my kids would still be alive. Can you imagine? As if my company's success had some direct bearing on Virgil Lesko's drinking habits."

"Do you still have any of those letters?" Josie asked.

"No," said Gloria. "I threw them away. They were awful. Nathan wanted to take them to the police, but there were no actual threats. Just hatred. Pure hatred."

"Have you received anything like that recently?" Gretchen asked.

Gloria shook her head.

"Mrs. Cammack," Josie said, changing tack. "We understand that Wallace often had trouble with the other students at school and on the bus. Were there ever any issues between him and Bianca?"

"You're going to go there, then? You think because my son, who has been dead for two years, had trouble with some other students in school, that it somehow has something to do with Krystal's murder?"

"We're not saying that at all," Gretchen told her. "We're just trying to figure out why his nickname would be at a crime scene. The most logical connection is that your children went to school together. Were there ever any issues between Wallace and Bianca Duncan?"

Gloria shook her head and sighed. "No. They weren't friends, but there were never any problems between them. Look, Wallace was bright, exceptionally so, and he grew bored very easily. His mind was always working at double the speed of everyone else's, even the teachers at school. I wanted to put him into private school where he might actually be challenged intellectually for once, but Nathan refused. He thought the cost was too high and that Wallace's issues with teachers and other students were to do with his personality, not his intelligence."

Josie said, "We understand there was an incident with Gail Tenney shortly before the crash."

Gloria waved a hand in the air. "That was horseplay. An accident. A misunderstanding. Dee and I discussed it. Both of the children were uninjured. It was fine."

"Did you talk to Wallace about it?" Josie asked.

"Of course. I had to make sure he wasn't hurt."

"Did the school become involved?" Gretchen asked.

"Well, yes, that's where the call came from on the day it happened. But I agreed I wouldn't pressure the principal to punish Gail, and Dee said she would do the same for Wallace. It was nothing, really."

Neither Josie nor Gretchen mentioned that Dee's story about the incident didn't exactly line up with Gloria's account. Dee had said that she and her husband had never had a chance to deal with it properly, implying perhaps that they had intended to press the school to take the matter more seriously.

"Mrs. Cammack," said Gretchen. "When is the last time you saw Krystal Duncan?"

"I don't know. A week ago? Two weeks ago? Her yard is right behind mine. I try not to sit out there if she's outside but occasionally I see her through the window. She mows her own lawn."

Josie said, "Can you give us a rundown of your activities and location from Thursday through Monday morning?"

Gloria gave another uncertain smile, as if they were trying to prank her. When it became clear they were waiting for an answer, she shook her head and laughed. Pushing up from the table, she said, "Whatever. Hang on while I get my planner. You can have my whole schedule." She left the room and returned with a large black purse. From its depths she pulled a black leather book and plunked it onto the table before them. She turned the pages until she came to the Thursday of the past week. "I don't have a copier here at the house. You can take photos with your phones or follow me over to the store and I'll make copies for you there. I imagine you'll need to talk to some of my staff if you want to verify that I was there when I say I was."

Gretchen was already snapping photos of the pages.

Josie said, "You were at work Thursday and Friday during the day."

"And into the evenings. We've had some big orders lately that have needed fulfilling and as you might guess from the phone call you walked in on earlier, my current staff requires a lot of overseeing."

"They'll be able to tell us how late you were at your store on each night?" Josie said.

"Of course. Come by after you talk with Nathan. I'll be there all day."

Gretchen said, "You had a yoga clinic on Saturday from eight to four?"

"Yes, that's right," Gloria said. She rattled off the name of the yoga place, which Gretchen scribbled down. "Weekends are hard," she added. "I used to ferry the kids everywhere. Now I just sit here. I try as much as I can to find things to fill the hours."

Josie said, "But Sunday you were here?"

"I went to the cemetery on Sunday. Then I went into the office for a while—although I was alone—and yes, then I was home."

"No one can verify your whereabouts on Sunday?" Gretchen asked.

Gloria looked surprised. "Well, no, I guess not."

"What about Monday morning? You went to work?"

"Yes. I was there by nine a.m. I would have been in earlier, but I didn't sleep well on Sunday night. The trial coming up—it just brought it all back, you know? The nightmares…"

"I understand," said Josie.

Gretchen stood up. "Thank you for your time, Mrs. Cammack. We'll let you get to work, and we'll be in touch later, after we've spoken with Mr. Cammack."

CHAPTER FIFTEEN

Frankie climbed the bus steps, watching Bianca and her brother shove each other as they went ahead of her, even though the principal told them not to fight. Wallace never listened. Not to anyone. Frankie stopped at the top of the bus steps and smiled at the driver.

"Hi, Mr. Lesko," she said with a wave.

He grinned at her. She waited for him to give his usual greeting. He always said, "Hi, Frankie," back to her and added the last name of a famous Frankie or Frank to the end of it. Yesterday he had said, "Hi, Frankie Valli!" and she had had to google Frankie Valli when she got home. Another singer. Apparently, there were a lot of singers named Frank or Frankie. Her favorite Frank that Mr. Lesko had ever come up with was Franklin D. Roosevelt, the president.

"Get in your seat, hon," said Mr. Lesko.

Frankie stared at him. "Are you okay, Mr. Lesko?"

Taking a step closer, she saw that his eyes looked funny. They reminded her of glazed donuts. Plus, he had a weird odor today. It was faint, but Frankie could definitely smell it. She wrinkled her nose. It reminded her of Gail's dad whenever she saw him at parties or barbecues.

"I'm frine," he responded. He reached over and pulled the lever to close the door. Frankie turned back to look out at the sidewalk in front of the school, but the principal was already gone.

"Do you mean fine?" she asked Mr. Lesko.

"Frankie!" Wallace shouted from the middle of the bus. "Shut up and sit down already. Just let him drive!"

Frankie looked back at Mr. Lesko, but he was already looking out the front window, squinting his eyes like it was hard to see. The bus lurched forward and she fell onto her knees. A moment later, Wallace was there, hooking his hands under her armpits and pulling her to her feet. He reached down and brushed off her knees. "Come on," he said. "You can sit with me."

CHAPTER SIXTEEN

In the car, Josie asked, "Are we going to talk to Nathan Cammack next?"

Gretchen put on her seatbelt and pulled away from the Cammack home, one hand adjusting the AC in the car. Even before ten a.m., the heat outside was punishing. "I want to stop somewhere first. Virgil Lesko's attorney is ignoring me."

Josie watched the streets of West Denton flash past. The memorial came into view again. She turned her gaze straight ahead. "Ignoring you? You just left a message for him last night."

"Right," said Gretchen. "I called again this morning and his secretary told me not to hold my breath for a return call. I don't think there's anything to the meeting Krystal Duncan had with Virgil Lesko that is going to connect to her murder but now that I've been told no, I feel compelled to get more information."

Josie said, "I think that telling the police no is one of the first rules in the defense attorney handbook."

Gretchen laughed. "True. The thing is that Krystal Duncan didn't have much human contact after her daughter died. It was work and the support group and that was it. That doesn't give us many avenues of investigation. If there is even the slightest chance that she said something to Virgil Lesko at their meeting that might lead us in the direction of her killer, then I need to know what happened at that meeting. I don't think there will be anything—"

"But you have to cross it off the list," Josie filled in. "I get it. You think Krystal knew her killer?"

"Don't you?"

Josie thought about it. "No sign of a struggle. All her personal belongings left behind. No sign of forced entry. Yeah, I think she probably did."

"If there is even a one percent chance that she said something to Virgil Lesko that could be helpful, we need to know about it. If she'd met with him three months ago or six months ago, I wouldn't be interested, but just over two weeks is too close to her murder."

"Fair enough," said Josie. "Who is the defense attorney, anyway?"

Gretchen slowed to a stop at a red light. Her head swiveled slowly in Josie's direction. A grimace twisted her features. "Andrew Bowen."

Josie's stomach lurched.

"I'm sorry," Gretchen said.

"It's fine."

"You don't have to come in with me."

"And miss an opportunity to make that jerk uncomfortable? I don't think so." She sighed. "This certainly explains a lot."

The light changed and Gretchen pulled through the intersection, heading into central Denton. Andrew Bowen's office was only a few blocks from city hall. "What do you mean?" Gretchen asked.

"Virgil Lesko admitted to drinking the day of the bus crash, right?"

"Yeah, although he retained Bowen as counsel before he was even discharged from the hospital."

"Smart," Josie remarked. Bowen was the best criminal defense attorney in the county. He also hated Josie and most of the Denton PD with a white-hot intensity after they'd put his mother away for a decades-old murder.

Josie said, "It had to be Bowen's idea to plead not guilty and force a trial."

"I'm sure it was," Gretchen agreed.

The bus accident had garnered a lot of news coverage and outrage in the community. No one wanted to see Virgil Lesko plead down. He was responsible for the deaths of five innocent children.

It was legal maneuvering, Josie knew, and Bowen was good at it. She didn't know what his defense was going to be, but she knew that whatever it was, he'd try to reduce or eliminate the number of years that Virgil would need to spend behind bars. There was always a chance Bowen could strike a deal with prosecutors in the weeks leading up to trial. No wonder he had agreed to let Krystal Duncan meet with Virgil with the trial only weeks away. It was exactly as Dee Tenney suspected. Bowen had hoped to get one of the parents on Virgil's side. If that didn't sway prosecutors, certainly it might sway a jury.

Gretchen parked in front of Andrew Bowen's office, which took up the first floor of an old brick building that reached four stories high. A small sign hung next to the imposing red door, marked "Andrew Bowen, Attorney At Law". There was nothing more. Not even a phone number. But an attorney as successful as Bowen didn't need to advertise. They got out of the car. Gretchen fed quarters into the meter along the sidewalk.

"You sure he's here?" Josie asked.

"Yeah. I called the clerk of courts to check his schedule. He's got a hearing at eleven, which is an hour from now. He'd have to be here prepping for it."

Josie followed Gretchen into the office. Gleaming hardwood floors stretched out before them. There was a small seating area to their right—one table and two chairs. No magazines. Bowen didn't want his criminal clients lingering. To the left was a large wooden desk with files stacked neatly two feet high on both sides. Between them was a laptop and behind that, a woman in her fifties, her graying brown hair tied back in a bun. Over reading glasses, she glared at them. "You don't have an appointment," she said. "You can make one or you can leave."

"Charming," Josie muttered under her breath.

From the look on Gretchen's face, Josie knew she was stifling a smile. They approached the desk and held out their police credentials to the secretary. She glanced at them and then looked back up at Josie and Gretchen, an expression of disinterest on her lined face. "So?" she said. "You want to make an appointment?"

Gretchen pocketed her identification and motioned to a large set of closed wooden double doors opposite the front entrance. "We want to talk to Mr. Bowen."

"You can't. I know you called here earlier. He's preparing for a hearing. He's not to be disturbed."

From behind the doors, Josie thought she heard muffled voices. Male. She cocked her head to the side, trying to make out some of the words. " … don't care…" said one voice. Josie couldn't tell if was Bowen or not. Turning back to the secretary, she said, "But he's meeting with someone right now."

The woman's jaw fell open for a second, then she snapped it shut. Instead of giving her time to recover, Josie walked over and rapped her knuckles against one of the doors. The muffled tones on the other side ceased.

"Hey," said the secretary, now on her feet, rounding the desk. "You can't just come in here, and—"

The door swung inward. A man stood before Josie. Not Andrew Bowen. This man was younger and dressed in what looked like a delivery uniform. Food delivery, judging by the smell of garlic and onions that wafted from him. His face was tan and covered in stubble. His frame filled out the door as he stepped toward Josie. He was easily six feet with the upper body of a weightlifter and the lean lower body of a runner. The white T-shirt he wore clung to his chest. His brown eyes panned downward, taking in the gun and badge at her waist. As he turned back to the inner sanctum of Bowen's office, Josie saw thick brown curls peeking from beneath a black baseball cap. "The police are here," he said.

Footsteps sounded behind him. Then Andrew Bowen's face appeared next to the man's shoulder. His look of surprise turned to a scowl. "You? They sent you?" he said to Josie.

"Yeah," she told him. "I'm a detective for Denton PD. Typically, I'm asked to handle police matters. That's kind of how this works."

Bowen's face flushed red all the way to his pale blond roots. He pushed a hand through his hair. His mouth worked but nothing came out. Gretchen stepped forward, edging in front of Josie. "Mr. Bowen," she said. "I need to talk to you about a meeting that your client, Virgil Lesko, had with Krystal Duncan just over two weeks ago."

The man next to Bowen said, "Well, shit." Turning to Josie, he smiled and extended a hand. "I'm Ted. Ted Lesko. Virgil's my dad."

Josie shook his hand, noting a tattoo between his wrist and the base of his thumb. Five dots. Four corners and one dot in the middle. "Detective Josie Quinn," she said.

"Krystal Duncan is the lady they've been showing on the news, right? She was one of the moms… from my dad's accident."

"She's been murdered," Josie said.

Ted's face went slack. "Oh shit. Are you—are you sure?"

"Her murder has been in the press," Josie said.

"I'm sorry," he said. "I've been working like crazy the last couple of days. Last I saw, she was missing. What happened?"

"We're not at liberty to discuss the details of an open investigation," Gretchen put in.

Ted shook his head. "That's really awful. I'm sorry to hear that."

"Did you know Krystal Duncan?" Josie asked.

"No. Not personally. I knew who she was, obviously. My dad's on trial for killing her kid. But I never met her. Speaking of my dad, you guys know he's been in jail for the last two years, right? If you're thinking he had something to do with her getting murdered, it's just not possible."

"We're aware, Mr. Lesko," said Gretchen. "We're not trying to put any stress on your father or you. We're only here to discuss the content of the meeting between your father and Ms. Duncan in case it may shed light on the murder case."

He looked at Bowen. The attorney shrugged. "We're under absolutely no obligation to share the contents of that meeting. Unless these detectives want to get a warrant, and they know as well as I do that no judge is going to grant one. Like you said, your father has been in jail for two years. There is no way that he could possibly have any connection to the death of Krystal Duncan."

Gretchen said, "If that's the case, then just show us the tape."

Bowen said nothing.

Josie said, "Do you want to be that guy, Andrew? Someone killed this poor woman just weeks before Virgil's trial. The mother of one of the West Denton Five. She was preparing to testify at the trial. The police just want to talk to anyone who had contact with her in the weeks leading up to her murder to try to establish her state of mind and find out whether she mentioned anyone giving her trouble. Your client was one of those people who had contact with her. Like you and Ted said, he's in jail so we couldn't possibly like him for this murder. We just want to talk. But his attorney said no. His attorney refuses to help in the investigation of the murder of the mother of one of his client's child victims. Is that the guy you want to be, Andrew? In the press?"

One of Ted's eyebrows kinked upward as he stared down at her. The slight curve of his lips told her that he was enjoying watching her get under Bowen's skin. "Yeah, Andrew," Ted said, drawing out Bowen's first name. "Do you want to be that guy? Is that what my dad would want?"

The flush covering Bowen's cheeks deepened. Through gritted teeth, he said, "You're not paying me to cooperate with the police on an unrelated investigation. I'm trying to keep as many years off your father's sentence as possible."

Ted shook his head. "Good luck with that. Even with a reduced sentence, he's going to die in prison."

"Not if I can help it," Bowen spat.

"Whatever," Ted replied. "Listen, I don't want my dad looking like a douche on top of everything else. Everyone already hates him. Don't make it worse. Just show them the tape of the meeting."

Andrew shook his head. "I have to discuss it with Virgil first."

Ted put a large hand to his chest. "Did my father just give you two grand or was that me?"

"Your father is my client," Andrew said, the pink hue of his cheeks now spreading to the tips of his ears. "And besides, you're two full months behind paying me. You know what? I'm not comfortable talking about this in front of the police."

He turned to retreat to his office. Ted followed, looming over him. To Bowen's back, Ted said, "Show them the damn tape."

Bowen whirled on him just as he reached his desk, nearly bumping into Ted's broad chest. He poked Ted's collarbone. "No."

Josie and Gretchen stepped inside the door. Gretchen said, "Mr. Bowen, if you show us the tape, we'll be out of your hair in time for your eleven o'clock hearing."

Ted said, "Why are you making something out of this when it doesn't have to be anything? Is it because you don't like that one?" He pointed at Josie.

"N-no," Bowen spluttered. "I'm a professional. I—"

"Then show them the tape," Ted said, sounding calm and reasonable.

"You don't know what's on it," Bowen pointed out.

Ted shook his head. He reached up, took his hat off, and pushed his thick brown hair around on his head before putting the hat back in place. Suddenly, his face looked haggard and tired. When he spoke, his voice was resigned. "I don't need to see it. In his whole life, my dad only committed one crime, and he's going to pay for it. No matter how much you try to stop it, no matter how much money you squeeze out of us, he's going away. As he should. You kill kids, you should go to prison. Period. He's okay with that. I'm okay with that. You should be, too."

Bowen squeezed the bridge of his nose between an index finger and thumb. "Ted, your father hired me to help him. My entire job is predicated on it not being okay for him to die in prison. If I recall, you availed yourself of a defense attorney several years back when you got in trouble yourself."

Ted pursed his lips. Turning his head toward Josie and Gretchen, he gave them a tight smile. Josie thought of the tattoo on his hand. The five dots. It was a common prison tattoo. The four dots represented the four walls of a cell. The fifth dot was the prisoner. She said, "Your defense attorney must not have been very good. You did time."

Ted nodded. "Yeah. I did time. No, my attorney wasn't very good. But I wasn't looking at murder charges. I had a girlfriend. We broke up. I didn't take it well. I did some stupid shit. Spent a few years inside. My dad made sure I got my head right after that. Now I work three different jobs to keep his house and pay his legal bills, and he still plans on going to prison for that crash." He turned back to Bowen. "Do what you have to do for my dad, but let the police see the stupid tape, would you? You heard what they said. One of those parents was murdered, Bowen. My dad would want you to cooperate in the investigation. We both know that. Besides, there can't possibly be anything on that tape that could be worse than what he's facing right now."

With a heavy sigh, Bowen pushed his way past Ted. "Fine," he said. "Come with me."

All three of them followed him through another set of doors to the right of his desk and into a hallway. He led them past two further doors. Josie saw that one was a bathroom and the other was a darkened conference room with boxes piled on the table and along the walls. The last door opened into a small room with a table and two chairs. In the center of the table sat a laptop. Bowen spent a few minutes booting it up and clicking away at its keys. Then he moved to the far wall where a television hung. He reached up, snagged a remote control from behind it, and clicked it on. The screen came to life, showing a carbon copy of the laptop screen. Bowen pressed the volume button several times and then returned to the laptop, clicking some more until a video began.

Josie recognized the private meeting room that most correctional facilities used for inmates to consult with their attorneys. Everything was drab gray—the walls, the tiles, even the table and chairs. Virgil Lesko sat on one side of the table with Bowen beside him. Across from them was Krystal Duncan with the telltale bump on her nose. She was dressed for work in a black skirt and purple silk blouse. Her brown hair hung straight down her back. The camera was positioned so that it only showed Krystal, Lesko, and Bowen in profile. Still, Josie could tell from Krystal's body language that she'd been nervous. One leg was crossed over the other at the knee. Both her arms hugged her chest and the fingers of her right hand tapped out a manic beat against her triceps.

Bowen spoke first, announcing who was in the room, where they were, the time and date, and the fact that the meeting was being recorded. Then he said, "Ms. Duncan, you requested this meeting."

"Wait," said Virgil.

Josie had seen his photos in the press following the crash and more recently now that the trial was in sight. He'd always been handsome in an old-school, dashing, Hollywood way with a tall, broad frame, angular features, and a thick head of black hair. He was only in his early fifties. But in this video, from what Josie could see, he looked much older. He had lost weight and his hair was more gray than black. He reached his hands across the table toward Krystal, but she recoiled, pushing her chair back abruptly. Virgil's hands retreated. "I'm sorry," he said softly. "I shouldn't have—I didn't mean—Krystal, I just want you to know that I'm so sorry—"

"Virgil," Bowen said sharply, cutting him off. "As we discussed, I advise against making apologies of any kind for what happened on the day of the crash."

Virgil's head fell. When he lifted it again, it seemed to take great effort. "Krystal, I want you to know that I would never intentionally hurt anyone. I made a mistake—"

Again, Bowen shut him down. "Virgil."

Krystal's body trembled violently.

Virgil shook his head. "I have a son. I know there's nothing I could ever say to you that would make up for what I—"

This time, Bowen silenced his client with a hand on his arm. "Ms. Duncan," he said. "I really must ask that you get to the point."

Her voice was barely audible at first. She stopped and started twice before pushing out the words. "I thought I could talk to Virgil alone."

"I'm afraid that's not possible," Bowen said. "Anything you have to say to him, you can say in front of me."

She glared at Bowen. "I don't have anything to *say* to him."

Virgil stared at her with interest.

Bowen said, "If you have nothing to say, why are we here?"

"I need to ask him a question."

"Then go on," said Bowen.

She stared into Virgil's eyes for a long moment. Josie watched her arms clench tighter around her body. Then she said, "The day of the accident, before you—before you—"

"Stop," Bowen snapped. "I'm afraid you cannot ask any questions about the accident or the day of the accident or anything leading up to it."

Krystal's knuckles went white against her shirtsleeve. "You said I could talk to him. You said I could ask questions. He killed my daughter. What the hell did you think I was going to ask about? Casserole recipes?"

Bowen stood up, cold eyes looking past her now. "I'm afraid this meeting is over."

Virgil put his head in his hands. Krystal sprang up and began to berate Andrew Bowen. Gone was her nervousness. Now there was only the fury of a mother denied answers about her daughter's death. For a moment, it looked like Krystal might even haul off and punch him, but then a correctional officer entered and escorted her from the room. Her shouts of "You bastards!" echoed in the tiny room. Then the video cut off.

"That's it?" Ted said, laughing. He swatted Bowen's shoulder. "You put up a fuss for that? You were the one who did all the damn talking. What a waste of time. I have to get back to work. I'll have more money for you next week. Detectives?" He took a moment to meet Gretchen's eyes and then Josie's. "I'd say it was nice to meet you, but I don't really like police. Let me just say I hope you find whoever killed Krystal Duncan."

He left them in the room. Gretchen thanked Andrew Bowen for his time and she and Josie trailed Ted Lesko out the front door, all three of them drawing harsh glares from the secretary. Josie watched Ted walk down the street until he reached a bright-red Prius. A magnetic sign attached to the passenger's side door read: *Food Frenzy*. Josie was familiar with it. It was a food delivery service like DoorDash or Grubhub. You ordered from just about anywhere using an app and the driver went to the restaurant, picked up the food, and brought it to you.

"You getting in or what?" Gretchen asked.

Tearing her gaze from Ted as he folded himself into the Prius, Josie looked at Gretchen. "Yeah," she said. "Turn up the air though."

Once they were seated in the car, Gretchen cranked the air conditioning up while Josie booted up their Mobile Data Terminal. Hot air blasted from the vents, quickly turning cool, much to Josie's relief. As she punched Ted Lesko's name into a database via the MDT, Andrew Bowen emerged from the building, dressed in a full suit, a briefcase in hand. He took a moment to scowl at them. Josie grinned and waved, and he turned on his heel and stalked off.

"What do you think?" Gretchen asked.

"I think he needs to get over himself. His mother is a murderer. I put her away. One of these days he's going to have to accept it."

"No," Gretchen said, checking her cell phone. "I mean about the tape."

"Krystal obviously wanted information from Virgil about something that happened the day of the accident. What that information was is anyone's guess now. I think that entire thing left us with more questions than answers, and I'm not sure any of those questions have to do with her murder. Ah, here it is!"

Gretchen leaned over and pushed her reading glasses up her nose. "What do you think of the son?"

"He seems devoted to his father," Josie said. "He was telling the truth about his prison time. He spent almost three years in prison for stalking. The case was initiated in Philadelphia County eight years ago. He would have been twenty-four." Josie kept scrolling. "Not so much as a parking ticket since."

Gretchen sighed. "And no connections to Krystal Duncan other than that his dad killed her daughter. Dead ends everywhere. Let's go talk to Nathan Cammack and see what he can tell us about the nickname 'Pritch.'"

CHAPTER SEVENTEEN

Nathan Cammack lived in a one-bedroom apartment over a comic book store in central Denton. It was not far from the police station. Most people in Denton thought of it as the business district of the city. The streets were laid out in grid fashion, and most of the buildings were huge brick structures that had been standing for more than one hundred years. Many of the buildings, like police headquarters, were on the historical register. Gretchen and Josie found metered parking a few doors down from the storefront and made their way around to the back of the building. A set of wooden steps led to a narrow deck on the second floor. In the center of it was an exterior door. As they reached the door, Josie noticed a tin bucket on the floor filled with cigarettes. A tattered paper that looked like it had been taped and re-taped onto the door multiple times read in scrawled letters: *Door sticks. Make sure you pull all the way closed.*

"Looks like he didn't get very much in the divorce," Josie muttered.

"I guess not," Gretchen said. "When the crash happened, he was some big-time marketing executive. You'd think he'd spring for a condo or a townhouse."

They pushed through the door, taking care to pull it all the way closed behind them. Gretchen said, "We're looking for apartment two or, as Nathan told me on the phone, the door on the right."

At the end of the hall was a door with a metal 2 just above the peephole. Josie didn't see a doorbell so she knocked. Seconds later, the door swung open. Nathan Cammack stood before them, barefoot in a pair of khaki shorts and a button-down, yellow, short-sleeved shirt. It looked as though he'd made an effort to look presentable except that his clothes were wrinkled, his sandy brown hair was long and shaggy, and there were crumbs in his long, scraggly beard. Josie knew he was in his mid-thirties, but he looked about ten years older. His blue eyes were a darker shade than his ex-wife's and they seemed hollowed out, as if he'd lost a lot of weight and his cheekbones had become more prominent.

"Hey Detective Palmer," he said, ushering them inside.

Gretchen introduced him to Josie as they settled onto a futon couch in his living room. The ceilings inside the apartment were high, the walls faded brick. A half wall made of brick topped by round, white wooden pillars separated the living room from the kitchen. Although both rooms were sizable, there was very little furniture. It looked as though a college student lived there except for the photos of Wallace and Frankie hanging on one of the living room walls. There weren't nearly as many as Josie had seen in Gloria's house, and the effect was even more heartbreaking. School photos of each child bracketed a candid shot of Nathan and both kids standing on a beach, all of them grinning, even Wallace. Below that was a framed child's drawing. Handprints in pink and purple paint made the shape of a heart. Above, it said "Happy Father's Day" and below, it read "We love you. Wallace and Frankie".

Frankie had drawn a heart where the dot over the I in her name should be.

Josie swallowed over a lump forming in her throat. Although Nathan clearly had the air conditioning cranked up, she felt a film of sweat on her skin. She squeezed her hands together in her lap so no one would see them shake.

Nathan stood in front of them, running a hand through his hair. "I can offer you water and, um, maybe some water. I'm sorry. All I've got is water. I haven't been shopping. I don't really go shopping now 'cause it's just me and I don't need a lot—"

"Mr. Cammack," Gretchen interrupted him with a warm smile. "We're fine, thank you. We just have a few questions."

Nathan went to the kitchen to grab one of the chairs from his table. Josie noticed he only had two chairs and they were mismatched. His laptop sat open on the table next to four coffee mugs, two water bottles, and an open bag of Doritos. He set the chair in front of them backwards, straddling the seat and folding his arms across the back. "I guess you're here about Krystal, right? Dee told me what happened. I mean, she said she found her in the cemetery, and she was dead. Is it true that someone murdered her?"

"Yes," said Gretchen.

"How can I help?"

Josie asked, "When is the last time you saw Krystal Duncan?"

"At our last support group meeting. Well, not the one that just passed, but the one before that. Dee told you about that, right? We meet Mondays."

"Yes," said Josie. "Did you speak with Krystal during that meeting?"

"Well, not one-on-one. It's a group. Dr. Rosetti kind of moderates it."

Gretchen said, "So you didn't speak to Krystal privately that evening? Either before or after the meeting?"

He shook his head. "No. Sorry, I didn't. What's going on here? You think I had something to do with her—her murder?"

"Mr. Cammack," Josie said. "We're talking to everyone who was close to Krystal right now."

He put a hand to his chest, straightening his back. "Oh, I wasn't close to Krystal."

Gretchen said, "Your wife told us about the affair."

His head reared back as if she'd slapped him. "Affair?" he said. "What affair?"

"Your affair with Krystal Duncan," Josie said.

He tipped his head back, looking at the ceiling, and then lowered his forehead onto his arms. "Jesus," he said, voice muffled. Lifting his head, he said, "Who told you that Krystal and I had an affair? Gloria? Where in the hell would she get that from?"

Gretchen said, "Krystal told her."

He leaped from his chair and began pacing. "What? When? Is this some kind of joke?"

Josie said, "Mr. Cammack, calm down."

He stopped pacing and pointed a finger at Josie. "You're telling me that Krystal told my wife that we had an affair? When the hell was this?"

"Gloria's not exactly sure. Sometime in the last few months."

His face twisted. The pacing resumed. "What? Are you kidding me? What? Why would she—what the actual f—are you sure? Krystal told my ex-wife that we had an affair?"

"Yes," said Gretchen. "Mr. Cammack, please sit down. Gloria said she's not upset about it. She said your marriage has been over for some time."

He threw his arms into the air and let them fall back to his sides with a loud slap. "Why would Krystal say that? Why? Listen, Krystal and I did not have an affair. Jesus. She told my wife that and now she's dead? So now you must think if there was something between us that I—I did something to her?"

Josie stood up and walked in front of him, forcing him to stop. "Nathan," she said firmly. "No one is accusing you of anything."

"My ex-wife is accusing me of having an affair!" he exclaimed.

Josie reached for the chair, dragging it along the floor and positioning it so that it was behind him. "Sit," she said. "Your wife didn't accuse you of anything. Why would Krystal tell her that the two of you had an affair?"

He plopped into the chair with a heavy sigh. Crumbs spilled from his beard as he used both hands to rub it. "Christ. I don't know. I have no idea why Krystal would say that, especially after all this time. And to Gloria. Jesus. I thought we were cool. It's been two years. The kids—"

Josie walked to the kitchen and opened the fridge. Nathan hadn't been kidding when he'd said all he had was water. There were two bottles. The rest of the fridge was filled with various takeout containers, some of which were pretty old given the smell wafting toward her. Quickly, she grabbed a water bottle and returned to the living room, handing it to Nathan. She said, "Were things 'not cool' between you and Krystal when the crash happened?"

He took a long pull from the bottle and then set it on the floor between his feet. "Krystal and I were always cool. We used to get together at night, after our kids were asleep. Gloria was always on her computer or doing some weird New Age beauty regimen that kept her in the bathroom for hours. I used to sneak out. Our backyards connected. Did you know that?"

"Gloria showed us," Gretchen said. "You used to go over to Krystal's house at night?"

He shook his head. "Hell, no. She said I could come inside the house, but I didn't want to. What if Bianca woke up and saw me? She'd have the wrong idea."

Josie looked down at him. "What was the wrong idea?"

Meeting her eyes, he said, "That we were having an affair! We weren't. I mean, yeah, okay, when the kids were really little, like when Bianca and Wallace were in kindergarten, we slept together. Once. It only happened one time. Gloria was away, Krystal let Wallace and Frankie come over and play in the playhouse. They loved it. Gloria never let them go over there."

"Why not?" asked Gretchen.

He rolled his eyes. "She was always afraid that Krystal would try to feed them fast food or something. Or, god forbid, peanut butter and jelly and—" he gave a dramatic fake gasp. "White bread! You know Gloria runs that all-natural family and child shop, right?"

"We're aware," said Josie.

"She's insane about that stuff. She never let the kids have anything good. I mean anything with dyes or preservatives or that was processed. Everything had to be organic and specially made. She made their lunches for school all those years. Do you know that Frankie came home one day and cried because she ate a cupcake at school? Some other girl had a birthday and brought cupcakes for the whole class, and Frankie couldn't resist. She came home crying—imagine it, a six-year-old filled with regret! She thought Gloria was going to punish her."

"Did she?" asked Gretchen.

"No. We didn't tell her. It wasn't worth it. Then it was our secret. Frankie loved that." Tears spilled from his eyes as a sudden, unexpected sob rocked his body.

Josie's breath caught in her throat. She stepped forward and laid a hand on his shoulder. His body trembled under her touch. He looked over at the photos of his children and used the pads of his thumbs to wipe away his tears. "I'm sorry," he muttered.

Gretchen said, "You never have to apologize for missing your children, Mr. Cammack."

He nodded and sucked in several deep breaths. "It's weird, you know? It's always the good memories that get me. I can talk about the accident, about that day. I can remember the funerals, those first awful weeks, and I feel dead inside. But then I think about the look on their faces when we did the really fun stuff together—just me and them, without Gloria—and I feel like I might die from missing them."

Josie gave his shoulder a squeeze. Another question was on the tip of her tongue, but she couldn't force it out. Gretchen picked up the thread for her. "Did you take the kids to Krystal's whenever Gloria was away?"

He shook his head. "No. Not every time. Not when they got older and stopped getting along."

"You said you and Krystal were intimate?"

"Right, but just that one time. I felt terrible and so did Krystal. She was single, but she wasn't that kind of person. She didn't go for married men. It just sort of happened. But like I said, that was it. It was a one-time thing. A mistake."

Josie let go of his shoulder and took a step away from him. Steadying her voice, she said, "Then why were you sneaking out at night to see Krystal?"

He sighed. "We smoked pot together, okay? In the playhouse. I caught her smoking up there one night, and she got all freaked out. She was afraid I'd tell people. I told her it wasn't my place to tell anyone anything and that if she wanted to smoke weed in the privacy of her own yard, it was none of my business. Then she burst into tears."

"Why?" said Gretchen.

"Work stress," Nathan said. "I don't remember specifically, but Krystal was always stressed out about something. She said pot was the only thing that helped her anxiety. Anyway, we were sitting up there so long, she offered me some. Then it became like a thing, you know? We met out in that tiny-ass playhouse, smoked weed; she complained about work, and I complained about my marriage."

Josie said, "How long did this go on?"

"I don't know. A couple years. After the crash, we never did it again. I never even talked to her alone after the crash."

Gretchen said, "That still doesn't explain why she would tell your wife two years after the bus crash that the two of you had had an affair."

"I know," he said. "I don't understand why she did that. I don't—I can't explain it."

Josie said, "Nathan, does the word 'Pritch' mean anything to you?"

"Pritch? Like pitch with an r in it?"

Gretchen said, "Like a combination of the words 'prick' and 'bitch'."

Nathan's shoulders slumped. "Wow. I haven't heard that in ages. Two years. If you're asking about it, I assume you know what it is—a nickname my son earned at school."

Josie met Gretchen's eyes briefly. Not only were Gloria and Nathan opposites in terms of appearance and their homes, but evidently in the way they had viewed their children as well. Josie said, "Earned it? How did Wallace earn a nickname like that?"

Nathan's chin dropped to his chest. After a deep breath, he looked back up, turning his head to meet Josie's gaze. "I loved my son. Deeply and unconditionally. I would have taken a bullet for him. For both of them. I would put myself in their place in a heartbeat if I could. But the truth is that we had some problems with Wallace bullying other kids at school. I'm not proud of it, okay? I thought we should work with him on it, but Gloria didn't see it that way. You ever hear of these 'not my son' parents?"

Josie had heard of them, but Gretchen said, "What's that?"

"These parents who raise their sons to be entitled assholes who think the world owes them everything and no matter what they do wrong, no matter how strong the evidence of their misdeeds, the parents refuse to believe it. 'Not my son,' they'll say. Their son couldn't possibly have gotten drunk underage and mowed down a bunch of pedestrians. Their son couldn't possibly grope some poor girl at a party. Their son couldn't possibly hurl racist insults. 'Cause their son is perfect. Get what I'm saying?"

"Yes," Gretchen said.

"Well, Gloria was kind of like that. It was one of the things we always fought about. I mean, don't get me wrong, Wallace wasn't near as bad as some of those examples I just gave you. He was only twelve. But I was worried that he was headed in that direction, you know? I mean, no one wants their kid to grow up to be a douche."

"How did you find out about his nickname?" Josie asked.

"He told us. Came home from school one day angry and upset. Refused to go to drum practice even though missing something on his mother's precious schedule was a cardinal sin."

"What happened?" said Gretchen.

Again, he rubbed at his beard. "Nothing. Nothing happened. I started to tell him he needed to take responsibility for his actions and think long and hard about why the other kids would call him that, and Gloria put a stop to that right away. She accused me of taking the other kids' sides when really, Wallace had been getting into trouble at school for months for picking on people. So ultimately, nothing happened. She shut me down. But regardless, I kind of thought it was a good thing. I know that sounds terrible, but that nickname got to him, you know? I hoped he would take some time to think about his actions and maybe try to be better."

"Dee Tenney told us there was an incident with her daughter, Gail, right before the crash," Gretchen prompted. "Your wife confirmed it. Did you feel like maybe he hadn't learned his lesson?"

Nathan nodded. "I did. I was really upset about that whole thing but you know, Gloria said she put it to bed, and she didn't want me getting involved. Which pissed me off because he was my son, too. I was going to talk to Miles about it, you know, father to father—but then the crash happened, and it didn't matter anymore."

"Did Krystal know about the nickname?" asked Josie.

"I don't know. Probably. Bianca probably told her. Bianca told her everything. They had a good relationship like that."

"Who else knew about the nickname?" Gretchen said.

"I don't know. Everybody, I guess. All the kids at school knew about it. Wait a minute. Why are we talking about my son's middle school nickname? Is that what you came here to ask me about? I don't understand."

They explained, as they had to Gloria, in the vaguest way possible, that his son's nickname had been found with Krystal's body.

"That makes no sense," he said. "Are you sure? It has to be a mistake. Why would Wallace's nickname be where Krystal was killed?"

"We don't know," Josie admitted. "That's what we're trying to find out. Nathan, can you tell us about your activities from Thursday night through Monday morning?"

He looked from Josie to Gretchen and back again before shaking his head. A small laugh escaped his lips. "Sure," he said. "I was here. I'm always here. I write website content now. Work from home. I went out for food a few times."

"Can anyone confirm that?" Gretchen asked.

"Nope," he said. "I'm all alone."

CHAPTER EIGHTEEN

Josie and Gretchen got takeout for lunch and headed back to the station. Amber popped up from her desk as soon as they entered the great room. She looked out of place in the detectives' area with her brightly colored maxi dress, her taupe wedge sandals, and her auburn locks cascading down over her shoulders. She smiled at them but Josie could see the tension pulling at the corners of her mouth. "I need an update on the Krystal Duncan case," she told them. "The press is going crazy. They know she was found dead. The Chief confirmed that, but wouldn't give them anything else, which has made it so much worse. They already ran a story on the twelve o'clock news that she had been found dead. My phone is blowing up. My email is practically full—"

Gretchen handed Amber a brown paper bag. "That's a Cobb salad. You like that, right?"

Nonplussed, Amber stared at the bag like it was a severed head. "Um, yeah."

"You'll eat that," Gretchen said. "Then you'll tell the press the following details: that Krystal Duncan's body was found in the cemetery on Monday morning. The ME ruled her a death a homicide. We have no further information. We're following every lead. If anyone has any information about Krystal's whereabouts from Thursday through Monday or about her death, they can call the main Denton PD number. That doesn't seem like much more than they already have, but it's something. Push for tips from the public."

Amber stared at Gretchen for a beat. Then a smile spread across her face. "Thank you."

Josie and Gretchen took their own lunches to their desks and dug in. Josie ate without tasting anything. The morning had taken more out of her than she anticipated. She was thinking about walking to Komorrah's for a cup of coffee when Chief Chitwood's door banged open. He strode into the great room, his flinty gaze landing on Josie immediately. "Quinn," he barked.

She stared at him. "Sir?"

He raised a brow and folded his arms over his thin chest. A single white hair floated over top of his balding scalp. "You got something for me?"

It took Josie only a second to realize he was referring to the rosary beads. What he was really asking was whether or not she was ready to give them back. She had no idea when that would be or how she would even know, but she was certain she still needed them. She felt their weight in her pocket. "No, sir," she told him. "Not now."

He nodded and turned his glare toward Gretchen. "Palmer. What's going on with the Duncan murder? The whole town's got its panties in a bunch over this—as they should, as they should—but I don't want a panic."

Gretchen gave him a rundown of hers and Josie's activities since Krystal Duncan's body had been found. "We've got to speak with Gloria Cammack's employees and see if we can confirm dates and times she was accounted for."

"But she's got a weak alibi," said Josie. "And Nathan Cammack has none at all, and he was close to Krystal—at least before the accident."

Chief said, "You think the Cammacks did this?"

"No," said Josie. "I don't, but we're just doing our due diligence."

"What about the cemetery workers? Did they check out?" he asked.

"They did," Gretchen said. "I ran all their names before we went to the morgue. No red flags."

"How about the Tenney woman?" said the Chief. "You think she could have something to do with it?"

Gretchen said, "I doubt it, but she's got a weak alibi, too. Noah took her statement yesterday. She doesn't work so she's home alone most of the time. Heidi Byrne can account for some of her time, and she's got receipts from some errands she ran on Monday morning, but other than that, no one can confirm whether or not she was really home alone for most of the time that Krystal was missing."

Josie added, "Plus she genuinely didn't seem to know what 'Pritch' meant."

"Or she lied," Chitwood suggested.

"Sure," agreed Josie. "She could have lied, but I don't think that's the case here."

Chitwood shook his head. "You're telling me you found out all this crap about this woman's pot habit and about this one having an affair with that one or maybe not but nothing that points you toward Krystal Duncan's killer?"

Gretchen frowned. "Pretty much, yeah."

"There was no DNA on the body? Nothing?"

Gretchen flipped through some pages in her notebook. "I'm sorry, sir. The ERT didn't find anything."

"What about the method? Carbon monoxide poisoning? Does that get us anywhere?"

"No," Josie said. "The only thing it tells us is that the killer would need access to an indoor area that he could fill with carbon monoxide and leave her there long enough to die from it. Maybe somewhere out of the way enough that no one would hear her screaming or trying to get out before the gas started taking effect."

"So, a garage," said Chitwood. "Probably in a single home with enough land around it that her screams would go unheard. That narrows it down. I hope one of you has a miracle in you, because otherwise—"

The rest of the sentence was cut off by the stairwell door banging open. Their desk sergeant, Dan Lamay, stood hunched over, trying to catch his breath. "We got a situation downstairs," he huffed.

Josie and Gretchen were on their feet. Chitwood said, "Lamay, you ever hear of a phone? I'm pretty sure we've got one down there for you to use."

"Yeah," Lamay said. "I'm gonna need a new one. This guy pulled it right through the opening in the plexiglass and out of the damn wall."

The three of them charged through the door. Dan limped along behind them. He was nearing seventy, overweight, and fighting a bad knee. Chitwood said, "Lamay, you should have locked down the station."

"He's not a threat," Lamay said, following them down the stairs. "He's not armed or anything, and he's on the other side of the glass, still. He's just distraught. It's Sebastian Palazzo."

Josie and Gretchen stopped at the door to the first floor and looked up the steps toward Dan. Gretchen said, "Sebastian Palazzo, the father of Nevin Palazzo, who also died in the West Denton bus crash two years ago?"

Dan nodded. "He said his wife is missing."

"Well, shit," said Chitwood.

Josie and Gretchen pushed through the door, into the first-floor hall, and jogged toward the lobby area. Sure enough, on the other side of the plexiglass that separated Dan Lamay's desk from the rest of the room, stood Sebastian Palazzo, surrounded by a mess. Dan's desk phone lay in the corner of the room, its wires frayed and torn like broken tree roots. Chairs had been overturned. The corkboard hung crooked, one side of it pulled out of the wall. Sebastian was tall, over six feet, with broad shoulders, and thick, wavy black hair. His dark eyes looked wild. The entire scene was incongruous with the rest of his appearance: charcoal gray suit pants, a white shirt and red tie beneath what looked like a lab coat. The words "Palazzo

Pharmacy" were embroidered on the left breast. A pin was affixed just below that with the name of a nationwide pharmacy chain over top of his first name. Josie seemed to remember the chain buying out the Palazzo Pharmacy a few years earlier.

When he saw them behind the window, he launched himself at the desk, his forearms banging against the glass until it shook. "I need help!" he shouted. "Help! Do you hear me? My wife is missing! Why doesn't anyone care that my wife is missing?"

Josie walked toward the door that led into the lobby. "Boss," Gretchen said.

But Josie didn't care how crazed the man was or how much larger he was than her. She entered the lobby anyway, picking her way over the detritus to meet him at the desk. "Mr. Palazzo," she said, her voice strong. "My name is Detective Josie Quinn. I'm here to help you. If you'd just calm down."

He pointed a finger at her nose and through gritted teeth, he said, "Don't tell me to calm down."

Josie heard the door open and close behind her and she knew that Gretchen and Chitwood were there. She sidestepped out of the way of his finger and met his eyes. "I won't tell you to calm down, but you must stop destroying our lobby. If your wife is missing, I'm not sure the best use of your time is sitting in jail on property damage charges."

He lowered his hand. "Are you going to help me?"

"Of course," said Josie.

"I called 911 and they said they couldn't help me because my wife hasn't been missing for twenty-four hours."

"For adults, yes, we typically wait at least twenty-four hours to take a missing persons report, but since you're here, why don't you come inside to our conference room and tell us what's going on."

The crazed look in Sebastian's eyes slipped away. He seemed to come back to himself. Looking around the room, he put both hands in his thick hair. "Oh my God," he said. "I'm so sorry. I don't—I'll pay for all of this but please, just help me find my wife."

Gretchen held the door to the first-floor hallway open. "Come this way, Mr. Palazzo."

Chitwood led him down the hall with Josie and Gretchen behind. The Chief stayed in the conference room with them, insisting that Sebastian take a seat, and then hovering near the door while Josie and Gretchen began speaking with him.

Josie said, "Your wife's name is Faye, correct?"

"Yes, yes," he said. "How did you know that?"

Gretchen leaned forward in her seat. "Mr. Palazzo, you probably don't remember me, but my name is Detective Gretchen Palmer. I was the investigator on the bus accident case."

He studied her for a long moment. "Yes, right. I'm sorry. I don't remember. Everything has been a blur. There were so many people. Police, lawyers, press, neighbors. Even people we didn't know who just wanted to express sympathy."

"It's fine," said Gretchen. "Tell us about Faye."

"I came home for lunch and she was gone," he said. "I come home for lunch from the pharmacy every day at eleven a.m."

"What time did you leave for work?" Josie asked.

"Eight thirty in the morning. I work six days a week now. Monday through Saturday. I always leave at exactly eight thirty, and I come home at eleven for lunch. It's so early because the pharmacy gets too busy after noon for me to leave. Faye and I have lunch every day at the same time. I mean, now we do, since Nevin was killed. I suggested it because she was so despondent after the crash that I was truly afraid she'd try to kill herself. She started seeing Dr. Rosetti after a few months, which helped, and then we started going to the group. That was very helpful, too, but we never stopped our lunch routine. Anyway, I came home the same time as always, but she wasn't there. I searched the entire house, our garage, out back. Everywhere."

Josie said, "Are you sure she didn't go for a walk or a drive or something?"

Sebastian shook his head. Tears gleamed in his eyes. "No, no. Her car was in the garage still. She wouldn't just leave like that. She wouldn't. She wouldn't do that to me. Not after Nevin."

Gretchen said, "Did you try calling her on her cell phone?"

His gaze flitted to Gretchen. "That's the thing. Why I know something is wrong. Her cell phone was there on the kitchen counter. Her purse was still in the foyer closet where she keeps it, and everything was still inside, including her anti-anxiety medication. Faye would never leave the house without it."

Josie looked at Gretchen. A sick feeling stirred deep in her stomach. Five days ago, Krystal Duncan had disappeared from her home, leaving her vehicle, cell phone, and purse behind.

Gretchen said, "Mr. Palazzo, would you mind if we came over to your house and had a look around?"

He shot up out of his chair, his face bright and earnest. "Yes, please," he said. "Please come. There's more. Something I need you to see. Like I said, I called 911 but they wouldn't send anyone out."

Josie stood up, pinpricks of fear piercing the length of her spine. "What do you need us to see?"

He walked toward the door. Chief Chitwood stepped out of the way. Looking back at Gretchen and Josie, he beckoned them to hurry. He said, "Something that wasn't there before."

CHAPTER NINETEEN

The outside of the Palazzo house looked like any other in West Denton—large, two stories, brick façade, three-car garage, and ample lawn space with carefully tended garden beds out front. The inside, however, was another story. The Palazzos had gone for a sleek modern look that seemed more in keeping with an upscale New York City apartment than a family home on the outskirts of a small, Central Pennsylvania city. All the furniture was black and white and so small it barely looked large enough to accommodate more than two people. The floors of every room were tiled in a black-and-white checkerboard pattern with fluffy white throw rugs throughout. Josie wondered if the house had always looked this way or if they'd remodeled after their son died. She could not imagine a child living here.

"I didn't see any signs of forced entry," Gretchen said as they passed through the foyer. "Was the door locked when you got home?"

"No, it wasn't. Which is unusual because Faye always comes in and out through the garage. I mean, at least when she uses her car. Here, I'll show you the entrance from the garage."

As they walked off, Josie took a look around the living room. Nothing was out of place. A white couch and loveseat formed an L-shape with a black end table anchoring the bend. A television was mounted on one wall. On another wall hung a massive black-and-white picture. At first, Josie thought it was wall art, but on closer inspection, she realized it was a photo of Faye Palazzo. Josie recognized her face from the news coverage of the bus crash. Faye had been a successful model in her early twenties. Any time she'd appeared on camera after the crash, even in her grief, she had been striking. The picture was a life-sized portrait. In it, Faye stood in high heels and a form-fitting dress. Her body was angled away from the camera, but her face was turned, looking over her shoulder. The backless dress showed off a wide expanse of skin. Her long, dark hair had been pushed to one side. A slit in her dress revealed one of her legs, slightly bent. It was an awkward position, to be sure, but her eyes showed no discomfort. They stared at the camera with an inviting and somewhat mysterious smile.

Behind Josie, Sebastian said, "That's her! That's my Faye. She used to be a model."

She turned to see that he and Gretchen had returned from the garage. "She's beautiful," Josie said politely, but she wondered whose decision it had been to have the photo enlarged and hung in their living room.

"That's my favorite one," Sebastian said. "She hates it."

"But she let you hang it," Josie said.

"She lost a bet," he responded. "Come to the kitchen. I'll show you what I found."

Josie turned away from the photo. In the hall leading toward the kitchen were even more photos of Faye from her modeling days, arranged in geometric patterns. Each one was in a small, square frame, and they were color. Faye modeling various dresses. Faye on a runway, presumably in New York. Or maybe Paris. Faye in a swimsuit, blowing the camera a kiss. Josie could tell by the quality of the shots that they had been professionally taken. There were no candid photos. Nothing taken in a happy moment by her husband. As they passed the dining room, Josie spotted a large portrait on the wall of the Palazzos on their wedding day. At least there was that.

Josie trailed Sebastian and Gretchen into the kitchen. Here, too, were white cabinets and countertops, white appliances. Only the table was black. One side of the table held two plates, each one with a sandwich on it, presumably for Faye and her husband. They sat diagonally. The other end of the table was stacked with boxes. Josie took a quick peak. One box held fliers announcing a vigil to be held for the West Denton Crash Victims the evening before the trial. The other boxes held thin candles and paper drip protectors. Block letters on the side of the two other boxes read: *6.5 inch candles with drip protectors. Quantity: 50.* Josie said, "Faye was organizing a vigil?"

"Yes," said Sebastian. "She has organized many since Nevin passed. She thought doing one on the eve of the trial would be good. Remind people of what was lost."

Josie looked over to see Gretchen standing before a small table in the corner of the kitchen. It was shiny black and on top of it were framed photos of the Palazzos' son, Nevin. Candid photos of a young boy who looked very much like his father except with his mother's long eyelashes and perfectly straight, narrow nose. In one, he played soccer. In another, he stood next to a Disney character at Disneyworld. A third photo showed him posing with his parents in Times Square. In the final photo, he grinned as his mother planted a kiss on his cheek. He looked so happy.

Josie took in a deep breath and reminded herself that she had a job to do. Turning back to Sebastian, she said, "What was it that you found?"

From the kitchen doorway, he bustled over to the table and pointed to one of the place settings. On the napkin beside it, Josie saw two sparkly earrings. Small, gold, diamond-encrusted hoops by the look of them.

"They're Tiffany," Sebastian said. "Very expensive."

"They don't belong to your wife?" Gretchen asked.

His arm shook as he pointed to them once more with force. "They do belong to my wife! But they've been missing for almost three years now. We thought they'd been stolen. I had to file a police report."

Gretchen took out her phone and fired off a text. Josie knew that Detective Mettner would be on shift by now and he'd be able to look up the report, if it existed, to confirm Sebastian's account.

Sebastian continued, "There was a time that things around the house were going missing. One of my power tools, some of Nevin's sports equipment, a necklace Nevin had given Faye for Mother's Day—it wasn't valuable but it looked very expensive. It had fake diamonds and said *#1 Mom* on it. His school had a pop-up Christmas shop every year where the kids could buy their parents inexpensive gifts and wrap them themselves. You know, to surprise us and make them feel independent. We just sent him with money in an envelope."

Gretchen said, "Did all these things go missing at the same time?"

"Oh no. It was over the course of about a year, I'd say, and not close together. It was one of those things where we each thought we'd simply misplaced things until the earrings went missing. Those were very costly. That's when we looked back and began to wonder if someone had been taking things all along. We started locking our doors and being more careful about monitoring anyone who came to the house."

Josie asked, "Did you ever report any of those other items as stolen?"

"No. As I said, we didn't realize at the time that the things were being stolen."

Josie looked back toward the earrings. "Is there any chance that your wife simply found these? Maybe they hadn't been stolen after all?"

Sebastian shook his head. "No, no. That's impossible. Those were three-thousand-dollar earrings. I bought them for Faye for our fifth wedding anniversary. She only wore them on very special occasions and always put them back into her jewelry armoire. Very top drawer, on the left. When we realized they were missing, we tore the entire house apart. They were gone. My wife is not a careless woman, Detective. She did not lose them."

Josie said, "Are you sure these are the same ones you gave to your wife?"

Sebastian's brows rose. "Oh. Well, of course I can't be sure. They're expensive, but they're not one of a kind. But how many people would just be carrying around three-thousand-dollar earrings?"

"Are you sure your wife didn't buy a replacement pair?" Gretchen suggested.

"Oh no. She was angry with me when I bought them. She said they were entirely too extravagant. There's no way she would buy a new pair. Besides, we submitted the police report to our insurance company. We did receive a payout."

Gretchen's phone chirped. She swiped and scrolled. "Our colleague confirmed that you filed a report two and a half years ago. Says here that your wife was getting ready for a night out, went to get them, and they were gone. She hadn't worn them for six months before that so there was no way to know when they'd gone missing or when they could have been stolen."

"Which explains why it never made it to a detective's desk," Josie said.

Sebastian spread his hands. "We knew there was no possibility of recovering them or finding who took them. We had had parties. We'd had work done on the house during that six months—a plumber to fix the downstairs toilet, some painters. We had a contractor build a custom shelving unit for Nevin. It could have been anyone. We were too trusting, I guess. Anyway, the officer who took the report told us that the best thing to do would be to present a claim to our insurance company so that's what we did. Faye didn't want me to spend the payout on another pair of earrings, so we put it into savings. We were going to take a trip. Nevin wanted to go to Universal Studios. Of course, then he died…"

Sebastian drifted off. His whole body went still, and his eyes took on a faraway look. Either he was staring into his past or he was dissociating from a present that was too painful to bear. Josie would bet her life savings on the latter. She waited a moment before touching his forearm gently. "Mr. Palazzo?" she said softly.

He shook his head, as if shaking off a trance. "I'm sorry," he said. "Sometimes I just… I remember all over again. That day. The reality. It hits me. Even after all this time, it hits me like a truck."

"Please," said Gretchen. "No apologies. Really. Did you touch these earrings?"

"No," he said. He looked back toward the hall. "I came in the front door. I thought it was odd that it was unlocked, but then I thought maybe Faye just unlocked it for me. I locked it behind me. I called out to her. Came into the kitchen and she wasn't here, but the plates were, so I thought everything was fine."

"Did you sit to eat?" Josie asked.

"No," he said. "I wanted to see my wife. I wanted to eat with my wife. I thought she went to the bathroom but when I looked, the door was open and it was empty. Dark. I searched the rest of the house, calling her name. Nothing. I checked the garage and the yard. Nothing. Then I came back here and called her phone, but it rang." He pointed to the countertop where a cell phone rested. "That's when I really started to panic. I went to the neighbors' houses on either side and across the street. Some people are at work so no one was home. One lady was but hadn't seen or heard anything."

Josie asked, "Do you or any of your close neighbors have security cameras of any kind?"

He shook his head. "No, I'm afraid none of us do. There has never seemed a need."

"When did you notice the earrings?" Gretchen asked.

"I came back in and checked Faye's phone—her password is Nevin's birthday—to see if maybe someone had called her or there was anything that might tell me where she went. There wasn't, but as I was looking, I was kind of pacing back and forth and then I saw them there."

Josie motioned toward Faye's phone. "Do you mind?"

"Of course not," he said. He reached for it, tapped in a code, and handed it to Josie. "But you won't find more than I did."

He was right. Josie searched all text messages, emails, and social media accounts and found nothing that sent up any red flags. In fact, Faye Palazzo seemed to do very little but stay at home and attend the support group. There were emails to and from the district attorney's office informing her of the trial schedule as well as emails between her and the city clerk regarding the vigil she'd been organizing, but other than that, nothing. Just as her husband said.

Josie said, "Did Faye have any close friends she might have gone to see? Family members?"

"Oh no," Sebastian responded. "Her father is a professor at Duke. They rarely speak. Her mother is an ex-pat living in El Salvador. They speak even less."

"She's an only child?" asked Gretchen.

"Oh, well, her parents fostered children back when they were together, but Faye never grew close to any of them, so yes, she was basically an only child."

"What about friends?" Josie asked. "Can you make a list of Faye's friends? Perhaps we can talk with them?"

"She doesn't have friends," Sebastian said. As if realizing how that sounded, he threw his hands up defensively. "I know, I know, it sounds awful, doesn't it? When Nevin was alive, she was very active in the Parent Teacher Association and she always had someone to meet with, have coffee with, go to Zumba with and all that, but even those relationships were very superficial. Then once Nevin was killed, well, that was the end of that."

"Faye chose not to continue her relationships?" Gretchen asked. Josie could tell by her kinked brow that she, too, was perplexed.

"No, no," Sebastian explained. "You see, Faye is very beautiful, and we found that other women were extremely intimidated by her beauty. It was hard for her to get close to people. That's why she didn't have friends. That, and, once Nevin died, she really didn't care about friendship anymore. She didn't care about anything, really."

"How does she spend her days?" Josie asked.

Sebastian looked around. "She spends her days here. She makes lunch and then she cleans or gardens or runs errands and then she makes dinner. Then after that, we spend time together before bed, and the days, they just... keep passing."

It sounded like a terribly sad life only because Josie imagined how much fuller their lives must have been when their son was alive. Faye Palazzo sounded like a woman who was just biding her time until death. But she wasn't here to speak for herself. They had only Sebastian to provide an accurate picture of Faye and her life.

Gretchen asked, "What about the other support group members? Did she speak to any of them? Outside of the group?"

"Oh, well, yes. Occasionally. I think she might have met Dee Tenney for coffee once or twice in the last couple of years. Although last night she talked about leaving the group. I'm sure you know about Krystal. Dee told us at the last group meeting. It's just devastating. Faye took it really hard."

"Was she close to Krystal Duncan?" asked Josie.

"Oh no. I mean, we had a boy and Krystal had a girl and they were in different grades. Faye knew Krystal before the crash because of PTA activities but didn't really get to know her until the start of the support group."

"Did they speak outside of the group?" Gretchen asked.

"No, no. But Faye still took the news very hard. We both did. We know exactly what Krystal went through losing her child—and then for her to be killed? It's unbearably tragic."

"Mr. Palazzo," Josie said. "Were there ever any disagreements within the support group? Any arguments about anything?"

He thought for a moment. "No, not generally. There was one time that Krystal told us that she had gone to meet with Virgil in jail. I'm not sure when but it was fairly recently. We all reacted badly to that, I'm sorry to say. But we're all very emotional and those meetings can be very—well, they stir up a lot of emotions. I'm sure you can imagine, things get heated sometimes. Grief is a rollercoaster ride that you can't get off no matter how badly you want to do so, but no, there was never any true animosity, if that's what you're asking. Even after we found out that Krystal had seen Virgil, by the next meeting, all of us were over it. I mean, we were all friends with him before the crash. Probably every one of us at one time or another has wanted to go see him and confront him about what he did. But Krystal didn't seem very satisfied by her meeting with him."

"We understand that at last week's meeting, Krystal Duncan was upset," said Gretchen.

Sebastian's chin dropped to his chest. "Yes, she was very distressed during that meeting. She lashed out at all of us, but we didn't think anything of it. We had been so hard on her about the Virgil thing. We kind of had it coming. No one took it personally."

Josie suppressed a sigh. Every minute that passed there was less and less to work with. She turned the conversation back to Faye. "What about your wife's hobbies? Did she have any?"

"No," said Sebastian. "Nevin was her whole life until he was killed. Since then, well, neither of us feels like getting out of bed in the morning, much less taking up any kind of activity."

Gretchen said, "Did your wife ever explicitly express any suicidal thoughts? Did she talk about killing herself? Maybe how she would do it if she was going to do it?"

He shook his head. "No, no. She only ever said that she wished she was dead."

Josie said, "Mr. Palazzo, what do you believe happened here this morning?"

He spread his hands. A pleading look came into his eyes. "I think someone took my wife. They came here and took her, and those earrings were left behind as some kind of message."

"What kind of message?" Gretchen asked.

"How should I know? But my wife is gone. You have to find her. You have to help me."

Josie held up a hand before he could become hysterical. "We're going to help you, Mr. Palazzo. I promise you that. Who would want to do something like this? Do you have any idea?"

He rubbed his hands down over his face. "I don't know. I have no idea."

Gretchen asked, "Were either of you having any issues with anyone recently? Feuds, bad blood, disagreements? That sort of thing?"

"No, no. We keep to ourselves."

"But someone was here," Josie argued. "In your home. They left behind earrings that they've either held onto for three years or that they bought as replicas of the ones that were stolen. What do you make of that?"

"A stalker," Sebastian said. "It has to be a stalker. Faye is a very beautiful woman."

"You've mentioned that," Josie said. "Has she had issues with stalkers in the past?"

"When she lived in New York she had trouble with someone. That was handled in the courts. Then when she first moved here, there was another gentleman that I believed was taking too much of an interest in her. A man at the gym. She reported him to the gym management and they expelled him. That was the last we heard from him."

"How long ago was this?" Gretchen asked.

"Oh, maybe fifteen years?"

Which meant there would no longer be a record of the man who'd been kicked out of Faye Palazzo's gym, and it was unlikely the same man would have stalked her for a decade and a half without making himself known to the Palazzos before this.

Josie asked, "Did either of you have any reason to believe that Faye was being stalked recently?"

"No, nothing. She would have told me. I know she would have. I have always been hypervigilant when it comes to her and I haven't noticed anything, but what other explanation is there?"

Josie had an inkling of another possible explanation for Faye Palazzo's disappearance, but she wasn't about to share it with Sebastian. "Mr. Palazzo," she said. "Detective Palmer and I are going to step outside for a few minutes. First, can you tell us what Faye was wearing when you left this morning. Was she still in pajamas?"

"She had already changed. It was, uh, like a jumpsuit. Shorts and blouse but one piece. Linen, pink, baggy."

Josie nodded while Gretchen jotted it down. Then she said, "We need to call in some more units and get things moving. If you wouldn't mind not touching anything here in the kitchen until our team has had a chance to go over it, we'd appreciate that."

His eyes lit up. "You believe me! Thank God. Yes, I mean no, I won't touch anything. Thank you. I can wait in the living room."

Josie thought of the massive, sultry photo of Faye on the living room wall. "Why don't you wait on the front stoop?" she suggested.

CHAPTER TWENTY

Sebastian Palazzo paced back and forth along his front walk while Josie and Gretchen stood several yards away near Gretchen's car. They had called for two patrol units to canvass the neighborhood although they didn't expect anything to come from it. The street was quiet, with very little traffic, and if the neighbors on either side and across the street hadn't seen anything of note, then it was unlikely anyone else had. Still, they had to try. Another unit would be assigned to search relevant places: the memorial site and anywhere else within walking distance. Josie also dispatched a unit to take a drive through the cemetery where Nevin Palazzo had been buried. Gretchen had called the Evidence Response Team to have them process the Palazzos' kitchen and front door.

"You're not getting prints from those earrings," Josie told her after she hung up with Officer Hummel.

"I know," Gretchen said. "It's a long shot, and if Krystal Duncan hadn't turned up dead two days ago, I wouldn't even be taking a report."

"But both Krystal and Faye were in the same support group."

"Yes," Gretchen said.

"Both were home until they weren't, and both disappeared and left their phones, purses, and vehicles behind."

"Yes," Gretchen repeated.

Josie glanced toward Sebastian, but he continued to pace. His head was down, and it looked like he was muttering something to himself. "He seems a little overbearing."

"He does," Gretchen agreed. "A little obsessed with his wife. Then again, they lost their son. For some couples, the loss of a child can destroy a marriage but for others, it can bring them closer. Maybe he and Mrs. Palazzo clung to each other. Maybe the experience changed their dynamic."

"Yeah," Josie conceded. "If I'd lost my son, I'd be pretty freaked out if my spouse disappeared. I don't think we're looking for a stalker, though."

Gretchen sighed. "No, not in the sense that he's thinking."

"The bus crash is the connection," Josie said. "The support group."

"I agree. We should check with Dr. Rosetti to see if she's heard from Faye."

"We still need to talk to Gloria Cammack's employees about the parts of her alibi that can be verified between the time that Krystal Duncan went missing and when she was found dead," Josie pointed out.

The work was stacking up.

Gretchen said, "I'm going to have Mett do that. I'll call him now. Why don't you take my car and head over to Dr. Rosetti's place? See what you can find out. We'll regroup later at the station. I'll have one of the patrol units drive me back."

Josie used her cell phone to call Dr. Rosetti and make sure she was available before taking Gretchen's vehicle. The doctor's sessions were over for the day by the time Josie arrived just after five p.m. Paige had told her to use the gate at the side of the house and meet in the garden. Josie made her way through the large wooden privacy gate and into the space she had only seen from the therapy room until now. It was even more lush and gorgeous in person. Paige was dressed in a pair of old khaki capri pants and a UPenn T-shirt. Her hair was pulled back off her neck as she knelt in the grass and pulled weeds from one of the flower beds, depositing them into a canvas bucket next to her.

She looked up and smiled at Josie, waving a hand covered in a thick, pink gardening glove. "Have a seat," she said.

Josie turned to see a stone bench beneath the window of the therapy room, across from Paige. She sat and watched Paige work for a few moments. The day was still hot but here in the garden there was a gentle breeze. The sounds of birds chirping, and the heady smell of flowers were soothing.

As if reading her mind, Paige said, "I like to come out here at the end of the day to decompress. Sometimes I just sit and enjoy the space and sometimes I work."

"It's wonderful," said Josie.

"You said you needed to talk to me about police business. I assume it must have to do with Krystal Duncan. You've probably discovered that she was one of my patients. I run a support group for the parents of the West Denton crash."

"Yes," Josie said. "Actually, I'm not here about Krystal. I'm here about Faye Palazzo."

Paige's hands froze in the dirt. When she turned to look at Josie, her eyes were wide with fear. "Has something happened? Is Faye all right?"

"She's missing," Josie said.

Paige removed her hands from the dirt and took off her gloves. She stood, brushed off her pants and came to sit beside Josie. "Can you tell me more?"

Leaving the part about the earrings out, Josie recounted what Sebastian had told them. Then she asked, "Have you heard from her today?"

Paige shook her head. "No."

"You've seen her privately and in the support group for a couple of years now. Do you have any thoughts as to where she might have gone or who she would have turned to?"

"You know I cannot violate the privacy of my patients, Josie."

"I understand that. If we believed she was in danger, would you be able to break your oath?"

"You think she's in danger?"

"Her husband believes she was taken by someone, possibly a stalker. We have no reason not to believe him. Did Faye ever talk to you about being stalked?"

Paige shook her head. "I'm only answering this because if she is truly in danger, I want to be helpful. No, the subject of stalkers never came up. Not in private sessions or in the group."

"How did she seem the last time you saw her?" Josie asked. "Did she seem more depressed than normal?"

Paige frowned, looking at her lap. "They're all more depressed, Josie. I can say this to you because it's public knowledge: the trial of the bus driver is on the horizon. Something like that creates a great deal of stress for the family members of victims. Not only are you asked to relive your trauma, but it can be frustrating that a trial is occurring at all."

"You mean because the evidence showed that Virgil Lesko was drunk, so why has he pled not guilty? Why force a trial?"

"Exactly. It's hard to explain to someone in the throes of grief and loss that there are legal nuances at work and that he is entitled to a defense no matter what. Faye seemed perhaps more stressed than usual, but if I thought she was a danger to herself I would have had her hospitalized. I do not believe she was at that point."

"I know you can't violate confidentiality, but we believe that Krystal's murder and Faye's disappearance may be linked. Can you think of anyone who might want to hurt the members of your group?"

Paige took a moment to consider this. Together, they watched an eastern bluebird flit back and forth on some low-hanging tree branches near the back of the garden. Then Paige said, "No, I'm sorry. I can't think of anyone. At least, there was never any discussion in the group or in any private sessions that I had about any threats. Obviously, if I had been told about any potential threat, I would have encouraged them to bring that to the police. Josie, these people are just grieving parents, nothing more."

"A couple of people have said that there was tension in the group between Krystal and the others because she had met with Virgil Lesko in jail."

Paige waved a hand in the air. "That had blown over. The other members were upset initially, but by the next week no one was even talking about it."

"I understand that Krystal was very upset at her last meeting. That she became very angry at the other group members and that she said that Bianca wasn't even supposed to be on the bus that day. Do you know what was behind her outburst?"

Paige stood and went back to the garden bed. She knelt down but made no move to put her gloves back on. She seemed to be considering something. She said, "I don't think it has anything to do with her murder."

Josie said, "That's the thing about solving murders. What might not seem important could be the thing that cracks the case. That's why you have to get as much information as possible. Why don't you tell me and let me decide whether it's helpful or not? Krystal is no longer with us so you're not violating her privacy."

Paige looked down where her hands rested in her lap. She sighed. "Krystal was extremely upset when she left her last group meeting. I felt compelled to check on her, so I called her at work the next day. She came in for a short session during her break. She apologized for getting so angry and yelling. I asked why she was so angry. She told me she couldn't say, so I prompted her by asking what she meant when she said Bianca wasn't even supposed to be on the bus that day. She tried to avoid the question at first, but finally said she'd been finding out about a lot of things lately—"

"Meaning what?" interrupted Josie. "What things?"

"I don't know," said Paige. "She didn't say. The only thing she told me was that on the day of the bus crash, she'd made arrangements for Nathan to pick up his children and Bianca fifteen minutes early from school. Evidently, Bianca and one of the Cammack children had orthodontist appointments at the same time, and Nathan had agreed to take them so that Krystal wouldn't have to leave early from work that day."

"But the kids were on the bus," Josie said.

Paige nodded sadly. "Yes. Nathan texted Krystal right before he was supposed to leave work and told her that the orthodontist had canceled all afternoon appointments, and he was stuck at work anyway."

Josie said, "Krystal must have agreed at that point for Bianca to take the bus just like every other day. Why, two years later, did she feel as though Bianca shouldn't have been on the bus? Had she intended to leave work to get her?"

"I don't know if I should tell you this as it involves one of the other parents," Paige said.

"Did you talk to that other parent about this? Whatever it is?"

Paige shook her head. "No. Krystal told me. I didn't try to verify it. I saw no reason to. It changes nothing."

"If it came from Krystal, you're hardly violating anyone else's privacy," Josie pointed out.

"But, Josie, I'm sure this isn't important. None of these things are important. That's the thing that Krystal struggled with—that many, if not all, people grieving struggle with. You know this yourself. All those tiny, seemingly meaningless decisions that we made on the day that our loved one was taken from us, we can go over them in our heads ad nauseam, but it changes nothing. Whether Krystal decided to wear a red skirt or a blue skirt that morning—Bianca is still dead."

Josie felt something shift inside her. An image of Lisette pushing her walker through grass toward the edge of the woods came unbidden into her mind. "There's a big difference between wondering if the color clothes I wore the day my grandmother was murdered would have saved her and wondering if I should have told her to stay away from the woods and go back to the hotel. If I had just told her to go back to the hotel, she would be alive."

"But you didn't," Paige said.

Josie felt as though she'd knocked the wind out of her. An avalanche of feeling crashed down on Josie's shoulders. Her body buckled. Her lungs fought for breath that wouldn't come. Suddenly, Paige was beside her again. Her hands were on Josie's shoulders. "It's just pain," Paige told her. "Breathe."

Josie opened her mouth to say that she couldn't breathe, but only a strangled cry burst forth.

Paige rubbed one hand in a circle on Josie's back. "Don't fight it, Josie."

I can't, she wanted to say. *I can't not fight.*

Paige kept talking. "Don't you see, Josie? All day, every day, we make these decisions, and we make them from a place that assumes that the world is reasonably safe. We make risk assessments all day long, and those assessments are based on experience and expectations that don't necessarily involve murderers or drunk drivers. When you walked with your grandmother to the edge of those woods to find the spot where a little girl had wandered off, why in heavens would you assume that a killer would be waiting on the other side and that he would fire a gun at you and your grandmother? You didn't let your grandmother die. Someone killed her. When Bianca had to take the bus the day of the crash rather than going to the orthodontist with the Cammacks, Krystal had every reasonable expectation that she would arrive home safely just like she had every other day of school for her entire life. Krystal didn't let Bianca die. The bus driver got drunk and chose to drive his route anyway. If Only is a dangerous game, Josie. A dangerous, pointless game, and it changes nothing. If Krystal had gotten drunk and driven with her daughter in the car, and Bianca had been killed that way, well, yes, Krystal would have had a lot of work to do in terms of forgiving herself and moving on. But it wasn't her fault, just like Lisette's murder wasn't your fault."

Josie finally gulped in a full breath. The scenarios weren't the same—Josie and Lisette, Krystal and Bianca—and Josie wasn't sure she would ever convince herself that she was blameless for what happened to Lisette. Now her grandmother was gone, and all Josie had left was this crush of feeling that was so heavy and so excruciating that it didn't seem possible to physically survive it. Was this how Krystal had felt? Had it been magnified because Krystal had lost her child and not a grandparent?

"What did she tell you?" Josie huffed. "What did Krystal say that you don't want to reveal?"

Paige's hand still moved in a circle on Josie's upper back. Josie kept her upper body folded, afraid she might throw up if she tried to sit up straight. Paige said, "Nathan lied. The orthodontist didn't cancel his afternoon appointments. The kids were a no-show."

"Why would he lie?" Josie asked.

She felt Paige shrug. "I have no idea."

"How did Krystal find out? Wouldn't this have been something she would have found out soon after the crash?" Josie asked, feeling the nausea in her stomach settle.

Paige said, "I really don't know, Josie. All I can tell you is what Krystal said. She said that she had just found out that Nathan had lied about the orthodontist and apparently about being stuck at work as well. She said he went home—without even picking up his children from school—to be with Gloria."

"But why?" Josie wondered out loud.

Paige sighed. "I imagine that's between Nathan and Gloria. I'm sure they have a great deal of guilt over it. It's not my place to speculate. If one or both of them wants to avail themselves of my services to discuss it, I would be happy to try and help but other than that, there isn't much I can say."

Josie finally sat up straight. Paige put her hands into her own lap. "How do you feel?" she asked Josie.

"Like someone put me in a trash compactor and didn't finish the job," Josie admitted.

Paige laughed.

Josie said, "Krystal must have been furious with Nathan. Why didn't she confront him?" Or had she confronted him, but he'd conveniently left that part out? "Did she tell you whether she had or not? Or whether she was going to?"

Paige shook her head. "She told me she had not discussed it with him. I don't know if she intended to or not."

In her pocket, Josie's phone trilled. "I'm sorry," she said as she looked at the screen. "This is my colleague. I've got to take it." She swiped answer. "Mett? What's going on?"

Detective Finn Mettner's voice sounded strained. In the background, Josie could hear a man yelling. "Boss?" he said. "Could you come over to the All Natural Family and Child store? We've got a situation here."

CHAPTER TWENTY-ONE

Gloria Cammack's store was housed in a converted auto repair shop close to central Denton. One half of it was filled with retail items for local shoppers and the other half looked as though it was being used as a shipping hub where employees packaged products and sent them out to customers and clients all over the country. A second-floor addition had been added at some point and as Josie pulled into the parking lot in front of the store, she saw Gloria Cammack standing in its window, staring down at the street below. Her arms were folded over her chest and a scowl covered her face.

A patrol vehicle sat across two parking spots, its lights flashing. Two uniformed officers and Detective Mettner stood about five feet away from the entrance to the retail store, surrounding Nathan Cammack. As Josie got out of her vehicle, she saw that Nathan was pacing in a tight circle, hands fisted at his sides. His shaggy hair was in disarray. Teeth gritted, he said, "I just want to see my *fucking wife!*" He shouted the last two words, loudly enough to startle a customer emerging from the store.

Mettner said, "Mr. Cammack, I've asked you to calm down twice already. Mrs. Cammack doesn't want to speak with you. She's asked us to remove you from the premises. I think it would be best for everyone if you left of your own accord."

One of the uniformed officers said, "And that doesn't mean stepping off the pavement into the street. It means go home and cool off."

"One conversation," Nathan said, addressing Mettner. "She can't have one conversation with me?"

He tried to step past them but Mettner put his hand on Nathan's chest. "She doesn't want to talk right now. She's made that clear."

Josie joined the fray. "Mr. Cammack?"

"You!" he said. "I talked to you this morning. You know what's going on. I need to talk to my wife. I need to tell her that Krystal lied."

It was then Josie smelled the alcohol on his breath. "Mr. Cammack—Nathan—Gloria is your ex-wife, and if she doesn't wish to speak with you, I'm afraid there's nothing that we can do about that."

Mettner said, "I was finishing up with the employee interviews and he showed up here like this. Ambushed Mrs. Cammack in her office—"

Nathan threw his hands in the air. "I didn't ambush her. Come on, man. She's my wife."

Mettner continued as if Nathan hadn't spoken. "She called 911 while I was in the building trying to get him out."

"You have no right!" Nathan hollered. "You can't kick me out of here! I have every right to be here."

Josie said, "Nathan, I really don't want to see you hauled away from here in the back of a patrol car. Why don't you come with me? We'll go get some coffee and we can talk. I've got more questions for you anyway."

He seemed to consider this for a moment. Then his lips firmed into a thin, straight line, and he tried to push past them. Mettner and Josie held him back. Mettner said, "Take him down to the station."

As the uniformed officers approached, he began yelling. "Get out of my way! I'm going to see my wife, and you can't stop me! I want to talk to my wife!"

From over her shoulder, Josie heard Gloria's voice cut through. "I'm not your wife anymore, Nathan."

He stopped struggling against Josie and Mettner and craned his neck to see Gloria better. She stood four feet away in her high heels and sharp pantsuit, arms crossed over her stomach. A Bluetooth was affixed to her ear. "Go home, Nathan," she told him. "We have nothing to say to one another."

"Krystal lied," he blurted out. "We never had an affair."

For a split second, Gloria's scowl loosened, replaced by a look of shock and dismay. She quickly regained her composure. With a heavy sigh, she said, "I don't care, Nathan. It doesn't matter. Nothing matters anymore."

"It matters to me," he said. "When we were a family, I was faithful to you and the kids."

Josie knew this wasn't entirely true given his admission of a one-time tryst with Krystal, but she didn't intervene.

"Were you, though?" Gloria said, taking a step toward him. "You fought me about everything. The food the kids ate, the clothes they wore, the medications they took, the vacation spots we chose. Everything. Nothing was ever good enough for you. Why should I believe you didn't cheat? If you were that unhappy—and I know you were unhappy—why wouldn't you have an affair?"

Nathan shook his head like a dog shaking off water. "Okay," he said. "All right. It's true. I was unhappy. I didn't like this whole organic lifestyle you wanted all of us to live by. It was too much. Sometimes me and the kids, we just wanted a damn cheeseburger or some candy. That's right, overly sugary, processed candy that has no place in the natural world. We wanted to have fun, Gloria."

Tears gathered in Gloria's eyes. Her voice cracked when she said, "I wasn't fun? After everything I did for our family, to provide for us? To make our lives better? I wasn't fun enough for you, Nathan? When are you going to grow up?"

She turned on her heel and began striding away.

Nathan lunged toward her, still held back by Josie and Mettner. "You were a good mother!" he shouted. "Gloria! You were a good mother. Please, listen to me. Please."

She stopped walking but didn't turn around. Her shoulders quaked.

Nathan said, "I'm an idiot, okay? I'm immature and I'm an idiot. I'm sorry. I didn't appreciate you, okay? I'm sorry. But I didn't have an affair with Krystal. We smoked pot together. That's it. I mean, come on, what's more believable? I was having some long-term affair with her or I was smoking weed with her in the evenings?"

Slowly, Gloria turned back to face him. She wiped tears from her cheeks. Some of the tension had left her face.

"Do you believe me?" Nathan asked.

"Yes," she said. "I do. But why did Krystal say you had an affair?"

His gaze dropped to the ground. Josie and Mettner lowered their arms tentatively and let him have some space. When he looked back up at Gloria, he said, "It was that stupid Student of the Month thing."

Confusion passed over Gloria's face. "Are you high right now?" she spat. "What are you even talking about?"

Nathan took a step toward her. "Remember Wallace's regular teacher went on maternity leave? They had that sub right before the crash?"

She gave her head a quick shake, urging him along. "I guess. Whatever. Get to the point."

"You don't remember Wallace coming home and announcing that he was Student of the Month?"

"Oh," Gloria said, her irritation draining away. "Yes, of course. He'd never been before."

"He wasn't that time either, evidently. Bianca was supposed to be Student of the Month. That's who their teacher had chosen before she went on maternity leave. Wallace took her planner and changed it so that he was Student of the Month. The substitute teacher had no idea. She just went by what was in the book that the regular teacher had left. The entire class knew about it, but no one wanted to tell. They didn't want to be tattletales, I guess, but Bianca was upset."

"I'm sure that's not true, Nathan. Besides, what does it matter?"

"Krystal wanted me to go to the principal and have it changed back. Bianca had just done all that fundraising for pediatric cancer research. She deserved it. No one in the class would stand up for her. Krystal said that she felt like a bitch telling on a twelve-year-old boy and that I—that we—should just do the right thing and make Wallace tell the truth and apologize."

"Why didn't I hear about any of this?" Gloria asked. "You never told me."

"Because I knew you wouldn't believe it unless Wallace told you himself. I confronted him about it, but he wouldn't admit it. Krystal told me to go to the school anyway, without you or him, but I wouldn't."

Gloria put a hand on her hip. "You were discussing our son with the woman you smoked pot with but not with me?"

Nathan took another step forward, hands up in a conciliatory gesture, but Gloria stepped back in time with him. "I'm not saying I was right. I'm just trying to tell you what happened. When I refused to set the record straight about the Student of the Month, Krystal threatened me. First, she said she would tell you that we smoked pot and when that didn't scare me, she said she would lie and tell you that we were having an affair. She was angry with me. She's probably always been angry with me. That's why she lied about the affair."

Gloria studied him for a long moment, appraising. Then she said, "She wouldn't be holding onto the stupid Student of the Month thing for two years after the kids died. She only told me recently that the two of you had had an affair. She wanted to hurt me, Nathan. Why? Why would she do that?"

Nathan's hands dropped to his side. Before their eyes, he seemed to deflate and for a second, Josie wondered if he was going to fall. In a small, defeated voice, he said, "I don't know."

Josie stepped forward. "I think I do."

CHAPTER TWENTY-TWO

It took some convincing to get both Cammacks to accompany Josie and Mettner to police headquarters. Once a news van showed up outside of All Natural Family and Child, it gave Josie a little more leverage. The last thing the two grieving parents needed was press coverage of them airing their dirty laundry with one another. Josie sent Mettner to Komorrah's to get Nathan some coffee while she secured a bottle of water for Gloria. The Cammacks waited in the first-floor conference room, facing off across from one another. It seemed like an eternity since Sebastian Palazzo had paced this very room talking about his missing wife to Josie and Gretchen when in fact it had been less than twelve hours ago.

Josie checked the time on her phone as she stood outside the door to the conference room. It was just after eight thirty in the evening. She hadn't eaten dinner. Her fingers flew across the screen of her phone as she asked Mettner to get her some pastries from Komorrah's while he was there. It would have to do. She answered the handful of texts that Noah had sent checking in on her and then messaged back and forth with Gretchen so that they could update one another on where things stood.

The search for Faye Palazzo was a bust. No one had seen her leave the house. No one had seen her walking around the neighborhood. She wasn't in any of the places that police looked, including the cemetery. The ERT had processed the Palazzo kitchen and front entryway but hadn't come up with anything. Sebastian Palazzo was so beside himself that Gretchen was considering taking him to the Emergency Room unless he calmed down. They promised to keep one another apprised of any and all developments. By the time Josie dropped her phone back into her pocket, Mettner was back with coffees for her and Nathan Cammack as well as several cheese Danishes for Josie to consume later at her desk.

"You're the best," she told him quietly as they went into the room with the Cammacks. Josie sat beside Nathan, pushing a cup of coffee in front of him while Mettner sat across from them beside Gloria.

Nathan said, "Are you gonna, like, read us our rights or something?"

Gloria rolled her eyes.

Josie said, "We're only here to talk, Mr. Cammack. Neither one of you is a suspect in any crime, but we are still investigating the murder of Krystal Duncan. Also, Faye Palazzo went missing this morning."

Gloria gasped, eyes on Josie. "What? What do you mean?"

"Just what I said. Faye Palazzo is missing."

Mettner said, "Have either of you spoken with her recently? Say, in the last twenty-four hours?"

Both Gloria and Nathan shook their heads. Nathan said, "I saw her at the meeting on Monday night. That was it. Jesus. Where do you think she is?"

Josie didn't answer, instead asking her own question. "In the course of our investigation into Krystal's murder and Faye's disappearance, it has come to our attention that Krystal had found out some items of information before her death."

"What does that mean?" Gloria said. "Could you be more specific?"

Josie said, "It has to do with the date of the bus crash."

Gloria tipped her head back, looking at the ceiling, and sighing heavily. "This again. When does this end? When will it be over? First, the trial and now you come around rehashing all of this shit. Why can't anyone let my children rest in peace?"

"Our children," Nathan put in. For the first time, he picked up the paper coffee cup and took a sip.

Gloria glared at him.

Josie said, "Like it or not, Krystal Duncan was found murdered and your son's nickname was found at the scene. Other than work, the only people that Krystal associated with were members of the support group for parents of the children killed in the accident. Now we have a second member of that group missing. The last time Krystal attended a meeting, she was visibly upset, and she said a number of things before storming out."

Gloria said, "I don't go to that group, so I don't see how this concerns me."

Josie kept going as if Gloria hadn't spoken. "On the day of the bus crash, Nathan was supposed to pick up your children and Bianca Duncan early from school to go to the orthodontist."

Silence.

"Nathan texted Krystal while she was at work and told her that the orthodontist had canceled all his afternoon appointments; that he was stuck at work; and that he would not be picking up the children."

"Stop," said Nathan, his voice suddenly raspy.

"But the orthodontist didn't cancel his appointments for the afternoon. Nathan called his office and canceled the appointments, and he was not stuck at work." Josie caught his eye. "You went home."

He pushed his chair back and buried his face in his hands, sobbing. The sound reverberated through Josie's bones like she was some kind of grief tuning fork. Across the table, Mettner lowered his gaze. Josie lifted a hand to touch Nathan's forearm, but then Gloria's voice cut through Nathan's cries. Her tone was carefully controlled.

"It was my fault. It was because of me," she said. "I called him at work that day. I was home. I had forgotten my planner, and I needed it. I came home after lunch to get it, and there was an issue. I called Nathan and told him to come home. He said he had to take the kids to the orthodontist. I told him to cancel the appointments. When he asked me what he should tell Krystal, I said I didn't care. I told him to just get his ass home immediately."

Nathan's sobs subsided to hiccups. He didn't lift his head. Mettner slid a box of tissues across the counter and Josie plucked two tissues from it and nudged Nathan until he took them.

Gloria's voice was cold. "Is that what you wanted to hear? That it's my fault that our children are dead? That it's my fault that Bianca Duncan died?"

Josie thought about the conversation she'd had with Paige Rosetti in the garden. *If Only is a dangerous game.*

"What happened to the children on that bus was not your fault, Mrs. Cammack," said Josie firmly. "No matter what happened. No matter what choices you made that day. It was not your fault."

Gloria looked surprised. Then, as tears filled her eyes, she turned her head away. Josie slid the box of tissues back to the other side of the table.

Josie gave both parents a moment to compose themselves. Then she began again. "What was the issue, Gloria? What happened that you needed Nathan to come home that day?"

"Does it matter?" Gloria asked.

"I don't know," said Josie. "Why don't you tell us what happened, and we'll decide whether it's germane to either of our investigations."

Gloria rolled her eyes but said, "Wallace's PlayStation had been stolen."

Nathan, finally regaining some composure, said, "We don't know that it was stolen."

"What do you think happened to it, Nathan? It was stolen. Just like Frankie's Roosevelt dime, my Saint Laurent clutch, and that stupid camping stove you never even used."

He shook his head. "You got rid of the Saint Laurent bag and my camping stove during one of your purges."

"I would not have gotten rid of that bag," Gloria insisted.

Mettner asked, "Why don't you take us through it? Which items went missing and when?"

Nathan said, "It was about four or five months before the bus crash. Actually, it was New Year's Eve, wasn't it, Glor?"

She shifted in her chair, folding her arms over her chest, a stance Josie had become used to seeing her in. "Yes. We had that party at the Eudora Hotel. The city Chamber of Commerce put it on. I was looking for my clutch because it went with my dress, and it was gone."

Josie asked, "Did you think it was stolen at that point?"

Gloria said, "If you're wondering whether or not we made a police report, no, we didn't. I thought I misplaced it. It never turned up."

"Then maybe a month later, maybe two months, Frankie's Roosevelt dime went missing."

Mettner said, "Roosevelt dime?"

Nathan answered, "My dad gave it to her. It's a rare coin. A dime from 1982 with the mint mark missing. She always kept it in this tiny blue pouch—like a change purse—with her initials on the front in glitter: *F.C.* She kept the pouch inside a box on one of her bookshelves. She had a friend over and wanted to show her, opened the box, and it was gone—the pouch and the dime with it."

"We looked everywhere," said Gloria. "She was so upset. We even took the vacuum apart and emptied out the filter because we were afraid maybe somehow the dime had come out of the pouch and had fallen onto her bedroom floor, and I had accidentally vacuumed it up. I did that more to appease her than anything else. I mean, the pouch was gone, too."

"But there was nothing in the vacuum," added Nathan. "We never did find it."

Josie asked, "The clutch and the dime. How much were they worth, do you think?"

"Combined?" asked Gloria. "Maybe six, seven hundred dollars."

"What about the camping stove?" asked Mettner.

"I never even opened the box," Nathan said. "It was a high-end stove, so probably three hundred bucks? When the weather got nice, I went to the garage to get it out. I thought that we could use it out back to roast marshmallows—" He looked at Gloria from under his lowered brows. "The vegan kind, in the yard. But the stove was gone. Gloria had taken some things to Goodwill, and I just assumed she had donated it."

Mettner said, "You thought she donated a three-hundred-dollar, brand new camping stove, and you didn't say anything?"

Nathan shrugged. "Not by that point. We'd fought over it several times before that."

"He spent entirely too much money on it," said Gloria. "He doesn't even like camping. He didn't even own a tent."

"I would have gotten around to it eventually," Nathan said.

"Oh, like you got around to kayaking and learning how to smoke meat?" She turned to Mettner. "He has a habit of buying overpriced things for hobbies he never takes up."

Before they could get any more off topic, Josie said, "But the day of the accident, you said you came home and Wallace's PlayStation was gone?"

"Yes," said Gloria. "It was set up in our family room, where the kids hung out when they had friends over and I could keep an eye on them. I walked past that day and noticed it was gone. That was the final straw for me. I called Nathan and told him to come immediately."

Josie said, "You thought these items were being stolen?"

Gloria nodded. "Yes. I did."

"Not at first, though," Nathan said. "Neither of us thought anything was being stolen. We just thought we were going crazy. Misplacing things. Getting rid of things but not remembering."

Mettner asked, "Do you think someone was sneaking into your house and taking things?"

"Or someone we knew was taking things," Gloria suggested. "Our neighborhood is very safe. There are a ton of families. All of our children played together. We all watched each other's kids."

Nathan added, "There was always some barbecue or kid's birthday party or book club… it was endless. Every family hosted things. There were always people in and out of the house. Even Virgil—the bus driver—came to everything. He was a good neighbor and friend to all of us before the accident."

Gloria glared at him. "Don't say his name, Nathan."

Josie brought them back to the topic at hand. "You thought it was someone you knew?"

Gloria shrugged. "We weren't sure. We weren't even sure it was really happening at first."

Mettner asked, "Could you make a list of people who had been in your house during that time?"

Nathan laughed. "You're kidding, right? Just make a list of almost all the neighbors in a ten-block radius. Not to mention that there were also a few times we had to have contractors at the house for repairs."

Gloria added, "There's no way to make a comprehensive list and if we did, it would be dozens of people. The point is that it never occurred to us that anyone would steal things from our home, so we weren't paying attention. That's why I wasn't sure until the PlayStation went missing. That was a big-ticket item. I mean, the clutch was more expensive, but I hardly ever used it. The PlayStation? Wallace lived for that thing. That's what I thought when I saw it was gone: he is going to be devastated. He played it almost every day after school—with time limits, of course. It was at that moment that things came together for me. I thought all of these things were related, and someone definitely had been coming into our house and taking things! I was freaked out, upset, so yes, I called my husband."

Nathan shook his head, not meeting her eyes. "And I came running. Ditched the kids. Ditched work. Came home."

Gloria said, "They should have been safe on that bus."

Josie said, "Did the two of you ever tell anyone about this? The missing PlayStation? The canceled orthodontist appointments? You meeting at home while the kids were finishing up school?"

Both parents looked at her. Gloria tried to speak but all that came out was a strangled cry. Nathan said, "No. We didn't. I mean we were talking about whether or not to go to the police when we got the call about the accident. We didn't even think about any of that until much later. We—we decided together not to tell anyone. It didn't seem… relevant."

Mettner said, "You were afraid you would somehow be blamed."

Nathan nodded. "Not just for our own kids' deaths but for Krystal's daughter, too. It was too much. Too horrible. Gloria was already getting so much flak in the press for being a mother and the head of a company—as if that had anything to do with anything. We just didn't think it was a detail that ever needed to come out. It didn't change the outcome."

"Then how would Krystal Duncan have found out two years after the fact?" Josie asked.

Nathan shrugged. "I don't know. The orthodontist, maybe?"

"What does it matter?" Gloria asked. "How does this relate to her murder? If she found this out, she had every right to be furious with us. If I were her, I'd want to kill us both. So why are we here and she's not?"

"That's what we're trying to figure out," Mettner said.

The real question was, why had Krystal started searching for information in the first place? Josie thought about what Paige Rosetti had said: that Krystal had found out some things. What else had she found out? What had she found out that had sent her to the East Bridge to ask Skinny D for painkillers? Had it been the revelation about Nathan canceling the orthodontist appointments or something else? Gloria was correct. The revelation about Nathan and Gloria meeting at their home on the day of the crash was not something that would result in Krystal's death.

What were they missing?

"Boss?"

Josie looked at Mettner and then realized all of them were staring at her. "Yes?"

Gloria said, "We asked if that was everything? Can we go? I'm exhausted, and I just want to go home."

"Okay," said Josie. "Yes. That sounds like a good idea."

Mettner drove Nathan Cammack home while Gloria left on her own. Josie scarfed down some cheese Danishes while finishing up her reports for the day. By the time she got home, it was almost ten o'clock. As she approached her front door, she heard Trout's claws scratch the other side along with his high-pitched whining. Exhaustion warred with regret. She'd gone from being home with the dog twenty-four hours a day to now being away from him most of the day. Added to that was the fact that today had been one of Noah's days off and she hadn't even made it home in time for them to eat dinner together. This was the job though, and it had never bothered her before. But the cloak of grief hung heavy on her. The West Denton bus crash parents not only shared the kind of trauma Josie was intimately familiar with, but they were a reminder to hold close the ones you loved most. They could be taken in a second.

As Josie reached the door, Noah swung it open. Trout rushed out at her, jumping at her legs and whining excitedly. She herded his wiggling body back into the foyer and gave him enough attention and praise to settle him down. When she looked up, Noah was grinning at her. She looked beyond him to see flickering light in the kitchen doorway.

"What's going on?" she said.

"I have a surprise for you. Come on."

The kitchen was lit by a dozen candles. The table was set with what looked like shrimp scampi. The smell was overpowering, and Josie's mouth watered at the prospect of a real meal. As Noah pulled out a chair for her and she sat, he told her, "I didn't make this, obviously. Misty did. She was worried about you, this being your first week back and all. She dropped this off. Mett texted me a while ago to say you were finishing reports so I heated it up."

"This is wonderful," Josie said, feeling some of the heaviness lift.

He sat across from her and that was when she noticed the wildflowers in a vase in the center of the table. Her breath caught.

Noah's gaze followed hers. "Your grandmother—before she died—she told me to gather wildflowers for you every now and then."

Josie took in a shaky breath. "Yes. We used to do that. When I was a teenager and I lived with her. We'd collect wildflowers and leave them on the foyer table for one another. It was silly. It was—"

She broke off, tears burning her eyes.

"I can get rid of them," Noah said. "If they're too upsetting."

"No, please," Josie said. "Don't."

Trout nudged Josie's leg and she reached down to touch his head. Assured that she was okay, he circled once and laid down near her feet.

Noah said, "She told me that you would need to be reminded of what she told you before she died."

Lisette had said a few things to Josie before she passed away, but Josie knew exactly which bit Lisette had meant when she gave Noah these instructions.

"You have to live with them both, dear," she had said. "The grief and the happiness. If you can't live with them both, you'll never make it."

Josie reached forward and turned the vase to get a better look at the wildflowers. "This one," she said, "With the tiny pink beads all clustered together is called lady's thumb. These flowers with the four white petals and the yellow starburst at the center are quaker ladies."

Noah laughed. "Do they all have the word 'lady' in their names?"

"No," said Josie. "A lot of them do, but not all. This little thing—" She pointed to a tiny purple flower that shot straight up from the green leaf below and then burst open with one petal dangling downward like a lolling tongue. "This is called henbit, and this—" She moved her index finger over to a gathering of flowers that looked like a bulb with clusters of purple petals erupting from every part of it. "Is called heal-all." She met his eyes, which sparkled in the candle light. "Did you know the names when you picked them?"

"Of course not," he said. "I don't know anything about wildflowers, but your grandmother said you could name every one of them."

"I can," Josie said.

"Do you want to talk about today?"

Josie picked up her fork. "No. I want to eat and then I want you to take me to bed."

CHAPTER TWENTY-THREE

Bianca's head slammed against the window as the bus swerved violently to the left. Before she could even cry out or check her scalp for blood, the bus veered the other way. Her body crashed into Gail's, nearly knocking her onto the aisle floor. A round of cheers went up. Someone said, "Way to go, Mr. Lesko!"

Bianca rubbed her head and looked out the window. Everything seemed to be going by entirely too fast. Normally, the bus ride was so slow, she felt like she could have walked home faster.

"You okay?" Gail said.

"I think something's wrong," Bianca told her.

"Are you bleeding?"

"No, not with my head. I mean with Mr. Lesko. This isn't normal."

Gail laughed. "Oh come on, he's just having a little fun."

"How can you tell from all the way back here?" Bianca asked.

"I don't know. Everyone's cheering."

"Because they're idiots," Bianca said. "People shouldn't drive like this, especially not adults in charge of a bunch of kids."

Gail rolled her eyes. "You sound like someone's mom right now, do you know that? If something was really wrong with him, would the principal have let him drive us? Relax. We're almost at our stop anyway."

CHAPTER TWENTY-FOUR

Josie and Noah stopped at Komorrah's the next morning before work to get coffees for themselves, Gretchen, Mettner, and Amber. As they parked in the municipal parking lot, Noah gave a low whistle. "Look at this circus."

Surrounding the door to the station, which was the private entrance for police personnel, were a handful of reporters. As Josie and Noah approached, they crowded in, thrusting their phones into Josie and Noah's faces. Questions came from every direction.

"Have you found Krystal Duncan's killer yet?"

"Is it true another mother of one the West Denton bus crash victims is missing?"

"Will this delay Virgil Lesko's trial?"

"Should the public be worried?"

"Is the killer targeting the West Denton bus mothers specifically?"

WYEP had sent a cameraman who moved in tandem with the crowd, capturing every "no comment" that Josie and Noah tossed out. Upstairs in the great room, Gretchen was seated at her desk, intent on something on her computer screen. Mettner and Amber were standing next to her desk, their bodies close, heads bent toward one another. As Noah dispensed coffees, Gretchen looked up. "You guys get caught by the paparazzi out there?"

Josie said, "Yeah. They've got a lot of questions."

Amber slid away from Mettner. "I think we should hold a press conference. That would quiet them down, at least for a little while."

Mettner said, "First we need to decide if we're going to tell them that Faye Palazzo is missing."

"They already know," Noah said. "Unofficially. Word got out. They know someone else is missing."

Josie said, "Gretchen, you're the lead. What do you want to do?"

Gretchen took off her reading glasses and leaned back in her chair, sighing. "I don't want to fan the flames here. If we take a lot of this public then we expose these families, and they've already been through more than anyone should ever have to deal with. We could potentially be creating a public panic."

"Or making the public safer by warning them," Mettner argued.

Gretchen picked up her coffee and took a sip. "True. That's a possibility, but I think the press will spin it as a West Denton bus crash parent thing—that would get them the most ratings. The issue here is that we have no leads in these cases. None. Absolutely nothing."

Noah said, "Let's go through it then, piece by piece."

Together, Josie and Gretchen brought him up to speed. Josie concluded, "We know a lot about what happened in the months and even the hours leading up to the West Denton bus crash now but connecting that in some way to Krystal's murder and Faye's disappearance is an issue."

"In that it doesn't seem to connect at all," said Mettner. "Except for the fact that Wallace Cammack's nickname was written on Krystal Duncan's arm. If it wasn't for that, there would not be any connection to the crash at all."

"Except that two mothers of children who died in the crash went missing," said Noah. "And one of them is now dead, and she was left on her daughter's grave."

Mettner replied, "Yeah, but I'm saying maybe you're looking too hard at the bus accident. Maybe that's a distraction. Boss said that in the months—possibly the year—leading up to the crash, things in the homes of the Palazzos and the Cammacks were going missing, right? But there were no break-ins. No police reports were filed."

Gretchen said, "Except for the one for Faye Palazzo's earrings, which were returned to her home when she disappeared, so far as we can tell. They could be replicas. I've asked the Evidence Response Team to see if they can verify whether or not they're real Tiffany earrings."

"Right," Mettner said. "But we're still looking at someone who was coming in and out of the homes of these residents with access to valuables—someone who definitely took things from at least two homes. I bet if you canvassed that neighborhood, you'd find a lot of similar stories."

Josie said, "You think we're looking at a thief turned murderer?"

Mettner shrugged. "Sometimes criminals escalate from non-violent crimes to more violent crimes. It's not unheard of, but what I'm saying is that we shouldn't be honing in on just one theory—like the bus crash connection."

"I agree with that," Noah said.

Josie and Gretchen stared at Noah, then looked to Mettner and back to Noah. Gretchen said, "Holy crap. That might be the first time you two have ever agreed on anything."

Everyone laughed. Then Gretchen said, "Well, Mett, why don't you work that angle? Get over to West Denton and start asking around. If the thievery was more widespread, there's a chance that someone saw something."

Josie said, "I think that the thief and the killer—whether they're the same person or not—was someone known to both the Palazzos and the Cammacks. Like Gloria and Nathan said—and even Sebastian—there were always people in and out of each other's houses for parties and other gatherings. Also, neither Krystal nor Faye put up a fight. There was no sign of struggle. Faye was about to sit down to eat lunch with her husband."

"Krystal had a half-finished glass of wine on her coffee table. We covered this when we started looking into her disappearance. Before you came back to work," Noah said to Josie.

Josie said, "You wouldn't be worried about walking away from a meal or a glass of wine or your purse or phone if it was just a neighbor popping over, wanting to talk to you or asking you to come outside for a moment."

Gretchen said, "Someone's got to make a list or a diagram or something of the families over there and their level of familiarity with one another."

"I'm on that," Mettner said. "I can run criminal background checks on everyone I speak with as well."

Noah said, "I can help Mett with that stuff. That's going to be a lot of knocking on doors. We've still got the issue of Faye Palazzo though. Speaking of which, the ERT did call with one very important detail this morning, which is that there were two boxes of vigil candles on Faye Palazzo's kitchen table when she disappeared."

"I remember," Josie said. "They were marked as having fifty in each box."

Noah nodded. "Except there were only forty-two in each box."

"Okay," said Josie. "When did Faye get them? Could Sebastian account for the missing sixteen candles?"

Mettner said, "She'd gotten them two weeks before she went missing and he said that to his knowledge, none of the candles had been used or given out to anyone else. There should have been fifty in each box."

"But there weren't," Noah said. "And an initial comparison between the wax from Faye Palazzo's vigil candles and the wax found in Krystal Duncan's throat showed that there's a high probability that it's the same type of wax. Of course, we have to submit the samples to the state lab and maybe even the FBI lab for a more in-depth analysis, which would confirm it for sure but that could take weeks."

Gretchen said, "Okay, then. Let's assume for a moment that the wax found in Krystal Duncan's throat did come from Faye Palazzo's vigil candles. What does that mean? Either Faye killed Krystal and is now staging her own disappearance or her husband, Sebastian, killed Krystal."

"And maybe Faye found out and he's killed her too?" Josie wondered out loud.

Gretchen pinched the bridge of her nose. "This is a mess. If Sebastian killed Krystal Duncan and did something to his own wife then he's putting on the most Oscar-worthy performance I have ever seen. He was so hysterical last night I had to threaten to have him involuntarily committed to the hospital to get him to calm down."

"Then maybe it's not him," Metter suggested. "Maybe someone else took Faye's vigil candles precisely to get us to look at Sebastian. Regardless, if the same person who took Krystal Duncan is behind Faye's disappearance, then she's in trouble."

Noah said, "Someone would have had to come into the Palazzos' house to get the candles though, if they were the same ones used in Krystal's murder. Who would that be? Your reports say that Faye didn't see anyone but her husband."

Josie said, "As far as her husband knew. She was home alone all day every day except when he came for lunch. She could have had someone over without his knowledge."

Gretchen said, "Then we're back to someone known to both Krystal and Faye, if that's the case. Faye wouldn't let a stranger into her home when her husband was at work."

"True," Josie said. "I think we need to look more closely at Krystal. That's where all of this started. Something made her go digging into aspects of the bus crash, and we know she found out at least one thing that upset her deeply. We know she arranged a meeting with Virgil Lesko so she could ask him something about the day of the accident although we have no idea what. Why was she digging in the first place and what else did she find out? Was it something that someone would kill her over?"

Mettner said, "I can call the orthodontist where Nathan was supposed to take their kids the day of the crash and find out if she'd been in contact with them recently."

Gretchen pulled her notepad closer and wrote something down.

Noah fingered a stack of documents on Josie's desk. "These are from Krystal's law firm? You didn't find anything in here?"

"Yes, those are all the cases she was working on," Josie said. "And no, we didn't find a damn thing. But you guys are welcome to have another look."

Noah said, "When Mett and I get back, we'll take a look. It doesn't hurt to have a fresh set of eyes. Besides, hopefully we'll have a new list of names of other neighbors and potential thieves by the time we get to this."

Gretchen interjected, "I want to put a unit on Sebastian Palazzo for now to keep track of his movements. He's home right now as far as I know. Someone will need to get his alibi for the time that Krystal was missing and then murdered."

Mettner said, "We're going to be over there canvassing anyway, we'll take care of it."

Josie said, "I know we don't want to focus too tightly on the crash, but I think it bears some examination. While Noah and Mett are working the thievery angle, maybe Gretchen can take me through the details of the crash since she was the lead."

Mettner said, "You think that will help find Faye Palazzo?"

"No," Josie said. "I think the best way to find Faye Palazzo is to notify the press. In the meantime, we can't sit around hoping for a break. We've got to keep moving forward. It makes sense to look at the crash. Maybe there's something we're missing. Maybe someone we're missing. Someone on the periphery."

Gretchen stood up. "The boss is right. Amber, let's prepare something. We'll run it by the Chief and then you and he can do a press conference while the rest of us are out running down these leads."

Amber smiled wryly. "Oh, working with the Chief. Happy day."

CHAPTER TWENTY-FIVE

Noah and Mettner left, dodging the press outside while Gretchen and Amber disappeared into the Chief's office. Josie booted up her computer and found the police files on the West Denton bus crash. The first 911 calls had come in between 3:30 and 3:45 p.m. as students were dropped off at their designated bus stops, ran home, and told their parents that Mr. Lesko had been slurring his words and driving erratically. At 3:47, a 911 call came in from a driver who had almost been sideswiped by the bus. Units were dispatched by 3:50 p.m. Before they could intercept the bus, the crash occurred. At 3:58 p.m. as the final six children were due to be dropped off—Heidi Byrne, Gail Tenney, Nevin Palazzo, Bianca Duncan, and Wallace and Frankie Cammack—the bus careened past the bus stop, jumped the curb, flipped once, and then the back half of the bus wrapped around a large sycamore tree in someone's yard. The first units arrived on site by 4:05 p.m. By that time, the owner of the house whose yard the bus ended up in had come out and started trying to pull the children from the wreckage.

But it was too late.

Gail, Nevin, Bianca, Wallace, and Frankie were all killed instantly. Heidi was transported by ambulance to Denton Memorial where she stayed for a week. She sustained a concussion, several broken ribs, and a laceration to her spleen, which, thankfully, healed. Virgil Lesko was unconscious at the scene. Gretchen spoke to him later in the hospital. At first, many people speculated in the press that he had had some kind of medical event, perhaps a stroke, but it became clear, at least to Gretchen and the hospital staff treating

Lesko, that he had been under the influence of both alcohol and oxycodone. In his first statement to Gretchen, he admitted to having one drink at lunch before going on his afternoon route but insisted that he hadn't taken anything else, certainly not any narcotics. When asked if he routinely drank and drove his school bus, he answered, "No, of course not." Gretchen asked him why he had had a drink that day. Her notes read: "Mr. Lesko relates that he was upset due to his mother being placed in hospice care that morning." More notes indicated that Lesko stated that his elderly mother lived with him and had been battling breast cancer for several years.

Josie continued to scroll through the materials in the file, the photos from the scene nearly bringing her breakfast back up. Clicking through those, she came to photos of Lesko's vehicle, which he had left at the bus depot when he took his bus for the afternoon route. There were no empty liquor bottles or prescription oxycodone bottles inside the vehicle. There was some sporting equipment—the gear he used to umpire Little League and softball games; a baseball cap; some fast-food wrappers; a crumpled receipt from a gas station; and a stack of opened mail, which included an electric bill and a statement from Denton Memorial Hospital.

"What do you think?" Gretchen asked, peering over Josie's shoulder.

Startled, Josie looked up. "Seems cut and dried. I could see why a killer might target Virgil Lesko or his family, but not the parents of the kids who were killed. I don't get this."

Gretchen sighed. "Maybe Mett is right. Maybe the accident business is a form of distraction."

"And what?" Josie asked. "We have a serial killer on the loose? Someone targeting grieving mothers?"

"Don't use the S word just yet," Gretchen said with a dry laugh.

"All right," Josie said. "But it can't be a coincidence that two of these mothers went missing in the last week."

"But the other thing we need to consider is that almost all the details about the accident were known to everyone in the community. Anyone in that West Denton neighborhood would have had access to the families and could potentially know things not reported in the press. Maybe this is someone using the accident as a smoke screen. Killing Krystal, taking Faye, and wanting us to look at the accident because then we're not looking for them."

"True," Josie agreed. "We don't want to get tunnel vision, put all our focus on the accident, and miss something right in front of us. But we should still look closely at the accident, even just to get it out of the way."

"You've got the file there," Gretchen said.

"No," said Josie. "I want to drive the route the bus took that day."

To her credit or maybe because they had no other leads, Gretchen shrugged and said, "Let's go."

The parking lot was mercifully empty now that reporters would get a full presser in an hour. Gretchen drove them to the bus depot, which was a large, gated lot in South Denton filled with big yellow school buses and a tiny, flat-roofed building that served as an office. Gretchen pulled up outside the gates, now locked since it was summer and schools were closed. "Virgil went home between his morning route and his afternoon route to tend to his mother."

"Is she still alive?" Josie asked.

"No. She passed two months after the accident. Ted Lesko took care of the arrangements since Virgil was in jail by then."

"So how does this go?" Josie asked. "He shows up, parks outside that building, and takes his bus?"

"He clocks in and then he takes his bus," Gretchen corrected. "There's usually a supervisor on duty, but he wasn't there that afternoon. His wife was having a baby, so he left the depot unattended for the afternoon shift. He didn't think it would be a problem—all the drivers knew what to do, and he had assigned one of the last drivers in to lock up the gate at the end of the day."

"Was anyone else here when Virgil clocked in?"

"No," Gretchen said. "He was late. All the other drivers had clocked in, taken their buses, and left."

"Jesus," Josie said. "If the supervisor had been here that day—"

"He might have noticed that Virgil was impaired," Gretchen filled in. "Yeah. Tragic."

Josie closed her eyes, feeling a vise tighten around her chest. If only, if only. If only the supervisor's wife hadn't gone into labor that day. If only Nathan hadn't canceled the orthodontist appointments that day at least three of the children would still be alive. If only Gloria hadn't forgotten her precious planner and gone home to get it. She wouldn't have seen the missing PlayStation and called Nathan, insisting he cancel the appointments. But how far did it go? Josie wondered. If only the person stealing things from West Denton homes hadn't taken the PlayStation that day. If only Virgil Lesko's mother hadn't been put in hospice care that morning.

If only she had told Lisette to go back to her hotel room the night she was shot.

"Boss?" Gretchen said. "You okay?"

Josie forced the images of Lisette's body jerking from the buckshot out of her brain and turned her attention back to the crash. Something was niggling at the back of her mind. "If only, if only," she muttered.

Gretchen's hand was warm on Josie's forearm. "Josie."

The pieces in her head shifted into place. Her eyes snapped open. "Virgil Lesko's mother didn't go into hospice care that day."

"What?"

"When I was looking at the file right before we left there were photos from Virgil's car. He had mail. The ERT took photos of it, and one of the pieces of mail was a statement from Denton Memorial. It was for home hospice care for the month before the accident."

"Are you sure?" Gretchen asked.

"Yes," Josie said. "I'm sure. I mean, we can check when we get back, but I'm pretty certain."

"Why would Virgil Lesko lie about the reason he had a drink that day?" Gretchen said.

"I don't know. Maybe he drank regularly and that was the first time he got caught?"

"He had a lot of oxycodone in his system."

"Which he denied taking," Josie pointed out.

A beat of silence passed between them. Then Josie said, "Let's keep going."

Gretchen pulled away and drove past Denton West Elementary School. "He gets to the school, where the kids are already waiting since he was late."

She moved on, weaving through the streets of West Denton, occasionally checking her phone for the coordinates of the various bus stops, which she had programmed into her GPS app before they left the station. "The stops are all on corners that are central to a three- or four-block radius. So each time he stops, he lets off between three and six kids and they either walk home from the stop or the parents are there, waiting. That day, no parents were waiting."

If only, Josie thought. If only one parent had been waiting at one bus stop that day. Maybe they would have seen something was off about Lesko and stopped him from going any further.

"This is the third stop," Gretchen said, pulling up to another idyllic corner in West Denton. "This is where the kids got off and ran home to tell their folks that something was wrong with Mr. Lesko."

She drove four blocks and rolled to a stop at a red light. "Here is where he almost sideswiped another vehicle. That driver called 911."

"How many more stops?" Josie asked.

The light turned green, and Gretchen accelerated through the intersection. "Two. The next stop he lets off three children, leaving only Heidi, Gail, Nevin, Bianca, Wallace, and Frankie on the bus. Then the stop after that—the final stop—he crashes."

Gretchen made a right onto a street named Tallon that was lined with houses on one side and trees on the other. Along the road a huge sign read "Land for Sale. Fifty Acres" with a phone number beneath it. Gretchen said, "This has been for sale forever. I read about it in the paper. Developers want to put apartment buildings up, but the local community wants green space. They've been fighting over it for ten years."

Near the end of the block was an opening in the forest where a span of packed mud led to a clearing on the other side of the tree line. A flash of pink caught Josie's eye.

"Stop," she said.

"What?"

"Turn around," Josie told her. "Go back to that clearing."

Gretchen checked her mirrors and swung the car around. She pulled onto the mud drive. They bumped along it until they came to the other side of the trees where a large swath of land had been cleared—now just grass and dirt.

Josie's heart skipped. Beside her Gretchen whispered, "Sweet Jesus."

In the middle of the clearing, on her knees with her head tipped back, dead eyes fixed on the sky, was Faye Palazzo.

CHAPTER TWENTY-SIX

As they got out of the car, Gretchen was already on her phone, calling for units, an ambulance, the ERT, and Dr. Feist, instructing everyone to keep the news off the radio. Josie approached Faye's body, feeling a chill despite the punishing August heat. Like Krystal Duncan, Faye's skin was pink. She looked alive and healthy until Josie got close enough to see the wax dried in droplets along her lips and chin and her milky, sightless eyes. Her brown hair hung loose down her back. A diamond stud earring sparkled in her right ear, but the one in her left ear was missing. Fingerprint-sized bruises lined the underside of her chin. Her arms were laid out on her thighs, palms and forearms up. More light purple bruises, these larger, marred her skin.

Faye Palazzo had put up a fight.

Along the inside of one of her forearms was a name spelled out in black marker: *GAIL*.

"Gail Tenney," Josie mumbled, letting out a breath she hadn't realized she was holding. Sadness swept through her.

Gretchen walked up behind her. "How did you see her? From the car?"

"I didn't," Josie said. "I saw something pink through the trees."

They both turned in the direction they had come and walked ten feet to the right where they had a clear view of the road and any cars passing by. Directly across from the mud drive was a wide space between two neighboring houses on the other side of the road. Faye had been displayed but not so prominently that she would be seen immediately by the first passing motorist. She also wouldn't have been seen from the window of one of the houses facing this area. Maybe not right away. It was possible that at some point one of the neighbors might have noticed the same ribbon of pink fabric through the trees and gone investigating.

Josie spun slowly, taking in the clearing. Behind Faye was a large dirt pile and then more trees. There were tire tracks in the mud, but they were numerous, each one running over the other, leaving only fragments. No clear tire tracks to cast. "Shit," she said.

Gretchen said, "I don't get it. What's the significance of this place?"

Josie said, "Maybe they didn't want to leave her at the cemetery because there was too much traffic? That was risky to begin with. Or maybe because this is on the bus route? Anyone in this clearing would have been able to see the bus pass that day."

"I don't—"

Gretchen's sentence was cut off by the sound of an engine revving. A white pickup truck swung onto the dirt path and came barreling toward them. The sun glared off the windshield, making it impossible to make out who was behind the wheel. It sped past Gretchen's car without slowing, heading directly toward Josie and Gretchen. Josie's body moved without thought, and she threw herself into Gretchen, tackling her to the ground. The pickup kept going. Josie rolled off Gretchen and pulled her Glock from her side holster in one fluid motion, positioned on her back, head up, both hands pointing the gun toward the truck, which smashed into the dirt pile in front of the trees.

Next to Josie, Gretchen struggled to breathe. The wind had been knocked out of her. Before Josie could tend to her, the driver's side of the truck swung open with a screeching sound. "Stop right there," Josie shouted, aiming for the truck's cab. "Freeze! Police. Put your hands up."

Heidi Byrne stumbled out of the truck and fell to the ground on all fours. Blood poured from a gash in her forehead. Josie lowered her weapon and jumped to her feet. Holding her gun pointed downward at her side, she ran to the girl.

"Heidi? What's going on? What are you doing?"

Josie looked into the cab of the truck, but it was empty. A thin column of smoke rose from the compacted hood. She holstered her weapon, reached into the truck, and turned it off, pocketing the keys, and then put a hand on Heidi's trembling back. Blood dripped from the girl's head into the dirt. She looked up at Josie. "Is that—is that Mrs. Palazzo?"

Josie's gaze turned toward Faye's body—still upright, kneeling, with her hands in her lap and her head tipped back. Josie moved until she was between Heidi and Faye. "Yes," she answered. Pulling at the hem of her polo shirt, she squatted and pressed it to Heidi's head, trying to stop the bleeding. "What are you doing here, Heidi? Whose truck is that? You're not even old enough to drive."

Heidi sat back and Josie followed, trying to keep the tail of her shirt pressed to the wound on her forehead. "What happened to her?"

"We don't know," Josie answered. She looked back to see Gretchen hauling herself to her feet and trudging over.

Heidi looked up at Gretchen as she approached. "I'm sorry. I'm really sorry. I didn't mean to—I wasn't trying to hurt you."

"Were you following us?" Gretchen asked.

Josie lifted her shirt tail, happy to see that the blood flow was slowing down. Gretchen pulled a tissue from one of her pockets and gave it to Heidi. "Thank you," Heidi said, replacing Josie's shirt with the tissue. "Yeah, I was following you. I'm sorry."

"From the police station?" Josie asked.

"I wanted to talk to you but when I got there, there were all those reporters. Then they left, but I still felt weird so I just tailed you. Then I got stuck at a light and lost you. I was passing this opening when I thought I saw your car. I swerved. I didn't mean to speed, but then I saw Mrs. Palazzo and I couldn't—I just lost control, and I—"

Josie said, "Whose truck is that?"

"My dad's," Heidi said matter-of-factly. She pulled the tissue away from her head, but it was still bleeding. Pressing it back in place, she said, "He's got two. He says the alternator is going on this one, but I've never had a problem with it."

Gretchen and Josie looked at one another, and Josie knew that Gretchen was thinking the same thing she was: "never had a problem" implied that Heidi had been using it often. "Heidi," said Josie. "How often do you drive your dad's truck?"

They all turned their heads toward the sound of tires over dirt. Several police vehicles pulled into the clearing, much like the caravan that had appeared at the cemetery the day Dee Tenney and Josie discovered Krystal's body.

Heidi said, "I don't know. I mean… sometimes."

The vehicles parked and Josie noted the patrol officers emerging from their cars, as well as Hummel and a couple of other members of the ERT. Gretchen jogged over to them.

Josie looked back down at Heidi. "Does your dad know that you drive his truck?"

From under the tissue, Heidi rolled her eyes. "Duh. Of course not."

"You're what? Fourteen? You know that driving around without a license or even a permit is illegal, right? You almost killed me and my colleague today, Heidi."

Her lower lip quivered. "I didn't mean to, I swear it. I am always very careful. I've never even had a problem until today. I would definitely have stopped, but I got distracted when I saw Mrs. Palazzo." She craned her neck to look around Josie. "Are you sure she's dead?"

In spite of herself, Josie looked back at Faye's body. Hummel was directing a couple of uniformed officers where to cordon off the perimeter of the scene with yellow tape. Beyond him, an ambulance and Dr. Feist's truck pulled in. "Yes," Josie said. "I'm so sorry, Heidi, but Mrs. Palazzo is dead."

Heidi bowed her head. A few seconds later, Josie noticed tears dripping from Heidi's chin. Her thin shoulders quaked. Josie knelt next to her and touched her arm. "Hey," she said. "I'm sorry. Why don't you come and sit in our car? We're going to need to get you out of here right away. I'm sure you know we'll have to call your dad, though."

Heidi nodded. With a sniffle, she looked back up at Josie. "That's fine. If you can even get in touch with him."

Josie glanced up at the truck. "How did you learn to drive?"

"Mrs. Tenney," Heidi said. "She taught me. But don't blame her, okay? I don't want her to get into trouble because of me. I've already caused her enough problems. Did you know her husband left her because of me?"

"What?"

"Yeah," said Heidi. "She'll never say it but I know it's true. I heard her husband yelling at her once when they thought I couldn't hear. He said it was sick what she was doing with me. Like she was trying to replace Gail with me. He left for good after that fight."

"I'm sorry to hear that," Josie said. "But grieving people say a lot of things they don't mean, Heidi. It's not your fault that their marriage broke up. I'm sure there were a lot of things going on. Most marriages don't survive the death of a child."

Another car pulled into the now very crowded clearing and Noah and Mettner hopped out. Gretchen waved them over to where she was and began gesturing animatedly.

"Whatever," Heidi said. "You can give me that adult bullshit all day long. I know what happened."

Josie turned her attention back to Heidi. "I didn't mean—"

"Forget it," Heidi said, cutting her off. "My point is that Mrs. Tenney is the only person who's treated me like a regular human being since the accident. She was only trying to help me. I was terrified of being in any vehicle after the accident. All those doctor's appointments I had to go to afterward? Back and forth, back and forth. I couldn't go more than a minute in a vehicle without a major panic attack. My dad didn't know what to do. Then one day Mrs. Tenney saw us on the side of the road on the way home from the doctor. I was sitting on the curb hyperventilating. That's when she offered to help. Which turned into her basically taking me in, you know?"

"I got that sense," Josie admitted.

"Earlier this year, I was having my usual panic attack in the car and Mrs. Tenney, she just stopped. I thought she was going to kick me out of the car. Like she was done with me or something. But she said, 'This isn't working so we're going to stop doing it.' Just like that. Then she took me to an empty parking lot and made me get behind the wheel."

Unexpectedly, tears sprang to Josie's eyes. Lisette instantly came to mind. Josie had had many fears as a result of her traumatic childhood, and Lisette had helped her face each one head-on. Sometimes it helped, sometimes it didn't, but Lisette was willing to try anything, and she never stuck with something that simply wasn't working, even if it meant bending some rules.

Heidi went on, "We started trying every day until I was good at it. Then I stopped being afraid. She made me swear I would never tell anyone though, so you have to promise you won't, like, arrest her or anything, okay?"

"I can promise not to get her into any trouble if you promise to stop driving without a license."

Heidi frowned but said, "Deal."

"Why were you following us?" Josie asked. "You never said."

Heidi stood and looked around, as if trying to decide where to go. Josie touched her arm. "We should take you to the hospital to get checked out."

"No," Heidi said. "I'm fine. I feel fine. I can make my dad take me later if you're worried, but I can't go now. I came because of Mrs. Tenney. She won't tell you but she's afraid."

Gretchen walked back over. "It's going to be a few hours here with processing and everything else. I've got to get in touch with Heidi's dad, and we'll probably need a tow truck."

"You won't get him," Heidi said. "He's on some job site somewhere. Anyway, I was just telling Detective Quinn that Mrs. Tenney needs help."

Josie said, "Why do you think she needs help? What is she afraid of?"

"She's been acting really weird. Like, always looking out the windows and double-checking that her doors are locked. This morning she was freaking out about something to do with her checking account and then I heard her on the phone talking to Mrs. Cammack."

"Gloria Cammack?" Gretchen said.

"Yeah. She said something about being watched and wanted to know if she could stay there for a few days. Then she told me to go to camp and that she would meet me at my house afterward instead of her house."

"Who does she think is watching her?" Josie asked, wondering why Dee hadn't called the police. Had she seen someone or was she just spooked by Krystal's death and Faye's disappearance?

"I don't know," Heidi said. "But if someone is really watching her, then she needs help. She won't ever ask for it, though. You have to protect her. What if she ends up like Ms. Duncan or Mrs. Palazzo?" A sob erupted from Heidi's throat. "Please."

She dissolved into tears. Josie reached out to touch her arm again but Heidi threw herself into Josie, wrapping her arms tightly around Josie's waist. Heidi cried into Josie's shoulder. "It's okay, Heidi. We'll talk to her," Josie said as she wrapped Heidi in a hug and rested her chin on her head. From across the clearing, Josie saw Noah staring. She managed a weak smile.

Gretchen said, "How about this, Heidi? We'll have one of the patrol units take you to the hospital while we go speak with Mrs. Tenney?"

Heidi lifted her face from Josie's shoulder. "No. I want to go with you. I want to make sure she's okay."

She held on tightly to Josie. Gretchen said, "Boss?"

Josie looked around. "You said yourself it will be hours. Noah and Mett are already here. Let them take over and we'll go to Gloria's house. Heidi can come with us until we reach her dad."

Heidi let go of Josie and used her bloodied tissue to dab at the tears spilling down her cheeks. "Thank you."

Josie smiled. "At least this way I know you won't be stealing cars."

CHAPTER TWENTY-SEVEN

On the way to Gloria's house, Josie left two messages for Heidi's father, Corey Byrne. Heidi suggested she text him instead. "He never answers calls," she told Josie. By the time Josie had fired off a number of texts to him, they were out front of the Cammack home. Gloria was at work, but Dee Tenney let them into the house. This time, they gathered in the living room with Dee curled on the couch, her feet tucked under her. Heidi sat beside her and Dee drew her in for a hug. As Josie and Gretchen explained the morning's events—from finding Faye Palazzo's body to nearly being killed by Heidi driving her dad's truck—Dee's expression went on a roller coaster of emotions: shock, grief, fear, anger, concern. Finally, she touched Heidi's hair, smoothing it back away from her face and gingerly touching the cut on her forehead. "Honey, you can't ever do that again, do you understand? I taught you to drive to help you get over your fear, not for you to take your dad's truck without permission."

"I promise it will never happen again," Heidi told her.

Dee smiled, though Josie saw tears welling in her eyes. She kissed Heidi's forehead. "I'm sorry that you were so worried about me. It's not your job to worry about me, or any adult, but I appreciate that you care for me so much. The feeling is mutual."

Heidi beamed. Josie tried to speak but her throat had closed up. She felt Gretchen's eyes on her. Taking over, Gretchen said, "Heidi, we really need to talk to Mrs. Tenney about our investigation and—"

Heidi cut her off. "You don't think it's appropriate that I hear what you have to say."

Gretchen said, "It would be better if we talked to Mrs. Tenney in private."

Heidi thrust her chin out. "Know how many dead bodies I've seen? Six. I saw five of my best friends die in that bus crash and today, I saw Mrs. Palazzo's body. Do you even know what that's like?"

Gretchen raised a brow, and Josie could see she was fighting not to laugh. Gretchen had probably seen more dead bodies than the entire Denton PD force combined. But she didn't laugh. Heidi was being earnest and trying to make a point. Gretchen sighed. "Well, I guess if you're mature enough to ride around town in your dad's truck with no license and no supervision, then you're mature enough to listen to this conversation. Unless Mrs. Tenney objects?"

Dee shook her head. "She'll hear it all anyway when I fill her father in later."

Gretchen took out her notepad and pen. "Let's start with Faye. Your daughter's name was found written at the crime scene."

"It was?" Heidi blurted. "I didn't see it."

Gretchen gave her a hard look.

"Oh right," she said. "Because I was speeding past in the truck. Sorry. I'll shut up now."

Josie found her voice. "Dee, is there any reason you can think of why Gail's name would be found at the scene?"

Dee shook her head. "My God, no. I have no idea."

"Were Gail and Nevin Palazzo close?"

"No, not really. I mean Gail had been to his house a few times and vice versa. All the kids grew up together, but no, they weren't particularly close."

"When is the last time you spoke to Faye Palazzo?" Gretchen asked.

"At the last support group meeting."

Josie asked, "Was there any bad blood between Gail and Nevin?"

Dee laughed. "Bad blood? They were kids!"

"No," Heidi interjected. "I know, I know, I said I'd shut up but I saw Gail and Nevin when they were just being kids, and they got along fine. Nevin was sweet. Everyone liked him, and Gail could be really sassy—and crazy funny—but she wasn't mean. She wouldn't take any crap, but she was kind."

A small gasp escaped Dee's mouth. One of her hands flew up and covered it. Heidi turned toward her, face filled with apprehension. "I'm so sorry, Mrs. T. So sorry. I didn't mean to upset you. I—"

Dee removed her hand from her mouth and grabbed Heidi's hand, holding so tightly that her knuckles went white. "Thank you," she said. "For talking about her. I never get to talk about her. No one ever tells me things about her. Things I didn't know. I mean, at the support group we talk about our kids, but not like this. Outside that group, it's like I'm invisible. No one wants to hear about your dead child."

Heidi said, "We can talk about Gail any time you want."

Josie and Gretchen let the two of them have a silent moment while each of them fought to compose themselves. Then Josie jumped back in, changing the line of questioning. "Why are you staying here, Mrs. Tenney?"

"I didn't want to make a big deal out of it but yesterday I thought I saw someone at the side of the house. Through the dining room window. I went out and crept around that way. I didn't see anyone but I heard footsteps—or what I thought was footsteps—running through the trees behind my house. Then today, when I let Heidi in for breakfast, my screen door lock was… well, it was destroyed. Like someone had tried to pry the door open."

"Why didn't you call the police?" Gretchen asked.

"I was going to, I was, but then the bank called to tell me that my account was overdrawn and I just, well, I got swept up in that. Since Miles and I separated, he deposits money into the account, and I take cash out from the ATM machine and buy myself gas and groceries and whatever else is needed. That's the agreement we came to. I tried calling him but I couldn't get in touch with him. I just—I was having a bit of a meltdown, okay? I couldn't get in touch with my husband; I thought someone had tried breaking into my house. I got afraid. I thought I'd call Gloria and ask her if I could stay here and then at some point, I would call the police, and I meant to, I really did."

Josie said, "Mrs. Tenney, both Krystal Duncan and Faye Palazzo were murdered this week. I don't need to remind you that both of them were members of your support group. If you feel anything is amiss—absolutely anything—you need to call us immediately. In fact, if you're going to stay here a few days, I am sure I can get approval from my chief to have a car stationed outside."

Dee put her hand to her chest. "Oh. Do you think that's really necessary?"

"Yes," said Heidi.

Gretchen said, "I think everyone concerned would feel better if we did that."

"Well, okay. I can let Gloria know."

Josie said, "Have you noticed anything missing from your house lately?"

"No, nothing."

Gretchen said, "What about something reappearing?"

Dee's brow furrowed in confusion. "Reappearing?"

Josie said, "Maybe some item that went missing a long time ago that suddenly turned up again?"

"Oh, no, nothing like that," Dee answered.

"If you don't mind me taking you back to before the bus crash," Gretchen said. "We have reports from several people that for a period of between six months and a year before the accident, valuables were going missing from their houses. Did you happen to experience that?"

"Oh," said Dee. "Um, yes. Sort of. Someone stole all of Miles' tools from the garage. It was about four or five months before the accident. I remember because it was freezing. It must have been after Christmas. Or maybe right before. Anyway, he reported it to the police."

Josie and Gretchen exchanged a curious look. Josie said, "Are you sure?"

"Yes, I'm sure. He said he'd get an insurance payout for it."

"Did he?" asked Gretchen.

"I'm sure he did."

"But you don't know," Josie said.

"Miles handles all our finances. That was the agreement when we got married. He was a hot-shot car salesman making a lot of money, and he wanted me to be able to stay home and take care of Gail. When we separated, as angry as he was, he didn't want my life to be turned upside down by having to move and support myself, he said."

"Did the police come to your house that day?" asked Gretchen.

"No. Miles went to the police station. He said he didn't want to tie up 911 for something that wasn't an emergency. Tools could be replaced."

"Did he replace them?" Josie asked.

Dee took a moment to think about it. "No, not right away. Well, no, not at all, now that I think about it. He meant to but then the crash happened and… well, it was hard enough for us both to just breathe in and breathe out all day. Tools were the furthest thing from Miles' mind. He barely used the ones that were stolen."

Josie's phone chirped. She took it out to find a text message from Corey Byrne. *Sorry. On job site. Can't talk. Can meet you at my house after work. Five p.m.* Josie shook her head as she pocketed her phone. His daughter had been in a car accident with his truck, and he was too busy to talk, or couldn't be bothered. No wonder Heidi had bonded so much with Mrs. Tenney. Josie had to wonder what life had been like for Heidi before the accident.

Gretchen said, "Mrs. Tenney, what if I told you that Miles never filed a report?"

"How do you know?" she asked.

"Because we were checking over all police reports made in this area going back three years. Your husband never made any police reports."

"I don't know," Dee said. "You'd have to ask Miles. I'll give you his phone number. Maybe he'll answer for you. I can give you his address as well. If you talk to him, tell him to call me."

"Going back to Faye Palazzo," Josie said after Gretchen had jotted down that information. "Her husband said that she didn't have friends anymore but that the two of you used to get coffee sometimes. Is this true? Is there anyone else you can think of that she would have spent time with? Or anyone she might have been having trouble with?"

Dee's mouth firmed into a thin line. She sat forward, unfurling her legs and glancing at Heidi as if she regretted her decision to allow her to stay. Finally, she said, "We used to have coffee, yes. Before the accident, not so much after. Both of us were stay-at-home moms, and we were both heavily involved in the PTA. Faye is a great organizer—was a great organizer. She always put everything together."

"Like vigils?" Josie said.

"Yes, exactly. She liked to organize those after the accident. I know she was planning one for the eve of the trial, but we had only talked about it at group. The only times we met for coffee after the accident were to discuss the vigils. That was it."

"Is there some reason you didn't continue to be friendly after the accident?" Gretchen asked. "Other than meeting in group?"

Again, Dee looked at Heidi who was now focused entirely on chewing the fingernails of her left hand. Dee lowered her voice even though Heidi could still hear her. "I shouldn't say. I don't want to say. It's—I don't think it matters, especially now."

"Please," Josie urged. "Why don't you tell us and we'll decide whether it's relevant to our investigation or not."

Dee closed her eyes and took several deep breaths, as if shoring herself up for something. They snapped open and she blurted, "Faye was having an affair."

There was a beat of silence in the room. Heidi's gaze moved to the side of Dee's face, but she continued to chew on her nails. She didn't look shocked or surprised, Josie noted.

"How do you know that?" Gretchen asked.

"She told me."

"When?" said Josie.

"A few weeks before the crash. We had met for coffee as usual to plan some PTA stuff. She was distracted and upset. I badgered her into telling me what was wrong. She said she had been having an affair, but that she wanted to end it. The guilt was consuming her. Sebastian is very devoted to her. She thought—and I must admit that I believe she was right—that it might literally kill him if he found out."

"Are you sure that's what she said?" Josie asked. "Was it possible she said that he might kill *her*?"

"Oh no," said Dee. "Sebastian is not like that at all. I mean, if you talk to him for even a second, you'll see how he worships her. He always has. To be honest, among the other mothers, we always felt it was kind of pathetic. Not that she didn't love him back. She most certainly did, but she always seemed to love him in a less passionate way than he loved her."

"Being devoted to someone doesn't exclude domestic violence or even murder," Gretchen pointed out.

"I know that," Dee said. "But I'm telling you that Sebastian just isn't that kind of person."

"He's a wimp," Heidi piped up. Everyone looked at her. She rolled her eyes. "Sorry, but he is. He's wimpy as hell. Even us kids couldn't understand what Mrs. Palazzo saw in him. I mean she was like some big, successful New York City model, and he was like this shy pharmacist who could barely speak."

"Heidi, really," Dee admonished. "That's mean."

"What?" Heidi said, eyes wide. "I'm not saying he's not a nice guy. He's a super-nice guy. He came on a class trip once and bought everyone ice cream. But once he was driving me and Nevin home from our practices—Nevin had baseball and I had softball—and this guy rear-ended him. Mr. Palazzo got out to exchange insurance information, and the dude just ripped him a new one. Like, the guy was just screaming at him when he was the one who hit us! We thought he was going to hit Mr. P. Nevin even started to cry. Then Mr. P just got back into the car and drove off. He never got the guy's information. He didn't call the police to report the crazy guy. He didn't even say anything. Just drove us home like nothing happened with half his bumper hanging off."

Dee tutted. "It sounds like the other driver was out of control and Mr. Palazzo was being smart by not engaging with him, especially with the two of you in the car."

Trying to take back control of the conversation, Josie asked, "Dee, do you have any idea who Faye was having an affair with?"

Dee shook her head. "I'm sorry, I don't."

Gretchen said, "Even if you're not sure, is there anyone you think it could have been?"

"I truly have no idea," Dee responded. "But I can tell you that I don't believe it went beyond the accident. She was already intent on ending it, and once she and Sebastian lost Nevin, well, like all of us, they were a wreck, and I think that unlike some of us, their shared grief actually brought them closer."

Gretchen nodded. "We're going to step outside for a few minutes to make some phone calls. I need to get a unit over here to keep an eye on you, Mrs. Tenney. Would it be okay for Heidi to stay with you until we meet with her dad later?"

"Of course."

Josie followed Gretchen out to the driveway. They stood beside Gretchen's car while Josie got both Mettner and Noah on speakerphone. Noah said, "We canvassed the houses on the other side of the road. No one's got cameras and no one saw anything. Dr. Feist says that Faye Palazzo is in full rigor—the same as Krystal Duncan, although in her case, livor is fixed. Probably the same cause of death, although there's some bruising on Faye Palazzo's face."

"I saw that," Josie said.

"We won't get a time of death or official cause until Dr. Feist gets her on the table," Mettner added. "But I think it's safe to say that this is almost identical to Krystal Duncan's murder based on the doc's initial observations: the pink color indicative of carbon monoxide poisoning, the wax in her mouth, the name on the arm. Given the state of her body and the heat out here, she was probably left here early this morning—probably before the sun came up—but as I said, the doc will try to narrow down a time of death after her exam."

Gretchen asked, "Did you guys get anywhere with your interviews before we called?"

"Not very far," Noah answered. "We managed to talk to Sebastian Palazzo, though. Like everyone else—Gloria, Nathan, Dee—he's got a spotty alibi. He can account for some of his time but not all of it during the days that Krystal was missing. Plus, Faye was his alibi for a great deal of the time and with her dead, she can't corroborate anything he says."

Gretchen sighed and shook her head. "Noted," she said. "The neighborhood still needs to be canvassed as we discussed."

Mettner said, "I'm going to go back over while Fraley stays here on-scene. No sense in both of us being here. The ERT will be here at least another hour or two."

"Great," said Gretchen. "We're going to go speak with Miles Tenney and see if he has any idea why his daughter's name was written on Faye Palazzo's body."

Josie looked back to the Cammack house as the front door opened. Heidi stuck her head out. "Hang on," Josie told Gretchen, pointing to Heidi.

"We'll keep you posted," Gretchen told Noah and Mettner before hanging up.

Heidi was already halfway down the driveway. Josie said, "Is everything okay?"

"I know something," Heidi blurted out. She looked back at the house but the door remained closed. "I don't know if I should tell."

"You know something about what?" asked Josie.

"About Mrs. Palazzo's affair."

"Okay," said Gretchen.

"But I don't want to get anyone in trouble. I mean, I don't want to get my dad in trouble."

Josie said, "Because you think that your dad was having an affair with Mrs. Palazzo?"

"No. Because I know that he was, but listen, this doesn't mean that he killed her, okay? He would never do something like that. They were actually—I think they were in love. But they stopped after the accident. Mrs. Tenney was right about that."

Josie asked, "How do you know your dad and Faye Palazzo were having an affair?"

Heidi rolled her eyes. "Because I'm not stupid, okay? Everyone always treated me like I was, but I'm not. I hear everything. I always heard everything. Adults figured I was either too stupid to know what was going on or that I just didn't care 'cause I was a kid. The way my dad works all the time—and I mean *all* the time—is the same as it was before the accident. The other parents were always driving me places or feeding me or having me over until he got home. It was like this whole neighborhood raised me. Like I'm some charity case or something—except my dad has plenty of money. I mean, he ought to, since all he does is work and never has time to spend any money."

Gretchen asked, "Did you overhear your dad and Faye Palazzo talking about an affair?"

"No," said Heidi. "They used my backpack to pass notes."

"What?" said Josie.

"Yeah. There is this super small pocket in my backpack that you could never fit anything in. Well, I mean, you could put like, an eraser, in it or whatever but other than that it was useless. On the days that I would go to Mrs. Palazzo's house after the bus dropped us off—until my dad got home from work—he would put a note in that little pocket. While I was at their house playing with Nevin or hanging out with him, she would take it out, read it, write a response and then send it back."

"How do you know this?" Josie said.

"Duh. Because I saw them do it. I mean, the first time I found a note, I didn't know what it was. I was in school. It was something about meeting in our spot at two o'clock. I didn't know what that meant. I thought maybe it was from my dad's stuff and somehow got into my bag? I don't know. I wasn't that bright then. I meant to ask him about it that night but then I forgot and when I was over at the Palazzos', I walked past the kitchen when Mrs. P thought Nevin and I were out back and saw her taking it out. Then I watched her read it, write something on it, and put it back."

"You didn't ask either one of them about this?" Gretchen said.

"Well, no. Like I said, I was a dumb kid. I made sure to read her note before my dad did but all it said was 'OK', and I was still really confused so I didn't bring it up. But I kept track after that of the notes they left for one another. They were super boring, though. It was just all about when they could meet in some spot. Except the last one."

Josie said, "What did the last one say?"

"That she wanted it to be over," Heidi answered. "I still have it if you want to see?"

"Where?" Gretchen asked. "Where do you have it?"

"At my house. I can take you there. It's just a block over."

CHAPTER TWENTY-EIGHT

Corey and Heidi Byrne's home was much like all the other ones in the neighborhood, a well-kept, two-story stucco house with a generous front lawn and a two-car garage. The landscaping was more practical, with bushes that stayed green all year and didn't lose their leaves. They would only require a minor amount of pruning. For someone who allegedly worked as much as Corey did, this seemed like a win-win. Heidi found a key under a flowerpot next to the front door and let them all inside.

"Wow," said Josie as they stepped into a huge open concept area. Where there might have been walls, there were instead thick beams throughout. Hardwood floors gleamed. The huge space seemed to be divided into four corners or areas: living room, dining room, kitchen and what looked like an office area with a desk. Several papers were stacked haphazardly on the surface of the desk.

"Yeah," Heidi said, watching them take it in. "Everyone who sees it has the same reaction. He's been working on this on and off for my whole life. Sometimes we've got walls and sometimes we've got this. He keeps changing it. I used to think that he couldn't decide what he liked, but now I think he just has to be working on something or he'll go crazy. Come on."

She beckoned them across the space to a door that led out to the garage. Josie and Gretchen followed through the door, down a short hallway and through another door into the cavernous garage. There were no vehicles but almost every square inch of wall was covered in tools.

"What kind of work does your dad do?" Gretchen asked.

"All of it," Heidi said in a disinterested tone. "Well, that's not true. He doesn't do plumbing. He says he's really bad at it. But he builds houses. He knows carpentry, electric, painting—all that stuff. I used to think he worked so much because he needed so much money to raise me and keep us in this nice neighborhood, but now? Now I just think he loves work more than me."

"I'm sure that's not true," Josie said.

Heidi shrugged and turned away, going over to a shelving unit with several plastic bins marked with her name. "Whatever. You don't have to do that adult thing where you try to reassure me by lying. Before the accident, when I had friends, I saw how other parents treated their kids. I know my dad loves me, but I'm not sure he was ever interested in being a dad."

She said it without emotion, as if she'd resigned herself to the fact a long time ago. Josie was suddenly glad that she had Mrs. Tenney to rely on now. At fourteen, Josie herself had landed in her grandmother's care after years of abuse and neglect, and it had made all the difference. Not that there were any signs that Heidi was abused, but it was clear she had been neglected for many years. All her physical needs had been met, but clearly that was as far as Corey Byrne's care of his daughter extended.

Heidi lifted her heels up and balanced on the tips of her toes, pulling down a mustard-yellow plastic bin. She dropped it onto the concrete floor with a *thwap* sound. She peeled the lid off and pulled out a blue-and-white backpack that was stained brown in some places and a faded rust color in others. Blood, Josie realized.

Heidi placed the backpack at their feet. "That's blood from my friends," she said in a somber tone. "The ones who died in the bus crash. It was already dried on there by the time I got it back. I don't know who brought it to the house but when I got home from the hospital, it was here."

Gretchen said, "Your dad didn't try to clean it off?"

"Actually, he threw it away," said Heidi. "I found it in our trash. He doesn't even know I kept it. I think he didn't want me to see it because he thought it would upset me, but an old bloody backpack? That can never compare to the pictures that are permanently in my head from that day, you know?"

"Yes," Josie breathed. "I know what you mean."

"You don't have to touch it," Heidi said. Kneeling, she moved the straps out of the way and found a small slit in the back of the bag, right where it would rest against the top of her spine if she were wearing it. It took some digging but eventually she came up with a folded piece of loose-leaf paper. Carefully, she smoothed the creases out, using the tops of her thighs as a surface and then handed the page to Josie.

There were two different types of handwriting on the page, though both were faded, and the creases had worn away some of the ink. One set of messages was made in blocky letters, almost all of them capital letters. The other set was written in a long, flowing cursive hand with tall, graceful loops. There were no names or even initials. Only short sets of instructions just as Heidi had said. *Meet me in our spot. Two p.m. Thursday.* In the blocky capital letters. Then beneath, simply: *OK* or sometimes: *See you then.* This went on for half a page. Then the short, simple responses of the graceful handwriting changed.

This has to stop. I can't do this anymore. It's not worth it. They saw us.

Below that was another blocky-lettered message that said: *We don't know that they saw us. Don't do this.*

Then: *If we saw them, they saw us. I can't risk this any longer. I'm terrified. This has to be over.*

Finally: *Please let's talk about this in person. Our spot. Two p.m.* That was it.

Heidi pointed to the boxy capital letters. "That's my dad's handwriting."

Over Josie's shoulder, Gretchen studied it. Quietly, she said, "Doesn't look like the writing found at the scenes."

"No," Josie said, allowing herself a small sigh of relief. "It doesn't." She couldn't imagine what it would do to poor Heidi, after all she'd been through, learning her father was a killer. "Still," she whispered to Gretchen. "We should check alibis."

"Absolutely," Gretchen agreed. To Heidi, she said, "You're sure this is Faye Palazzo's writing?"

"Yeah. I mean, pretty sure. I did see her write stuff on the paper and put it back in my bag."

Gretchen said, "Do you know who the 'they' is that they're talking about?"

"No."

Josie asked, "Do you have any idea where this 'spot' is that they're referring to?"

She shook her head. "Sorry. No idea. I'm in school at that time. I don't know where they met."

"Did you ever see Mrs. Palazzo here?"

"Only if she was picking up Nevin after he came to hang out, which was rare."

"Heidi," Josie said. "We're scheduled to talk with your dad here, today, at five o'clock. We're going to have to ask him about this."

"I know," Heidi said. "If you're worried about me getting in trouble, don't be. He's not that kind of dad."

CHAPTER TWENTY-NINE

Josie and Gretchen dropped Heidi Byrne off at Gloria Cammack's house, leaving her in the care of Dee Tenney until later that afternoon when Corey was off work. A patrol car had already been stationed outside the home. They grabbed lunch from a nearby fast-food restaurant, pulling over in the parking lot to quickly eat their meals while they discussed the latest developments.

Gretchen said, "What do you think about Corey?"

Josie popped a French fry into her mouth. "Hard to say without meeting him, but I'm not sure he looks good for these murders."

"Based on the handwriting? He could have tried changing his writing when he wrote the names on the arms."

"True," Josie agreed. "But why would he be killing off the mothers of the bus crash victims? It makes no sense. His daughter survived, and by the looks of it, he's long depended on that network of mothers to care for Heidi while he spends ninety percent of his time at work."

Gretchen sipped soda from her straw. "Yeah. You're right. Unless he wanted to kill Faye because he was upset with her for breaking off the affair, and Krystal was some kind of decoy."

"That's pretty elaborate," Josie said. "And it doesn't sound like Corey Byrne is the type of guy to go out of his way, even for the people he cares about. Still, I get what you're saying. Due diligence and all that. We'll get alibis from him when we talk to him today and verify them with the people he works with. What's next?"

Gretchen picked up her phone from the center console. "Mett is still on the street tracking down our thief. I think we should pay

Miles Tenney a visit. I left him two voicemails already today but no answer. Let's just head over there."

They finished eating, Gretchen punched the address into her GPS, and they headed to Southwest Denton, where Miles Tenney had rented an apartment in one of the seediest parts of the city. His apartment was on the first floor of a four-story building that was sandwiched between two much larger, multi-story buildings. None of the structures on the block were well maintained. Paint peeled from the façades. Some of the windows on the upper floors were boarded up with plywood and cardboard. As Gretchen and Josie got out of the car and made their way to the front door, they dodged weeds poking from the cracked sidewalk, broken glass, garbage, and a few hypodermic needles. The front door was glass, as if it had once been an entrance to a store. Some light-colored fabric affixed to the other side of it prevented them from seeing inside, but a badly handwritten note taped at face-level indicated that the apartment entrance was around back.

There was only one alleyway leading to the rear. Cockroaches scattered before their feet as they rounded the back of the building. What might have once been a backyard was now an empty lot littered with broken blocks of concrete, the remnants of discarded furniture, and a handful of large, dented appliances that were probably older than Josie. A chain-link fence separated the lot from a parking lot that held three cars. Accessing the map of this part of Denton in her head, Josie remembered there was a pawn shop on the next block over that probably owned the parking area.

"It stinks back here," Gretchen groused.

"Miles Tenney left his wife to live here?" Josie muttered, walking up to the single door at the back of the building. Beside it was a dumpster overflowing with trash. The smell, made worse by the intense summer heat, was enough to churn her stomach.

Gretchen said, "This makes Nathan Cammack's apartment look like a palace."

"Cammack's place wasn't bad," Josie said. "Very modern. It definitely didn't smell this bad."

The door was solid, with a single doorknob. No deadbolt. Gretchen looked at Josie who shrugged as if to say, "Give it a try." The knob turned easily in Gretchen's hand. They walked through the door into a dark, narrow hall with hardwood floors. A musty, unpleasant smell filled Josie's nostrils. "Did Dee give you an apartment number?"

Gretchen shook her head. "She just gave the street address, followed by 'first floor left'."

"The door on the left."

"Seems that way. Tell me again what Miles Tenney does for a living?"

"Car salesman," Gretchen answered as they moved more deeply into the building. "At least, that's what he was doing when I investigated the crash."

"He must not be very good."

They passed a door on the right and kept going. Almost at the end of the hall was another door, standing ajar. Gretchen pulled up short and Josie stopped behind her. "Well, this is never a good thing."

"Not in our business," Josie agreed. Her hand moved to her holster, unsnapping it.

Over Gretchen's shoulder, Josie could make out what looked like a small sitting area. An old brown couch that sagged in the middle sat across from a small, overturned table. A television rested on its face. Beside it was a lamp on its side, the shade crumpled. The bulb gave off a dim yellow glow. The wooden paneling of the wall straight ahead was dark but not so dark that they couldn't make out the blood spatter arcing across it. Josie smelled cigarettes and blood. She pulled her gun from its holster, the weight of it reassuring in her palm. Holding it downward, she tapped Gretchen's shoulder. Gretchen, too, pulled her weapon. With her free hand, she rapped on the door. "Mr. Tenney," she called in a loud, clear voice. "It's Detectives Palmer and Quinn from Denton Police. Mr. Tenney? May we come in?"

Josie ticked off the seconds along with the beats of her heart. Five seconds. Ten.

"Miles Tenney," Gretchen yelled, louder this time. "This is the police. We need to speak with you, sir."

Five seconds. Ten.

"If anyone is in there, please come out now with your hands where we can see them."

No response. Not even a sound. Josie tapped Gretchen's shoulder again, indicating for her to move forward. They moved as one unit with Josie slightly behind, each one of them taking a different side of the room, sweeping their pistols across the area, searching for any movement. There was nothing. The living room and kitchen were all in one room. The couch back separated the two. A table barely large enough for two people to sit was covered in takeout containers. Two wooden chairs lay next to it, both of them over-turned. One had lost two of its legs, large splinters jutting out like daggers where they'd broken off. Covering almost the entire square of tiled floor in the kitchen were pages and pages of what looked like various types of documents. Josie saw more droplets of blood scattered across the papers. At the foot of the fridge was a smashed cell phone, smears of blood dappling the broken pieces.

Turning her attention back to Gretchen, she saw her make a motion toward the left-hand side of the room, indicating a corner with two doorways. Both doors were open. The first was obviously a bathroom, no bigger than a closet. Not even big enough for a full bathtub. There was only a standing shower, no curtain, toilet and sink all crammed together. The next room was a bedroom. A twin mattress lay on the floor, sheets crumpled on top of it. Along the walls were cardboard boxes—rows and rows of them stacked almost to the ceiling. There was no closet.

"Clear," Gretchen said.

They holstered their weapons and went back into the first room. "I think we're standing in a crime scene," Josie said. She took out her phone and called Noah. He would get the team out here to process the apartment and keep the entire thing off the police scanner so that the press didn't pick up on it. "If there was any doubt that Krystal's and Faye's murders were about the bus accident," Josie said after hanging up. "This puts that to rest. One week, three parents of bus crash victims?"

Gretchen stood near the open apartment door, surveying the scene. "Except Miles didn't go willingly. He fought. The killer wounded him. Or he wounded the killer, maybe. We don't actually know whose blood this is."

"I'm sure Dee can tell us Miles' blood type. The ERT can type the blood here at the scene to see whether it's a match or not."

Josie walked carefully back toward the kitchen area. Something blue and sparkly peeked out from behind the fridge. It stood out against the wood paneling and dull, drab green of the fridge. Whatever the object was, it looked as though it had fallen from the top of the fridge and gotten lodged near the base of the wall. Leaning down, she saw the shimmer that had caught her eye from across the room was a glittery letter on the outside of a small blue pouch. A capital F. Josie didn't touch it. She didn't want to contaminate the crime scene, but she was positive that once the ERT retrieved the pouch from behind the fridge, there would be another silvery letter: a capital C.

F.C. for Frankie Cammack. This was the pouch in which young Frankie had kept her treasured Roosevelt dime. What the hell was it doing in Miles Tenney's rundown apartment on the wrong side of the city? Josie straightened her body and opened her mouth to call it to Gretchen's attention, but Gretchen spoke first.

"Ravioli."

It took a split second for Josie to process the word, completely out of context. It was their panic word. Meant for emotional panic, not to signal physical danger, but Josie immediately knew what Gretchen meant by it. She turned her head to see Gretchen facing the open apartment door, hands up. The barrel of a pistol was pointed at her forehead. All that was visible from where Josie stood was a meaty hand wrapped around its handle. No sleeve, only the black band of a wristwatch. The rest of the gunman's frame was blocked by the door, which meant that he couldn't see Josie either.

He said, "What?"

Josie's heart thundered as her body launched into action. Silently, she took two large steps and fit herself behind the door with her back against the wall so that she couldn't be seen through the crack. Her Glock was in her hands, pointed upward.

The man said, "Did you say 'ravioli?'"

"I said, 'Don't shoot me.'"

Josie watched as the pinky and ring finger of Gretchen's left hand slowly folded down toward her palm. Then her thumb tucked in after them until only two fingers remained, pointing toward the ceiling. Two. There were two men.

Gretchen said, "I'm a police officer."

Laughter. "Sure you are, sweetheart."

"Put your guns down," said Gretchen.

"Where's Miles?" the man asked.

"My colleagues are on their way."

"Sure, sure," said the man. "You're with the police, and all your police buddies just happen to be on their way here. If I put my gun away, will they turn around and go back to the station?"

"Let's find out," Gretchen said flatly.

More laughter. "This one's a pistol. You're a pistol, you know that? Now, we came for Miles, and if he don't come with us, we're taking you."

There was another male voice, this one lower and raspier. "She don't look like the wife."

"So she's the mistress," said the first man. "We take her instead."

The pistol pointed at Gretchen's head wobbled while the man talked to his friend. Gretchen took the second to meet Josie's eyes. Josie took one hand off her gun to give Gretchen a signal, hoping she would know what Josie intended. They'd been in some dicey situations before, and they'd always been on the same page. Gretchen gave a curt nod and looked back at the pistol as it stopped wobbling and pointed once more at her face.

"What if she's really a cop?" Raspy asked.

"I am really a cop," said Gretchen.

Josie took in a breath and on the exhale, she yelled, "Police! Drop your weapon!"

As expected, there was a second of shock from the other side of the door. The pistol wavered. Gretchen dropped straight down and then rolled to her left, out of the way of the door. Josie lifted her leg and kicked the door as hard as she could. The gunman cried out as his wrist was slammed between the door and its frame. Josie kicked twice more until the pistol dropped. Before Josie could step forward to open the door, a gunshot exploded from the hall. Then another, and another. Wood splintered from the door. A bullet lodged in the wall opposite. Josie's body had already dropped down. Gretchen was behind her, gun now drawn as well.

Another gunshot came, followed by a grunt. The door swung open, and a large man fell forward onto the floor. White T-shirt, jeans, black sneakers. Blood blossomed from a hole in his back. Had his buddy shot him on purpose or by accident? There was no time to figure it out. The echo of the shots reverberated in Josie's ears. It wasn't until she heard the slam of a door that she realized that the shooter, Raspy, had run out of the building.

Josie looked back at Gretchen.

"Go," Gretchen said. "I'll tend to this guy and call the cavalry. Let them know we've got a shooter on foot."

Josie jumped up, gun pointed downward and took off, jumping over the body of the first man and sprinting down the hallway. She shouldered her way through the door, the sun momentarily blinding her. The smell of the dumpster was just as overpowering as it had been when they arrived. Trying to orient herself, Josie panned the back lot until she spotted Raspy running across the pawn shop parking lot, gun tucked into the back of his waistband. He was taller and thinner than she expected, wearing a pair of khaki cargo pants and black T-shirt. Josie yelled, "Police! Freeze!" but he didn't even look back at her.

She covered the lot quickly and vaulted the chain-link fence. In her four months of suspension, Josie had run almost every day, sometimes twice a day, punishing her body to keep her mind off Lisette's murder. Now it paid off. She gained on him quickly, but he was so much taller than her. In a few more strides, he would be out of the parking lot. An old Honda Civic sat between the two of them. Without breaking pace, Josie holstered her weapon, jumped onto the hood, ran up the windshield, and leapt from the roof of the car onto Raspy's back. He went down face-first with a grunt. Josie straddled him, yanking the gun from his waistband, and tossing it out of his reach.

"Are you crazy?" he screamed beneath her as she pulled his wrists to the small of his back.

"You're under arrest," Josie said, cinching handcuffs around his wrists. She read him his Miranda rights as he squirmed beneath her.

"You broke my nose, you stupid bitch!" he complained.

As he lifted his face from the ground, blood poured out of his nostrils.

Josie said, "I'm going to help you stand up now so we can tip your head back and try to stop some of that bleeding."

"Screw you," he shouted.

"Let's go," Josie told him, sliding a hand under one of his armpits. "Get on your knees and then we'll stand."

He wriggled away from her. "Get away from me! You're not a real cop! This is some bullshit!"

Josie heard footsteps behind her, from the back lot of Miles Tenney's building. She looked back to see Noah hop the chain-link fence and stride toward them. He looked down at Raspy and grimaced. "I'm sorry to tell you, my friend, but she is a real cop and you should do as she says."

CHAPTER THIRTY

After writing up their reports back at the station, Josie and Gretchen were sent home for the evening. Chitwood instructed them to put off their interview with Corey Byrne until the following day. Both of their assailants were being held in the hospital under guard, and it was going to take the ERT hours to process Miles Tenney's apartment, which was now the scene of two crimes—whatever had happened to Miles, and the shooting that took place while Josie and Gretchen were there. Noah and Mettner stayed on-scene to canvass neighbors and check for any video footage at nearby properties to see if they could determine what had happened to Miles. At home, Josie soaked in a hot bubble bath while Trout slept on the mat next to the tub. In her mind, she catalogued all the investigative steps that would need to be taken moving forward, trying to keep her mind off what had happened at Miles Tenney's apartment.

It wasn't the first time she'd ever been shot at, but it was the first time since Lisette's death. Across the film screen of her mind, the scene in the apartment was flash cut with scenes from Lisette's murder. Over and over again, she heard that first, unexpected shot in her head. When her mind's eye saw Lisette fall through the door to Tenney's apartment, bloodied, Josie's body jerked, the water, now lukewarm, sloshing around her. Trout whined and stood up. He rested his chin on the edge of the tub, ears pointed straight up in the air, big brown eyes filled with concern.

"I'm sorry, buddy," she told him. "I fell asleep."

She'd been in enough danger for one day, she decided. Once out of the tub, dried off, and dressed, she sat on the bed and checked her phone for any word from Noah. Nothing yet. With a sigh, she put the phone back on its charger. She meant to wait up for him, but once Trout hopped onto the bed and fit his warm little body against her hip, Josie fell asleep almost instantly. Her dreams were filled with gunshots, with Lisette's body falling at her feet. Sometimes they were near the forest where it had actually happened, and sometimes they were in the pawn shop lot behind Miles Tenney's apartment. Always, just as Josie was about to scoop Lisette's lifeless form into her arms and run for help, a wall of water came crashing in on them from every direction, as if the East Coast had experienced a tsunami so massive that it was cresting in Denton—in the center of Pennsylvania. Beneath the wave, Josie fought for air and tried to hold onto Lisette, but she never could.

Josie woke gasping and clutching at her throat. Trout stood over her, pawing at her arm and licking her face. Sunlight streamed into the room. Once she caught her breath and assured Trout that she was just fine, Josie looked at the clock. It was almost ten a.m. Noah's side of the bed was empty. Yet, she had slept through the entire night for the first time in four months. New nightmares, different nightmares, but for one night at least, these had allowed for some rest. She snatched up her phone to find a text message from Noah. *Got in late. You were out. Didn't want to wake you. When you get up, come to the station. There's news.*

A half hour later, Josie was dressed and pulling into the municipal parking lot of police headquarters. Amassed around the entrance were four times as many reporters as the day before. Was this just because of the incident at Miles Tenney's place or had something else developed overnight? Her heart stuttered in her chest as she parked and got out, noticing for the first time that there were several FBI vehicles in the lot. She hurried out of her car, battling past the throng of reporters shouting questions.

"Is it true that Faye Palazzo was found murdered yesterday?"

"Do you believe there's a serial killer targeting the parents of the West Denton bus crash children?"

"Were you involved in the shooting yesterday in Southwest Denton?"

"Is it true that Miles Tenney was found murdered in his apartment?"

"Who are the men you have in custody? Are the charges related to the murder of Krystal Duncan?"

"What does it mean that there is such a large FBI presence here today?"

"What does this mean for the trial of Virgil Lesko?"

"Are the other parents of the bus crash victims in danger? Or should the public be worried?"

Josie threw out "no comments" like a broken record until she was safely through the door. She ran up the steps and burst into the great room to find the entire team, including Amber and Chief Chitwood, gathered around the detectives' desks along with FBI Agent Drake Nally, dressed sharply in a gray suit and blue tie.

"Well," boomed Drake. "If it isn't Mrs. Noah Fraley!" He strode over and grabbed her in a hug, lifting her off her feet momentarily. Josie squeezed him back, always happy to see him, no matter what the circumstances. "Nice to see you. How are you doing?"

Drake had come from the New York City field office. He lived in Manhattan and dated Josie's twin sister, Trinity Payne, a famous television journalist. Josie managed a smile for him when he released her. "Fine," she said.

Drake was tall and rangy, and he had to lean down to look closely at her face. In a low voice, he said, "You sure?"

Josie kept her smile plastered on her face. "If I wasn't, I sure as shit wouldn't tell you."

He laughed and squeezed one of her shoulders. "Trinity said you would say that."

"What are you doing here?" she asked, walking past him to her desk. Noah kissed her cheek and pulled out her chair for her. When she was seated, he handed her a paper cup of coffee.

"I knew I married you for a reason," she told him.

Across from her, Gretchen nodded a greeting. Mettner was on the phone, but gave her a small wave. Amber typed away at her laptop, and Chitwood presided over all of them from the side of the room, a silent sentry.

Drake perched himself on the edge of her desk, folding his arms over his chest. "Those two guys you and Palmer had a run-in with yesterday? They're part of a pretty large crime syndicate based out of New York City. They call themselves Cerberus."

"I've heard of them," Josie said.

"We've had a task force looking at Cerberus for two years now. They started out loan sharking and as they expanded, they got into gambling rings, prostitution, and now they're dabbling in drugs. They've got their hands in just about everything now as far south as D.C. and as far north as Boston."

Chitwood said, "We haven't seen them here until now."

Drake nodded. "They're active in Philadelphia. We believe that's where Miles Tenney came into contact with them."

Noah said, "The boxes you guys found in Miles Tenney's bedroom were filled with what we believe are stolen items. Everything from electronics to jewelry to power tools. Anything and everything you'd be able to sell or pawn for money."

"The pouch behind the fridge," Josie said. "Were you able to confirm that it belonged to Frankie Cammack?"

Mettner hung up his phone. "I met with Gloria Cammack at her office last night and showed her photos. She confirmed it."

Josie asked, "Was the dime still in there?"

Noah shook his head. "Nope."

Gretchen said, "Miles was stealing things from his friends and neighbors and selling them."

Mettner said, "Looks that way. It's going to take a long time to track down the owners of the items that were still in his possession and to contact pawn shops to determine if any of the items reported missing were brought in by him." He pointed to a thick stack of papers on his desk. "This is a list of items that West Denton residents within a fifteen-block radius of the Tenney household told us yesterday had gone missing in the two years prior to the bus crash. Almost none of them had been reported to the police."

Noah said, "It was the same story again and again—each resident thought they misplaced these things, got rid of them, or loaned them to someone who hadn't returned them, but no one could remember clearly enough to say yes, the item was definitely stolen. It was usually something they didn't notice right away or didn't use that often or never used."

"Like Gloria's clutch purse," Gretchen said. "Or Nathan Cammack's camping stove."

"Exactly," said Noah.

Josie raised a brow. "We now know Miles was taking things. You think he stopped after the crash?"

"No," Noah said. "Not given all the items in his apartment. He just changed areas. We think he stopped stealing from people he knew and moved on to strangers."

"I thought Miles Tenney was a successful car salesman. Their house is beautiful, and it has to be worth a fair bit of money," Josie said.

Mettner said, "I just got off the phone with his old boss. Miles was fired six months after the accident."

"For stealing?" asked Gretchen.

"For suspicion of stealing. A large amount of money went missing from the dealership's petty cash. Apparently, several employees' personal items had been going missing for some time so the owner had additional security cameras installed. They caught Miles going into the safe."

"And didn't have him arrested and charged?" Chitwood asked.

"They felt badly because his daughter had just died. They told him if he returned all the money within twenty-four hours, they'd let the whole thing go. They fired him, of course. He returned the money, and that was that."

"I don't think his wife knows about any of this," Josie said.

Noah said, "She doesn't. We went over to Gloria Cammack's to talk with her last night. We had to let her know about Miles. The blood at the scene matches his blood type. Someone had to tell her that he's missing and likely injured. Somehow the press already has wind of it. Technically, they're still married. Plus, we needed to know if she had any information on where he might be or who could have taken him—other than Cerberus. She knew nothing. Everything was a complete shock to her."

"Miles was lying to her," Josie said.

"On a pretty grand scale," Mettner pointed out. "Evidently, sometime in the last three or four years, Miles Tenney developed a pretty bad gambling problem. He didn't have very good luck. He ended up in a lot of debt. He's been trying to pull himself out of it ever since."

"That's how he ended up in touch with the Cerberus syndicate," Drake said.

"Was Miles Tenney already on your radar?" Josie asked.

"No, but the two men you met yesterday? Leon Tartaglia and Joseph Bruno? They were. When they were taken into custody, we were notified."

"But you're not here because of Miles Tenney," said Gretchen.

Drake smiled. "No. I'm hoping to turn one of these guys."

"So they're out of our reach now?" Chitwood said.

"We talked to them both this morning," Drake said. "One is cooperating, the other isn't."

"They both survived," Josie said.

"Yeah," Noah interjected. "Bruno started shooting when you disarmed Tartaglia and he hit his buddy in the back. Tartaglia spent a few hours in surgery last night but he's in stable condition."

"They were looking for Miles," Gretchen said. "There's no way that they know where he is. But they were talking about taking his wife."

Chitwood said, "We've had a detail on Dee Tenney, and we'll keep one on her for the time being."

Drake said, "Bruno told us that Miles was into Cerberus for over three hundred thousand dollars. He was supposed to deliver cash to a bar in Philadelphia that acts as a Cerberus front a week ago. This wasn't the first time he failed to show or to pay back what he owed. Bruno and Tartaglia were sent to get him and take him back to their boss. If they didn't find him, their orders were to take his wife. They were going to hold her to flush Miles out."

"But Miles is gone," Josie said. "Either he got away or someone besides Cerberus found him. Dee is still in danger, and I'm not sure we have the resources here to protect her long-term from a syndicate like Cerberus."

Drake frowned. "I can't get her witness protection if she didn't actually witness anything."

"She's a sitting duck, Drake. She's innocent." She looked around the room, thinking of Heidi and how bonded she had become to Dee Tenney. "We can't do nothing."

No one spoke. In the silence, there was only the sound of Amber tapping away at her keyboard. Soon, that stopped as well. Then came Amber's voice. "If I could make a suggestion?"

All heads turned toward her. She stood up from her desk and leaned her hip against the edge of it. "This crime boss—he only wants Dee Tenney to flush Miles out, right?"

Drake nodded.

"Then if you make him think that Miles is gone, he'll have no reason to go after Dee."

"Theoretically, yes," Drake answered. "But guys like this—like the people running Cerberus—they don't always operate on the honor system. They could take her anyway and kill her just because they feel like it. Or if they think that Miles ran off, they'll take her to lure him back in."

Mettner said, "But we could decrease the chances of that happening if we do what Amber says: take this to the press. Tell them that Miles is missing but he's believed to be dead."

"No one has said anything about him being dead," Gretchen pointed out.

Josie said, "No, but his blood was found at the scene. If nothing else, we know he was injured. He could be dead."

"How much blood loss?" Noah asked. "Can we make a case that he lost too much blood to have survived?"

Amber said, "I'm not sure you need to. You could just say there was blood found at the scene that matches Miles' blood type and let the public fill in the rest. We don't have to lie about what happened to him—we really don't know and it's okay to say that. The important thing would be telegraphing to this Cerberus group that he's gone and that he didn't go willingly. But if you really want to protect Dee you need to tell the whole story—that he lied to her, left her destitute, and she had no idea what he was into."

Gretchen said, "You want to air her dirty laundry to the whole city?"

Josie said, "It's the only chance we've got of protecting her." *And Heidi*, Josie added silently. "If we talk to her, explain the situation, I'm sure we could get her to agree to it."

Drake said, "I'm willing to talk to her and tell her what we know about Cerberus. Maybe try to drive home the seriousness of what we're dealing with here. We'll be taking over the Miles Tenney case from here."

"Thank you," Josie said. "But it's not just protecting Dee that we need to worry about. Did the team catch you up on what's been happening here?"

"How the parents of the bus crash victims have been turning up dead?" Drake said. "Listen, I know this looks like a pattern, but you have to consider the possibility that whatever happened to Miles had nothing to do with that."

"You don't think whatever happened to Miles is related to the murders of the other two parents?" Josie asked.

Mettner said, "There were a lot of documents in Miles Tenney's apartment. The ERT is still sifting through them and uploading them to the file, but none of it is good. We have to consider the possibility that Cerberus wasn't the only outfit looking to take out some repayment from Miles in blood."

Gretchen lifted her chin in Noah's direction. "You guys find any leads on Miles Tenney? Video? Car? Anything?"

Noah said, "No video. The pawn shop had a camera, but Miles wasn't on it. We found his car a few blocks away. Nothing. Neighbors all claim they saw nothing, heard nothing."

"Of course," Josie muttered. This was a typical response in that area of Denton. It was better to pretend you had seen and heard nothing than to put a target on your own back ratting out criminals. "You didn't find any candles in his apartment, did you?"

"No," Mettner answered.

Gretchen said, "We really can't say for sure that Miles' disappearance is related to the murders of Krystal Duncan and Faye Palazzo."

Noah said, "Not unless his body turns up in a day or two with wax in his throat and a name on his arm."

Chitwood cleared his throat, and everyone startled. Josie had nearly forgotten he was there. "Regardless of whether Miles Tenney's disappearance is part of the Duncan and Palazzo cases or related to some hot water he got himself into, we have a killer on the loose in this city right now. Someone who is targeting grieving parents. Someone who is clearly trying to send a message of some kind."

Gretchen said, "So let's take Miles out of consideration for now and look at the cases."

"No," said Josie. "We were meant to talk to Miles. Actually, we were meant to find out his secret."

"What do you mean?" Mettner asked.

Josie looked up from her coffee cup to see she had everyone's attention. "Think about this. Krystal's body led us to Gloria and Nathan Cammack. What were their secrets?"

Gretchen said, "That Nathan was smoking pot with Krystal for years behind his wife's back. That he slept with Krystal at least once. That on the day of the accident, he canceled his children's and Bianca Duncan's orthodontist appointments to meet his wife at home."

"Those are all the husband's secrets," Noah pointed out.

"No," said Josie. "Gloria's secret is that she made Nathan come home early and leave the kids at school that day, and they got on the bus."

"Faye was next," said Chitwood.

Noah said, "Gail Tenney's name was written on her arm."

"Which led us to Dee first," Josie said. "She didn't have any secrets, or at least, we haven't found them out yet."

"But she did tell us that Faye had been having an affair," Gretchen pointed out. "Maybe it's not necessarily their personal secrets but something they knew about one of the other parents."

"Yes," said Josie. "That could very well be. But for now, let's follow the trail this killer has left. The next logical person we would interview would be Miles."

"His secret is the years of stealing, the gambling debts, getting fired," said Mettner. "His own wife didn't know about any of it."

"You sure about that?" Chitwood asked. "You sure Dee Tenney's not just lying to save face?"

"According to fourteen-year-old Heidi Byrne who is practically living with Dee right now," said Gretchen, "Dee had a meltdown the morning Faye was found because her bank account was overdrawn. I think we can assume that Heidi is an independent witness. If Dee was lying, she might put on a show for the police, but I don't think she would for Heidi. From what Heidi told us, Dee had no idea there were any financial issues. When we talked with Dee yesterday, she said that Miles just deposited money into their bank account and she went about her life."

Noah said, "But absent the bloody scene at Miles' apartment and the Cerberus lugheads, how would you have found out about Miles' big secret? You think he would have just told you?"

In Josie's mind, two words whispered on a loop. *If only, if only.*

Gretchen said, "We'll never know, but he had a secret. If we had dug deeper, we might have uncovered it or if we waited long enough, his web of lies would have reached critical mass like it did last night with those guys coming after him."

Chitwood said, "You can't run forever when you're in that deep. It would have come out sooner or later."

"But so what?" asked Mettner. "This one canceled doctor's appointments. This one smoked weed. This one had an affair. This one was in debt to a loan-sharking crime syndicate. What does any of this have to do with the bus crash?"

If only, if only.

Josie said, "If Miles hadn't been stealing things from his neighbors' houses for all that time, when Gloria went home to get her planner on the day of the accident, her son's PlayStation would have been there that day. She wouldn't have called Nathan at work and demanded that he come home. He wouldn't have canceled the orthodontist appointments. Instead, he would have picked up the kids—at least three of them—and they'd still be alive."

Noah said, "You think this is revenge of some kind?"

Gretchen said, "If that's true, then why kill Krystal or Faye? Why not kill Nathan, Gloria, and Miles?"

Josie said, "Because those aren't all the secrets. There are more. Plus, Faye did have a secret—her affair with Corey Byrne."

"Whose kid survived the crash," Mettner pointed out.

Chitwood gave a frustrated sigh and waved a hand in the air. "We're not asking the right questions, people. If someone is targeting the parents of the bus crash victims, who has the most to gain from their deaths?"

"No one," said Noah. "Virgil Lesko was drunk the day of the accident. Toxicology showed that, and he admitted to it. The parents weren't even due to be witnesses at his trial. Killing these parents does nothing for him. He's guilty whether they're alive or dead."

"But he lied," Josie said. "He lied about why he had a drink that day. In his initial statement he said he had a drink because his sick mother had been admitted to hospice care that day when in fact, she'd already been in hospice care for at least a month. In the case files there's a photo of an explanation of benefits for hospice care, which was found in his car. It's dated a month before that."

She leaned forward and clicked her computer mouse until she had accessed the Virgil Lesko case file and found the photo again. Enlarging it on her screen, she pointed to two lines. "Patient: Luray Lesko. Billing Period: April 1 through April 30. The bus crash took place on May 18th."

Gretchen and Mettner got up from their seats and came around to look at her screen. Chitwood walked over as well and peered at it.

Perched on the edge of Josie's desk, Noah had a good view of it. He said, "Why would he lie? He admitted to drinking. Why lie about the reason?"

Gretchen took a step back and slid her reading glasses up onto her head. "Because he was well-respected in the community. He took his job seriously, and he would never take a drink before driving a bus full of schoolchildren around. He told me that. He took pride in that."

"What would be so bad that would make him take a drink that day and then lie about it?" Mettner asked as he too, stepped away from Josie's computer.

Silence.

Josie said, "We could ask his son, Ted. He was pretty cooperative when we met him at Andrew Bowen's office."

Mettner said, "About his son…" He shot a look at Chief Chitwood, sucked in a deep breath, and kept speaking. "I know the Chief thinks that these murders are about gain but what if Noah is right and this isn't about gain at all but about revenge? The person who would want revenge most against the parents would have to be Ted Lesko, don't you think?"

They waited a beat for Chitwood to holler, but he remained silent, arms folded over his chest. Gretchen said, "That does make sense, except there is no way that Ted Lesko would know all these intimate things like the nickname the other kids gave Wallace Cammack or the thing about Nathan Cammack canceling the orthodontist appointments and lying to Krystal about it. We should be looking at people who had access to these families, someone who could glean these details."

"We're back to the support group, then," Noah pointed out. "Or someone else in the neighborhood."

Chitwood clapped his hands, drawing their attention. "All right, all right. Let's bring in Ted Lesko anyway and see what he's got to say for himself. Someone else interview Corey Byrne. I know he's not in the group but maybe he knows something that no one else does. Mettner and Fraley, I know you've got leads left to follow up on from yesterday, like Krystal Duncan's work files and the orthodontist. Squeeze those things in, too. Drake, you can have Amber for the day. Head over to see Dee Tenney and see if you can get some kind of story together for the press to keep the heat off her. Quinn, this business you're talking about with everyone having a secret—who's left? Who's got secrets we don't know about?"

"Dee Tenney and Sebastian Palazzo," said Josie. She turned to Mettner. "Speaking of Sebastian, who gave the death notice?"

She could tell by the pained looks on both Noah's and Mettner's faces that they had done it. Mettner said, "It was bad. Really bad."

Noah said, "We were going to drive him to the emergency room and get him admitted to the hospital for seventy-two hours on suicide watch but then a coworker from the pharmacy came over. She promised to stay with him and call 911 if he got agitated again."

Mettner added, "I told her to just go outside since we've got a unit stationed out front of his house anyway. He hasn't left since his wife went missing."

Gretchen said, "Chief, what do you want us to do? Bring Dee and Sebastian in and ask them point blank if they've got secrets?"

"Not yet," said Chitwood. "Both of them are under police guard so if either of them is the kidnapper/killer, they're not going to be in any position to hurt anyone else for now. Let's focus on the other things for today and see what breaks."

The phone on Josie's desk rang. She snatched it up. "Quinn."

On the other end, Dr. Feist said, "I've finished Faye Palazzo's autopsy. You have time to stop by for a few minutes?"

CHAPTER THIRTY-ONE

The scene at the morgue was almost identical to the one from the other day when Josie and Gretchen had visited after Krystal Duncan's autopsy. Faye Palazzo's body lay on the same exam table, a sheet pulled to her neck. Dr. Feist strode in from the door that connected the exam room to her personal office. Today, her scrubs were salmon-colored. As Josie and Gretchen entered, she waved and pulled off her skullcap, shaking her silver-blonde hair loose. She gave them a grim smile and beckoned them closer to Faye's lifeless form.

"I know you were both at the scene," she said. "Which means you already saw the pink color of her skin, indicating carbon monoxide poisoning, as well as the wax on her lips and the name on her arm."

Josie and Gretchen both nodded.

Dr. Feist pointed to the bruises along Faye's jawline that Josie had noted at the scene. "You saw these?"

"Yes," said Josie. "She struggled."

"She did but I didn't find any skin under her fingernails or any kind of bruising anywhere else on her body."

Gretchen said, "Meaning she was restrained except for her head?"

"I don't think so. I think if she had been restrained, we would see evidence of that. Ligature or tape marks or something somewhere on her extremities. I think that by the time the killer poured the wax into her mouth, she was too weak to put up enough of a struggle to leave us any evidence. But given the burn patterns on the inside of her mouth and throat, the killer didn't get his timing exactly right the way he did with Krystal Duncan."

"The wax was poured into her mouth before she died," Josie said.

"Yes. I think she instinctively tried to turn her head away, even in her weakened state from the carbon monoxide poisoning, and the killer had to hold it in place."

Josie's stomach burned. She couldn't help but think of Sebastian Palazzo. He would find out the details of his wife's murder eventually. It would be torture for him, although he already seemed as though he was in agony. He'd lost his son and his wife now within two years of one another. How would he survive this, she wondered. Clearly Faye had been his entire world. How did anyone survive losses like this? How was she surviving the loss of Lisette? How had it already been four months since Josie had watched her take her last breath? How was Josie still walking and talking and moving through life when such a large part of her soul had been torn away from her?

"Josie?"

She blinked and looked up from Faye's face to see both Dr. Feist and Gretchen staring at her. She wasn't sure which one of them had called her name. Slowly, as if she was afraid to startle Josie, Gretchen extended a hand. In it was a tissue. Josie didn't take it. Instead, she touched her fingers to her cheek and came away with moisture. Quietly, almost reverently, Dr. Feist said, "I'm not sure I've ever seen you cry."

"I'm not—" Josie began but more tears spilled out. Reluctantly, she took the tissue from Gretchen and wiped at her face.

"I cry, you know," said Dr. Feist.

Josie blinked again, annoyed by the pressure behind her eyes, wanting to let the tears fall to relieve the feeling if nothing else. "What?"

"I cry," Dr. Feist repeated. "All the time. Privately, of course."

Josie stared at her blankly.

A warm smile spread across the doctor's face. "You think I can do this job every day and not get upset? I have to autopsy children. Sometimes infants. I did the autopsy on this woman's son and on Krystal Duncan's daughter. I don't know what's worse: the violence that human beings are capable of inflicting on one another or the fact that even if you stopped all that violence, people would still die and their loved ones would still be left behind with huge holes in their hearts and lives." Dr. Feist stared down at Faye, a somber expression on her face. With one finger, she traced the bruises along Faye's jawline. "So I cry," she added. "In the car, in the shower, in the bathroom. Sometimes a good hallway or even an elevator will do. I don't do it because I need comfort. There is no comfort for this. I cry because it lets some of the tension out. It helps me let go of some of the sadness and sorrow. It reminds me I'm still human."

Josie's throat was thick with mucous. She coughed to try to clear some of it and said, "That works?"

Dr. Feist shrugged. "For me, yes. I'll never be okay with murder and death and loss and grief, but it gets me through the worst days."

Josie pressed the tissue to her cheeks again, but it was soaked through. Gretchen handed her another. She turned away from them, dabbing at her tears again, trying to compose herself, but the harder she tried, the more tears came. "Jesus," she muttered.

Josie didn't know how many minutes passed but after several more tissues were soaked through, the tears abated enough for her to turn back to her colleagues. Dr. Feist smiled kindly. "It doesn't have to leave this room, Josie."

Gretchen nodded.

Josie sucked in a shaky breath and walked back to the table. "I'm fine," she said. "Let's get back to work."

"Okay," said Dr. Feist. "What I can tell you is that the immediate cause of death was asphyxiation from the wax in her airway although, given the cherry red of her viscera, just like what we saw with Krystal Duncan, even if the killer hadn't poured the wax into her throat, she would have died from carbon monoxide poisoning. No sign of sexual assault. Nothing else remarkable on exam or autopsy. She was a very healthy woman. A little underweight, perhaps, but in great shape, physically."

"What did you want us to see?" Josie asked.

"A couple of things." She moved to Faye Palazzo's feet and then slowly peeled the sheet up, folding it at Faye's knees so that her shins were exposed. At first, Josie only saw angry red lash marks across both of Faye's legs. Then she realized they weren't lash marks. It was the shape of something imprinted on her skin. Dr. Feist said, "I know what you're thinking—these horizontal red marks across her skin look like someone either whipped her or that her legs were resting against something slatted for a long period of time, but remember when we talked about livor mortis?"

Gretchen said, "How the blood settles in the lowest parts of the body, turning the skin purple or black—"

"Or cherry red in the case of carbon monoxide poisoning," Dr. Feist interrupted. "Livor mortis is when that settling becomes fixed and no amount of manipulating the body changes it. The red you see here is where the blood settled."

Josie said, "What about the white marks? It looks almost like she's got red and white stripes across her legs."

"The white is contact blanching. Where you see the white is where her legs were resting against something that prevented the blood from settling in that area. It does look like stripes—or, as I said, slats of some kind. Livor was fixed when you found her, which means she had been dead for eight to twelve hours before she was moved to the location where you found her."

"Which means she had to have been killed pretty soon after disappearing from her home," Gretchen said. "At least within a twelve-hour window."

"The killer didn't keep her," Josie said. "He didn't need anything from her. He only meant to kill her."

Gretchen nodded. "He wanted something from Krystal. Information. That's why she was gone for so many days and why she logged into her work database. Or why he made her log in."

Josie took out her cell phone and fired off a text to Noah. "I'm asking Noah if he and Mett have had a chance to check back in with the law office yet. I'll tell him to look beyond the cases that Krystal was working on. If you're right, Gretchen, then there was something in that law firm's files that the killer wanted."

Gretchen nodded and turned her attention back to Dr. Feist. "You're telling us that Faye Palazzo died while kneeling on something slatted?"

"Yes," said Dr. Feist.

Josie said, "Where would you find slatted floors? A deck of some kind? The bay of an auto repair shop?"

"Or a barn," supplied Dr. Feist. "Come look."

She covered Faye Palazzo's legs and walked toward the counter at the back of the room, beckoning for them to follow. Her laptop sat next to several evidence bags. Usually at this point in any conversation about an autopsy, Dr. Feist opened her laptop to show them results of x-rays or read off other notes about her exam. This time, she bypassed the laptop and went straight to a small paper evidence bag, which she had already labeled. "Hummel is coming by for these shortly. I can't leave here until he's taken them into custody. Before I show you why I think she might have been kept in a barn of some kind, I just want to bring this to your attention. In this bag is a single diamond stud earring."

Josie said, "I noticed at the scene she only had one."

Gretchen asked, "Had the other one been torn out? Maybe in the struggle with the killer?"

Dr. Feist shook her head. "No. There was no tearing at all of the lobe of her other ear. I think she took the earring out herself. Either that or it fell out but there's a good chance that she took it out and left it wherever she was held."

"What makes you say that?" Gretchen said. "I lose earrings all the time."

Dr. Feist lifted an index finger in the air, as if to tell them to wait for it. Then she snapped a pair of gloves on and picked up a larger evidence bag. Carefully, she took the contents out and placed them onto the stainless-steel counter. A pair of tan ballet flats. "These are the shoes that Faye was wearing when she was found. They're flats so they didn't have any tread on the bottom that might produce trace evidence, but on the inside of both shoes I found hair."

Gretchen's brow furrowed. "Hair?"

From yet another bag, Dr. Feist pulled two clear plastic baggies with several strands each of a pale-yellow hair. Each strand was two to four inches in length and kinked in unruly curls. Josie leaned down, bringing her face within inches of the bags so she could get a closer look. "Animal hair?"

"I believe so. It has to be sent to the lab for analysis, but I am fairly certain you're looking at animal hair."

"She stuffed her shoes," said Josie. "She knew she was going to die. She took out her earring and left it and then she stuffed her shoes with animal hair."

Gretchen said, "The killer would have known to brush off her clothing and skin. He probably did. That would explain why there was nothing on either Krystal or Faye when the ERT processed their clothes and when Dr. Feist did her exam. The killer cleaned them both up."

"But he didn't take their shoes off," said Josie. "Why would he?"

"She took a risk," Gretchen said. "Ballet flats fall off easily."

"Even if the killer had found the hair inside her shoes," Josie replied. "She would already have been dead. The only risk was that forensic exams wouldn't turn it up."

"What kind of animal do you think we're looking at here?" Gretchen asked Dr. Feist.

The doctor shook her head. "Oh, Detectives, I'm no animal expert. I just knew something was off when I removed her shoes. I've done a lot of autopsies in my time, and I've never seen that before."

"A goat," Josie suggested. "Sheep? It's too long and curly to be from a cow."

"Alpaca, maybe?" Dr. Feist said.

Gretchen nodded. She took out her notebook and started scrawling words down.

Josie said, "The only problem now is that we're in the middle of Central Pennsylvania. Do you have any idea how many barns there are just on the outskirts of Denton alone? How many farms?"

Gretchen looked up. "I'm gonna say a lot."

Dr. Feist laughed. "More than a lot."

Gretchen took out her phone and checked the time. "Everyone is out on the street working this case. We've still got to interview Corey Byrne and either Mett or Noah should be out tracking down Ted Lesko. Checking on area barns could take hours."

"Get Lamay to do it," Josie said, referring to their desk sergeant, Dan Lamay. "He can start the list while he's manning the lobby. He'll do it if we ask."

"Great idea," said Gretchen, dialing Lamay's desk phone. As she gave Dan instructions, Josie turned to Dr. Feist and smiled. A real smile. "This is brilliant," she told the doctor. "Thank you."

Dr. Feist nodded. "Let's hope it helps you find this killer. I don't want to see another one of these cases ever again."

CHAPTER THIRTY-TWO

As they approached the next stop, the bus pitched to the side. There weren't as many kids on it now. No one cheered. Gail looked over at Bianca who had gone silent and paler than Gail had ever seen her. Her hands were clenched around the backpack in her lap. Gail heard one of the kids who was getting off the bus say, "Dude, I think I'm gonna be sick."

She lifted herself out of her seat a little so she could see the bus stop. No parents waited. Once the kids hit the asphalt, they scattered, running home. A loud grinding noise came from somewhere under them. The whole bus vibrated.

Behind them, Nevin said, "What's he doing? Did the bus break down?"

Gail felt a shiver start in her legs and work its way up her entire body. This wasn't fun, and she didn't like it anymore. "Maybe we should get off," she said to Bianca.

"You mean off the bus? Here? This isn't our stop."

"You said something is wrong with Mr. Lesko. Maybe you're right. We should just get off. I can call my mom."

Bianca said nothing. She looked frozen like a statue.

Nevin said, "We could probably just walk from here. It's not that far."

Their bodies jerked forward and then back and the bus lumbered on, picking up speed so fast that the scenery outside was just a blur.

"It's too late now," said Nevin.

CHAPTER THIRTY-THREE

Gretchen had gotten to the station hours before Josie that morning and had a chance to speak with Corey Byrne's boss to both verify the dates and times that Corey had been at work since Krystal Duncan went missing, and to find out precisely which job site he would be on that day. Again, Gretchen drove, weaving through the streets of Denton as if she'd lived there her entire life. Frigid air blasted into Josie's face, cooling the sweat that had formed on her upper lip in the time it took to walk through the hospital parking lot. Josie tried to muster some anger toward Noah for letting her sleep so late, but it was the best rest she'd gotten in four months. She felt more clearheaded than she had since Lisette died. For the first time, she had fleeting seconds where she thought of her grandmother without experiencing utter devastation; instead, seeing Lisette's knowing smile in her mind's eye and hearing her voice: "I know, I know. You've got to get back to work. Go, go!"

Corey Byrne was working in a new apartment building being erected on the northern end of Denton University's campus. Gretchen parked in a dirt-strewn lot behind it among a row of pickup trucks Josie guessed belonged to construction workers. The skeleton of the building was intact and one side had walls while the other was still open. As they rounded the front of the site, a sign announced that the building was destined to be new housing for graduate students. They worked their way through the site, talking to three different people and climbing four floors before finding Corey hanging drywall in one of the rooms on the closed side of the building. He started to tell them they couldn't be there until Gretchen flashed her badge.

He put down his tools and wiped his palms on his jeans before shaking both their hands. "I didn't know you were coming," he said. "My boss—"

"Gave us permission to speak with you," Gretchen filled in.

A yellow hardhat rested on his head. He reached up and took it off, revealing thick, golden-blond hair. Josie's first thought was that he didn't look like the father of a teenage girl. He barely looked old enough to have a fourteen-year-old, but then Josie remembered how Heidi had told them that her mother was only nineteen when Heidi was born. It was probable that Corey had been around the same age at the time, which would make him younger than the average parent in his area of West Denton. Not only that but he looked nothing like the other people living in his neighborhood. Most of the residents were college-educated and in their late thirties or early forties—even their fifties like Virgil Lesko—with white-collar jobs. Corey was an outlier—young and handsome, working a physical job each day. The seemingly endless work hours had sculpted his body into something gym rats could only dream about. His white T-shirt was tight and soaked with sweat, revealing every muscle of his arms, chest, and washboard abs, which rippled every time he moved. Josie could see why Faye Palazzo would have been attracted to him.

But surely, as a successful model, Faye had had her pick of the most physically attractive men on the planet, and yet she had chosen Sebastian to marry. Not that Sebastian was unattractive, but he was the polar opposite of Corey Byrne. Was that the reason Faye had risked her marriage to be with Corey?

"Heidi told me what's been going on," Corey said, holding his hardhat in both hands. "I'm real sorry to hear about Krystal and uh, Faye—I, uh, is it true? Is she really dead?"

"I'm afraid she is, Mr. Byrne," said Josie.

His gaze drifted to the floor. A muscle in his jaw quivered. In his hands, the plastic of the hardhat cracked.

"Mr. Byrne," Gretchen said. "Do you need a moment?"

He shook his head but still did not speak.

Gently, Josie said, "We know that you cared for Faye. We know about the affair."

Now he closed his eyes and tipped his head back. His Adam's apple bobbed as he swallowed several times. He tossed his hardhat into the corner of the room and swiped at his eyes before opening them again and returning Josie's gaze. "Does her husband know?"

"No," Josie said. "Not that we're aware of. We found out through other channels."

Corey raised a brow. "Other channels, huh? So, Heidi then." He shook his head. "Dammit. Can't get nothing past that kid."

Gretchen said, "She did the right thing by telling us, Mr. Byrne. We've got a murderer in this city, and he appears to be targeting the parents of the children who died in the West Denton bus accident."

He jammed his hands into his jeans pockets. "Okay, but then why do you need to talk to me? My kid survived that accident."

Josie said, "In investigating Faye's murder we have to look at every facet of her life. When is the last time you saw her?"

"The funerals," he answered instantly. "I did go to the kids' funerals."

"You haven't seen or spoken to her in over two years?" Gretchen asked.

"That's correct. I wanted to—man, did I want to—but it didn't seem right. She wanted to end it before the accident anyway, and I knew what Nevin meant to her. I knew that there was no room in her life for me anymore. Plus, it was so awkward, you know? I was the one parent whose kid survived. I told Heidi we could move anywhere she wanted but she wanted to stay here, so we did. The only parent from the crash who still talks to me is Dee. Thank God for Dee."

Josie said, "When was the last time you saw Faye before the funerals?"

"The day of the crash."

"You met?" Gretchen asked. "At 'your spot'?"

He blinked. "Yeah. How'd you know that?"

"We're in possession of a piece of notepaper that you and Faye Palazzo had been using to communicate during your affair. Your 'spot' was mentioned several times," said Josie.

One side of Corey's mouth lifted in a half-smile. "Heidi again," he guessed. "Yeah, we were at our spot that day. Same time as always. Two p.m. We actually—we saw the bus pass us by, and I thought it looked like it was swerving. I told her, let's follow it, but she said no, we couldn't risk being seen together. There would be too many questions. I told her, 'Who cares? What about the kids? We'll say we ran into each other and I gave you a ride,' but she insisted. We were arguing that day. She was dumping me. We stayed longer than usual, and then, well then both our cell phones started blowing up because the bus crashed. It was—it was horrible."

His eyes had gone glassy with a distant look, as if he were peering back into the past, watching the events of that day replay again and again.

They gave him a moment and then Gretchen said, "Mr. Byrne, where was your spot?"

He gave his head a little shake, as if to bring himself back to the present. "Oh, it was this undeveloped tract of land not far from our houses actually. It's been vacant for years. Every time there's something about to be built there, the city council shuts it down. There are houses across from it, but there's enough tree cover that you can park back there without being seen. We used to meet there in my truck. Faye would never go to either of our houses. It always had to be the truck."

Gretchen looked at Josie. They were both thinking the same thing. Josie named the street on which they'd found Faye Palazzo's body. "That place on Tallon Street?" she asked.

"Yeah," said Corey. "That's the spot. Hey, how'd you know that?"

Josie didn't answer his question. Instead, she asked her own. "Who else knew about your affair?"

"No one," he said. "Faye was insane about keeping it a secret. Her husband's not wrapped too tight, you know?"

"Was she afraid of him?" Gretchen asked.

"I think she was, a little bit, but she always just said she didn't want him to divorce her because Nevin needed his father."

Josie said, "Did you tell anyone about the affair? Ever? Even after it was over?"

"No. Never. I promised Faye."

"In the note we have, she says that someone saw you," Josie said. "What did that mean? Someone caught the two of you?"

Again, Corey's head tipped back, and he looked up at the ceiling for a moment. On a heavy exhale, he met Josie's eyes again. "I don't know if anyone saw us or not. Faye thought they did but I was never sure. I didn't think it mattered anyway."

Gretchen said, "Tell us what happened."

He shrugged. "We were in our spot, you know? We were, well, you know—going at it in the cab of the truck but we always parked off to the side—like, behind these trees so that if anyone pulled in, they wouldn't see us at first. No one ever pulled in except this one time."

"When was this?" asked Josie.

"I don't know. Like, a couple months before the accident?"

"Who pulled into the clearing?"

"Two cars," he said. "Two guys. They parked next to each other and got out, started moving shit from the trunk of one car to the other. We recognized Miles right away and Faye started freaking out. She was scrambling so fast to get herself together and hide that she accidentally hit the horn. That's when they looked over. We just sat there completely frozen. Then, real slow, Miles and this guy closed their trunks, got into their cars, and left. Faye was sure they saw us and that Miles recognized us both, but I didn't even make eye contact with either of them. I mean I'm sure they saw us but I don't know if they recognized us or realized what we were doing. I saw Miles a couple of times after that when I dropped Heidi off or picked her up, and he never said anything."

Josie said, "You didn't recognize the other guy?"

Corey scratched the back of his neck. "He looked really familiar but no, I didn't recognize him. Maybe if I had been closer, I would have, but no, not from where we were parked. I recognized Miles right away because I saw him all the time and he had that shiny shaved head and drove that silver Lexus sedan that he leased from his dealership."

"Did Faye recognize the other guy?" Gretchen asked.

"I think she did but we never got around to really discussing it. That wasn't really important, you know? The thing was that someone saw us together. Then she dumped me and the accident happened, and we never spoke again."

Josie said, "What were they transferring from car to car?"

"I don't know. I wasn't really paying attention that much. Like I said, Faye was freaking out."

"What about the car the other guy was driving?" asked Gretchen. "Do you remember what kind of car it was?"

"I remember it was red. Red and small. I don't know, like maybe a Prius or something. I can't say for sure, though."

Something sparked to life in the back of Josie's mind. She turned to Gretchen. "I know someone who drives a red Prius."

Gretchen said, "Let's go."

CHAPTER THIRTY-FOUR

Twenty minutes later, Josie and Gretchen stood inside one of the CCTV rooms at Denton Police Headquarters staring at a television screen that streamed live footage of one of their interrogation rooms. On the screen, Ted Lesko sat at the scarred wooden interrogation table and scarfed down a tuna sandwich like he didn't have a care in the world. Next, he guzzled the can of Coke that Mettner had provided him and let out a healthy belch.

"It cannot be this easy," Gretchen said.

"It's not," Mettner replied. "If you're looking at him for the murders, he's got an alibi for most of the time we're talking about here. During the three-hour window during which Faye Palazzo was taken from her home—between the time Sebastian left for work and came home for lunch—we've got him out on deliveries on the opposite side of town. I've got GPS coordinates, receipts, and even video of him arriving at various houses and businesses with his food deliveries. He also works for Downey's Grocery Market and WheelShare, the ride-sharing app, and those work hours account for most of the rest of his alibi for both the time that Faye was missing and the time that Krystal was missing."

Gretchen said, "But all we really know for sure is that he couldn't have taken Faye. It's possible that he could be working with someone else. He's still got time where no one else can verify his whereabouts during which both Faye and Krystal were missing."

"True," Mettner conceded. "But he's got GPS on his car and it was where he says it was during all of those times."

Josie asked, "Is it the only car registered to his household?"

"Yeah. Also, we checked out his house. He gave us permission. He's got a garage like everyone else but a tree fell into the roof a few months ago, did some serious damage that he hasn't been able to afford to have fixed. There's no way he could hold someone in there with the place sealed off well enough to cause carbon monoxide poisoning."

"Shit," Josie said. Something was bothering her, like an annoying paper cut that burned every time she washed her hands, but she couldn't figure out what.

Mettner said, "He gave us permission to search his house and car and even to have the ERT come in and look around, take whatever they wanted."

"Did they find any candles by any chance?" Josie asked.

"Yankee candles," Mettner said. "No vigil candles."

Gretchen said, "And he hasn't asked for a lawyer?"

"No, but I haven't read him his Mirandas yet."

"Doesn't look like you need to," said Josie. "Let's find out what he was doing with Miles Tenney two years ago, and then we'll cut him loose."

Josie walked from the CCTV room into the interrogation room. Ted's face lit up in a smile when he saw her. "We meet again," he said. "You know you're the only person who can piss off Andrew Bowen more than me?"

Josie laughed and took the seat across from him. "Is that so? You don't like Bowen?"

"Does anyone like that guy?"

"Good point. Ted, did Detective Mettner tell you why we asked you to come here today?"

"It's pretty obvious from all the questions he asked," Ted replied. "This is about the Krystal Duncan thing—and he said another parent was murdered. Pretty messed-up shit."

"You're not worried about being brought in for questioning?"

He shook his head and leaned back in his chair, stretching his arms over his head. He brought them back down and rested his elbows against the table. "Nah. I didn't kill anyone. No reason to be nervous."

Josie tilted her head to the side, regarding him skeptically. "You're not worried that we'll try to pin these murders on you? Plant evidence? You're the only person we can think of who might have a beef with the bus crash parents."

He leaned in, bunching his shoulders up toward his neck. "I'm not the trusting type, if that's what you're getting at, but I've been through the system. I've seen how it works. No matter what you cops plan on doing to me, my best play right now is complete transparency. Take that however you will."

"All right," Josie said. "I need to ask you something about before the bus accident."

"Shoot."

"You met with Miles Tenney, at least once, in the empty lot on Tallon Street. You two were moving things back and forth from the trunks of your cars. What were you doing? How do you know Miles?"

Ted's eyebrows shot up in surprise. Then he laughed. "That is going way back. Is Miles dead too?"

"We don't know."

"If you don't know then he probably is dead because that guy was in deep to some pretty nasty people. Owed a lot of money. I was helping him out 'cause he didn't want to be seen pawning stuff. Big, important car salesman. Supposed to be rolling in money. Could barely keep up with his mortgage. I had to lend him money for gas a few times. You believe that?"

When Josie didn't respond, Ted kept talking. "He was too embarrassed to go into pawn shops and sell stuff so he asked me to do it for him. We'd meet now and then so he could give me whatever he had to sell. I'd take it and pawn it at shops anywhere from here to Philadelphia. I kept a small cut and gave him the rest. Nothing illegal about that."

"Except that the stuff he was giving you was stolen. Did he tell you that?"

Ted was not fazed. "No, he didn't tell me where he got it and I didn't ask. You can try to pin me with theft by receiving stolen property since the statute of limitations on that is five years, but you'd have to know the value of the property that was received and be able to prove that I knew it was stolen in order to make that one stick."

Josie knew that a theft by receiving stolen property charge without a solid witness or more definitive details would be next to impossible to prove, but she wasn't interested in arresting Ted at this point. All she really wanted was information about Miles, and he was giving that freely. "Why did Miles ask you for help?"

Ted laughed. "Come on, Detective. You saw the neighborhood Miles lived in—that my dad and I lived in—you think anyone there has ever set foot in a pawn shop? When I first got out and moved back in with my dad, he would take me to parties and barbecues so he could keep an eye on me. Once he realized I wasn't going to go batshit crazy if he left me alone, I didn't have to go sit around eating shitty food with strangers for hours at a time. But I met Miles at one of those barbecues and so he knew who I was. Then I delivered food to the dealership a few times. Talked to him there. He knew the deal. Knew I'd been in prison. He asked me if I knew how to pawn stuff or sell stuff on the black market. I said, 'Sure, if you're willing to cut me in.'"

"How long were you and Miles doing this?"

"I don't know. A couple of years? Maybe three?"

"Did it stop after the accident? Because of the accident?"

Ted gave her a dry look. "Well, it would have been pretty fucking awkward, don't you think? Hey, my dad killed your kid. You still want my help selling shit? Yeah, it stopped after the accident, because of the accident. I never talked to him again."

"Did you ever see anyone else in the clearing when you met up? Did anyone ever see you two together?"

"I don't think so. There was one time we heard someone beeping but we couldn't tell where it was coming from, so we just closed everything up and left."

"Miles didn't see anyone? He never mentioned anything?"

Ted rubbed his jaw. "He said that he thought he had seen someone he knew parked farther out in the clearing and he wanted to go. I looked but didn't see anything. But just to be on the safe side, we left. After that, I would wait till after dark and go to his house, wait outside the garage in his side yard."

Changing topics, Josie said, "Did you ever talk to your dad about the day of the accident?"

"You're kidding me, right? Bowen would have a shit fit if he knew you were even asking about the accident. I'm not allowed to say shit about that."

Josie plunged ahead anyway. "At least tell me why your dad would lie about the reason he took a drink that day."

"What are you talking about?"

"He told investigators he had a drink that day because he was upset that his mother had been admitted to hospice care that morning. But that decision had been made at least a month before that, and your grandmother had already been receiving hospice care for all that time. Why lie about that?"

"I honestly don't know," Ted said. "Look, between you and me, I've asked him a few times what happened that day. Like, why did he throw his whole life away like that? I know he had more than just alcohol in his system. Bowen told me. It was in the news. I said, 'After you rode my ass all these years to get on the straight and narrow, you down a bunch of pills and booze and kill a bunch of kids? What the hell for?' He won't talk about it. Even to me."

"Ted," Josie said. "I just have one more question. Do you or your dad own any other property besides the house you live in? Something out in the country? Maybe something your grandmother left you? A farm or something?"

It would be easy enough to check the property records, but Josie wanted to know how he would answer. He laughed again. "Another property? Please. Anything that's not nailed down has been sold to pay for my dad's fancy lawyer. No, we don't own any other property but my dad's house, and I'm barely making the payments on that because Andrew Bowen gets almost every dime I make."

CHAPTER THIRTY-FIVE

Back in the great room, Josie sat at her desk, clutching the rosary beads in one hand while Gretchen, Mettner, and Chief Chitwood stood in a semicircle a few feet away. Gretchen gave Chitwood a report on Faye Palazzo's autopsy and the interview with Ted Lesko. Dan Lamay brought up a partial list of area farms and any other property that had a barn on it. None of the owners' names stood out to Josie, Gretchen, or the Chief, but the Chief dispatched Mettner to start visiting each farm to look for slatted floors and barn animals with pale-yellow hair.

Gretchen said, "That's probably going to be just about every barn, Chief."

Chitwood huffed, glaring at her. "You have a better idea, Palmer?"

Gretchen didn't respond, instead sitting down at her desk and booting up her computer to write up some reports.

Mettner said, "I'll be on the lookout for a diamond earring as well."

Chitwood added, "Anyone who won't let you take a look around their barn is a red flag, you got that?"

"Sure thing," Mettner said, jogging off to the stairwell.

Chitwood disappeared into his office, door slamming. Josie's cell phone chirped with a text message. "It's Noah," she told Gretchen. "He's bringing early dinner, and he said he went over to Krystal Duncan's law firm and started going through the files that they didn't give us—the files Krystal wasn't working on directly. Apparently he found something in those files."

"Well, I hope it's good," muttered Gretchen. "The lead, not the dinner. Actually, both better be good."

The stairwell door swung open, and a short whistle sounded. Josie looked over to see Drake motioning toward her. "Hey," he said. "I've got Dee Tenney downstairs if you want to talk to her. You know, about any secrets she might be hiding?"

Josie laughed as she walked over to him and followed him into the stairwell. "It's not usually that easy," she told him. "People don't generally like to tell their secrets to police."

Drake led the way down to the first floor. He pulled up short outside the door to the conference room and turned back to Josie. "Amber's in there with her now finalizing what we're going to say to the press."

"She agreed to go public with what Miles was doing?"

Drake nodded. "It was a hard sell. She's still in a little bit of denial that Miles had let things get so bad without her knowing anything at all. She also has zero desire to deal with the press. All the parents had enough of that after the bus crash, she said."

Josie put a hand on her hip. "How'd you convince her then?"

"Not me," Drake said, pointing to his chest. "Your crack press liaison in there did the job. She told Dee it was strictly an issue of safety, to keep herself and anyone else she cared about alive and unharmed."

"It was Heidi, then," Josie said, thinking of how many times Corey Byrne had said those words when they interviewed him.

Drake laughed. "Yeah, that kid's something else. Wouldn't leave Dee's side. Listened to every word. Mouthed off like crazy." His appreciative smile told Josie that he wasn't annoyed by Heidi in the least. In fact, Josie detected a note of admiration in his voice. "Honestly, if Dee didn't care about that girl so much, I think she'd stand outside waiting for Cerberus to come kill her."

"Yeah," said Josie. "I got that impression, too. Is Heidi here with her now?"

"No, she had to go to camp for the day. She said she'd stop by Gloria Cammack's house to see Dee tonight."

The door to the conference room swung open and Amber stepped through it, her laptop tucked under one arm. "She's all yours," she told them.

Drake motioned for Josie to go inside. "After you."

Dee sat in one of the executive chairs, looking small and insubstantial. Her skin was sallow, her hair greasy. Josie wondered if she had slept or bathed since they last saw her. She looked up at Josie, hope filling her wide eyes. "Did you find Miles? Is he okay?"

Josie sat down next to her while Drake lingered near the door. "I'm afraid not, Dee, but the FBI is looking for him and they've got a lot more resources than we do."

The hope in her eyes extinguished. She fingered her wedding band. "I don't even know if I want to see him again. We weren't together anymore but not because I stopped loving him. It was just that once Gail died, everything fell apart."

"Unfortunately, that's very common following the death of a child," Josie said. "I'm so sorry, Dee."

"Do you believe me?" Dee asked, her voice taking on a sudden aggressiveness. "'Cause if you don't believe me, how will anyone else? The press, the public, this… this crime syndicate?"

"Believe you about what?" Josie asked.

Dee leaned closer to Josie. "That I didn't know what Miles was doing or how bad things were financially."

"Dee, it's not my place to—" Josie began.

"No one is going to believe I didn't know, but you have to understand, I was a housewife Gail's entire life. Miles worked. He handled all the finances. That was his job, his role. My job was to be Gail's mother. I never wanted for anything. Neither did Gail. Anything we asked for, Miles made it possible. We were happy. I had no reason to doubt, to suspect—" She broke off as a sob erupted from her throat. She buried her face in her hands.

Drake slid a box of tissues along the table. Josie caught them and held them in her lap, waiting for Dee to look back up. She said, "You trusted your husband, Dee. There's nothing wrong with that. I don't think anyone can fault you for that. People don't usually marry people they don't trust."

Dee looked up and barked a little laugh. She took a tissue from the box and wiped her cheeks. "I guess that's true."

Josie cast about in her mind for a subtle way to ask Dee if she had any secrets that a killer would want exposed, but came up short. She decided to ease back into the subject of secrets by continuing on with some of the things Miles had kept from her.

"While I'm here," Josie started. "I just wanted to ask you about Ted Lesko. Someone told us that before the accident, they saw him and your husband together. When we asked Ted about that, he admitted that he'd been helping Miles sell or pawn things to make money. Did you know Ted as well?"

Dee put her hands in her lap and sniffled. "No, no. Ted wasn't helping Miles. Oh, and yes, I knew who Ted was because Virgil had brought him to a couple of parties at our house when he first got out of prison. Did you know he was in prison?"

"Yes," Josie said. "He mentioned it."

"Oh, I'm sure he did. What did he tell you it was for? Jaywalking? Virgil told me about it, you know. Years ago, right before Ted came home. He was so embarrassed and so worried that Ted would be worse off once he got out than he was when he went in. There was some girl Ted became obsessed with while he was in college in Philadelphia. He used to watch her through her windows, like a peeping Tom. He followed her everywhere, stalked her on social media. He even stalked her friends. It was an ugly situation. He stole things out of her apartment, too."

Josie asked, "Did Virgil tell you how he met the girl? Was it someone he'd been dating?"

Dee waved a hand in the air. "I don't know. Virgil never said. I just know it was bad. Creepy." She shuddered. "Ted Lesko is creepy. I still can't believe they didn't put him on the sex offender registry, although I know Virgil was grateful for that. I always thought, what if he escalates from stalking to attacking some poor woman? But he was Virgil's son and when it comes to your kids, you just want what's best for them, no matter what. But Ted still gave me the creeps."

"Well, you knew he was an ex-con," Josie pointed out. "What makes you think he wasn't helping Miles?"

Dee stared at Josie as if she was missing a very obvious fact. "He was in prison for stalking women, not for selling stolen goods."

From the doorway, Josie heard Drake stifle a laugh. She kept her own expression neutral. "Sometimes criminals branch out," she told Dee.

Dee shook her head. "No, no. He was up to his old ways. I—I didn't want to say anything to anyone because it's over now and it doesn't matter, and it stopped after the accident, but I saw him. I saw Ted."

"What do you mean?" Josie asked. "Saw him where? Doing what?"

"Outside of our house. In the evenings. He would just be out there, lurking. I sent Miles out there a few times to talk to him—I didn't want to call 911 because of Virgil—but he always left as soon as Miles went out there. The other day when I heard someone out there, for a moment, I thought maybe it was Ted again, but I didn't see anyone. The FBI thinks it was probably someone from that criminal organization. Cerberus. But I'm telling you, before the accident Ted was regularly stalking me."

"Dee," Josie said. "Ted wasn't stalking you. He was waiting for Miles. Someone had seen them exchanging goods at their old meeting place so they stopped going there. Miles told Ted to come to the house."

Dee folded her arms across her chest. "Who told you that? Ted? You're going to believe him over me? I know what I saw, and besides, Virgil told me I was right."

"What do you mean?"

"Like I said, I didn't want to call 911 and get Ted in trouble. I knew how badly Virgil wanted him to get better, to lead a normal life. I was a parent, too. I understood that. When I saw him hanging out around the house, I went to Virgil instead of the police. I told him what was happening, and he told me he would look into it. He even thanked me for coming to him first. About a week later, I talked to him at the bus stop. Our kids were always the last to be dropped off. He asked me to stay for a minute. I sent Gail walking the rest of the way to the house and talked with him. He was upset. Really upset. He said he'd found proof of what I said. Proof that Ted was stalking again."

"What kind of proof?" Josie asked.

"I don't know. I didn't ask. I didn't want to know, to tell you the truth. He just told me that he would handle it and if he couldn't, he'd definitely get the police involved. I trusted him. Then the accident happened, and well, I could care less what Ted Lesko does to me or anyone else."

Josie's heart raced. She said, "When was this? What day did you have this conversation with Virgil?"

Dee took a moment to think about it. Then she said, "The day before the bus crash."

CHAPTER THIRTY-SIX

Back upstairs, Josie found Gretchen and recapped the conversation with Dee Tenney. Noah appeared with bags of takeout and started spreading them across the desks, listening to the update. Even as Josie talked, the smell of food wafted toward her, making her stomach grumble. As soon as she finished speaking, she dug into one of the takeout containers, letting Gretchen take in the new developments.

Gretchen said, "Either Ted Lesko is lying about what he was doing at Dee Tenney's house on those nights or Dee Tenney completely misunderstood what was happening."

"That's what I thought," Josie said. "But if that were true then what the hell did Virgil find that made him think that Ted was stalking women again?"

Noah plopped into his desk chair and threw his feet onto his desk. "We have an independent witness in Corey Byrne who confirmed Ted was helping Miles and Ted admitted to it. Why else would he be at the Tenney household?"

Gretchen shrugged. "Because deep in his heart, he's a stalker? You know, it's possible he was assisting Miles in his criminal enterprises and stalking women on his own time."

"That is true," Josie said.

"What about the original case against Ted Lesko?" Noah asked. "Didn't you say that Ted told you the whole thing came about as a result of a break-up? You just told us that Dee Tenney said he was stalking 'some girl.' It would be easy enough to check on that and find out if Ted was lying about it being an ex-girlfriend or not."

Gretchen said, "But he still stalked her."

"Yeah," Noah agreed. "I'm not suggesting it was right, but someone who stalks an ex-girlfriend may not go on to stalk strangers or casual acquaintances. It's very possible that Dee Tenney was biased against Ted because Virgil had confided so much to her about his criminal history. She also didn't know that Miles was using Ted to sell stolen goods. She could have misconstrued that entire situation, and Miles isn't here to disabuse her of the notion that Ted was stalking her. Either way, whether Ted lied about the origins of the stalking case against him would tell you a lot about him."

Josie said, "I'd also like to know what Virgil found. He had this conversation with Dee the day before the accident. He was upset. Isn't it possible that whatever it was he found was the thing that drove him to drink on the day of the accident and that he lied about it so that he didn't incriminate his son?"

Gretchen said, "I think that's not only possible but probable. I'll call Andrew Bowen and demand a meeting with Virgil Lesko."

Josie laughed. "You're not going to get it."

But Gretchen was already dialing. After a curt exchange of words with Andrew Bowen's secretary, she hung up. Josie turned back to Noah. "What did you find in the files at Krystal's firm?"

Noah put his feet onto the floor and leaned his elbows on his desk. "It's about the orthodontist that Bianca Duncan and the Cammack kids went to—they had to close the practice. They're facing a huge malpractice suit, and guess who's bringing it?"

Josie said, "Gil Defeo."

Noah shook his head. "No. His partner, Richard Abt. That's why Krystal wasn't working on it."

"But she would have had access to the file through the firm's database," Gretchen supplied.

"Yes. About a month before she went missing, Krystal was having lunch with the other legal assistants in the office, and they were complaining about the case. Evidently there are a lot of clients—but not enough for a class action suit. Anyway, when Krystal heard the name of the orthodontist, she mentioned to the other women that that was where Bianca had been going. She even wondered whether, if Bianca had lived, she would have been one of the medical malpractice clients."

"Did they let her go through the files?" Josie asked. "Where is this going?"

Noah said, "Her going through the files never came up, but Abt and Defeo got a copy of the orthodontist's patient database through the discovery process so it was there if Krystal ever wanted to access it. It would have been easy. I did it while I was over there. Carly let me use her login credentials to go through the firm's server. I was able to then get into the orthodontist patient records and look up Bianca Duncan's name. Guess what I found in her chart?"

Josie felt a prickle along the back of her neck. "A cancellation for an appointment on the date of the accident."

"Right. Made by parent, not by the orthodontist."

Gretchen said. "Which means that when Krystal looked it up, she knew that Nathan had lied about why the appointment was cancelled that day and why the kids ended up on the bus. Was that the thing that sent her to the East Bridge looking for something stronger than pot to calm her nerves?"

Josie said, "We'll never know but you said that she found out about the file from her coworkers at least a month before she went missing, right? She didn't get upset enough to ask Skinny D for something more potent than weed until a couple of days before she went missing. I think there was something else she found out. Something that bothered her more."

Gretchen said, "What could be worse than finding out that your friend and neighbor caused your kid to be on the bus the day of the accident?"

Josie shook her head. "I have no idea, but I think there was more. There had to be more."

Noah stood up and stretched his arms over his head. "I'm going back over to Abt and Defeo. They're all going to be there pretty late 'cause they're prepping for a trial. Multi-car accident. If there's something else that Krystal found out from the work files, I might be able to find it. I can search for the names of the other parents in the other attorney's files, see what comes up." He looked at Josie. "You okay at home without me?"

She smiled. "I'll survive."

CHAPTER THIRTY-SEVEN

Nevin had the whole seat to himself. He had tried talking to Gail and Bianca, but they weren't talking at all anymore. Actually, the entire bus had gone eerily silent. For a minute, Nevin wondered if everyone had died or something. But that was a weird thought. He had to sit up really straight in order to look around the whole bus. Everyone was still alive, although they looked kind of sick. Now it was just the last of them: him, Gail, Bianca, Wallace, Frankie, and Heidi. Usually, the girls were talking or Wallace was messing with one of them, but not today.

Nevin looked out the window. He recognized the vacant lot that came right before their streets. A flash of color caught his eye. There was a truck or something back there today. He wondered if they were finally going to build something there. He really wanted a skate park or an arcade or something, but his mom always said they'd only build houses there if they built anything at all.

Suddenly, the bus shook. Nevin's whole body jerked side to side. A weird sound like metal scraping came from the outside. Then the bus sped up.

Wallace said, "Holy crap, you guys. I think Mr. Lesko just hit someone."

CHAPTER THIRTY-EIGHT

The rest of the evening was spent writing up her reports and listening to Gretchen argue with Andrew Bowen over the phone about getting a meeting with Virgil Lesko. After that, Gretchen called some of her old contacts in the Philadelphia Police Department to get more details on the stalking case that had sent Ted Lesko to prison for three years. After a full hour of muttering "mm-hmms" and "uh-huhs" into her phone receiver, Gretchen hung up and looked at Josie. "Ted Lesko was telling the truth. It was an ex-girlfriend."

"But Dee was right that his behavior was pretty bad," Josie said. "Or he wouldn't have gone to prison."

"Yes. I think after what Virgil shared with Dee about Ted, she was right to be concerned. I would have been."

"Where do we go from here?"

"Home," Gretchen said. "We've been at this all day. It's almost eight p.m. Mett and Noah are still running down leads so things are still moving."

Josie could not deny the exhaustion weighing her limbs down. The thought of sprawling across her couch in a pair of sweats was more than enticing. Of course, once she was on the couch, she didn't feel tired at all. As if sensing her restlessness, Trout ran over, put his two front paws on the edge of the couch and dropped his Kong into her lap. Then he stared at her intently.

Laughing, Josie sat up and took the Kong. "I swear, if you could talk," she told him. "I think you'd be saying, 'this Kong isn't going to throw itself.'"

For that she got a full-throated bark. He hopped around, anxiously awaiting the game of fetch he had initiated. Josie lowered herself onto the floor and tossed the Kong across the room. Trout brought it back again and again until they fell into a rhythm. Josie's mind went to the Duncan and Palazzo cases, turning all the information they had over and over in her head. Their team was still missing pieces.

Krystal Duncan had been digging for information about the bus accident, even going so far as to visit Virgil Lesko in prison. What had she been after? More importantly, what had she stumbled upon that had gotten her murdered? Had she told Faye Palazzo about whatever she found? Was that why Faye had died next? But if both women had been killed to silence them, why leave the names of the bus crash children on their arms? If the killer was killing to keep the secrets that Krystal had unearthed then why go to so much trouble to expose everyone else's secrets?

If only, if only.

Was someone out there playing the If Only game with the parents of the West Denton Five? If so, where did it start and where did it end? Josie tried to follow the convoluted path of if onlys in her mind, starting with the information Krystal had dug up.

If only Nathan hadn't canceled the orthodontist appointments that day, Bianca and the Cammack children would not have been on the bus. If only Gloria hadn't called Nathan and demanded that he come home, then he wouldn't have canceled the appointments. If only Miles Tenney hadn't been stealing from his neighbors, then Wallace Cammack's PlayStation would have been exactly where it was supposed to be when Gloria forgot her planner and came home to get it. Then she wouldn't have called Nathan, and he wouldn't have canceled the appointments.

Josie couldn't find the connection between Krystal or the Cammacks and Faye Palazzo, but Faye had been murdered next. Faye had seen the bus swerving that day—or rather, Corey had seen it and told her—but she had chosen not to go after it because she didn't want to be seen with Corey. If only she had not been so worried about hiding the affair, she would have agreed to go after the bus. Maybe Corey could have flagged Virgil down or detained him at one of the earlier bus stops, perhaps they could have prevented the accident altogether.

Who was left?

Dee and Sebastian, just like Josie had told Chief Chitwood. Josie didn't know the thing Sebastian hadn't told anyone—if there was a thing at all—but Dee had told Josie something that she hadn't told anyone and that was about Ted. What if Dee was wrong about Ted? What if Ted was telling the truth? He'd been at the Tenneys' house not because he was stalking Dee but because he was involved in a criminal enterprise with Miles. But, as Josie and the team had been over, why would Virgil think that Ted was stalking someone again? What had he found?

The answer was so obvious it was laughable. "Stolen property," Josie said out loud. Trout skidded to a halt on the living room carpet, Kong hanging from his mouth, ears pointed straight up, head tilted to the side as if to indicate for Josie to keep talking. She laughed. "Stolen property," she told the dog. Unimpressed, Trout dropped the Kong in front of her again and she tossed it. Then she picked up her phone and called Noah.

"Ted was receiving stolen property from Miles to sell," she said when he answered.

There was a beat of silence, then Noah said, "Yeah. Go on."

"Property that Miles had taken from his neighbors' homes, including jewelry. Ted was living with Virgil. Dee saw Ted lurking outside the home and sent Miles out to get rid of him but really he was there to pick up stuff from Miles."

"Which he took home with him until he could move it," Noah said. "Okay, I see where you're going with this. Dee told Virgil she thought Ted was stalking her. Virgil conducted his own investigation and probably found women's jewelry among Ted's things."

"Yes," Josie agreed. "Virgil had no idea that Ted was just making a little extra cash helping Miles Tenney move stolen goods. If he found women's jewelry, like Faye Palazzo's earrings or a women's purse like Gloria Cammack's clutch, immediately after Dee accused Ted of stalking, he would naturally have come to the conclusion that Ted was stalking someone again."

"Virgil had worked hard to get Ted back on track. He would have been upset. Upset enough to have a drink with lunch," Noah said.

"If only Dee hadn't misconstrued Ted's presence outside her house," Josie muttered. "She wouldn't have told Virgil that she thought he was stalking her, and Virgil wouldn't have looked through Ted's things and found something that seemed incriminating. Then Virgil wouldn't have felt compelled to have a drink that day."

Noah said, "What are you saying? That the accident wouldn't have happened?"

"Yes," Josie said. "I think so." She took a moment to explain what Dr. Rosetti referred to as the "If Only game."

Noah took a moment to think when she finished. In the background, Josie heard the rustling of paper and the clack of a keyboard. Finally, he said, "You're forgetting about the narcotics. Virgil Lesko tested positive for a large amount of oxycodone that day, and that makes sense. One drink—even two or three or four—would not have accounted for him driving so recklessly even before the crash. He was really wasted that day."

Josie said, "True, but he told Gretchen that he hadn't taken oxy."

"So he lied," Noah said. "We already know he lied about why he had a drink that day. Why not lie about the oxy?"

"But he admitted to drinking. Why admit to drinking but not taking narcotics? He wasn't going to make it any better for himself. The labs don't lie. Unless—"

She broke off as more pieces of the puzzle clicked into place. "Unless what? Josie?"

She worked through it in her mind twice before she spoke again. "Of all the parents alive and accounted for, the only person who doesn't have a game piece in the If Only game is Sebastian Palazzo."

"So? Maybe he didn't know anything. Maybe he had no secrets. The guy is pretty pathetic, Josie."

"Maybe he is but that doesn't mean he didn't have a secret. Noah, Sebastian Palazzo is a pharmacist. He owned his own pharmacy until pretty recently—within the last couple of years—when a larger chain bought him out."

"What are you saying? You think Sebastian Palazzo gave Virgil the oxy? Is that his secret? If only he hadn't slipped Virgil the oxy, Virgil wouldn't have been so wasted that day and maybe he wouldn't have crashed? Why would Sebastian give Virgil oxy before he drove the bus?"

"I don't know," Josie said. "But it would fit with the overall pattern of the case. If Krystal Duncan somehow found out that Sebastian gave Virgil the drugs that led to him crashing that bus, that would have sent her completely over the edge. Don't you think?"

"And she tried to stop herself from going over that edge by asking her pot dealer for the same kind of painkillers?" Noah said with a small laugh.

"Not necessarily," Josie argued. "She told Skinny D she needed something to take off the edge. I don't think it mattered to her what that something was. Noah, we need to focus on Sebastian. Can you search the Abt and Defeo records for his name?"

"I already have. He doesn't come up at all. Not as a client or a defendant or a witness or anything."

"Hold on," Josie said. Leaving Trout in the living room, she ran to the kitchen and opened her laptop. Her heel tapped tile floor as she waited for it to boot up. Once she got her internet browser up, she searched for Palazzo Pharmacy and scrolled through the results. "Looks like Sebastian sold the pharmacy to the larger chain about two and a half years ago and turned a tidy profit while still working there and drawing a salary. But last year, the pharmacy got into hot water because one of the pharmacists filled a prescription with the wrong pills and almost killed a lady."

She heard clicking on the other end. Noah said, "That would have fallen under a personal injury lawsuit. Hang on, I'll search by the chain pharmacy name." A few moments slipped past. Then he said, "Yep. Richard Abt represented that woman against the pharmacy."

"Which means that Abt and Defeo would have gotten all kinds of records in discovery," Josie said.

"Right and although Krystal wouldn't have worked on that case, she would have had access to the files."

"She found something in those files, Noah. I know she did."

"Well, I'm not coming home until I find what she found," Noah said. "But Josie, this doesn't get us any closer to finding the killer."

"Sebastian Palazzo could *be* the killer," Josie argued. "If we find whatever Krystal found and confront him with it, then—"

"Hang on," Noah interrupted. "I'm getting a call from Mett."

Josie heard the beep of an incoming call on her own phone. Pulling it away from her face, she saw it was Chief Chitwood calling. "I've got one from the Chief," she said. "I'll call you back."

But Noah was already gone.

"Chief?" said Josie after swiping answer.

"Quinn," he barked. "I need you to get your ass over to Gloria Cammack's house, pronto."

Josie's stomach tightened. Her first thought was of neither Gloria nor Dee, but of Heidi. "Sir? Is anyone hurt?"

"Hurt? No, Quinn. They're missing. All of them are missing. Gone."

CHAPTER THIRTY-NINE

Gloria Cammack's street was awash with the glow of red and blue lights from police cruisers. Josie parked as close to the house as she could. She counted three marked vehicles: the Chief's truck, Gretchen's car, and a pickup truck Josie remembered seeing at Corey Byrne's job site. Along the pavement opposite Gloria's house, neighbors had lined up to watch the show. A WYEP van pulled up behind Josie. Quickly, before any reporters noticed her, she jogged up the walk to Gloria Cammack's house. A uniformed officer stood sentry outside with a clipboard. Butterflies fluttered in Josie's chest. "You've got a crime scene?" she asked him.

"I don't know. The Chief said not to let anyone who's not the police inside." He waved the clipboard. "And to make sure I keep track of who goes in and out."

Josie nodded. He wrote her name down and she went inside. It looked like someone had turned on every light in the house. She didn't see anyone from the ERT but in the living room, Corey sat on the couch, staring up at Gretchen. His jeans and T-shirt were stained and grimy. "What happened?" Josie asked, drawing up beside Gretchen.

Corey said, "I came to get Heidi. Let myself in because the door was unlocked. No one was here."

Josie said, "It's almost eleven o'clock at night."

"Long day," Corey said. "Besides, I got here an hour ago. Like I said, no one was here. Not Heidi or Dee or even Gloria."

"He tried calling all of them," Gretchen said. "But their phones are in the kitchen."

A sick feeling roiled Josie's stomach. "Purses? Heidi's backpack?"

Gretchen nodded. "In the kitchen. Everything was left behind. Bags, phones, laptops. Gloria's planner."

Just like Krystal Duncan and Faye Palazzo.

"There was freshly popped popcorn in the microwave," Corey said. "And a movie playing on the TV. It's like they all just got up and left."

"What about the unit out front?" Josie asked Gretchen.

"They didn't see anything. They didn't even know anything was amiss until Mr. Byrne came back outside and told them everyone was gone."

"Which means they left through the back," Josie said.

"Right. Chief's got people out back right now. The ERT is over in Krystal Duncan's yard, searching for any clues that might be over there. They already printed the kitchen. We've got a couple of cruisers driving around the neighborhood and some units canvassing neighbors on Krystal's street to see if anyone saw anything."

Corey said, "Where the hell is my daughter?"

Ignoring him, Josie asked, "Did anyone check their phones? Maybe one of them texted someone or left something on their phone—a clue of some kind? Has anyone checked to see where Nathan Cammack is? What about Ted Lesko?"

Gretchen said, "Nothing on the phones. Nathan Cammack is home. We sent a unit to his place already. We pulled Mett from the property search and sent him to track down Ted Lesko. He only had a partial list to begin with. Dan Lamay is still looking up property owners of barns in the county."

"Where's my daughter?" Corey repeated. "I don't understand what's going on here."

Josie turned in a slow circle, as if the room could offer her answers. "Is this Miles?" she said. "Cerberus? Why would all three of them leave with someone?"

"A gun," Gretchen offered. "They'd leave with someone if that person had a gun."

Corey stood up, his tone strident now. "Are you telling me someone came here and took my daughter away at gunpoint?"

"We don't know," Josie told him. "We're just speculating. They could have gone with someone they knew."

"Like who?" Corey said.

Josie said, "What about Sebastian Palazzo? Has anyone checked on him?"

Gretchen said, "The unit is still out front of his house."

"Out front," Josie said. "'Cause that worked out so well here."

"Shit," said Gretchen. "Mr. Byrne, I'm afraid I'm going to have to ask you to go to your home and wait there until we have news."

"Are you kidding me? Someone took my daughter, and you want me to just go home?" he shouted.

Josie said, "The Palazzos are only a block over from Krystal's house."

"Go," Gretchen said. "I'll handle this."

The Cammacks' screen door slammed shut behind Josie. She took off, running in the opposite direction of the press, which was now a cluster of reporters and cameras instead of a single WYEP news van. She passed the top of Krystal Duncan and Dee Tenney's street. More police vehicles crowded the front of the Duncan house. Josie noted the ERT vehicle and Chief Chitwood standing in the middle of the street directing people. Some of the press had found their way over to the secondary scene and were crowding in on police.

Josie made a left onto the next street. A single police cruiser was parked halfway down the block in front of the Palazzo house. Josie rapped on the window when she reached it. "I'm going in to check on Mr. Palazzo. Is there anyone in there with him?"

The officer shook his head. "He had a friend here almost all day. She left a few hours ago. No activity since then. I know that Detective Palmer was worried about this guy trying to hurt himself. I asked his permission to stay with him inside the residence, but he wouldn't grant it."

Josie took out her phone and dialed Sebastian Palazzo's cell phone number. No answer. Same with his home number. She hung up and pocketed her phone. "I'm going inside."

"You want extra units?"

"No," she said. "Everyone's spread thin right now. I'll call you if I need you."

Josie ran up the walk and knocked on the front door. She called out for Sebastian several times but heard nothing. More calls to his cell and landline went unanswered. No sound at all from inside the house, although she could see that there were lights on inside on the first floor.

"Hey."

Josie whipped around to see Noah jogging toward her. Beyond him, parked behind the cruiser was his car. She hadn't even heard him pull up.

"What are you doing here?" she asked.

He moved to the opposite side of the door and unsnapped his shoulder holster. "I found what Krystal found. Came out here, talked to Gretchen. She's busy with Corey Byrne who left the Cammacks house and went right out to the press and blurted out everything."

"Oh great," Josie groaned.

"You shouldn't go in here alone."

She was about to ask what exactly Noah had found when a strangled cry came from inside the house. It sounded like an animal caught in a trap. "Come on," Josie said.

She pulled her weapon at the same time as Noah. The door knob twisted easily in Josie's hand. Sebastian hadn't locked the door. The keening was even louder inside the foyer. Josie swept one corner of the entrance with the barrel of her gun while Noah panned the other. "The living room," Josie told him. He signaled her to go first. Josie crept forward along the right-hand wall until she came to the entryway leading into the Palazzos' black-and-white art deco living area. The room was utterly destroyed. Furniture had been overturned. The lamps and small tables were splintered and crushed. There were gouges in the walls. There was even a dent in the ceiling. The only thing untouched was the life-sized portrait of Faye. Kneeling before it was Sebastian. His thick, dark hair jutted out in every direction. He stared up at the picture of his wife, mewling like a creature that had sustained a fatal wound. His chest heaved beneath a white T-shirt. There was a tear in his khaki slacks along his left thigh.

"Mr. Palazzo," Josie said, speaking loudly to be heard over his cries.

The wailing stopped. Then his left arm shot up and in Josie's direction. Too late, Josie realized it held a gun. She stepped back, out of the doorway, bumping into Noah behind her, but no shot was fired. "Gun," she told Noah. "Sebastian," she called. "It's Detective Josie Quinn. I'm here with my colleague, Lieutenant Noah Fraley. We're here to talk to you."

"Go away or I'll shoot."

"Please, Sebastian, put the gun down. We only came to talk."

"I don't want to hurt you," he yelled. "I was only going to kill myself, but if you try to stop me, I'll kill you, too."

"I'm calling this in," Noah whispered in her ear. "State Police can get a SWAT team out here in twenty minutes."

"I'm not sure we have that long," Josie mumbled. "But do it."

From the Palazzos' living room came quiet sobs. Josie peeked around the doorway to see that Sebastian had lowered the gun to his lap, but not relinquished it. She spoke in a gentler tone this time. "Sebastian, I want to come in there and talk with you, but I need you to put the gun down and kick it over to me. Can you do that?"

"You think I'm stupid?" he yelled.

"No, not at all," Josie said. "I'm just worried about you. I don't want you to hurt yourself."

"Why shouldn't I? I have nothing to live for now. My son, my wife. I tried everything, and it wasn't enough. She lied to me, you know. After everything I gave her, she lied to me. Betrayed me."

"I'm so sorry," Josie said. "But Mr. Palazzo, really, I'd feel much better if I could see your face. If we could just talk to each other, face to face. No guns."

His hand shot up again but this time, he aimed the gun at the photo of Faye and pulled the trigger. The gunshot boomed inside the house, its concussion bouncing off the walls. For a few seconds, Josie heard only silence, then the sound rushed back. Sebastian was muttering something. She couldn't quite make it out.

"Sebastian," she called.

Behind Noah, the uniformed officer rushed through the door, gun at the ready. Noah signaled him to hold.

Turning back to the living room, Josie watched Sebastian lift the gun again and empty the magazine into the photo of his wife until her alluring smile was nothing but a cluster of bullet holes. Once pressure on the trigger failed to launch any more shots, he tossed the gun aside and began to rock back and forth. When the ringing in her ears subsided, Josie heard his words.

"She got what she deserved. She got what she deserved. She got what she deserved."

Josie used her index finger to point toward the living room, signaling Noah to move in. The uniformed officer followed. Josie rushed forward, zeroing in on Sebastian's gun and kicking it even farther from him.

"Hands up," Noah instructed him.

Slowly, Sebastian lifted his palms. Something silver sparkled against the skin of his right hand. Noah kept his pistol trained on Sebastian while Josie leaned in for a better look. It was a necklace with a charm that said *#1 Mom*.

Josie said, "Your son gave that to your wife as a Christmas gift, didn't he? He bought it at the holiday shop at school, you said. You also told us it had been stolen."

As she spoke, Noah motioned for the uniformed officer to come closer. Together, they got Sebastian to his feet and cuffed his hands behind his back. His head lolled on his chest. The necklace fell to his feet. "It was stolen," he replied.

Josie picked it up. "Is this a duplicate?"

"No. That's her necklace. I found it in Virgil Lesko's house. It was maybe a week before the bus crash. I went there to drop off his dying mother's medication from the pharmacy as I had done at least a dozen times as a courtesy to him. I felt badly for him because his mother was dying."

"Where was it?" Josie asked.

"In his bedroom. His mother was in a lot of pain that day. She got sick all over herself. I walked in right as it was happening. I knew she had been prescribed some anti-nausea medication, but Virgil couldn't find it. He said to look in the bathroom but it wasn't there. I called to him and said it wasn't in the bathroom and he said to check the dresser in her bedroom. I was flustered—she was so sick—and I just started opening doors. I didn't even realize it was his bedroom and not hers until I was standing in front of the dresser and there were no pill bottles. There was a wallet and a belt and some loose change and with the loose change, there it was—the necklace. It was right there with his things! That's when I knew. I knew it was him. I didn't know what to do so I took it. I went to the next bedroom, which was the right one, and found the pills. He was so consumed with getting her settled and cleaned up, I didn't have a chance—I didn't talk to him. I didn't know what to…"

He stumbled and it occurred to Josie that he might have been drinking, although she hadn't smelled alcohol on him. Or had he taken something? Something to help him work up the nerve to kill himself? To Noah, she said, "Call an ambulance and let's get him seated here."

The uniformed officer grabbed a piece of the couch and righted it, testing it to make sure it wouldn't topple if they sat Sebastian on it. Satisfied that it would take his weight, he helped Josie lower Sebastian onto it.

"Sebastian," she said. "What did you take? What medication did you take tonight?"

A lazy smile curled his lips. "I'll never tell."

Noah put his cell phone back into his pocket. "Ten minutes," he said.

Sebastian used his chin to motion to the necklace twisted around Josie's palm. "You keep it. You have kids?"

"Sebastian," Josie said. "What did you take tonight?"

"If you had kids, you would know," he went on, oblivious.

Josie looked at the uniformed officer. "Go search the house for any prescription pill bottles."

He nodded and sprinted for the door.

Sebastian said, "When you have kids and your wife has an affair, it's worse. So much worse. And Virgil Lesko. A bus driver! What did she want with a bus driver? I had my own damn business. Was it because I sold the pharmacy? I think she started the affair after that. I knew all along. I could tell. She acted differently. She didn't think I paid that much attention to her, but I noticed everything. Every little thing. I just couldn't figure out who it was until I saw the necklace. Before that, I had even hoped I was wrong. I told her what would happen if she ever cheated on me."

Noah said, "What would happen?"

Sebastian looked up at him. "I told her if she ever cheated on me, it would be the end of everything. Everything. I told her I could never handle that. Not that. She was my whole entire world. I did anything she asked. I worshipped her like a goddess. I gave her my life, and she said this was what she wanted. She didn't want New York City anymore. She didn't want these superficial assholes with flat abs but nothing in their brains. She wanted a regular life. A normal life. A family. I gave her all of that. But I told her, I said, she could never cheat. If she cheated, it would just be total destruction. The apocalypse."

Josie said, "Is that why you killed her? And Krystal?"

He went perfectly still and lifted his eyes to meet hers. What looked like genuine confusion rippled across his face. "What?"

"Total destruction," Josie said. "That must have meant killing Faye, and who knows? Everyone else she considered a friend? Krystal Duncan? What about Gloria, Dee, and Heidi? Where are they, Sebastian?"

"What?" He blinked. "No. No, no, no. I didn't—how could you think that I would… I would never kill anyone. I would never hurt anyone."

Noah said, "But you did."

Sebastian's head whipped in Noah's direction. "What are you talking about?"

"The day of the bus crash. You hurt someone that day, didn't you?"

Josie watched Sebastian's face crumple as his mind slowly put the memories together with Noah's accusation. A sob wracked his body. "I didn't mean it. I never meant for him to get on the bus. I just wanted him to be fired, to be humiliated like I was. I knew he would go to the bus depot to clock in. I never thought for a minute that his supervisor would let him drive in his condition!"

Josie looked at Noah, who explained, "The records from Abt and Defeo show that on the day of the bus crash, Sebastian created a prescription for Virgil Lesko for oxycodone. The prescribing doctor was a guy who had passed away a few days earlier so his license hadn't yet been flagged. Sebastian used that doctor's license to put the prescription through. It was marked as delivered."

"I didn't mean it!" Sebastian howled. "I didn't mean for anyone to get hurt. Virgil was having an affair with my wife! I had delivered his mother's medication for months. I was good to him, and he betrayed me."

Noah said, "Was Virgil drinking when you got there?"

Sebastian looked up, eyes glassy with tears. "No. He wasn't. But I could see he was upset. I was just going to put the crushed oxy into his coffee or something, but he was visibly upset. I tried to get him talking so he wouldn't catch on to what I was doing, and he started saying all this stuff about his son being a stalker or something. He made me promise not to tell. I told him that I understood. I understood that kind of betrayal because Faye was having an affair. He didn't even blink! He was so fake, telling me how sorry he was, how I could always come and talk to him. The audacity! I couldn't believe it. He always kept vodka at the house. That was his thing. I suggested we share a drink. I could mix it with fruit juice. He always had that for his mother."

Josie said, "But he had to drive the kids that afternoon."

"Yes, of course," said Sebastian. "It was very hard to convince him, but eventually, I did. I made the drinks, mixed the oxy into his, but I'm telling you, I only meant for him to get caught drunk by his supervisor and get fired. That's it. No supervisor in their right mind would have let him drive in his condition."

Josie said, "But the supervisor wasn't there that day because his wife was having a baby."

"I didn't know!" Sebastian cried. "I didn't know!"

Sirens sounded from outside. The ambulance. Josie looked at Noah. The silent flood of communication between them lasted only seconds. They could tell him that he'd gotten the wrong man; that it wasn't Virgil Faye had been having an affair with, but Corey.

If only, if only.

If only Sebastian hadn't gotten the wrong man. He wouldn't have convinced Virgil to have a drink and dosed him with oxycodone before sending him on his afternoon bus route. But would it make a difference at this point if Sebastian knew the truth? Did they have anything to gain by telling him?

Noah said, "Mr. Palazzo, where are Gloria, Dee, and Heidi?"

Sebastian shook his head. "I don't know what you're talking about!"

"What did you do with them?" Josie asked. "Where did you take them?"

"I didn't take them anywhere. I didn't take anyone anywhere!"

The uniformed officer skidded into the room, an orange pill bottle in his hand. "Here," he said. "It was in the room leading from the house to the garage. Anti-anxiety medication, looks like, prescribed to his wife. Empty."

The front door banged open and two EMTs burst into the house with a gurney. She and Noah gave them a full report and waited for them to leave with Sebastian. Standing outside on the Palazzos' lawn, Noah turned to her. "I'm not sure he's our guy."

Josie felt that old tickle of discomfort she got when the puzzle pieces of a case weren't fitting together quite right. "Me either," she said.

Noah held up his phone, which showed an incoming call from Mettner. He swiped answer and listened. His phone volume was set high enough that Josie could hear Mettner's words from where she stood.

"I'm at the supermarket in Southwest Denton where Ted Lesko was supposed to be working an overnight shift. He's not here. He was a no-show. Boss called his phone but he's not answering. He said it's not like Ted to do something like this because he owes his dad's attorney so much money."

Josie met Noah's eyes. "Tell Mett we'll meet him at Lesko's house."

CHAPTER FORTY

Josie hopped into the passenger's seat of Noah's vehicle. It took almost ten minutes for Noah to thread his way through the crowd of press, onlookers, and now a state police SWAT truck that had gathered in front of Sebastian Palazzo's house. The Lesko house was only a few blocks away, just as Gloria Cammack had told Josie and Gretchen when they first interviewed her. Mettner's vehicle was already parked in front. He got out as they pulled up behind him. Unlike most other homes in this area, the Lesko place was only one story, sprawled across two acres. It had gray siding, a narrow porch, and a one car-garage that, as Mettner had previously reported, had a partially caved in roof covered with blue tarps. A single bulb next to the front door cast a weak circle of light that barely reached the edge of the porch but even from the sidewalk, Josie could see that the front door was ajar. Beyond it was only inky darkness.

Beside her, Noah sighed. "Well, after the night we've already had, I would expect nothing less. Let's get some flashlights, and after the scene at Palazzo's, we should probably wear our vests, too."

They popped their trunks and used the flashlight apps on their phones to dig out the necessary gear. Luckily, since Josie and Noah were married, they always carried gear for one another in their vehicles. He pulled one of Josie's bulletproof vests from the depths of his trunk and handed it to her, together with her extra flashlight. Once all three of them were suited up, they formed a line and moved quietly across the lawn to the front door. Mettner took the lead, pausing at the door to announce themselves and call for Ted. There was no answer.

Josie watched the beam of Mettner's flashlight pan across the entryway before he stepped inside. She followed, using her own flashlight, positioned just under her pistol, to sweep the opposite side of the room. The first thing she noticed was the smell of blood, vomit, and something else. It was death, she realized, as Noah glided past her, leading them into an open area on their left. Josie knew what they were going to find in that room before she followed him.

He called out, "Bodies."

She and Mettner stepped over two prone forms as they trailed Noah, each of them leapfrogging the other as they cleared the entire house. Once they were satisfied there were no immediate threats, they went back through the house, using gloved hands to switch on some lights. As they came back to the room with the two bodies, Josie said, "Get the ERT out here."

Mettner took out his phone, swiped, scrolled, swiped again, and put it to his ear. He stared at the ugly tableau before them until his face turned a pale shade of green. Josie motioned for him to go into the other room, and he immediately obeyed, gulping and then talking into his phone.

She took a step closer to the bodies, noticing that both were male, face down, their hands bound behind their backs with duct tape. Both had gunshot wounds to the backs of their heads—right to the brainstem—with black stippling around the holes, indicating that the gun had been pressed against their skin when the killer fired. Noah stood beside her and pointed to the man with the curly brown locks, now soaked in blood and brain matter. "That's Ted Lesko, isn't it?"

"I believe so," said Josie.

"And that?" Noah pointed to the other man who was taller and thinner and whose shiny shaved scalp was now covered in blood spatter.

Josie sighed. "My money's on Miles Tenney, but it will be up to the medical examiner to make a positive ID."

Noah said, "This isn't the killer we're looking for. This was a professional hit."

Josie nodded. "Looks that way. Maybe Miles came to Ted looking for a place to lay low and Cerberus or whatever other outfit he was into for money caught up with him. I'll wake up Drake and have his team get over here instead of ours."

"Yeah," Noah agreed. "Our ERT is pretty overworked right now."

"Mettner," Josie called, walking into the kitchen. "Cancel our team. We're going to get the FBI's evidence response people out here. We think one of those bodies belongs to Miles Tenney." She stopped when she saw him standing still, phone at his side, staring at an empty insulated food delivery carton on the table. Ted had likely been using it for Food Frenzy deliveries to keep the food as fresh and as hot or as cold as possible until it was delivered. Josie raised a brow. "Mett? What's wrong?"

"Come over this way," he told her. "I'm not going to touch anything since this is a crime scene, but you'll want to see this."

Josie walked over and stood beside him where she had a better view of the inside of the insulated bag. It wasn't empty after all. In the bottom of it were four vigil candles.

CHAPTER FORTY-ONE

It was almost four a.m. by the time they all reconvened at police headquarters: Josie, Noah, Mettner, Gretchen, the Chief, and even Amber, who had a press nightmare on her hands thanks to the chaos in West Denton the night before. For once, she wasn't tapping away at her computer. Instead, she sat at her desk, her chin resting in one palm. She still wore the clothes she'd had on almost twenty-four hours earlier except now they looked wrinkled. Someone had made coffee in the first-floor breakroom. Now the four detectives sat at their desks, drinking from old ceramic mugs. No one spoke. There was too much to process and none of them had slept in what felt like days.

Chief Chitwood emerged from his office, striding over to their desks, red-faced. Loose white hairs floated around his scalp. "I just got off the phone with Drake. He's got a preliminary positive ID on the bodies at the Lesko residence. Just as you suspected, Quinn and Fraley. It's Ted Lesko and Miles Tenney, and yes, Drake believes that was the work of Cerberus. Miles had a few superficial stab wounds to his arms and one shoulder, which look to have been sustained before death. His face was pretty bruised up. Drake thinks that someone other than Cerberus roughed him up at his apartment right before you and Palmer showed up there. That would explain why his blood was found there. He must have been on the run but it looks like Cerberus caught up with him."

"Or a similar organization," Noah muttered.

"Could be," Chitwood agreed. "Regardless, the FBI is taking point on the murders of Miles Tenney and Ted Lesko."

"What about Gloria, Dee, and Heidi?" Josie asked.

"Drake says that Ted and Miles hadn't been dead for very long. Cerberus probably came late at night, did what they had to do, and got out fast. They wanted Miles. They got him. There's no reason for them to have gone after Dee, much less take Heidi and Gloria as well."

Noah said, "But Gloria, Dee, and Heidi had been missing for hours before Ted and Miles were killed. What if Cerberus took them out of the house so they didn't alert the police unit outside and executed them somewhere else?"

"We would have found them by now," Gretchen said. "They wouldn't hold onto two women and a teenage girl. They would have killed them right away and left them. I think whoever killed Krystal Duncan and Faye Palazzo took those women."

Chitwood said, "But it's not Sebastian Palazzo?"

Josie said, "No. We don't think so."

"Based on what?" asked Chitwood.

"My gut," replied Josie.

"Don't come at me with gut feelings, Quinn," Chitwood snarled. "I've got three missing persons right now. We need to find them yesterday—if they're not already dead."

Noah said, "For what it's worth, I think Detective Quinn is right."

Chitwood snorted. "You're her damn husband, Fraley. Of course you think she's right. I need evidence, people. Evidence. This isn't your first day on the job. Now come on, what've you got for me?"

Unfazed, Noah continued, "Sebastian Palazzo had a nervous breakdown in front of us tonight. He admitted to manipulating Virgil Lesko into drinking vodka that he spiked on the day of the bus crash. The crash that killed his own son. I think if he had more to confess, he would have just told us. He thought he was dying from an overdose."

"Well, he didn't die," Chitwood said. "I called the hospital. He's hanging on. Maybe when he wakes up, you can take another crack at him. We need to find these women."

Mettner cleared his throat. All eye turned to him. "I searched the county property records for anything that either Sebastian or Faye Palazzo owned, and there's nothing but their home. No farm. No barn. No other property. I even checked records in the adjacent counties just to be sure."

Josie said, "You're forgetting that Ted Lesko had vigil candles in his home."

Chitwood shook his head. "That doesn't mean Sebastian didn't do it. Maybe they were working together."

Gretchen said, "I do think that Ted was working with someone else. It makes sense. His alibi for Faye's disappearance was airtight."

Mettner said, "But not Krystal's. Although, his alibi is based on the GPS coordinates of his car, Palmer. That's not that solid. When he wasn't working, he could have left his car in his driveway and found other ways to get around."

"Yeah," said Josie. "Like hitching a ride with an accomplice."

"His accomplice would have to live in the neighborhood," Chitwood said. "Which has been your theory all along: that the killer was someone known to the families or a member of one of the families. Sebastian Palazzo fits that bill. He also had access to the vigil candles. His wife was the one who bought them!"

"No. It's not him." Josie spun in her chair and faced her computer, booting it up. "You said look at the evidence, right? What else have we got here? What else?" She started scrolling through the case file. Noah leaned over her shoulder and watched the pages of the file—reports, photos, evidence logs, and warrants—flash across the screen. Josie looked up to see that no one else had moved. "Come on, guys," she said. "Let's take another look at everything we know."

Mettner said, "Everything we know isn't going to tell us where Gloria, Dee, and Heidi are or who has them. We've been over all this. Nothing has changed since the last time we scoured the file."

Noah said, "We've got warrants here for stuff that should be coming in. Check your emails."

Mettner remained still, but Gretchen moved her mouse across her desk. A few minutes later, she said, "I've got something. The results for the IP address search from where Krystal Duncan logged into her law firm's database the Saturday before she was murdered."

"Print it out," said Josie.

Gretchen clicked twice and the ancient printer across the room whirred to life. Pushing her reading glasses up the bridge of her nose, she leaned in closer to the screen.

"What's it say?" Josie asked.

Gretchen read off the street address.

Mettner jumped out of his chair. "Holy shit."

Josie's tired brain worked to remember why she knew the address but before it got there, Noah said, "That's the address of All Natural Child and Family. Gloria Cammack's store."

CHAPTER FORTY-TWO

The sun was creeping over the horizon as Josie led the caravan to the All Natural Child and Family building, tires squealing every time they took a turn. At sixty miles per hour in light traffic, they got there in less than ten minutes. They deployed from their vehicles in tandem: Josie and Noah; Gretchen and Mettner; Chief Chitwood; and three uniformed units behind them. Adrenaline surged through Josie's veins as she strapped on her bulletproof vest once more. Once everyone was ready, Chitwood gathered them around the hood of his car. Mettner had managed to rouse one of Gloria's employees from bed who was only too happy to meet them at the store. Josie watched as he drew a diagram of the building on a piece of computer paper and then handed Chitwood a key to one of the back entrances. "I hope you're right about this," said the man. "If not, Gloria's going to kill me. Oh, shit. No pun intended."

Gloria.

Josie struggled to focus on Chitwood's instructions. Her mind kept wandering back to every interaction she'd had with Gloria Cammack, looking for the signs she had missed. Why hadn't she looked closer at Gloria? She was the only parent who didn't go to the support group. Even Miles had gone from time to time. She was highly organized, efficient, and driven. She was a control freak. It wouldn't have been that much of a challenge for her to orchestrate the killings or even bring Ted into the fold. In fact, by pointing the police in her direction with the very first murder, she'd practically eliminated herself as a suspect. Plus, she'd been able to control the narrative practically from hour one of the investigation by painting her and Krystal as rivals. But how did she know about everyone's secrets?

"Quinn!" barked Chitwood. "You paying attention or what?"

"Sorry, sir," Josie said. "Yes. I'm ready."

Chitwood raised a bushy eyebrow. "Bullshit. Let's go over this again."

This time, Josie paid attention to the plan. She and Gretchen were paired up. When the Chief gave the order, they went to their assigned entrance and waited for one of the other teams to let them inside so they could help clear the rooms. The place was larger than Josie had realized. As she and Gretchen cleared several rooms in their quadrant of the building, one part of Josie's mind was tuned to the other officers calling out "Clear!" every few seconds. Within minutes, there was only silence, and Josie knew they'd hit a dead end. They followed the sound of Chitwood's voice to the lobby. He stood just inside the doors with the employee. Under the fluorescent lights of the interior, Josie saw he was in his twenties, probably just out of college given his Penn State sweatshirt. Mesh shorts and slides completed the youthful look.

"What's your name?" she asked him.

He took a step back as they formed a circle around him, and Josie realized how it must look—a dozen police officers in tactical gear with guns drawn closing in on him. She turned back to the others and said, "Search the entire place for anything that might help us find where Gloria took them. Desks, file cabinets, documents. Anything at all."

Gretchen and Chitwood stayed behind as everyone else dispersed.

"You won't find anything," said the employee. "Everything's electronic and the computers are all password-protected."

"We still have to search," Josie said. "What's your name?"

"Mason Brock."

"Mason, my team searched the property records for this county and all the counties surrounding it to see if Gloria, her ex-husband,

Nate, or this company owns any other buildings or land other than this. We didn't find anything. Does that sound right to you?"

He shrugged. "I don't know. I guess. This is the only place I know about."

Gretchen said, "How long have you worked here?"

"About a year."

"In that time did you ever hear Gloria talk about any other place she might go besides here and home?" Gretchen asked.

"No. I'm sorry. I don't know where she went."

Josie turned around, taking in the shelves of organic products. She thought about the building. While it was big and had garage bays that Gloria could have used to kill someone with carbon monoxide poisoning, there were no slatted surfaces and no place that was rife with animal hair. Where in the hell had Gloria taken Krystal, Faye, and now Dee and Heidi? They could go back to working their way through every farm and barn in the area but in the time that would take, Gloria would kill Dee and Heidi.

Josie's gaze landed on a shelf of caps for infants made in several different colors. She walked over and fingered them, searching for a label, but of course there was none. They were handmade. "Mason," she said. "What are these made from?"

He walked over. "Oh, I'm pretty sure alpaca fur."

Gretchen came over as well. "Do you make them here?"

"Well, I don't make them, but we do have a lady who comes in and makes them. I can show you her work area if you'd like."

"Not necessary," Josie said. "Where do you get the alpaca fur?"

"I don't know. Gloria just brings it in once a week. She gets it from someplace local."

"Would the supplier be in your computer system?"

"I can check," he said. "Hang on."

They followed him into another room where several employee desks were spread out. He went to one in the middle of the room and opened a laptop. After several minutes, he frowned. "It looks like she used to get it from some farm in upstate New York till about a year ago. Then the shipments stopped. I don't see anything after that at all. If she was buying it local, she didn't put it into the system."

Gretchen said, "How many alpaca farms could there possibly be around here?"

"Not that many," Josie said. "But we don't have time to run them all down. Heidi and Dee could be dead already. It doesn't take that long to die from carbon monoxide poisoning."

From behind them came Chitwood's voice. "You're coming at this wrong, Quinn."

Josie turned to him. "Sir?"

"Gloria Cammack was getting the fur from someone. She couldn't have been running this place and an alpaca farm by herself. But if she was using a building on that same farm to kill people, she wouldn't want a record of ownership or of purchasing the fur from someone."

Gretchen said, "But she'd have to pay someone unless they were in on it, and I don't see an alpaca farmer with no ties to the bus crash going in on something like what Gloria and Ted were doing—assuming that we're right that finding the vigil candles in Ted's house means he was involved."

"But—" Josie stopped, her mind puzzling it together. Turning back to Mason, she said, "Can you check the company records for anyone she was paying rent to, or any person listed as an employee or subcontractor who doesn't come to the office?"

"Sure," he said. He worked for a few more minutes and then waved them over. "Here. She pays monthly rent to a woman named Marilyn House."

"For what?" Gretchen asked. "Does it say?"

"No," said Mason. "But I've got an address here."

CHAPTER FORTY-THREE

Marilyn House was a spry eighty-year-old Denton resident who owned several tracts of farmland to the southeast of the city. She didn't bat an eye when Josie and the other detectives rolled up into her driveway at seven thirty in the morning. She was on the porch of her large, white farmhouse, drinking coffee with a fat gray cat in her lap.

"Gloria Cammack?" she said when they asked her about the rental income. "Yeah, she pays me to rent this little old house and old barn out past the alpaca farm about three miles from here. I haven't got many alpacas left but the ones that are there produce some wool. 'Course Gloria usually buys it all up. Pays cash."

Josie said, "Do you take care of the alpacas yourself?"

Marilyn laughed. "Goodness, no. I've got a few young men who tend to them. They rotate according to their personal schedules. So long as the animals are taken care of, I don't care who's there when. Of course, I haven't seen the one gentleman for weeks now. I'd hate to have to fire him."

"What's his name?" asked Gretchen.

"Teddy," said Marilyn. "Teddy Lesko."

From the porch steps, Mettner let out an audible gasp. Marilyn craned her neck to have a look at him. "Something wrong, young man?"

"No," he said. "I just—was Teddy already working here when Gloria rented the building or was it the other way around?"

"You want to know who came first? Teddy. He'd been working here a few years before Gloria showed up wanting to rent that old house and barn. I said, 'Why do you want that old place?' and she said she wanted to raise her own alpacas eventually. The plan was for her to learn from my little operation and start her own. She asked if she could make renovations to the barn. I said, 'Why not?' Any renovations to those two buildings would be an improvement. As long as it doesn't come out of my pocket, I don't mind."

Noah said, "What kind of renovations?"

Marilyn shrugged. "Air conditioning for sure. Other than that, I don't know what all she got up to back there. I saw Teddy bringing back some drywall now and then. Figured they were repairing some of the old walls. Tell you the truth, I suspect Gloria just wanted the place so she could get away. I saw her staying over at the house a few times."

Gretchen thrust a phone into Marilyn's face. "This is Google Earth. We're right where that little red thing is. Can you show us where your alpaca farm is in relation to that?"

It took a few minutes of Marilyn zooming in and out and then Gretchen re-centering the map but eventually, she gave them some directions. Seconds later, they were back in their vehicles, speeding down the road until they came to the dirt turn-off Marilyn had told them about. A long, rutted driveway wound its way through several fields before the alpaca farm came into view. Josie held onto the dash as they bounced mercilessly over the unpaved path. "Keep going," she told Noah. "Gloria's rental should be behind that grove of trees to the left."

The dirt path gave way to flattened grass. To their left was a large, more modern barn with two smaller buildings next to it and a gated area where several alpacas grazed. There were two old pickup trucks next to the barn with faded letters that read: *House Farms*. No one emerged from any of the buildings as the police caravan sped past, heading toward the copse of trees behind the alpaca farm that Marilyn House had shown them on the map. As they rounded the wooded area, Josie saw exactly why Gloria and Ted had chosen this place for their activities. Not only was it hidden away from the rest of the world, but it was even hidden from the small alpaca farm. There would be no reason at all for anyone to come to this place, even the other people Marilyn had hired to tend to her alpacas.

"There," said Noah, veering left.

The house that Marilyn had told them about wasn't much more than a one-room cabin, its wooden walls dull and gray with age and dirt. Beyond it was the barn, a dilapidated white thing with a red roof. A fence made of four-by-four posts and chicken wire ran between the barn and the house. Two dead walnut trees sat across from it, their spindly branches reaching skyward, as if begging the heavens to just take them already.

"There she is!" Noah said.

Josie looked up and saw Gloria emerging from the barn. She was dressed in sweatpants and an oversized Food Frenzy T-shirt. Her hair was loose and mussed. Heavy boots weighed down her feet. She spotted the two vehicles and took off in a dead run, following the fence to the back of the house.

Josie said, "We can't let her get inside. What if she's got a gun in there?"

Noah gunned the engine, bouncing them so hard over the terrain that Josie's head hit the roof, but they were too late. By the time they pulled up to the house with Gretchen and Mettner in tow, Gloria had already disappeared into the back door.

Noah stopped in front of the house, his vehicle turned sideways. Mettner and Gretchen followed suit. As they got out, Noah called, "Take cover behind the vehicles. We don't know if she's armed or not."

As she crouched on the other side of Noah's car, watching the front of the cabin, Josie said, "I've got to get to the barn. That's where Dee and Heidi are."

"You don't know if she's armed or not, Josie. You could run to the barn, and she could pick you off like it's target practice."

From behind the other car, Mettner yelled, identifying them as the police and instructing Gloria to come out of the cabin with her hands in the air. A minute ticked by. Then two. Then three. Josie's heart was in overdrive. Were they too late? Were Heidi and Dee already dead inside the barn, kneeling with wax in their throats? Josie tried to push the images from her head.

At the five-minute mark, Mettner started his spiel again but halfway through it, Gloria emerged from the front of the cabin, strutting toward them with a pistol at her side. She grinned at them. "I'm here! Is this what you wanted?"

Gretchen called, "Put the gun down."

Gloria looked down at her hand as if seeing it for the first time. "Oh, this? I'm not going to use this on you guys. No worries."

Noah said, "Throw it as far away from you as you can."

"I'm afraid I can't," she said. "This is how this whole thing ends. If you're here, then you've figured out my little project: exposing all those lying pieces of shit for their part in murdering my children. I never intended to get away with it, you know. I only wanted to make them pay."

Josie said, "Gloria, you don't have to do this. We can get you help."

She threw her head back and laughed. "Help!" she yelled. "Help!"

Mettner said, "Just put the gun down and we'll talk."

Ignoring him, Gloria said, "There is no help. Surely you've figured that out already." Her expression turned sad for a fleeting moment. "My Teddy never came so I assume you've got him already. Did he tell you how we cooked this whole thing up? Did he tell you how we met? He delivered food to my house! Can you believe that? We recognized each other. It was awkward but there was also this… strange attraction. We were definitely not ever supposed to be with one another. That caused a lot of chemistry."

From the side of his mouth, Noah whispered, "Should we tell her Ted was killed?"

"No," Josie said. "Not now. We have to get that gun and get her into custody so we can check the barn."

"She doesn't seem like she's going to shut up anytime soon," Noah said.

Gloria continued, "… obviously, he told me about what he'd been doing with Miles. I mean, that was crazy. He also told me about seeing Faye with Corey Byrne. That bitch. She always acted so high and mighty at those PTA meetings. Former model and all this bullshit. But the idea to start killing didn't even occur to us until I had this argument with Krystal in the yard one day. We were fighting over that stupid swing set, like I told you, except she confronted me about the whole orthodontist thing and me and Nathan having been home the day of the accident. I was upset but more than that, I was curious about how she found out. We vowed never to tell anyone, but it didn't matter. Krystal put it together by accessing some files at work. I decided to try to be her friend instead of her enemy. It took some doing but eventually I even introduced her to my Teddy, and we came up with this plan to find out everyone's secrets. Krystal and I both were so tired of everyone acting like they were so perfect…"

Josie nudged Noah and lowered her voice. "She's trying to buy time. Dee and Heidi are in there. I bet she was turning on the carbon monoxide to whatever chamber she's got rigged up in there. That's why she was coming from there. If she talks long enough, they'll die."

"Can we risk her shooting one of us or herself, though?" he said.

"… of course then Krystal didn't want to be a part of killing anyone when it came right down to it. She chickened out so we just said hey, let's make her the first victim. She was going to call the police and tell them what we had planned. We couldn't let that happen. So my brilliant Teddy built two chambers—one to keep them in and another to keep the car in. One feeds into the other. It's very clever, actually. I had stopped at Faye's house by chance around the time he was building the chambers because she wanted to talk about the vigil, and I had this idea to take some candles. Pretty savvy, right? Sealing their lips shut? Teddy had kept her Tiffany earrings from way back when he was helping Miles. We thought it would be a nice touch to leave them at the scene. By that time, we had found out Sebastian's little secret. Actually, it was Krystal who found out from her work records. Well, she pieced it together when she saw he had pushed through a script for oxy for Virgil on the day of the crash. She was pretty damn upset about that when she realized what it meant. She was really off the rails—threatening to just go to the police with the whole thing so we had to take her. Then we had her login to her work database while we had her, just to make sure. I needed to see for myself. Hey!"

She swung the gun upward, pointing it in the direction of the nearest vehicle. "Are you guys listening to me or not? I know I said I wouldn't shoot you, but at this point, what have I got to lose? Why shouldn't I take one or all of you with me?"

Mettner called out, "We're listening, Gloria, but you don't need the gun. Just put it down and we'll listen to everything you have to say."

She swung the pistol back and forth, as if she was searching for a target, but they were all ducked out of sight behind the vehicles.

Gloria laughed again, sounding more unhinged by the second. She kept talking. "It was so easy to get them to come with me. Faye, Dee, Heidi. They all trusted me. I had to invent some emergencies to get them to leave everything behind and go with me quickly, but they all followed."

Josie huffed. "I can't wait any longer, Noah. You guys are going to have to distract her while I make a break for the barn."

She inched her way over to where Gretchen and Mettner stood behind his car and told them her plan. Gretchen nodded and then turned her attention to Gloria, shouting, "Your plan was to avenge your kids' murders by killing more people?"

"Not just people," Gloria insisted. "They deserved it. They all bear some responsibility for what happened that day…"

Josie didn't look back or listen to another word. She kept her body crouched as low to the ground as she could and followed the fence to the barn.

She was almost to the door when a gunshot boomed across the valley.

CHAPTER FORTY-FOUR

Josie didn't look back, but she prayed that no one on her team had been hit. She kept running until she came to the barn doors. Luckily, they weren't locked. Josie pushed through them, falling as she reached the other side. Cold air rushed at her face. The smell of barn animals and gasoline fumes stung her nostrils. Jumping to her feet, she looked around, taking in the space. On each side of the structure was a series of stalls. Each one had slatted floors, just like Dr. Feist had predicted. Each one was littered with hay and animal hair. Obviously alpaca or other animals had been kept here at one time. Josie ran past all the open stalls until she came to the end where two stalls had been converted into one large enclosure with two garage bay doors. They'd been sectioned off with drywall and even a ceiling—like a large box within the barn. Josie went to the first door and pressed her ear to the metal. From inside she heard the low hum of a car engine. Josie reached down and gripped the door handle. Using her lower body as leverage, she pulled as hard as she could. It didn't give. She ran to the second door and pressed her ear against it. No sound.

It was then that she noticed the thick rows of duct tape sealing the bottom of the door to the concrete under it. Sealing everything inside. This was the chamber where Dee and Heidi were being kept. She tried to pull the door open, tugging with all her might, but it didn't budge. She banged both forearms against the door.

"Dee! Heidi! Are you in there?"

Still nothing. Were they restrained? Or was Josie too late?

Josie banged against the door again, throwing her entire body into it. "Heidi! Dee! Answer me!"

Nothing.

She dropped to her knees and started peeling the tape away. The margin between the concrete and the door was no more than a sheet of paper at best but still, Josie rested her head on the ground and pressed her mouth against the bottom of the door. There, just beyond the other side of the door, a diamond sparkled. Faye's earring. "Dee! Heidi! Are you in there? It's Detective Josie Quinn!"

Finally, a faint voice came. "Hello?" It was weak but it sounded like Heidi.

"Heidi," Josie yelled into the bottom of the door. "Heidi!"

She heard the sound of something dragging along the floor and then a thump on the other side of the door. Heidi was close. She was on the other side, and she was still alive. Josie jumped up and grabbed the door handle again, pulling until her hands ached and sweat poured off her entire body. The door gave a little but it wasn't much, barely a half inch, and as soon as Josie let go of the door, it slammed shut again.

"Shit."

She needed something to wedge under it. Maybe then Heidi could try to breathe through the crack until Josie figured out how to get the chamber open. She looked around but everything in the barn was too thick. She catalogued her gear, but everything was too bulky to fit under the door.

"Heidi, hold on!" she hollered.

She took off her vest and put it onto the ground. Pulling up on the handle with her hands, she used one foot to try to wedge the vest under the door, but that was too thick as well. Sweat poured down her face in sheets, burning her eyes. This couldn't be it. She couldn't be this close and not be able to break into the chamber. Where was the rest of the team? Surely, they could find some way to get in. Maybe they could just ram one of their vehicles through the door of the other chamber and at least turn off the running car—the source of the carbon monoxide. Josie patted her pockets, looking for her phone but not finding it. But her fingers passed over something hard and round.

The rosary bracelet. The beads were much thicker than the average rosary. But they might just fit under the door. Josie placed the bracelet onto the floor next to one of her feet. Then she pulled up on the door again with all her might, using the toe of her sneaker to move the beads beneath the door. They slid under easily. Josie let out a whoop and got back onto her hands and knees. She could fit her pinky finger through the crack now.

"Heidi!" she called again. "Heidi!"

The weak voice came again. "I'm… here."

"Get onto your stomach and put your mouth and nose against the crack at the bottom of the door. You have to breathe through the crack."

A moment later, Heidi's voice was closer, louder. "I'm herrr," she slurred.

"Take in as much air as you can," Josie instructed. "Can you get Dee over here, too?"

"She's passed out. I don't think I can move her."

"You have to try. My team will be here any minute. I'm going to try to get you both out of there. Stay with me, Heidi."

Another gunshot sounded from outside. Josie squeezed her eyes shut, praying everyone was all right. When she heard the barn door bang open, she opened them. Mettner stood there, gun in hand, looking haggard.

"Noah," Josie squeaked out. "Is he okay?"

"Everyone's fine," he said. "Gloria tried to shoot herself. Gretchen dove for her and managed to get there just in time, but Gloria went crazy. Thrashing and trying to hit them. Gretchen and Noah are restraining her now."

Relief that her husband was fine was fleeting as the problem at hand came rushing back. "The car is inside that chamber, Mett.

Running. They're inside this chamber. Both are locked. They're dying in there. I can't get either door open."

He ran over and studied the door to the chamber holding Dee and Heidi, eyes traveling from the bottom to the top and then all four corners.

"Now, Mett," Josie screamed. "Now!"

He holstered his gun and pointed to the two upper corners. "There are pins," he said. "Lesko custom fit pins to keep the door closed. If one of us can get up there and pull them out, we can get the door open. I've got pliers in my car."

"Well, go get them!"

He ran outside. It felt like an eternity that he was gone. Josie laid down on the floor and tried to get Heidi to respond to questions. Her speech was slowed and inaudible. Finally, Mettner returned with a pair of pliers in hand. He reached up toward the top right corner of the door but couldn't reach. He handed her the pliers. "Here," he said. "You stand on my back. You're lighter."

Before Josie could react, he got down on his hands and knees, making a bench out of himself. She put a foot on his lower back and stood shakily. It took several tries but finally, the pin slid out. They repeated the process on the other side just as Noah burst into the barn.

"Help us," Josie yelled.

The three of them lifted the door and Heidi tumbled out. Several feet away, Dee Tenney lay face up, unmoving, on the slatted floor. Fumes hissed from a vent on the wall adjacent to the other chamber. It was far too high for either Dee or Heidi to reach and try to block it. Noah said, "I'll hold the door. You guys carry them outside."

Josie and Mettner made quick work of it, carrying Dee first and then Heidi out into the grass. Noah followed.

"She's got a pulse!" Mettner said excitedly, fingers pressed into Dee's neck.

"Is she… ish he gerring to be okay?" Heidi tried.

Josie and Noah knelt down on either side of Heidi. Josie smoothed the hair away from Heidi's face and stared into her eyes while Noah pressed two fingers into the inside of her wrist, checking her pulse. "It's strong," he told Josie.

Relief swept through her. It was so powerful that for a moment, she felt as though the wind had been knocked out of her. "Yes," she choked. "Dee is going to be okay. You're both going to be okay."

"The Chief's here," Noah said, pointing toward the copse of trees that separated the alpaca farm from the tiny house and barn. Josie turned to see Chief Chitwood's car bouncing through the flattened grass toward the house. He had stayed behind with the marked units to secure the scene at Gloria's store.

Shouts carried from the house to where they now gathered in front of the barn. Josie's eyes panned the area surrounding the house until she saw Gretchen, on the ground between the house and their vehicles. She lay on her back, rolling side to side and holding one of her knees. She was crying out in pain, Josie realized, and Gloria was gone.

CHAPTER FORTY-FIVE

Noah said, "Mett, stay here."

He jumped up and sprinted toward the house. Josie gave Heidi one last look and then followed him. He reached Gretchen before Josie, dragging her over to one of the vehicles and propping her against the side of it. Her face was stark white. Sweat poured from her hairline down her cheeks. She clutched at her left knee. "She got me," Gretchen huffed. "She threw up in the back of my car. Since she was sick, I let her out and she stomped right on my knee!"

Noah dropped down and began to roll up Gretchen's pant leg, but she swatted him away. "No. No. Go get her. She's still cuffed. She won't get very far. Just find her."

"What the hell is going on here?" came Chief Chitwood's voice.

He stood before them, hands on his hips, one bushy eyebrow raised. Josie didn't answer. Instead, she asked Gretchen, "Which way? Did you see which way she went?"

"Through the trees. Headed back to the alpaca farm. There might be vehicles there. Go! Go get her before she gets off this farm!"

Josie took off in a run. Without her Kevlar vest, she was light and fast. She headed around the trees and back toward the alpaca farm. Gloria wouldn't hide in the grove of trees. Either the police would locate her quickly or they would simply surround the area and wait for her to come out. Gloria was too smart for that. As the gated area with the alpacas came into view, Josie spotted Gloria running along the fence line with her cuffed hands behind her. She didn't look back. Josie wasn't sure where exactly she was headed—to the vehicles or one of the buildings—or what her plan was, but she wasn't about to let her get away.

Again, Josie was grateful for having punished her body over the last four months, running even on the hottest days of summer, because she gained on Gloria quickly. When she was only a few feet away, she shouted, "Gloria! Stop!"

Gloria glanced over her shoulder at Josie and sped up, heading now for the trucks. Fleetingly, Josie wondered if she'd considered that she didn't have keys to either truck. Or did she, and how the hell did she think she was driving anywhere with her hands cuffed behind her back? Just as Gloria reached the door of the closest truck, Josie caught the collar of her shirt. She whipped her around and slammed her back into the truck door.

"Stop," Josie instructed.

Gloria's blue eyes were wild. She pulled her head back and then thrust it forward, trying to headbutt Josie, but Josie stepped deftly out of range. Gloria lunged toward her, head down, trying to drive one of her shoulders into Josie's hip. Josie stumbled back and out of Gloria's reach. She grabbed Gloria's shoulders, keeping her upright. "Gloria, stop!"

"Just shoot me," Gloria snarled, pushing against Josie, trying to headbutt her again. "I know you've got a gun. Just shoot me."

"No." Josie shouted to be heard over the guttural wails coming from deep in Gloria's throat.

"Shoot me!" she screamed. "Just do it. If you don't, I'll kill you. I'll kill everyone."

She thrashed, breaking Josie's hold, and Josie quickly wrapped her in a bear hug. She smelled like sweat and vomit. She kept struggling but Josie held her tightly. Into her ear, she said, "Stop. I'm not going to shoot you."

"Please," Gloria begged. "Please."

Josie cinched her arms more firmly. Slowly, Gloria's body went limp until she felt like a heavy sack of bones in Josie's arms. The moisture from her tears soaked through the shoulder of Josie's shirt.

"I'm going to let go now," Josie told her. "I want you to sit down."

Gloria didn't protest as Josie released her and guided her into a seated position next to the truck. She looked up at Josie. "I can't do this anymore. I can't do it. I can't take it. Do you have any idea what this feels like? To lose your whole world? To be so broken inside that you feel like you'd do anything to make the pain go away? To avoid feeling it?"

Josie sighed. "Yes," she said. "Yes, I do."

A vehicle pulled up behind them. Josie turned to see Chief Chitwood emerge. He walked over and looked down at Gloria. "Everything secure here, Quinn?"

Josie let out a long breath and looked down at her shirt, which was now covered in puke from having been pressed against Gloria. "Yes, sir."

"More units are en route," Chitwood said. "Plus the ERT and some ambulances."

"Thank you, sir," Josie said. She stared at the top of Gloria's head. Josie could see her frame shaking with silent sobs.

"Quinn," said Chitwood.

Josie looked up at him. He held out a hand to her. In it were the rosary beads. "You left these back there."

"Oh, shit. Sir, I'm sorry, I just—I used them to—"

"Shut up, Quinn," he said. "Shut up and take them back."

"Sir?"

"You still need them. You're not ready to give them back yet."

Josie took them, clutching them in her fist. The beads were warm and smooth. Familiar. Comforting. "But how will I know when to give them back?"

Sirens wailed in the distance.

A slow smile spread across Chitwood's face. "That's not something I can decide for you, Quinn." He glanced at Gloria, his grin fading. Almost to himself, he said, "Everyone's different."

Then he walked off to meet the caravan of emergency vehicles bouncing along the drive.

CHAPTER FORTY-SIX

Two Weeks Later

Josie stared at Paige Rosetti, whose pen had gone still a long time ago. She was pretty sure the end of their session was near, but the doctor hadn't checked her watch or her phone once. She simply stared at Josie.

Josie waited for her to interrupt but she didn't, so Josie kept talking. "Gloria already reached a plea deal with the district attorney's office. She'll go away for a long time. Sebastian is being charged for spiking Virgil Lesko's drink the day of the bus accident. He'll lose his license as a pharmacist. He's already got an attorney. Evidently, he plans on fighting the charges. Virgil Lesko's trial is off. Andrew Bowen is working with the DA to reach an agreement on lesser charges than what he was facing, especially since without Sebastian Palazzo spiking his drink, he would have been fine to drive the bus. I mean, he shouldn't have had the vodka, but one drink would not have been enough to impair him to the point where he crashed. Dee and Heidi are doing well. Dee has to sell her house to pay off some of the debt that Miles accrued, but Corey Byrne said she could move in with him and Heidi until she gets on her feet. The FBI is still working on the Cerberus connection and the murders of Ted and Miles—"

"Josie," said Paige. "You're not paying me to talk about your cases."

"Oh," said Josie. "I just thought that I would—"

"You owe me a list," Paige said. "You missed last week's appointment, but I haven't forgotten."

Josie shifted in her chair, crossing and uncrossing her legs.

"Did you write it down?" Paige prompted.

"No," Josie answered. "I didn't need to write it down." Every single thing that had made her feel out of control in the last few weeks was emblazoned on her mind. All of it spilled out of her mouth, the words rushed and heavy.

By the time she was finished, both of Paige's eyebrows were arched. "That's quite a list."

"I know you only asked me for three things that make me feel out of control," Josie said. "But the truth is that I feel out of control a lot. Almost all the time."

"What does feeling out of control mean to you?" Paige asked.

"That is such a psychologist question," Josie responded.

Paige smiled. "Don't deflect. Tell me, what does feeling out of control look like from Josie Quinn's perspective?"

Josie looked away, eyes drawn to the garden outside. The eastern bluebird was back, flitting from branch to branch of the dogwood tree in the corner of the yard. "It looks like me letting my feelings in—or out—or in. I don't know. It looks like me feeling them. I'm afraid of them."

"They're just feelings, Josie," Paige said. "We've talked about this before. If you sit with them—"

"I'll die," Josie blurted. "That's what it feels like. When I think about my grandmother and how I'll never be with her again; how I have to live an entire lifetime still that is completely devoid of her; how I watched her get shot; how I sat there while she took her last breath and there wasn't a damn thing I could do; how I am probably responsible for her getting shot—it all comes crashing down and it doesn't feel… survivable." Tears sprang to Josie's eyes. In spite of her best efforts, a few of them slid down her cheeks. "I know I've been walking and talking and eating and sleeping and living in the months since my grandmother died, but this? Living without her? Knowing she's gone? Long-term, this doesn't feel survivable at all. I don't even actually know how I'm sitting here in front of you right now."

"It is survivable, Josie."

Josie swiped at her tears and put a hand to her chest. "By me. Survivable by me."

Paige smiled again. "It's survivable by you if you feel your feelings, Josie. I won't lie to you. It's going to be painful. Losing a parent—which is essentially what Lisette was to you—is always very painful. It takes time and work to get to a place where you feel like you're functioning at some level of normal again, but you can get there, Josie."

"I don't know."

Paige set her notepad aside. She walked over and sat in the chair next to Josie. "I'm going to sit here beside you and for five minutes, you're going to let those feelings in and then you're going to let them out. I'll be right here with you. Will you try?"

Josie's heart beat so hard it felt like it might burst from her chest. Her hands fisted in her lap. She could feel those awful feelings at the periphery of her mind and heart, pulsating like an angry blob just waiting to consume her. She'd faced down more killers in her life than she could count. Why was this so hard? Lisette had done this multiple times in her life—grieved the loss of someone she loved; someone essential to her. Josie still marveled at it. She had a sudden flash of Lisette's face, smiling, her silver curls bouncing. It was a memory. They were on the beach. Josie was a teenager, but she'd never been to the beach before, never even seen the ocean. Now Lisette wanted her to get into it. The pounding, rushing waves terrified her.

Lisette held out her hand. "Come on, Josie."

"I can't," Josie said.

"You can," Lisette told her, laughing. "You have to try."

"Josie," Paige said, pulling her from the reverie.

"Okay," said Josie. "Let's try."

A LETTER FROM LISA

Thank you so much for choosing to read *Her Deadly Touch*. If you enjoyed the book and want to keep up to date with all my latest releases, just sign up at the following link. Your email address will never be shared, and you can unsubscribe at any time.

www.bookouture.com/lisa-regan

As always, it is my privilege to bring you another Josie Quinn book. If you're reading this, I am glad that you returned after what happened to Lisette in *Hush Little Girl*. This was an incredibly difficult book to write, not just because of the subject matter, but also because my father passed suddenly and unexpectedly while I was writing it. Josie's grief is my own. Still, as always, I tried to bring you a page-turner that would give you a few hours of nail-biting entertainment as you try to put the puzzle together alongside Josie. That is always my main goal! Hopefully, I have succeeded.

I absolutely love hearing from readers. I will never tire of it! You can get in touch with me through any of the social media outlets below, including my website and Goodreads page. Also, if you are so inclined, I'd really appreciate it if you'd leave a review and perhaps recommend *Her Deadly Touch* to other readers. Reviews and word-of-mouth recommendations go a long way in helping readers discover my books for the first time. Again, thank you so much for your support and your enthusiasm for this series. I am astounded and deeply moved by your passion for Josie! I hope to see you next time!

Thanks,
Lisa Regan

f LisaReganCrimeAuthor

🐦 @LisalRegan

🖥 www.lisaregan.com

ACKNOWLEDGMENTS

Lovely, passionate readers: thank you for reading this book. My dad died when I was two-thirds of the way through writing this book. My dad was to me as Lisette was to Josie. He loved me with ferocity from the day I was born, and he always fought for me, always advocated for me. He was also fun, mischievous, and wise like Lisette. He was my anchor, my North Star, and the person I could always rely on in life no matter the circumstances or what personal demons I was struggling with—a lot like Lisette was for Josie. He was, and is, forever the voice inside of my head. Even as I continue to grieve deeply for him, finding myself beneath miles of emotional sludge, I hear him saying, "Go to work." That work was finishing this book for you fabulous fans and readers. He would not want me to let you down. He would not want to be the reason I stopped doing what I have loved so passionately since I was eleven years old. So here is Josie's twelfth adventure and my most deeply personal book to date. I hope that you enjoyed it.

Thank you, as always, to my husband, Fred, and my daughter, Morgan, for picking me up and dusting me off and being so brave and steadfast during the worst time of my life. Thank you to my first readers: Dana Mason, Katie Mettner, Nancy S. Thompson, Maureen Downey, and Torese Hummel. Thank you to Matty Dalrymple and Jane Kelly—two of the most wonderful humans and writing friends I know! Thank you to my grandmothers: Helen Conlen and Marilyn House; my parents: Donna House, Joyce Regan, Rusty House, and Julie House; my brothers and sisters-in-law: Sean and Cassie House, Kevin and Christine Brock and Andy Brock; as well as my lovely sisters: Ava McKittrick and Melissia McKittrick. Thank you as well to all of the usual suspects for your spreading the word—Debbie Tralies, Jean and Dennis Regan, Tracy Dauphin, Claire Pacell, Jeanne Cassidy, Susan Sole, the Regans, the Conlens, the Houses, the McDowells, the Kays, the Funks, the Bowmans, and the Bottingers! As always, thank you to all the amazing bloggers and reviewers who continue to stick with Josie or who met her somewhere in the middle of the series and have been so vociferous with their support! It means the world!

Thank you to Katie Mettner and Carrie Butler for that special, perfect personalized gift that got me over the hump and will remain on my desk for the rest of time!

Thank you so very much to Sgt. Jason Jay for answering all of my crazy questions in such great detail over and over and over again. Thank you to the team at Coroner Talk for answering all my elaborate algor mortis questions.

Thank you to Jenny Geras, Kathryn Taussig, Noelle Holten, Kim Nash, and the entire team at Bookouture including my lovely copy-editor and proofreader, and last but certainly not least, my incredible editor, Jessie Botterill. You have made what could have been one of the most painful processes in the world—writing a book that, at its core, is about grief while experiencing the worst grief of my life—feel effortless. Thank you for your kind words. Thank you for shuffling the schedule around endlessly. Thank you for checking in on me and also for giving me space. Thank you for listening to me. Thank you for holding me up. Thank you for believing in this book. I could not ask for a better, more empathetic, or more wonderful editor or publishing family.

CPSIA information can be obtained
at www.ICGtesting.com
Printed in the USA
BVHW081156110821
614085BV00007B/465

9 781800 196339